Runaways

Author: Justin Avery

Illustrators: Kimba & Hailey Jack

Justin Avery
Contents

Justin Avery

ISBN: 978-1-7373261-0-6

Chapter 1:
Fire & Brimstone

"Alright Justin, we'll see you tomorrow in class"!

My friend group shouts before we split up, heading in opposite directions.

I beam excitedly, eager to go home and relax now that school is over for today. I rush to meet up with my friends Donshay and Elijah at the Field house. Once everyone arrives, we all talk about how today was wild.

"Did you see the senior prank all over the 300 hall"? Don exclaims loudly.

I fold over laughing so hard that tears come to my eyes.

"Yeah! How long do you think it's gonna take for them to clean up all that baby powder"?

We all just laugh as we make our way slowly walking down the bus ramp.

"I can't wait for our senior year bro." Elijah chuckles.

I glance at him grinning ear to ear.

"Just a couple more weeks man, then we'll be the big dogs around campus." I beam proudly.

As we walk home, we laugh and joke about everything that went on during our day and we discuss our plans for the upcoming weekend. Once we get to Don's house, we wave goodbye to each other, and Elijah turns around to run back towards his place. I continue down my own street.

Once I get home, I sling my backpack over my bed post and plop down exhausted. I pull out my phone and text Ava.

"You got any plans tonight"? I question.

Moments later she replies. "Nah, I'm free, what do you wanna do"?

Laying back on my bed I try and think of something clever. Nothing comes to mind, so I suggest we head to the lake and grab some food. My concentration is snapped at the sound of my mother moving in the kitchen. She calls me out into the living room. When I see her, she suffocates me with a giant hug.

I try and push her off screaming. "Mom no! I'm still sweaty"!

She laughs and hugs me tighter. After greeting me she tells me to grab a shower and that dinner will be ready soon. I hesitate and make an awkward face while staring up at the ceiling, hoping she will notice and question why I have not moved.

"What? Do you have something better to do"? She inquires.

I nod my head nervously admitting that I might have made plans with Ava to get food already.

My mom smiles.

Runaways

"Text her that she can come over for dinner instead of the lake."

My mom moseys back into the kitchen and starts stirring what smells like ground beef and refried beans.

"Enchiladas"? I ask eagerly.

She nods her head slowly. As I begin to walk back towards my room, something clicks. Freezing for a moment, I turn staring at my mother.

"Wait, how did you know we were going to the lake"? I question, completely appalled.

Without even glancing up from the pot, she continues stirring. A few moments pass before she finally answers.

"Son, I'm your mama, it's my job to know."

I cross my arms and roll my eyes accepting that as my answer. I go back to scrolling through my phone, I click my messages seeing that Ava asked if we could go somewhere besides the lake. I promptly invite her over for dinner tonight. Slyly, I smirk knowing this will make me look more prepared.

Ava responds back quickly. "Bet, I'll be there soon."

Around an hour later I hear Ava giggling outside the front door. Racing to the door I open it eagerly and she rushes inside. Ava kicks off her shoes and places them neatly by the entrance before she greets my mother as we both head toward the living room.

"Awww, look at how cute you two are." My mother cheerfully exclaims.

Ava blushes and shuffles towards me. I welcome her affection and I suggest we grab a couple plates before getting comfortable again.

"So, what do you think of those Sathon wielding freaks"?

Ava questions as she sips pink lemonade through her bendy straw.

I recline back onto the couch and stare at the ceiling.

"Honestly, I wish I had their powers. I know they all end up getting put into private schools or must be raised from birth as an Elite. But I just like the idea of being able to control whatever situation I would be put in. I definitely wouldn't abuse my strength like those snobs at school". I comment.

Ava sits up completely and gives me a surprised expression. "Wait who are you talking about"?

I stare at her annoyed by her ignorance.

"Julien and Adrian. You're telling me you haven't heard of the most popular duo in Joviality? You know, the ones who only switched to our school to steal the valedictorian spot from our class president." I spout.

Her intrigue stops there, and her interest drops.

"Oh, those two bullies. Yeah, I heard they only switched into our school because we scored the highest on the final exams out of the entire school district system in Nero. Something about it looking better on their resume." She murmurs.

I clench my fist frustrated by their very existence.

"Those two are spoiled and irritate me to no end. They prance around school as if they own the place. Especially Julien, that pretty boy makes me sick." I growl, animosity building.

Ava stands up doing her best impression of him.

"Oh, look at me, I'm cool because I can shoot golden light out of my fingers and my hair is blonde". She mocks playfully.

We both burst out laughing. My mom chimes in.

"If we're being honest. They practically do own the place. Their father owns so much land in Nero he might as well be a king himself." She admits candidly.

Over the next few hours, we laugh as we talk about school and life goals after graduation next year. Ava looks down at her phone and screams loudly.

"Whoa, what's wrong Ava"! I shout nervously.

Ava hops off the couch and grabs her things quickly before she starts putting on her shoes. She shows me her phone and I realize that it's late and she has ten minutes to be home before curfew! We rush out the house and race down the road towards her neighborhood.

"Justin, you don't need to run home with me, I know where I live. You're risking missing curfew yourself." Ava warns wearily.

I smile at Ava and stay by her side.

"I just want to make sure you make it home without getting pulled over by some corrupt Lumin officials." I chuckle innocently.

Finally arriving at her house, I give her a quick hug and say hello and a quick goodbye to her mother before sprinting back towards my house. I glance at my phone seeing I only have four minutes left. Starting to round the corner and make it back to my house I see two Lumin officials getting ready to start their headcount. I try to avoid them but then I spot a wild Bingo lurking around the surrounding trees and houses. I freeze, weighing my options anxiously.

"A giant dingo with bat wings or two potentially corrupt officers who could beat me up and claim I attacked them." I think aloud.

I decide to race past the two Lumin officers as calmly as I can.

"Hey you! Stop running, you look suspicious"! One of the men barks aggressively and I start to speed walk to my house.

Both Lumin officers snicker at me as I pass them by. Once I get far enough to be out of their sight, I sprint down the road and make it into my house as the bell in the middle of town sounds violently. Breathing heavily, I slide down the door onto the floor as my heart pounds rapidly. My mom stares at me disapprovingly and sighs.

"You should be careful, Lumin officers don't need a reason to make an example of a Lustro. Please do not give them ammunition son." My mother warns.

I dismiss her statement mentally but nod my head agreeing with her. I drag myself into the kitchen cleaning everything up for my mom and then trudge to my room exhausted from the entire sequence. Plopping down onto my bed and curling up in my blanket, sleep encases my body within minutes.

I wake up to the sound of crunching leaves, looking around slowly I quickly recognize that I am surrounded by Crocodile fused Wolves, but I lay silent and lifeless patiently awaiting the pack's next move. One of the predators moves in closer only to be slapped away by another. Assuming he must be their leader I watch him and try to anticipate his movements, or they could be the last ones I witness. I notice that his scales are significantly darker than the rest of his pack, also that this individual has a scar on the left side of his body. Almost as if he were clawed by something much bigger than he was. I hear more leaves crunching behind me and the Wocodile scatter from my sight. I roll over to see a huge Hippo fused Lion marking a tree with his claws. In a panic I grab my bag and scurry up a tree in the opposite direction, peering down to see if the big cat noticed my frantic dash.

"Dude why are there so many of these exotic animals! Joviality has never been this hectic. Actually, where am I"? I think to myself.

Either from laziness or exhaustion the king of the jungle does not even turn his head an inch as he lays down and falls asleep. I look at the sky and long to cry out for help. Knowing that doing so will only attract unwanted attention, I sit back and attempt to recuperate.

"How did all of this start"? I ponder.

Frustrated, I punch the tree trying to remember.

It all started back when there were only five remaining countries on the earth. Due to the constant Scepin and plasma wars, most of the planet was rumored to be destroyed. Well, almost everything. The ravenous war left Lustro untouched along with Yintago and a couple other countries. At the tail end of the war, there were a few nations that survived. Hypor, Matiya, Roi, Syuble, and Mirra all crumbled from the merciless battles against one another. Scepin, a powerful chemical, ravaged all lands, pushing humanity to the brink of extinction. Eventually the surviving countries got together and signed a Forever treaty, stating that all the remaining people would live together in Lustro, peacefully.

The war also had devastating effects on the wildlife and the ecosystem around the planet. Some animals ended up becoming fused with others in their habitat because of the Scepin fallout, unfortunately it even extended out towards bugs, fish, and almost all mammals.

This did not go over very well with the Lustronese people, who fought to keep life as they knew it and did not want to sign the Forever treaty. They told the remaining countries that they were not involved with the war and that they would not give up their land.

After weeks of arguing, the countries' supplies got dangerously low, and they were forced into a desperate mindset. The last five countries agreed to make Lustro an enemy of all surviving nations and any undiscovered settlements that had made it through the Scepin war. In a quick and brutal battle, Lustro was defeated. Most of the men were killed and the uncooperative women and children were sadly exiled from their homes to go live in the wastelands.

The nation was renamed Nero, meaning ("strong or vigorous"). At least that is what my mother always told me.

I live in Nero where my friends and I want to become adventurers. Here, my people are slaves to the ruthless Lumin forces. I long to leave this cruel place we begrudgingly call home. Ava, Donshay, and I, have plans to explore the world and see what happened to the other continents. However, it is forbidden to leave this country and it is highly illegal to even have such an idea to escape.

If someone were to leave Nero, their way of escape would be destroyed without any hesitation, and it would be considered treason. Change was not acceptable in our country, no matter the age, race, sex, or social status. Things in my city, Joviality, were different from the other four cities in Nero. The laws here are stricter since our city has one of the biggest Lustronese populations.

As a child I would always ask my mother what life was like back before our people were enslaved, she would never change her answer.

"Different from the kings in control now."

I never knew what she meant by that, and she would never expound on her answer. I pondered about what it meant from time to time, but now that I am older, I have other things to worry about that are much more important.

Now, seven-teen years old, I am doing my best to stay out of trouble for my mother. School is tiring and all teens aged fifth-teen and older are forced into a "career field." My people are forced to work so much harder than the Lumin civilization and to make things worse, most of our income is taken up by corrupt Lumin soldiers or taken by taxes. My people barely have enough to make it day to day.

My mother tells my friends and I that the government overseeing Nero will not allow us the time to revolt again. So, they keep us busy.

Always referring to the government as "The Light." My mother states that they believe any teen without a "job" is more likely to try and escape with so much free time on their hands.

Nobody dares to fight the law of the Lumin forces, not after Joviality had over two hundred citizens executed for committing treason. I was eleven when I lost my father. Most of my friends lost at least one parent.

Occasionally a child would lose both parents to the Lumin kings and their strict laws. The five kings once ruled over each city, but now they live up north in one of the more sophisticated cities. They made this move after tensions boiled over into what our people call the first revolt.

After the Scepin war, one king was appointed their power from each surviving country. Each king has a governor, and that family has overwhelming power over their respected city, basically replacing the power that the kings left when they moved into the new city. The governors have always been known to host feasts and provide higher paying jobs to members of the Lumin civilization.

It takes three Lustronese households to equal the income of one Lumin household. That is, if both Lustronese parents are still alive. The hard labor in the mines killed most young teens if the starvation didn't wipe them out. This unbalance has gotten worse over the past few years and the failed revolt has put a stranglehold on Lustronese families around Nero.

A warped cry comes from the distance and for some reason my brain tells me to ignore it. Then I hear it again, and what sounds like my mother screaming wakes me from my slumber. Looking around confused I lay back down.

"I don't even remember falling asleep, how is it morning already? Why did I recall the painful past? I wish all that was a dream too." I murmur to myself.

Hearing a knock at my bedroom door I sit up annoyed. I roll out of bed slowly as someone repeatedly bangs on my door like a madman. Irritated and groggy I throw the door open in a hurry screaming at them to knock it off. I open my eyes to my best friend Jade. I spring out of my drowsiness as soon as I mentally register his face.

I have not seen Jade for five years after his family was taken out of Joviality due to the scandal going on with his father and his company. Most of the men and boys that were executed for treason worked in his father's company, they were caught planning on revolting but never got around to executing their brilliant plan. Once exposed they fought like crazy to gain our freedom to leave this cursed land. However, with the Lumin forces already aware of our plan, our premature revolt failed miserably and so did my people's spirit. Jade's father was rumored to have plans trailing back months before he converged from a Lustro, to a Lumin citizen.

Jade tells me that he was granted permission to come back because the High Court deemed him innocent.

Unfortunately, his parents were taken and were not spared. Jade does not explain much at all as he expresses his pain.

"It's just a lot to talk about right now." He laments.

Jade also tells me that his parents admitted to treason in court to save him from any questioning or punishment. I sit back bewildered.

"But we were eleven years old. How would you have anything to do with the revolt"?! I shout, unaware of my volume.

My mom hushes me, aggressively gritting her teeth. I shyly tell Jade that he is not the only one who has lost a loved one, reminding him that my father and most of our peer's parents had also been killed.

"We're all here for you man." I comment wrapping my arm around Jade.

He smiles painfully.

"It's alright man. Our shared pain strengthens our bond." I comment.

Runaways

"It sucks though, we were so close. Our parents had an amazing plan to take our city back." He groans.

"It's so sad that they were hastily arrested and were executed by a firing squad in view of the city to set an example for everyone"! Jade shouts.

My mother stares at us with an icy glare.

"If you two don't shut up, it won't be long before Lumin guards are over here making a new example. Quiet hours aren't up for debate." She hisses.

Jade shudders and at first struggles to change the subject. He suggests we take a walk outside for a fresh breath of air. I nod and walk outside. Both Jade and I see some people running near my neighborhood screaming.

"There's a fire"! People shout belligerently.

Jade's eyes widen and he freaks out before he takes off running.

"Come on Justin, there is a fire"! He shouts.

"Jade, normal people run away from enormous flames." I yell back.

Jade continues his race towards the flames and dark smoke pluming from the houses.

As I pursue after him, worried that I might not be able to catch up, we both stop abruptly when we see what is on fire. Jade falls to his knees as his parents' expensive home and a couple others close by, succumb to the relentless flames.

"All my memories, my clothes, our pictures, everything is gone." He mutters shakily to himself.

Jade picks himself up and sprints into the house! I grab his arm, but he throws me off as he tries desperately to save everything he has ever known. I scream at him to come back before watching him disappear into the smoky building.

I get off the ground, dusting myself off and pursue him. Instantly I am hit by the smoke and paralyzing heat right after entering the house. Looking around the living room frantically, I attempt to spot Jade. I partially see a shadow rush upstairs and I blindly follow it.

With no plan on how to get Jade out of this house. I panic, hyperventilating. The longer we are in this environment, the longer the toxic smoke continues to abuse my lungs. My coughing becomes uncontrollable, but I catch up to Jade and attempt to drag him downstairs. It does little to slow him as he twists, and I lose grip of his shoulder.

Collapsing onto the staircase I helplessly watch him dash up the rest of the stairs and I cough erratically in his wake. I try to follow in pursuit again but the smoke on the stairs is too thick and it stifles my breathing, rendering me to a powerless state.

Heavy chunks of the ceiling start to fall and one piece tears down the staircase, I quickly go tumbling into a downward spiral, slamming hard on the tile floor. The wood from the ceiling and staircase falls onto me soon after. I try to pull myself out, but I struggle to rip myself free from the rubble. My eyes become heavier and heavier until I can keep them open no longer.

A few moments pass as I am in complete darkness, and I don't recognize where I am. I walk around trying to find my way, but no matter where I turn, there is nothing but a vacant darkness. Turning left I spot a dim light glowing faintly. I walk cautiously towards the eerie light and flinch whenever it flickers like a candle.

A new feeling overcomes me as I stare into the light. It seems to show my reflection as if it were a puddle. However, it looks more like a flame the closer I get to it. I feel a strong urge to grab it, but I feel as if I am being watched.

Noises of something clashing echoes around me but I ignore the distractions and I grab the flame off the podium. It flickers around in my hand, dancing like tulips in the wind. Surprisingly, it does not burn. I'm shocked and my jaw drops.

Instantly the flame jumps into my body!

Everything changes from the dark abyss to a seemingly endless white plain. I hear Jade's voice and a couple others as if they are right next to me. I look around but I do not see any faces that match the familiar voices. I feel the white plane shaking violently as everything floods with a surge of water! As I am swept away by the current, I wake up lying in a cold sweat on my bed.

Jade is pacing my room impatiently, worried. Ava sits next to my bed with her hand on mine. Playfully, I squeeze her hand, she shrieks before she hugs me aggressively. Jade runs over, waiting until she frees me to get his turn. Ava glares at me and begs me to never run into a burning building again. I laugh and sarcastically tell her I will try not to make it a habit. Ava lightly punches my arm and giggles to herself. Jade apologizes repeatedly before getting super excited and shows me what he went to get. I wait as he leaves the room for a moment and returns with a small white box.

I want to get up and slap Jade when I see the box but the unbearable pain in my left leg brings me back to the forgiving cushions. Jade opens the box and there is an electronic map inside and some other items that look very suspicious.

Jade takes a ring out of the small white box and puts it on. He grins brilliantly and as the ring slides on, a small flash of lime glimmers in the room.

"Whoa! Jade, what is that"? I question.

Jade turns to me and smiles again.

"This is the ring of power. My father had this created when he became the richest Lustro in all the land. Obviously before we were born. He told me he had this ring since he was a boy. This ring has Sathon abilities of its own. However, my father said it only works if the wearer already possesses the ability. Regardless, I couldn't let it burn in that fire. I needed this piece of my father, to remember him by." Jade states.

"So, it's just jewelry to you, since you can't refract light"? Ava inquires.

"Right." Jade nods.

"Let me hold that." Ava replies as she reaches out, attempting to pull the ring off Jade's finger.

Runaways

"Don't touch"!! Jade scolds as he tosses her to the floor.

Ava gets up and closes the door just to ensure that my mom doesn't walk in on us. I sit up on the bed looking carefully at the map and the instructions on it. As I read down the lines, there is one part that sticks out like a sore thumb.

At the bottom corner of the map it says, "Different from the kings in control now."

I freak out and call out through the wall to my mother. Ava eyes me oddly but I hold her hand and assure her I know what I am doing.

My mother walks in and Jade shows her the map and instructions. Surprisingly, she does not seem to be shocked by the items in the box or the quote at the bottom that she so frequently uses. My mother closes the front door and pulls the curtains over all the windows. When she returns to my room, she closes the door, asking Jade for the map. She slowly tells us that we cannot tell anyone about what we are looking at or we will all perish.

My mother then turns to Ava and calmly states.

"Not even your parents, alright"? My mother warns.

Ava nods her head, and my mother continues to tell us the real story about what has been going on in Nero.

"The Sacred Council has been hiding a lot about the past from us. The five kings are the great grandchildren of each continent from the Scepin war. They have been in control and will pass the power down to their children to keep us from controlling our own futures. People aren't allowed to leave Nero for a fear of them finding out of what happened back then. The kings know that if someone comes out with the truth. Their wrongs will be out for everyone to see and not just the Lustronese people will revolt against them, but also the people who came from those outside countries. The loyal upper-class citizens believe the lies they have been fed. If someone were to expose the kings for what they have done, there will be no difference between us and the Lumin residents. We will all see that we are just pawns. You kids need to understand that we have to take our freedom back."

She hesitates, taking a deep breath and muttering something. I can't make out what is said before she continues.

"The Lumin forces turned our proud race of people into their slaves! They tax the Lustronese households and basically take everything we have worked so hard for! And the dimwitted Lumin citizens, they believe that we attacked them. That they're righteous for enslaving and murdering our people! They have been living this lie since I was a little girl, and their entire life is a façade"!

Crying bitterly now, my mother continues.

"The Lumin forces execute most of our vocal leaders to try to keep us quiet, but you three will be the ones to leave Nero and show everyone what happened." She exclaims, staring at the floor.

"Mrs. Avery, why are we the ones who have to do this"? Jade questions.

Runaways

"Jade, your parents were the ones who had saved this information that was hidden in that box you have there." My mother quickly answers.

"I'm so sorry that this has fallen to you, your father was planning on changing life in Nero for all of us. Now it is your responsibility to finish what he started." She states grimly.

"Jade, it isn't like we can give this to anyone else, nobody is going to believe us anyway. Even if they did, they would report us to save their own skin." I chime in.

Jade takes a minute to process everything that he has been told. Shortly after he grins softly and grips the box tightly.

"Yeah! This is my destiny. I swear I'll avenge my father and our people"! He shouts encouragingly.

He looks at me and tells me that we need to get started now. Ava slows him down and asks my mother what else we need to know.

"All you need to know is that wherever that map takes you, be careful. All of you are crucial to the survival of the people of Nero. No, the world is depending on you all." She comments calmly.

"We can't leave for an adventure. My leg is shattered"! I shriek nervously.

"My entire life I have only wanted to leave Nero and now that the opportunity finally arises my left leg is useless."

Justin Avery

Ava looks at me and shakes her head. "Sorry Justin, what can we do about it though"?

My mom says that my injury is not a problem because she has something special for my leg. Her voice sounds warped, and I look around but nobody else reacts to it. It's almost like I was the only one who heard it.

"Her voice was super distorted, what's going on"? I ponder.

When she returns to the room, she has this weird turquoise liquid on a cotton ball. I stare at her and she seems to fade in and out.

"What the heck, now my vision is acting weird." I think to myself.

For mere moments I see an unrecognizable man and then my mother. When the liquid touches my leg, I get that overwhelming feeling again.

Everything clicks, and I remember the flame I saw earlier when I had passed out. Struggling to separate reality from the dark abyss with the flame. I fade in and out of both locations. When I snap back to the real world, my leg feels perfectly fine. I thank my mom for the treatment, and she looks at me confused. However, the cotton ball is gone.

Ava asks me if I am alright, and I hop out of bed.

Jade is amazed at my quick recovery.

Runaways

"Whoa! How are you jumping around already man, you broke your leg"!? Jade spouts perplexed.

I stop and look at him to tell him it was the turquoise liquid my mom brought in just a second ago.

Everyone just looks at me as if I am going insane. Even my mom looks lost on what I just said. Attempting to escape this awkward moment I shake my head and tell them to forget it. Ava hugs me and asks me how I am walking.

"I just told you. My mom gave me some turquoise liquid and it healed me." I laugh as she squeezes me tightly.

No luck, she just shakes her head and asks how hard I really hit my head on that tile floor. Jade puts the items back into the box and says that we will head off tomorrow.

"Mrs. Avery, can we stay here until lunch because, well you know, my house kinda doesn't exist anymore."

Ava giggles.

"Sure sweetie, you and Ava can both stay since you're already here." My mom cheerfully responds.

Jade looks at me and laughs to himself when he hears that Ava was over here yesterday. I look at all of them, thinking to myself about what just happened.

"I shattered my leg but then it was healed by that turquoise substance. The issue is that nobody recalls this happening but me.

Remarkably they remember everything else we just discussed." I worry.

"Ring Ring Ring"!!

As the phone goes off loudly, my mom exits my room to answer it.

Ava looks at me and eyes me seductively. I look to Jade for help, but he throws his hands up and walks out of the room leaving me to my own devices. She gives a tantalizing smirk before leaning in to kiss me. I close my eyes awaiting the moment where our lips touch for the first time.

Nothing happens and I glance up at her, now opening my eyes. She laughs at me for a moment.

"Wow, you really were going to kiss me, huh"? She teases.

Without another word she hugs me tightly and then rushes out of the house to grab her backpack.

I walk into the kitchen and tell Jade we should bring some other friends we know so that it won't be just the three of us on a trip. I ponder for a few moments before I tell him that two more friends would be fine and all five of us could leave tonight if he was down for the idea.

Jade shrugs and laughs saying he doesn't care at all, and we can leave whenever I felt comfortable.

"My leg is fine Jade"! I spout, annoyed by the constant protective behavior everyone keeps giving me.

Runaways

I hear a hard pound at the door and flinch, once I check the peephole, I see its Officer Wilson.

I let him in and look at Jade motioning to him with my eyes to hide the box. Jade walks casually to my room and moves the box under my bed with his foot. Wilson sees him kick something and asks him what he's doing.

"I am just helping Justin clean his filthy room, because you know he's too lazy to do it himself." Jade cleverly answers.

I play along and glare coldly at Jade.

"Bro, why you gotta call me out like that." I growl.

Officer Wilson starts laughing at us and tells us he remembers when he was a teenager.

"You should honestly be grateful that you have a friend that will call you out on your issues and help you become a better person." He preaches.

I roll my eyes. "Yeah, I'll uh, keep that in mind sir."

Wilson nods his head as he walks around the house checking off his list and lets us know we are all good. I watch him walk towards the door as he is still looking at us, from the corner of his eye. Officer Wilson is blocking the doorway and I see Ava walking towards the door!

Jade and I mentally panic, knowing he'll instantly bully her because the Lumin guards always find a reason to taunt Ava. The last time they saw her, they roughed her up and wouldn't stop, repeating that she didn't deserve both parents and should lose one just so she can match the rest of us.

They threaten to kill one of her parents, or her daily.

Ava sees Wilson and dives in the bushes off the porch. Unfazed by the rustling of bushes, Officer Wilson keeps chattering to Jade and me.

Ava sneaks around to the left side of the house and pulls at the window.

It's locked.

To my surprise Wilson still isn't alerted to the noises and keeps on talking to us. Jade asks him how many houses he has left before morning headcount is finished.

Officer Wilson's eyes get wide as he takes off very quickly to his next house. We all sigh, knowing that Ava dodged a bullet just now. Finally, she races around the front of the house and comes inside. I close the door shortly after and we both laugh nervously. She sinks down to the floor sighing deeply, stating.

"Those Lumin Officers always bully me whenever they get the chance. Thanks guys."

Chapter 2: Become the hunted

As the next couple hours go by, we do our best to relax and devise a plan to escape Joviality. For a moment there are a few loud voices, and we pause the tv, hearing some commotion from outside.

Three Lumin officers are headed in our direction. We freeze and all rush around the house trying to look busy.

They knock twice before Officer Kelly's voice booms through. "Open up"!

I scurry over to the door and open it hastily.

Officer Kelly grabs me by my shirt, screaming his head off and spitting in my face.

"You should be at school young man! I hope you aren't trying to play me for a fool. I know your little friends are here too." He barks.

"Wait, there's school today? But it's a weekend." I whimper.

Officer Kelly mocks me as I struggle to speak.

"Not for you Lustronese scum, school is in session today." He growls.

My mother speaks up confidently.

"The schedule says they're off today, Sir. Now please leave my home."

"Well surprise! There was a fight, and the principal decided all students would be at school today to make everyone aware of our standards." He smirks.

"They just updated the schedule five minutes ago and normal school start time was hours ago! How were any of the students supposed to know about this update to be at school on time"?! I shout angrily.

Officer Kelly notices this and grins devilishly.

"Well, that's simple worm. You weren't. We wouldn't be able to kick your teeth in if you knew about the updates. Your kind has a habit of staying out of trouble and it makes me sick." He snarls.

My mother yells at him to put me down and he drops me on my face.

"You better grab your two friends and get to school, or your house might accidentally catch fire like a few did yesterday." One of his subordinate's chuckle.

"That was you"!? Jade steps out from the corner screaming angrily.

He charges at the Officer, not thinking clearly and Officer Kelly smirks before drop kicking Jade to the floor.

Runaways

He then stomps on Jade's chest, causing him to spit up blood! As Officer Kelly stands above Jade, he whispers something only Jade and I can hear.

"The next time you speak to me, or my men out of turn. I'll have you join your parent's you brat." Officer Kelly growls.

I freeze nervously and Jade clenches his teeth, restraining himself.

My mother yells at Kelly to leave and he stands up, staring at us for a few moments before finally exiting, knocking down a glass bowl on his way out.

The fruit from the bowl spills and rolls around the kitchen table.

My mother helps us to our feet and calls out to Ava.

"Come on kids, I'll drive you all to school." She mumbles.

When we arrive at the front of the school my mother waves goodbye to us and yells that she will be back to pick us up after school. Ava, Jade, and I all walk to the 200 hall before splitting off towards our classes. When I finally make it to class, I am greeted cheerfully by all my friends. Elijah gets up from his desk and we do our typical handshake before I take a seat beside him and a few others.

Mrs. Ross speaks up when the class's roaring comes to a halt.

"Okay class, you all know what to do for your projects. I hope you enjoy the groups I put you in. If anyone needs any help just let me know."

She takes her seat quietly.

As I glance around my small group, I familiarize myself with the faces quickly.

"Justin why were you late today." Elijah questions.

Making up something on the fly I blurt out that I woke up late but send him a text saying I will explain later when there are less ears around.

"Okay well let's get started." A voice giggles.

I look to who that comment came from. When I turn around, I see a short girl with curly dark brown hair, carrying a lot of paper and folders. Clumsily she almost drops everything, and I grab a couple things from her arms so she can sit down. As she places all her paperwork down, she straightens her glasses.

"Hey Alivia, could you go grab some of the glue sticks from the extra table in the back." Phillip asks.

I make a mental note that her name is Alivia and continue scanning my textbook. Elijah leads the group as we look through the textbook for answers about World history.

Conveniently, all the information about the Scepin war that was used to obtain Nero is left out. As I look through the book now knowing the truth, I notice that anything related to the war is gone.

Either that or edited heavily. Ignoring this, I press forward, and we finish finding all the information we need for our project. I grab everyone's packets and turn them in to Mrs. Ross's desk. As I make my way back to the group.

Alivia waves me over frantically. I jog over and she quickly bombards me with multiple questions.

"Can you write in sharpie on the poster boards I brought? Could you also draw a couple things as well? Pleaseeeee. I heard you have great handwriting and you're an artist in your spare time."

Shocked that she has even heard of my art, I hesitate for a moment.

"Of course, I don't have a problem with that." I agree.

She smiles brightly and turns back to another girl. I follow her gaze and before I know it, the girl looks up at me. We lock eyes. The girl gives me a disgusted expression.

"I honestly hate working with Lustro's." She mutters.

Neither of us back down as she keeps staring at me. I do not feel even slightly intimidated by her presence and I stand up.

"Do we have a problem"!? I bark angrily.

The girl has long black hair, her eyes look to be hazel, and she stares back with a serene expression.

"What are you staring at"? I scream.

Justin Avery

As my words blast across the classroom everyone stops, directing their attention towards us. I pause, realizing that now all eyes are on me. The girl covers her face and begins to bawl her eyes out. Dramatically knocking things off her desk. She sells her acts so well that people start to give me the stink eye and a couple girls run over to comfort her.

"I was just spacing out. I'm so sorry. I didn't mean to upset you." She cries.

Before I can even say anything Mrs. Ross scolds me harshly and escorts me out of the classroom. As I peer back, I can see the girl snickering at my expense and rage builds up as I am forced out of the class.

"Justin, what has gotten into you"?! Mrs. Ross yells.

"Melissa is a quiet and respectful child. You have no reason to blow up on her like that. I want you to apologize to her and the class immediately! Do you understand me"?

As I acknowledge her demands the bell sounds for the end of 3rd period.

I fight back a mischievous grin knowing I just slithered out of an apology, and I quickly grab my backpack.

Instantly turning to exit the classroom I hear some of the girls including Alivia and Melissa bickering about me, but I ignore them and walk out the class. On my way down the 100 hall, I hear the girls exit the classroom and start shouting.

"There he is."

34

Puzzled by this, I turn around to see who they are pointing at, when I see Julien.

Julien is the son of Joviality's governor. His father has more power than any other governor in Nero, they call the shots for the entire city but if he chooses to, he could overrule another governor's say in any situation. Julien has a twin brother, Adrian who is in my next class. They both were born with the ability to refract light into a solid force or objects. This ability is extremely rare in most cases and astronomical in their case considering both twins have the Sathon ability. What makes things worse is that nobody will call them out for using it against other people. Even teachers or Lumin officers! Everyone fears that the twin's father, the governor, will destroy their lives and families. Not even the Lumin guards give the boys trouble after one of their men shoved Julien. Later that night the Lumin force found his body mutilated by a river! What's odd about that is that they're apart of the Lumin civilization.

The only figures above their father on the totem pole are the kings of Nero and the royal guardians.

"Hey Justin"! Julien barks.

I flinch nervously as his voice booms down the hall. Never could I have imagined that Julien's anger and rage would be directed at me. All that mocking Ava and I did a two days ago isn't all that funny.

I turn and face him, not backing down. He rushes me and slams me into a set of lockers, knocking the wind out of me!

35

Justin Avery

As I sit down trying to catch my breath, he grabs me, lifting me by my shirt and tearing it in the process before slamming me into the lockers again.

"You put your hands on my girlfriend"? He shouts, spit hitting my face.

As I look on, his girlfriend Melissa, smirks and flips me off.

A teacher sees what's going on but closes their door and walks away from the window! I steam over in anger thinking of how they could've helped but ignored me.

Julien slams me against the lockers a third time demanding an answer.

Now agitated I argue back with him. "No, I didn't even touch her."

Julien reels back for a punch. His fist glowing golden, but I instinctually headbutt him.

He stumbles backwards holding his eye and I land on my feet. Most kids would run right about now. However, I am way too prideful to backdown to anybody, especially not to anyone like him.

Now tossing all caution into the wind, I chuckle softly as I see a small blood stream trickle down from his gashed eyebrow.

"What's wrong Julien? Scared of losing to a Lustro"? I taunt.

Enraged, Julien rushes me, but he is sloppy. I duck his glowing punch and he crushes the lockers behind me!

"Wow, if that would've connected, I might not have a chest cavity anymore." I think to myself.

Rolling to the left I clench my fists tightly, ready to take him down. Before I know it, everyone is watching us.

Julien is about to rush me again when Adrian steps between us both, yelling at everyone to knock it off.

Jade also steps in, being bigger than Julien and myself. His size intimidates everyone cheering on the fight.

"This isn't over Justin." Julien comments before backing off.

Internally I sigh as he heads in the opposite direction.

I turn to Adrian and give him a nod and for once, a Lumin and Lustro agree on something.

I race off and catch up to Jade who's already departed the hallway.

Jade and I both start sauntering to lunch together.

"You know you can't take him Justin." He starts to lecture.

Justin Avery

I roll my eyes and jokingly boast.

"I had him until you interrupted me. I could have been a legend bro"!

Jade stares at me in disbelief.

"I hope you're joking dude. The guy has like fifty pounds on you."

I laugh loudly.

"No wonder his punches weren't landing. He needs to push back from the table."

Jade eyes me curiously. "And what's that supposed to mean"?

I backtrack quickly.

"I mean he isn't fat, just maybe he should hit the gym and maybe he could hit me."

"Nice save." Jade chuckles.

We enter the cafeteria as the late bell sounds.

We walk over to the line, cutting almost towards the front and grab our trays. Some first-year students start to speak up about us cutting them and I turn around staring the group down.

"Seniority, lil boy." I growl with an arrogant grin.

Justin Avery

The three first-year students glare back as if they want to fight for the spot.

Jade turns around staring at them, awaiting their reaction and they back down ignoring our presence entirely. We purchase our food and head to the snack bar. I walk around with Jade knowing I cannot afford anything in here, but it is nice to just admire the desserts. The lady at the counter gives me a look of confusion and calls me over to her.

"You can go ahead and get you something sweetie, just don't tell anyone I told you so."

Amazed, I thank her and rush over to the milkshake machine, pouring chocolate and vanilla into my cup as high as it can hold and follow Jade on our way out.

We head to the back of the new cafeteria, plopping down at our table. Lunch flies by as we eat and laugh about our crazy day. Jade brings up my fight with Julien and the table erupts, we start to get into what happened while everyone salivates over the juicy story like it was their final meal. They debate the validity of the story, and the guys argue until the bell rings.

Heading back to class, Elijah cannot seem to get over the story and continues to badger me about every detail until we get to Ms. Jordan's class.

This is my favorite class of the day and Ms. Jordan is the best teacher I have ever had. Not to mention I absolutely love Marine biology.

Runaways

As we watch a movie about Mocking otters, (Motters), and what they do for the ecosystem. I write my notes down. However, I become distracted by some loud snoring.

A few others and I all turn around to see who is sleeping. To no surprise it is Adrian. A couple girls giggle at him and I turn back around annoyed by his lack of effort. Adrian is Julien's twin brother but being born on the same day is where the twins similarities stop.

Ms. Jordan does her best to ignore his snoring. However, she hops up to confront him once again.

"Umm Mr. Ibiza, would you please wake up and be attentive in my class"? She questions.

Adrian glares at her coldly and sits up annoyed, rolling his eyes he wipes the sleep slime from his face.

Finally, I settle back in and focus on the video. A half hour or so passes and I hear a desk dragging on the floor. I turn back and Adrian is getting up to leave the class.

"Adrian, where are you going"? Ms. Jordan calls out to him.

Adrian makes his chair glow purple, it levitates, and he launches it at the projector screen!

As static ripples around the screen He chuckles and tosses her the bird.

He continues his way out the classroom.

Justin Avery

The final bell rings soon after his exit and the class erupts excitedly, eager to head home.

Jade and I head down the main hallway towards the bus ramp. On our way, Julien spots me. He screams out my name and starts charging my way before someone steps in his way.

It's Adrian.

"Bro, this is not the time. Can we just go home already? School is out." He pleads.

Julien hesitates before obliging to his younger brother. Adrian looks back at me and we both nod to each other again.

I have never spoken with him before, but he's earned my respect from this day forward.

After Jade and I travel towards the outside basketball courts, we find Ava. We smile and chat as we head back towards my house.

"You should stay at home and spend some time with your mother, we plan on dipping later today." I inform Ava.

She nods.

Some time goes by and Jade splits on his own path to get to a friend's house.

Ava lets herself inside the house and greets my mother kindly.

"Hey, I hope you had a great day at work". Ava cheerfully states to my mom before plopping down on the couch.

Runaways

We all count all our things as we repack our bags for the fifth time. Eventually Jade arrives with his bag and Ava grows tired of my perfectionism. She starts complaining about the time.

I look towards the clock.

It is around 5pm. I decide to side with her, and we take our small bags filled with two sets of clothes. One set for any hot areas we will encounter and one more for any area where we could freeze at night or if it rained hard. With a bunch of other small items and the white box Jade risked his life for, I take the lead as we sneak out the back door and head off down a trail that will take us towards the nearest forest.

Jade stays behind us just far enough to keep an eye out for any followers. As we're just getting into our trip, I hear someone sprinting down the trail we're taking.

"It's like they aren't even trying to be stealthy." I think to myself.

We rush behind a group of trees to hide. I stretch my head around the wide trunk, and I notice it is my mother! She's carrying a sizable bag.

I come out from my cover, and she hands me the bag telling me we have plenty of food, water, and a great waterproof tent all inside. She also hands us a lot of money saying we are going to need it when we get to other towns. Ava begins to question how much money she gave us, but my mom rushes us off to start our journey.

Justin Avery

As we head deeper into the forest Jade shifts to the middle and then towards the rear of the group. Each of us keeping a wide eye out for any guards or any predators that may attack us for our food.

After about an hour of consistent hiking we make it to a huge hill. When we get to the top, we all look down to see nothing but endless desert.

Jade gives me a childish smirk as he drops his bags and rolls down the hill screaming.

"Wheeeee"!!

I chuckle and look to Ava for help, picking up his two bags. It's no use as she flies down the hill shortly after Jade.

I scramble to grab her bags as they start to slide down the hill behind her. Scooping up everyone's items, I'm about to start down the steep hill after them, when I hear someone moving behind me!

Dropping the bags, I whip around ready to defend my friends from the guards. I stare nervously at the rustling bush when a teenager I recognize steps out with his hands up.

When his hood drops, I shout his name.

"Donshay! What's up man"?

I drop my guard and walk over to welcome him. Don tells me that we don't have any weapons and that he could help us with that problem.

Runaways

"Of course, man! Please come along with us"! I attempt to convince him.

His eyes widen as he takes off towards the bush. I stare at him, harder than before, wondering where he's going.

He grabs a bag from the bush. Don runs back towards me with uncontrollable laughter and a smile that could be seen from miles away. I return the smile and we grab the extra bags as we head down the hill carefully. Jade waves to Don as Ava makes a sarcastic comment about me being afraid to roll down the hill. I roll my eyes and toss her sling at her.

Don suggests that we hurry and get moving because it will get hotter as the day goes on.

We hike close together and keep an eye out as we continue to go forward. As we walk, I explain to Don about what we found in that box and what the map says to catch him up.

Jade takes the lead and keeps glancing up and down as if something is wrong. Ava takes the map from him with a perplexed expression painted across her face. We all stop to take a brief break, sitting under a nearby tree, we go over the map together. We see that we need to collect a special ruby before moving on to our next location. After moving from each "RubySpot" we must collect a new gem. Each gem serves a purpose to our adventure and what they hold inside is special but is not specified at all.

Even after going through everything in the box, we gain nothing new about why we should collect the gems.

Justin Avery

Donshay hops up in excitement and starts jumping around. I can tell he's been waiting to leave Joviality ever since we were kids, and now we have the chance to do something amazing. It's obvious that he's elated to be in this situation. I get up after him and everyone starts to walk again.

We chat and keep a great conversation going as the group keeps moving. Don points out that the map has a time stamp that appears when you look towards the top left corner but fades away when you roll the digital map back up.

"That's a trippy effect, it's wild what technology we have now." He comments.

"Too bad we're going to have to face this same technology when we expose the truth about the kings." Jade dishearteningly mutters.

Donshay drops his head, looking embarrassed.

About an hour of walking later the temperature skyrockets.

One look at Donshay and it's obvious for everyone to see that his excitement has vanished and evaporated along with any water that should have been in the nearby area to replenish our energy. Even if only momentarily.

Ava suggests we take a break in our tent. Jade puts the bag my mother gave us down and unzips it. As he places it on the scalding sand, we all stand around as the merciless sun beats down on us.

Runaways

I see that my mom has packed us some storage pods. I rummage through the items in the bag and notice my mother packed us tents, extra clothes, and a plethora of food and water.

Ava tosses one down and the pod begins dancing rhythmically, as the small flash dissipates a platter of crackers, ham, Swiss cheese cubes, and a few water bottles settle in its wake.

I turn around to see Ava beaming when she spots the meal. As we all eat, we roll out a towel and finish up our water.

We relax for about thirty minutes before I start zipping up the bag and tossing it around my neck onto my back.

I lead the group back onto our journey knowing that the headcount tonight will certainly have the guards on the move to pursue us.

Shortly after we get started again Don stops us and silently points out a small camp built up ahead. Jade also shows us that there is a small water hole by the camp.

We huddle up to decide if the fresh water is worth the risk of being caught.

"For all we know, that could be anyone in that settlement. Let's just lay low and keep moving. It's too risky and we already have our own water." Donshay states.

I look to everyone for their perspective when I realize Ava has already taken off towards the camp! Jade takes off after her but screeches to a halt when he sees wild Bingoes walking around the camp near the water hole!

Foolishly Jade shouts at her to come back our way.

The predators are alerted to his cry and begin to search for its source.

Two adult Bingoes spot Ava and sprint at her. Don races to her rescue pulling out two daggers. I don't know how to react and freeze in my tracks.

Don effortlessly throws a dagger into the animal's shoulder, the other Bingo turns from Ava and charges Donshay, who does a flip over the creature and slashes its back. I drop my bags to charge while its back is turned to Don.

Suddenly I feel as if my body is a metal rod that has just been struck by lightning!

I launch myself forward to slam the Bingo on its injured backside but a turquoise aura leaks from my hands eerily. I stop myself a few feet away from the injured animal and stare at my hands in disbelief.

"What- what is this"? I mutter to myself.

Everyone around me stops and just watches anxiously. Even the Bingo stops, looking bewildered.

The pause in our struggle does not last long before its instinct kicks in and he lunges at my throat! I take a step back and punch the animal as hard as I can!

"Ping"!!

Runaways

The deafening noise goes off as I crush the savage beast's muzzle, the Bingo goes flying past Donshay and goes crashing into the sand mound not too far back behind us.

The other Dingo scampers off after hearing the frightening noise.

Ava runs up and holds my arm in the air. A stream of turquoise light follows from my hands, illuminating the air where my hands had just passed through.

Gasping, she waves my arm around wildly, being mesmerized by the color.

Jade makes his way to me, amazed at what I just did. He questions how I even managed to pull that off. I laugh and respond to everyone, stating that I got my leg healed from the same turquoise liquid too. Once again, they stay silent eyeing me, hesitating on whether to believe me.

"Do you not see me right now? I'm glowing guys. What would I gain by lying about this"? I jokingly yell at them.

Donshay rests a comforting hand on my shoulder.

"I have no idea what happened, but I'll always believe you bro. That was absolutely amazing"! He states cheerfully.

I nod, accepting his answer.

We look at Ava who's now going through the tent for supplies. I gaze at her and ask facetiously.

"So, we're stealing now"?

She stares back disgusted. Before I get any more attitude, I walk away silently with my hands on my hips.

"Forget it." I mutter, annoyed.

Jade runs over to the water hole and starts to fill his canteen bottle. I start walking north from our position knowing in an hour the heat will hit its peak and most likely stay like that until midnight.

"Why is it never this hot in the city"? Ava whines.

Donshay quickly responds.

"Well, the city has an outside barrier that blocks out unnecessary heat and the city roads are actually pumping cooled air into the streets. It's wild but yeah, it usually never goes above seventy-five degrees Fahrenheit."

She rolls her eyes.

"I knew that brainiac, I didn't need your stupid lecture, I was just saying it because it's unbearably hot right now."

I make conversation with Don as we continue trekking through the desert. Glancing down at his knives I question where he got the beauties. Donshay informs me that he made them with his father.

Astonished, I keep my pace but gander down to get a closer look. Don grabs the map from me and hands me his dagger so I can study his weapon.

Runaways

I notice not only that it has a very sturdy handle, but that Donshay encrusted his initials into his dagger as well. I hand it back over. He exchanges the map for his weapon, stating we need to stop in a couple zones before finding a way out of Nero.

As he gives me a pleading look, he murmurs. "There are a couple things I'd like to do before we go."

Before I can even respond, Jade and Ava run up heavily breathing all over us. I eye him and we both somehow acknowledge that we will have this conversation later.

As we trek along for hours the heat picks up and our pace worsens. I look to Jade who now is profusely sweating, and I try to encourage him with a joke.

Jade's head doesn't budge, but he keeps trudging along, not too far behind me. Nobody says anything for a while as we continue hiking, a heavy silence hangs in the air. As we climb another hill, I begin hearing something whistling towards us. Instantly I whip around to defend my friends. A spear lands to my left. If I wasn't paying attention, it could've skewered me!

Everyone turns tentatively, and our worst fears are confirmed.

"Lumin guards"! I quickly shout to the others.

Chapter 3:
Blanco haired Bandit

"Around fifteen guards are headed our way." Donshay barks.

Don then taps a button on his belt, it drops to the ground before it straightens out into a staff. Don then kicks the staff to Ava and tells Jade that he has spiked knuckles in his bag. When Jade grabs his weapons, he lines up beside me. I shout out at Donshay to toss me something.

He shakes his head, and his facial expression doesn't change at all.

"You better figure out how to use that turquoise aura again. That's all I got." Don shouts.

I sigh, and we prepare to fight for our lives.

A truck drifts across the sand and abruptly stops. The first guards hop out of the truck and rush us. Splitting off into two groups, giving them a three on two advantage.

Ava and I are forced backwards as they charge, the other nine guards stand by with fully automatic weapons on their hip.

Ava swings for the bleachers knocking a guard out cold with a swift blow to his skull, his head gear slightly crushed.

Runaways

I wrestle with a guard and try to bring out my hidden power. No luck. The grown man picks me up effortlessly before slamming my body into the hot sand.

Ava sends the staff rifling into the man's ribcage and he lets me go. Winded, I try to stand and help her out. The guard quickly sweeps my legs and lunges on top of me. I flip him and start swinging wildly on his face. Before I know it, the third guard grabs me and throws me off his partner.

"Can you six, really not handle a couple of children"?

One of the Lumin official's growl as he fires his weapon, killing one of his own men!

Both engaging parties stop and turn to the other officers holding guns. One of them steps forward clutching his weapon tighter.

"We weren't approved to use lethal force but if you guys can't corral a couple of silly teenagers, I'll use it on you"!

His steely gaze makes my nerves rattle.

"Did he just kill one of his own men? Just like that? There was no warning whatsoever, he just spilled his subordinates' blood." I panic internally.

I quickly decide to make my move while everyone is distracted.

Rushing over, I drop kick both officers in their chest and Ava comes down hard on them with the staff again and again until they stop moving. She rushes over to help Donshay and Jade who seem to be holding their own against the officers. The lead Lumin official shakes his head disappointingly as he signals the other eight to follow him. With their weapons trained on us we begrudgingly surrender.

Jade looks to me and we all know that there is nothing we can do. They surround us and the leader orders us down on our knees. They confiscate our weapons as a larger van pulls up beside us and a guard hops out.

On his waist he seems to have electric bands of some sort. Unable to read the guards expression through his mask, he uses the electric bands as if they were handcuffs. One by one we're patted down and thrown into the back of the van.

The Lumin guard approaches me lastly for a pat down. All hope seems to be lost when at the last second, I notice something small in the air, flying towards us at breakneck speed.

My eyes widen as I realize it is a girl! She hops off her glider and drop kicks the leader in his head, he whips back and collapses onto the sand lifeless!

I quickly hop up and kick the gun out of a guard's hands. It goes off wildly, hitting him and an officer to his right.

They roll around writhing in agony and the girl yells at them.

"Shut up! The bullet barely caught your shoulder you big babies."

Runaways

The others duck for cover as I grab the assault weapon. The Lumin officers know now that we have all the leverage, and they surrender.

I slam the butt of the weapon onto each officers' head until they are all out cold.

Now turning to the girl, I gaze at her astonished. Without a word she takes everyone's electric bands off and pockets them. I thank her, and she chuckles.

"You know if you wanna find the truth you're gonna need help along the way." She claims.

I nod as she picks up her glider.

"Follow me with that van, and make sure it isn't bugged"! She orders as she turns her back to us.

As she opens her glider and waits on us to get settled, Ava questions what does bugged mean. Don explains that the truck may have a tracking device in it and for some reason Ava rolls her eyes at him again.

"I just can't win with this girl"! Don shouts in frustration.

As Jade moves around the vehicle, we both check under it and find nothing. We slide out from under the vehicle and give our new friend a thumbs up before starting the van up to follow her.

We drive for about a good ten minutes and we end up in a slightly less sandy valley with mountains all around.

Justin Avery

"Wow, who knew Nero had such great scenery." Ava comments in awe.

Once we snake our way around what seems to be a maze of trees and rocks, we make it to this cave.

We pull in slowly and park deeper inside the cave, as Ava grabs our stuff and gets out. I speed up to talk to the new girl.

"Hey, so what's your name? Or at least give me a nickname so we can address you by something."

She glances at me before giving me her name.

"You can call me Jacqui. Listen loser, there are some lightweight suits in a room down the hall, it's the third door on your left. If that spear hit, you...."

Her sentence trails off, leaving it to linger in the air.

"Just go grab a suit so you'll be safe if something dangerous occurs." She states grimly.

Attempting to make a joke of the situation I think of something clever.

You know what's weird? It's funny how they weren't allowed to use lethal force but threw a spear at me"! I chuckle nervously.

Jacqui gives me a small laugh and I wave for the others to follow me as I thank her.

Runaways

Everyone searches around the room until we all stop as we spot this large machine. I tap the screen and we all drop our jaws when we see the unique customization of each suit.

Some options allow you to have thicker material around the chest area or wherever you'd prefer to attach it. As I rapidly click through the screens, eager to see what my suit will look like. The machine buzzes as smoke pours out before my suit rises in a clear container out of the floor!

As the glass container rises above us, a small door opens, I grab my suit. The glass retreats into the floorboards. I leave the room and quickly put the suit on under my clothes.

I look around and find a nearby mirror and stare myself up and down.

Getting hype from seeing how great I look. I scream in a hushed tone to myself.

"Look at yourself man"! I chant.

I beat my chest and flex my muscles in the mirror. Making a higher pitched voice, I act as if I'm Ava.

"Oh my gosh Justin, you look so ripped." I shriek, still in a hushed voice.

Now replying to myself in the mirror I laugh and arrogantly spout out.

"Oh, I haven't even been working out."

As I turn to leave the room, I realize Jacqui has been at the door laughing silently.

I beam brightly and spring at her trying to corral her before she tells the others!

She whips around the corner and heads in the opposite direction toward rooms farther down the hall that I have not explored. As I race after her laughing loudly, I do my best to keep up, but she is too quick.

Jacqui turns into a random room. I manage to cut her off and I am blocking the only exit. I grin widely knowing she has nowhere to go. Her smile falters and she raises her arms in defeat.

"Okay, okay, you win. Your secrets safe with me you loser." She laments candidly.

I laugh, letting my guard down for just a moment. Jacqui's suit glows purple and she rockets over me! I duck and fall backwards, and she takes off down the hall. I reach out attempting to grab her leg, but she hops out of my reach and sticks her tongue out at me as she runs off.

Suddenly, I feel energized and when I reach out a second time, the turquoise light fires towards her. It forms into a hand and grabs her firmly!

I freak out realizing my power is back.

Before she has a chance to escape, I yank my arm back and Jacqui comes flying towards me. Laughing hysterically, I levitate her over my shoulders and toss her back in the room that she had previously escaped from.

Opening my hand now, Jacqui is quickly released from my grasp and the turquoise energy dissipates. Astonished, she sits on the floor staring at me.

"What in the blue random was that"? She shouts appalled.

"Turquoise random." I correct her and she stares at me.

"That was awful. Don't do that again." She chuckles.

"But it made you laugh"! I insist.

She rolls her eyes and I help Jacqui to her feet before catching her up on the entire story on why my friends and I are leaving Nero. I also explain how I got these esoteric abilities.

Jacqui goes on to explain that her family used to live in Stembis, one of the cities in Nero, but tried to escape a couple weeks prior.

"We ended up getting split and I'm not too sure if everyone is okay." She admits.

After a few moments she decides to go into detail about the situation.

"My family is pretty well known in the city of Stembis. My mother was an insanely intelligent scientist, and my father was an up-and-coming journalist. My father had told the family that he had discovered something terrifying, and we needed to pack up and leave the country immediately. Once we left though, the Lumin officers came after us and even though we tried to fight back, we ended up being split apart. I have not seen them since the Lumin guards attacked a few days ago. When I saw the same thing happening to you and your friends, I had no choice but to intervene. I try not to think of the worst, but I think they might be dead."

Jacqui's eyes dart away from mine and then she looks towards the floor before she mumbles something I cannot understand. I ask her to repeat herself and she blurts out that she does not want to be here in Nero with the corrupt kings anymore.

I attempt to comfort her as Jacqui is visibly flustered.

"Hey, think of it like this, you are the only reason my friends and I are even still here. We are in debt to you for saving our lives and if the opportunity arises, I promise I will help you find your family." I spout with confidence leaking from my words.

"You promise Justin"? Jacqui questions as she puts her pinky finger out tentatively.

"I promise." I grin at her softly.

She smiles warmly before giving me a small hug. "Thank you, I don't wanna be alone anymore."

Surprised by her affection, I hug her back before she lets go. Jacqui, beaming now asks me how we even plan on leaving Nero.

"I mean we don't have a boat or a plane." I reply nervously.

Runaways

"We don't now I mean, but there is a port near Comely, I'm sure we could find a boat since Comely is a much smaller town than Joviality." I comment.

Not fully convinced, Jacqui shrugs indifferently.

"If you say so loser. I'm down to follow your lead." She replies.

"Why do you keep calling me that"? I inquire.

Jacqui places her hands on her hips and chuckles.

"Because I think it fits you. To me, you're a cute little loser." She replies.

"She thinks I'm cute"?! I almost scream aloud.

As she leads me back to the others, we both notice everyone has their own armor design.

Jade spots me at the door and comes over to tell me about his suit. I analyze his unique design and show him my much slimmer suit design.

"No, you guys are not going to walk around with me, looking like a bunch of bozos in shining armor." Jacqui laughs.

As she makes her way to the machine and presses a few buttons, the machine whirls loudly before all our suits change into clothes!

"Don't worry though, the clothes are just as affective. Maybe just a little less actually, but the stealthy and stylish look is worth it.

We would stick out like a sore thumb if we walked around with blatant armor on." Jacqui chuckles.

Everyone thanks her and we all decide to settle in her place. Hours go by as we all acquaint ourselves with Jacqui, we all tear into the food that Jacqui and her family somehow stole from the small shops in Stembis. As night falls, we start to pack our stuff to head to Comely in the morning.

Jacqui heads to her room early and Jade lays down in the back seats of the truck to sleep. I walk out and notice Ava is sitting at the edge of the cave, stargazing.

I slide down beside her. She gives me a puzzled look and I ask her if she's doing alright.

A couple ravens shrill in the distance as the wind blows softly.

Without making eye contact with me she tells me she is worried about what could happen to us on this adventure.

"Ava… I know it's scary, I mean we could've died today, but we." I start nonchalantly.

Ava snaps her head towards me with tears streaming down her face as she cuts me off. Her voice breaks.

"That's the issue Justin! I could have lost you today. I think we should go back and just be normal teenagers again." She sobs.

I hug her and speak softly.

Runaways

"Ava, I need you to be strong with me, I understand that death is a constant threat, but Jade lost both his parents and I have no clue where my father disappeared off to. There are rumors that he's alive, but it's been almost a half a decade and I've just accepted the worst. I'd rather die avenging what so many people sacrificed themselves for, than to just sit here doing nothing." I spout heroically.

"Don't say that." Ava whimpers.

"Well, it's the truth, we can't go back to being normal teenagers again. I know the truth is hard to digest." I reply bluntly.

Ava shakes her head softly before whispering.

"I know."

We stare into each other's eyes for a minute before Jacqui walks over towards us, questioning.

"Hey, is everything okay guys? I heard yelling."

Ava wipes her tears quickly and does her best to put up a façade.

"Yeah, everything is fine. We were just laughing about old stories." She lies.

Jacqui tightens her eyes annoyed at the blatant and unnecessary lie.

I'm sure she sees through the front instantly. Surprisingly, Jacqui chooses not to comment.

I get up and walk back to the kitchen exhausted. Eventually I move towards the couch to finally get some rest.

Before I get too far into dreamland, Donshay whispers.

"Get the big sleep and I'm not talking about the Salvador Dali painting." He comments.

I chuckle to myself and respond quietly while curling up on the couch.

"Good night homie."

Sleep zooms by, as I awaken, I feel extremely groggy. Moments later I find myself in the kitchen after poking my head in a couple of rooms, I see Jacqui and Ava chatting at the table. Jacqui spots me at the doorway and invites me in to grab some cereal and talk with them.

"I have some off-brand stuff in the cabinet so I'm sorry if you're a little too bougie for that, loser." Jacqui warns.

Smirking at me, both the girls giggle and continue eating. I look around not knowing what to grab, I see a box with a walrus on it and decide it couldn't be too bad.

After pouring a bowl I take a seat next to Ava.

"So, Justin, what are we doing next? Comely has a port but we need to figure out a way to get there undetected." Jacqui questions.

Runaways

Ava chimes in saying something along the lines of me needing to plan something smart since I am the one with superpowers.

I struggle to resist dropping a sarcastic remark, because I do not see any correlation with the two things. After a few moments of weighing if my joke is worth getting punched, I keep my mouth closed and answer the question.

"Well for starters, I think that we should wait out the day and then head there at night."

They both eye me cautiously, awaiting my reasoning. Jade speaks up from the doorway slightly startling us.

"I agree with Justin, Comely is a lot less active at night and they don't have guards roaming the city at night like we have in Joviality. Or at least there aren't as many guards." His voice booms.

The girls nod their heads in agreement and Donshay speaks up, vehemently disagreeing with my idea. His voice cuts into the silence and agreement like a warm knife through butter.

"It won't work, I am sure that Comely is on high alert looking for some teenagers in a stolen truck. Especially considering that it's the nearest city from Joviality and those guards that we attacked probably have reported back what happened". Don growls.

I pause briefly, before arguing with him.

"They'll spot us easily if we head there right now and they'll shoot us down. We need to be stealthy"!

Donshay gets annoyed and raises his voice.

"No amount of stealth is going to help us when they're expecting our arrival! Not to mention that our friend over here decided to spill their leader's blood! And don't get me started on how staying here in this smelly cave makes us sitting ducks for a search party"!

Jacqui stands up, sporting an irritated look on her face.

"Well, I don't care! If you don't like my makeshift home, then you can sleep your ungrateful tail somewhere else. Perhaps the Lumin prison? We're gonna get out of Nero even if I gotta go through eight hundred more Lumin officers"! She hisses angrily.

I smile softly. Thinking to myself.

"I like the fire Jacqui brings to the group. It is oddly therapeutic and gives me hope. Although I wish she would stop calling me a 'loser' so much."

Donshay rolls his eyes and storms out of the room. We decide to load up and leave in a couple of hours to avoid being in the same area. We walk around the cave, packing up what little items Jacqui owns.

As I am cleaning up, I bump into Don, and we start to head outside to talk.

"Hey Justin, I don't know if we genuinely have a shot at stealing a boat. The Light will have as many guards stacked by the ports around town with guns as they can. They could easily annihilate us without even flexing their massive military muscles."

Runaways

I assure him I know the risk of attempting to force my way out and we will come up with something when the time comes.

"Honestly though, Donshay, do you have a better plan? We are going to have to escape barely holding onto our lives no matter what we decide to do."

Unconvinced he shakes his head, upset and heads back inside.

After about twenty minutes Jacqui calls us all into the kitchen.

"Listen guys, I hate the idea of going in broad daylight, like a lot. We are not gonna take that risk, I would much rather go by the cover of night and try to sneak off with a boat. I have a plan for us to get in and out undetected, but I'm going to need a volunteer to go with me." She states confidently.

Nobody raises their hand, so she grabs mine, yanking me up from my chair.

"So, you and I are going to go scout the area together and try to set up check points prior to going tonight."

I smile, enjoying the idea of getting away from the tension inside the cave. I follow Jacqui out to the truck.

"I wonder what this city will look like." I ponder.

As we climb into the truck Jade warns me. "Hey Justin, be careful, I really don't like this idea to go scout the city. Although I know it's best if we have a layout considering none of us have ever been in Comely long enough to identify the area. Just be careful bro." He calmly comments as he gives me a fist bump.

"We will be safe"! Jacqui shouts at the group waving goodbye frantically.

Don and Jade look on unenthusiastic but wave back.

She then slams her foot onto the gas pedal, and we zip out of the cave! She speeds through the sand as we head towards Comely. I attempt to make conversation, but Jacqui's quieter than I expect. When we get around a half mile out, she slows to a stop.

"Okay, so I have a secret to tell you. However, you have to promise to keep it from the others. I only trust you with this information Justin so please promise you won't say anything." Jacqui pleads.

"Stop calling me a loser." I attempt to bargain.

"Not a chance, loser. Just promise me." She whines.

I hesitate before agreeing to keep it between us.

Jacqui reaches into her bag in the backseat and pulls out a container of pills. I mentally note that they are a hot pink color and seem to glow.

"These are Perdu pills. They grant us the ability to stay concealed from everyone's sight." Jacqui states calmly.

"So, invisibility pills." I reply.

Jacqui stares at me smiling.

"No silly, these are much better than just becoming invisible, they hide our Ki, or life energy as well. Not to mention that our footsteps can't be heard either. Be careful though, it functions well with body heat so try to stay warm and keep moving. If your body heat drops drastically, you'll become visible again." She warns.

Jacqui smiles briefly before she tosses me one, without breaking eye contact I catch it with my left hand and quickly pop it into my mouth. She swallows one as well, closing the jar before securing it in her bag again.

"They last for a little more than an hour, so we gotta move." She also tosses me a backpack to carry, and it blends in with my 'camo.'

"Whoa, so whatever we touch turns invisible too"? I ask.

"Just objects smaller than us, so we can't carry anything huge. That's why you should bring the backpack." Jacqui replies.

I nod in agreement as Jacqui smiles softly.

We decide to park the truck and take off for the entrance. Somehow, she notices that there is a newly built gate.

"Hmm, this girl gives me weird vibes. Why did she want me to keep this information from the others, and where did she get such sophisticated pills"? I ponder to myself.

As I brush these thoughts away, I focus on the entrance to the city. I look around nervously as the gate resembles a military base, where they limit who all is granted access to the community.

Justin Avery

Jacqui scratches her head in disbelief.

"How long has this gate been up"? She inquires.

Her confusion leads me to start wondering if Joviality has a gate being built and how long Comely has had this one up, considering Jacqui claims she escaped a few weeks prior.

Jacqui gives me a look of worry and we both sneak past the gate and armed guards.

"Wow, these Perdu pills actually work! This is so crazy"! I think to myself.

As we get a little deeper into the town, we find what we are looking for. The port is large enough for us to hide in a plethora of spots and stay unnoticed.

As we both hear a loud horn sound, we freeze in our tracks. A man with a dark helmet stands in the center of Comely with Lumin soldiers all around. A crowd begins to gather and bow as well. I realize that this is the king of Comely!

I see more people rush to bow before him as his men stand behind him proudly. Even our fellow Lustronese people begrudgingly bow.

The cities governor, and council, cower before the king. Each one of them visibly petrified and sweaty.

"Justin, look, they're scared of him." Jacqui whispers.

Runaways

I nod my head and we watch as now the entire city is now gathered around the king and his men.

A smaller man comes forward speaking for the tyrant.

"As you all should know, there are a few fugitives out and about from your neighboring city Joviality, if anyone has seen them or has any information on who they are, you will be rewarded for your loyalty." He states before promptly standing down.

The king now steps forward and the governor, along with his council become more antsy.

"Well, hello there, it's a pleasant sight to see my Lumin citizens." The king chuckles, holding back a sinister grin.

The governor greets the king and thanks him for blessing the city with his presence.

"Oh, believe me, the pleasure is all mine." The king snickers as his steely gaze pierces the council's psyche.

The tyrant drops his smile as he steps closer to the governor.

"It seems you may have some teenagers running amuck in your city. They aren't anywhere to be found in Joviality and I promise you if they escape Nero, I'll have heads roll. Are we clear"? He questions.

"Yes sire." The governor whimpers pathetically.

The king walks around patiently, circling the council, like a vulture surrounds its prey. Just awaiting death to arrive.

"You see, I hate having Lustronese bugs squirming around, but what I despise more than anything, is when they make me feel uneasy. These teenagers pose a threat to my mental health, and I won't stand for any insubordination. So, to ensure you won't fail. I'll be leaving you one hundred more guards to help you secure the city. For your sake, I hope you exceed my expectations." He snarls.

The king then comes to a stop in front of the group staring at the governor and his council, emotionless.

Suddenly a man charges the king! Wielding a sword, the Lustronese man has a determined look painted across his face.

"You die here scum. We'll be your slaves no longer"! The man shouts.

Without even breaking eye contact with the governor, the king stretches his arm out and the man implodes! A bright flash of colors shine as his skeleton is vaporized instantly!

"My husband! You... you're a monster"! A woman in the crowd wails.

"Daddy!! No"! her tormented child cries.

As a distorted cry leaves the man's dissolving corpse, the king then points his finger behind his back and without looking, the woman and her young child are also vaporized!

"Great, now they won't miss him." The king sneers with a cynical expression and malicious laughter.

"What was that! He erased them like they were nothing. How…how can anyone be that strong"? I shout, panicking inside my brain.

Jacqui stares at me in horror and the king speaks up again.

"I love children, they usually don't make that much of a mess. Anyway, as I was saying, I feel as if one hundred soldiers are more than enough. If you feel so inclined to believe that's unfair, feel free to complain, otherwise we're done here."

The king snaps his fingers as he smirks and he, along with his men vanish into thin air.

"Come on Justin, we have to keep moving, we already have wasted too much time sitting here." Jacqui comments.

"Yeah, right." I agree, doing my best to process what we just witnessed.

"We should just steal a bunch of food and load it in the boat we're gonna steal tonight." Jacqui grabs my arms, and we race off towards the boats.

We scamper around the pier looking for a quality boat that we would love to take. After looking for about fifth-teen minutes, Jacqui calls out for me, and I hop off my boat. Searching around for a few moments before I spot her, when I do find her, she's dancing in the front of a decently sized boat.

Her delicate silky white hair flowing smoothly in the wind.

Runaways

Mesmerized by her beauty, I watch her for a few moments, as she awaits my arrival. Impatiently, she turns around questioning where I am at before she catches me staring and giggles.

"Look at this boat, I think this is the one." She says softly, almost goading me to agree on her choice.

She shows me around the whole thing almost as if she was a tour guide.

Jacqui is extremely animated, and she really gets into her character, when I tell her it would be funnier if she used a Lumin accent. She starts crouching down, pointing at things the boat has, explaining why I should purchase it.

Really putting the emphasis into the Lumin accent, she simply pronounces words with so much exaggerated pizzazz, that I start to cry from holding in my laugh.

"Don't you laugh at me worm! My accent is a gift from the Gods. An underling like yourself wouldn't understand." She says bluntly while containing her own laughter.

"Act like a car salesman now." I laugh.

She chuckles, struggling to not break character and then gets super touchy on me and the boat.

"You see this wood here on the deck, eh? That's some quality mahogany right there."

Justin Avery

Jacqui slaps the floor, rubs it, knocks on it as if it were a door before over dramatically rolling towards the railing. She eyes me suspiciously.

"Are you sure you can afford this beauty? Buckaroo, after giving you this here tour, I think I'm gonna up the price thirty thousand big ems."

I burst out laughing and she gives in as well. Both of us roaring with happiness, we laugh so hard we collapse to the floor.

After finally recovering, we stare into each other's eyes. A short moment passes before she gives a soft smile and breaks off.

"Come on, we gotta grab some food to fill this beauty." She comments as she puts her hands behind her head, walking away from the port.

"Wait up"! I shout trailing after her.

Once I catch up, we talk all the way until we make it into this small grocery store.

I take control and lead Jacqui around the store. We grab a shopping cart, and she hops in. Racing around the store we grab lots of fruit, water, bread, and other essentials. Most of the items we grab are nonperishable. As the cart fills up, Jacqui spots a customer pointing in our direction. At first, I think the woman is just asking for assistance when I remember we are invisible!

"Loser, the cart is bigger than us! We need to go now"! She shrieks terrified.

Runaways

Almost on instinct I take off pushing Jacqui who is in the cart through both the customer and out the doors! We weave between a couple buildings, and I keep pushing the cart, racing as fast as my legs will allow me.

Once I feel confident that we lost anyone who may have been tracking us from the store, we both head back towards the pier. I stop abruptly, and Jacqui hops out. She tosses the whole cart full of our stolen goods into a room on the boat. Jacqui yells at me to move and we take off rushing back past the gate.

Jacqui hurries and I follow close behind. Passing dozens of the new Lumin soldiers on our way out, we don't stop running until we get back into the truck.

When we get there, we just lay on the seats breathing heavily, I look at Jacqui and she starts to laugh.

"I'm sorry, I forgot we were invisible." She rubs her head nervously admitting that she should have known better.

I brush off any blame from her feet and lay back in the seat worn out and laughing. Too tired to even be mad I just shake my head calling her crazy.

As if on cue, we slowly fade back into the reality of being visible again.

"We should just hurry and get back to the others and move tonight when hopefully there won't be much activity." I state.

Jacqui nods and starts the truck up.

Chapter 4:
The calm before the storm

After arriving back inside the cave, I collapse on the couch.
Jade saunters over questioning what happened and why I look
exhausted. I start to tell him but stop myself instantly as I remember
Jacqui's secret. Now stopping in the middle of my sentence,
realizing my near blunder, I say nothing and stare at the floor. Jade
peers at me even more perplexed than he was before. He repeatedly
asks me what I'm hiding, I deny him every time he badgers me, as I
shuffle away nervously.

Out of my peripheral vision, I can see Jacqui giving me a nod
of approval. When Jade finally quits, Ava approaches me and asks
the same question. I decline her as well.

Ava looks up at Jacqui making a disgusted expression.

The silence hangs for a couple seconds as they continue to
stare each other down. Jacqui doesn't falter and when the staring
reaches its climax, she gets in Ava's face.

"What! What are you looking at"! She shouts aggressively.

Ava flinches at the sound of her voice but tries to argue back.

Jade grabs Ava and takes her outside to calm her down. I walk
over to Jacqui to calm her. She puts a hand up waving me off, but I
press forward ignoring her and blanket her in a warm hug.

Runaways

"You guys don't need to be so confrontational about everything. Just ignore her and move forward." I comment amicably.

She tries to fight my hug off, but gives in, hugging me back.

"You're so annoying sometimes Justin, I hope you know that." She begrudgingly admits with a smile on her face.

Jacqui doesn't let go for a moment. She beams harder as she reluctantly releases her grip.

Donshay walks past us shaking his head disconnected from the entire sequence.

He struggles to hold back a raging grin.

I lead Jacqui over to the living room area and we take a much-needed rest on the couch.

"Just give me some time to relax on this forgiving couch." Jacqui moans, reclining back into the cushions.

She presses a pillow to her face and lays down before passing out. I smile and decide a quick catnap couldn't hurt anything.

After an hour or so everyone walks back into the kitchen, and we sit down at the kitchen table.

I greet everyone and start the conversation before the silence settles in.

"Is there anywhere you guys want to go before we head out to Comely? It's getting close to the time where it would be best if we departed." I comment.

"How about the place where we needed to pick up that ruby." Donshay replies.

I reach for the map, sitting on the counter and show him that the RubySpot is a little off the continent.

"We'll have to go for it after we escape Nero." I state.

He leans back against the wall and slouches down mumbling his gloomy thoughts to himself again.

"By the way, we need to be careful. There are one hundred more guards in Comely." Jacqui admits.

"What? See, this is why I said we needed to leave earlier"! Donshay scolds.

Jacqui turns to Don with a steely glare, he backs down lowering his voice.

"Just shut up Don. There was this king in the city and his power eclipses anything you could fathom. He obliterated a man, his wife, and child without a second thought. If we would have departed the cave when you wanted, we would be dead right now." Jacqui hisses.

Jade sits up, his curiosity aroused.

Runaways

"Wow, he's that strong, huh? I guess liberating our race from slavery is going to be harder than we thought." He admits candidly.

"Let's just focus on one thing at a time, where do you all think, we should go to, so we can clear our heads"? Jacqui inquires.

"Maybe we could head for the beach just outside of Comely, to relax." Jade replies.

Everyone agrees that a mini vacation before we go on our stealth mission would be great.

"Honestly, this group needs some bonding after uh, recent events." Donshay chuckles while his eyes dart between Ava and Jacqui.

We all pile in the truck and Jade hops into the driver's seat, with everything already loaded in the back, we decide it is best if we don't return.

Jacqui takes some of her machines and collects them with the storage pods. We drive through the shifting hot sand and for most of the ride, Ava and Jacqui stare out the window. As we finally slow to a stop, everyone cheers that we have finally arrived.

Ava rushes out first and everyone follows.

Jacqui taps her suit twice behind her shoulder and it quickly morphs into a bikini. Amazed, I stare at her in awe.

"Yo, how did you do that?" I question shocked.

Justin Avery

"Here loser, let me help you. These suits can switch from armor to casual clothes, to puffy winter gear, and into comfortable beach attire." She states, visibly proud.

As she approaches me, she does the same to my clothes and they transform into some tropical shorts.

"Okay Jacqui. I need to know where you get all the sublime gear. Like this is some high-tech stuff that only high-ranking officials of Nero would have." I joke playfully.

She gives me a small smile, ignoring my question and Jacqui begins walking towards a shady part of the beach where a couple palm trees are. She rolls out a pair of towels and plops down on the purple one. Jacqui gives me an inviting smile and gestures for me to lay down beside her.

I return the smile but turn away from her, jogging over to Jade. He and Ava are tossing around a volleyball and are making small conversation as they go. I decide to skip over towards Don, and I attempt to build sculptures of Jade and Ava with the sand.

As I get into the details of creating my friends in the gritty sand, I hear Ava shout.

"Heads up"! She shrieks.

I glance up and see a volleyball hurtling towards my sand people! I try to catch it but react too slow as the ball proceeds to destroy the statue versions of my friends.

An annoyed tone radiates from Jade as he stares at Donshay and I. Glancing up, I notice not only Jade but also Ava have irritated expressions painted onto their faces. Even their body language is stale as their hands rest comfortably on their hips.

"Can I help you"? I respond facetiously.

Jade and Ava stare back impatiently.

"Is there something you two want"? I question, confused now.

"We're supposed to be relaxing, so come play some volleyball against Jade and I. Unless you two just wanna draw in the sand." Ava laughs, belittling my work.

Don and I smirk at each other and spring up, quickly we rush onto the opposite side of the net to play against them.

Ava serves and launches the ball at me, but I pop it up high and Donshay slams it down into the hot sand for our first point.

Fist bumping, we start our trash talk.

"You couldn't even return the ball once?" I yell out.

We start to chuckle and poke fun at the two.

Before we can even finish our joke. Disgruntled cries come flying back at us.

"Hurry up and serve the ball back already!" Ava shouts already fed up with our overconfident attitudes.

Ava's determination glistens in the sun as she stares us down awaiting the return.

Justin Avery

I switch to the back of our play field and prepare to serve to Ava.

As I send the ball hurtling over the net, she hits it back and I watch as Don handles her return with ease.

I intensely follow each hit and prepare myself to join in when the ball flies out of his reach.

Unfortunately, this goes on for some time and I eventually crouch down, becoming bored with Ava and Donshay only playing against each other.

Almost as if she were awaiting my lack of focus, Ava launches the ball out of Don's range, and it goes flying over his head! I clumsily flail at the volleyball as I try standing up and chasing the ball, all at once. Nearly missing my target, I end up slapping it back up into the air. Donshay jumps up and spikes it into Jade's face and he falls back into the sand rubbing his eyes furiously.

"Oww! You got sand in my eyes you idiot"! He barks frustrated.

Donshay reels back. Laughing harder than ever, we collapse onto the sand and start mocking Jade.

Now enraged, he pops up instantly and heads to the back where he can serve.

Jade rifles the ball past me to Don! The volleyball smacks Donshay and he flies back gripping his face in agony.

Runaways

"Yo, that sand really does burn"! He shouts trying to clear it from the bottom of his eyelid.

His efforts do little to help and actually have a reverse effect, causing more sand to end up in his eyes.

I head over to his aid when I realize that Ava and Jade are now mocking us.

"Ow my eyes, it hurts so bad" Ava mockingly whines.

"That's a terrible imitation of me, I sound nothing like that." Don shouts finally clearing the sand from his eyes.

I help Don up and he walks to the back, so he can serve. Almost to add insult to injury Don hits the ball which hits the net and falls to the ground in the most pathetic way I have ever seen.

"2-2." Jade starts to chant and then Ava joins in.

Ava takes the ball and backs up to her line to serve it when she chuckles.

"I hope you both know that this is game point." She devilishly smirks.

She sends the ball flying over and we send it back, each of us takes our turn. We go back and forth, competitively forcing our opponent to push themselves.

This goes on for some time and Don starts to tire out.

Justin Avery

"Bro, I'm just gonna let them have this, I'm exhausted." He admits.

"Don't you dare quit on me. Come on, we got this"! I shout encouragingly.

Eventually he collapses and allows the volleyball to follow him to the sand. I look gloomily over at Jade and Ava as they rejoice their victory.

I shake my head as I begin to lumber over to the towel beside Jacqui and plop down as if I were a child, salty about losing.

"I hate being humbled. We should have won that." I growl to myself, still tethered to the stinging defeat.

I lay there groaning with my face down in the towel before I then feel a pair of soft hands rubbing on my shoulders.

"Whoa, that actually feels really good. I should've asked you for a massage earlier." I murmur wistfully.

"Oh, shut up, you're such a baby." Jacqui chuckles as she continues working on my shoulders.

Jacqui now moves to my lower back, massaging every muscle. Driving her thumbs into my back roughly, I tense up.

"Relax Justin, you're going to be fine." She reassures me as her fingers soothe my muscles.

I slowly relax and lay flat on the warm towel. I soon notice that Jacqui's hands are small but extremely soft and comforting. She continues and I start to drift further and further into the blissful feeling.

I try to move but she keeps me still and runs her hands down my sides. Jacqui continues as I murmur silently to myself.

"Do you want me to stop"? She leans in and whispers into my ear.

I struggle to spill out my words and she giggles, continuing to massage my back and sides. This continues for forever it seems, and she finally ends her session and lays down on her towel beside me.

I roll on my side, and we just stare into each other's eyes smiling. As the sun sets, we chat briefly about her past before she was living in caves or trees.

"So, what was your life like before all of this? I want to know what you used to do." I question.

"Well, I was a kid roaming around school aimlessly. I was an average student when I felt lazy and when forced to, I could conquer anything I put my mind to. And I'm not talking about the trashy lies all adults tell uninspiring kids. I mean like I could do it. I underachieved purposely just to fit in and played volleyball for the school's team. I didn't live in Joviality like you all though. I was more east coast. You've heard of Stembis right"? She questions.

"I've heard it wasn't a good place to be, since the city is so far isolated from everything else in Nero, I've heard Lumin guards can get away with pretty much anything." I respond.

Jacqui rolls onto her back and stares into the sky.

"Yeah, it was honestly the worst. Lumin guards would kidnap children that spoke out of turn and make examples of them. I don't wanna get too deep into it but once someone found the bodies, they weren't recognizable. Any small inconvenience for the soldiers could mean the end of your life. It was depressing if I'm going to be totally honest. I want to help free our people as well and that's why I'm so glad I met you, Justin. You and your friends give me hope. That's something I haven't had in a long time." She states bluntly.

Intrigued by her mysterious past, I long to question her more. However, Ava walks over informing us that we should probably get ready, so we can grab the boat and leave Nero.

Jacqui rolls her eyes, ignores Ava's presence, and then tells me she thinks it is time for us to pack up and leave to grab a boat. Ava clenches her fist and storms away. Jacqui gives a small grin before smothering it again.

"I don't know why, but I just love irritating her. Sorry I'm not more mature." She comments before sitting up and dusting herself off.

We hop up and roll up the towels before reactivating our armor back into normal clothes.

I walk with Jacqui back towards the truck and she does her best to not burst out laughing as we head to our seats in the back. As we pass, Ava stares us down and folds her arms while turning away so she doesn't have to look at me.

Once we click our seatbelts, Jade starts the truck up and we start heading towards Comely.

Runaways

Don starts the conversation about what we need to do.

"Alright, keep your clothes on for now but if we're discovered, do not hesitate to change it into your battle armor. There is no mission failure here. By the end of tonight we'll either have a boat and be on our way, or we'll be in Lumin custody. Or maybe even worse than that". He murmurs grimly.

Jacqui chimes in and starts giving everyone our plan and what we are going to do. I help her navigate the conversation as questions flood in from the others.

"Don't worry guys, we're going to get the perfect boat, just follow our lead." She assures them.

I look out the window and it is now completely dark outside.

Jade parks the truck around the same spot as when Jacqui and I had stopped earlier. Everyone starts to grab a backpack and we rapidly empty the truck. Jade takes the lead, and we walk towards the gate when Jacqui pokes me and pulls me to the side. She slides me another Perdu pill.

"What about the others? What if they get caught and we don't? We should ensure everyone is safe." I whisper, pleading with Jacqui.

Jacqui shakes her head and forces the fuchsia pill into my hand.

"Shut up loser. Take it, you are my priority. I can't trust them with these, not like I trust you." She growls in a hushed tone back to me.

"What does trust have to do with an invisibility pill." I ponder to myself.

Reluctantly, I take it, and Jacqui chuckles softly in the back of the group.

Ava glares back at her and pushes one finger over her own lips, signaling for Jacqui to be quiet.

Jacqui ignores her and tells me to pocket the pill for later. As I do so, I slide towards the front of the group, and we all crouch down by some huge stones at the front of the gate. I ask what we should do to get past the two guards at the gate.

Ava stands up without saying a word to us and rushes towards the officers. She pleads desperately with the Lumin officers.

"Please sir, could you help me? I don't know where my pet went." She cries, pathetically slumping over like a candy cane.

We all promptly shuffle back behind the boulders nervous of the outcome.

She even starts to get tears in her eyes as she questions if they've seen her puppy.

Both guards look at her confused and hesitate for a second. This small hesitation is what Ava was looking for as she lunges forward! Ava rams the gun into the first guard's chest before smoothly turning and ordering the other to the ground. We all quickly surround the officers and tie them both up with the electric bands.

Runaways

Jacqui pulls a knife to slit his throat and I grab her arm.

"What are you doing!? We can't just kill them." I shout as quietly as I can.

I then make my hand glow turquoise and punch the soldier in his temple. He goes limp, passing out but he's still breathing.

The turquoise light dissipates from my hand and Jacqui rips her arm from my grasp.

"They will kill us if you give them the chance. Remember that." She scowls and continues moving forward.

We all rush from the gate and start to make our move for the pier. Everyone races after Jacqui, who takes the lead.

It looks as if we are going to make it uninterrupted. Moments later, I notice that a group of Lumin soldiers are sprinting towards us! It isn't hard to tell that they will arrive at the boats before we do.

Jacqui immediately puts on the brakes and pulls out a gun of her own!

"Where did she get that from"!? I think to myself nervous of what our immediate future holds.

She fires at the soldiers taking a dozen or so down, they dive looking for cover.

I race towards the boats when I hear my friends screaming at me to stop. I see one of the soldiers raise his weapon at me and instinctively I put my hand up to block his fire. A turquoise light leaks from my hand and drapes down to my feet blocking the gunfire like a shield! Amazed, I keep my hand up and keep running towards our boat. With bullets whizzing by my body, I stop at a different boat from the one we picked out and hide inside. Donshay and Jade hide around a building and jump three unsuspecting Lumin guards. They quickly dispose of them and stay hidden. Ava rushes out attempting to hide behind a car further ahead and a bullet nicks her side!

Our attackers press forward and sluggishly make their way towards my friends. I try to escape from my hiding spot to assist. However, eight soldiers keep their fire on me!

"Help us"! They wail frantically.

"Guys hold on, I'm coming"! I scream as I desperately search for a solution.

I shape my hand into a gun and fire small Sathon blasts at the guards. I hit one and he flails backwards. More guards train their weapons at me, and I no longer can come out from behind my barrier.

An idea comes to mind, and I create a small Sathon spark. Almost like a TNT fuse, the turquoise line slithers its way towards a huge group of men.

KA-BOOM!

At least thirty guards are annihilated!

"Well, so much for not killing any guards, Justin. I hate it, but it had to be done." I argue with my moral compass inside my head.

Runaways

As I glance over again, I feel my energy drop rapidly!

"That attack took a lot more out of me than I thought." I mutter, vexed with my own limitations.

Several trucks of Lumin guards arrive on the scene and fifty or more armed men rush out.

"They just keep coming! I don't know what I can do to get rid of them all." I surmise, deeply dispirited.

I start to stress heavily, even though I block most of the bullets, there isn't a clear path for me to get towards my friends to save them!

Donshay, Jade, and Ava, hide behind a concrete barrier scared for their lives. More and more cracks start to form in my Sathon shield, and all hopes of success begin to fade. Suddenly twelve guards go down, screaming in agony. I look around but don't see anything.

Before I can register what is happening, something begins pulling me into the lower floor beneath the deck! I try to fight it, but it wraps my left arm tighter than before and drags me to the floor.

As I fall and slam onto the floor, I hear a soft voice.

"Ouch, why are you so heavy"?

As I look to where the voice came from, I feel a finger cover my lips shushing me. It clicks immediately.

"Jacqui, you used your Perdu pill to save me"! I try to spout excitedly.

She covers my mouth and I listen to her instructions.

"I want you to go to the wheel, start this boat up and leave in the next sixty seconds. Not one second more! I don't care who's all on, you need to go, you have the map in your backpack, right"? She asks hurriedly.

I nod my head slowly.

"Jacqui, please let me follow you up there. I'll use my Perdu pill and I'll help you save everyone." I beg, pleading with her.

"No! You're not going back up there when I already got you to safety." She scolds me in a hushed yell.

There is a short pause where nobody says anything. I open my mouth to thank her, but she pulls me into a soft kiss.

"Be safe, loser." Jacqui chirps happily.

Before I can get another word out, I hear her shoes clanging up the metal ladder and she's gone.

I start to count to myself as I run towards the front of the boat. When I reach the wheel, a wave of anxiety hits me.

I start the boat up.

"Thirteen...fourteen ...fifteen." I count to myself silently.

Runaways

Once the boat is started, I hear the fighting and yelling get louder.

"Twenty-seven…twenty-eight…twenty-nine. Where are my friends"? I whimper nervously.

My hands start to sweat and then out of nowhere Donshay slams to the floor in the room by the ladder! More gunshots ring off and then I hear a soldier cry out. I begin to lose my cool for a moment, then Jade falls to the floor!

I start to relax, having faith in Jacqui and continue getting the boat ready.

As the seconds tick by, an indescribable heat builds up inside of me, almost making me nauseous. It gets worse as neither Ava nor Jacqui come down the ladder.

"Fifty-four…fifty-five… fifty-six. Come on guys! Where… are… you"!? I scream internally.

Donshay freaks out telling me he was dragged here, and he doesn't understand what's happening. I calm him down saying everything will be alright.

I look back towards the wheel knowing it is time to go and start to back away from the wheel.

"I can't! I refuse to leave them behind." I wail nervously.

Now tears start forming in my eyes and my vision blurs.

Jade and Donshay scream at me to drive the boat away, but I'm frozen with fear, until I hear what sounds like two women fighting. I glance up and see bright fuchsia bursts of light flash repeatedly. The boat shakes as something explodes, and I fall backwards. Suddenly Ava slides down the ladder, screaming we need to leave.

"Where's Jacqui?" Jade asks.

Ava pushes me to the ground and slams the boat into its forward gear. We speed off. I climb to the top of the ladder and onto the deck. I spot Jacqui unconscious, being dragged away by Lumin officers!

I scream frustrated as the foggy night takes away my vision. I drop down and reach for the wheel when Ava slaps my hand and pushes me away.

"We have to go back for her!" I scream desperately reaching for the wheel.

Jade steps in front of me, blocking off my path.

"Justin, it's not wise to go back, we won't make it back to Comely alive. We certainly won't be able to grab Jacqui and escape again! We barely escaped just once"! He shouts.

"They'll kill her! We must go back and save her guys! We wouldn't be alive if she didn't risk her life to come save us"! I scream, tears streaming from my eyes.

Jade frowns, but he does not budge.

"Well, that was her decision, and this is ours"! Ava yells at me.

Runaways

Jade pleads with me, asking for forgiveness, as he stands in my path guarding Ava.

I rush him, trying to squeeze by, and he throws me back violently. My hands glow turquoise, fueled by rage, I sprint towards Jade, punching him in the face!

I go under his arms and grab the wheel, spinning it around to return to Comely.

Everyone slams into the wall and floor from the quick change of direction. I stand up securing my claim to the wheel of the boat.

As I try to stay on the wheel, Jade grabs me, and slams me into the floor, knocking the wind out of me.

Ava reclaims the wheel and slowly spins us away from Comely. As rage fills my body. The heat is so indescribable that I almost feel as if I might blackout.

"Stop it you guys"! Donshay shrieks nervously.

I try to stand, but Jade shoves me hard! I fly back and bang my head on the ladder. The turquoise disappears from my hands and as I gaze around slowly, I hear Don screaming at Jade to stop.

Everything looks fuzzy and I get a numb taste in my mouth before my surroundings go dark.

Chapter 5:
Cave into Betrayal

As my eyes open, some intense lights attempt to blind me.

Annoyed and disoriented, I roll over to escape the glare, but it seems as if the lights are everywhere.

I stand up, trying to locate where I am. It's no use. After failing to figure it out, I squint and try to shield my eyes from what feels like the sun.

Nothing helps.

I blink and that is when the memories hit me, the entire environment becomes pitch black.

Just like before, I see something glint in the distance and I am drawn towards it. Stalking towards the light slowly, two hot pink figures race past me and I jump back startled by their presence. I follow the two with my eyes and see that the figures are Jacqui and myself! I walk towards the two individuals, spectating their movements. They sit down laughing and talking. I slowly meander over, taking a seat down beside them. I call out Jacqui's name, hoping for the two to acknowledge me, but it is as if they don't see me.

I begin reaching out to the hot pink version of myself, curious of what's going on.

Runaways

When I tap his shoulder, he dissipates into a pink gust of air and the wind blows, carrying his particles away.

I glance over to the other figure, and I can see that she is crying. With a depressed expression painted on her face, she begins looking around frantically. The pink figure begins yelling, but her cries sound distorted. I try and understand her cries, but the broken noise begins to make my head pound. Struggling to make out what she is saying, I step back feeling dizzy from this entire experience. Her cries get louder, and louder! This continues until something in my head feels as if it is going to burst!

I try to cover my ears and block it out, but it gets louder.

"Maybe if I touch her, she'll vanish just like the pink version of myself did. I can't take much more of this distorted screeching." I think to myself as my head begins to do backflips from the pain.

I stand up from my kneeled stance. Rushing to shove Jacqui down, I prepare for a blissful silence. However, we collide!

Surprised by this, I freak out as we both tumble violently to the ground. We stare at each other for a moment and then Jacqui jumps onto me hugging me tightly and sobbing uncontrollably.

"I'm so glad you found me." She repeats between gasps.

After she finishes sobbing, Jacqui releases her death grip on me.

She then stares at me, and an icy glare takes over as her beaming grin disappears.

Justin Avery

"Justin. You have to go back". She states bluntly.

"Go... where"? I question her confused.

My blood runs cold as I put two and two together. I nod and stand up before staring at the floor. I look Jacqui in her eyes, and she frowns.

"Go back Justin, save me." Jacqui whimpers desperately.

She stands up and hugs me for a moment. Without another word being said, she smiles and takes a step back.

Jacqui then taps my forehead and I wake up on a bed.

I look around and realize I am still on the boat. I lay there trying to gather my thoughts for a moment. Finally, I stand up slowly and then walk around looking for everyone else.

Now stumbling around the main area, still groggy, a small holographic screen glows, showing the boat's coordinates have been locked.

Glancing around, it's clear nobody is operating the ship and a sneaky idea manifests itself inside my mind.

"If I move the wheel slowly, I can flip the boat around." I think to myself, tempted to change the ship's course.

I tiptoe over to the boat's wheel, eyeing it like a starving hound eyes its meal.

"Oh Justin! You're awake."

Runaways

I snap around, quickly pulling my hands away from the wheel. Ava stands before me, smiling.

Not knowing if she caught me, or even how to respond I just stare at her.

Finally, I find my words.

"How long have I been out"? I muster as my eyes search the boat tentatively.

Joyfully, she skips over and hugs me.

"Not too long, just two days, sleepyhead." She beams at me.

My eyes widen as this statement snaps me completely awake.

"How long"!? I shout again.

Quickly, I pull away from her hug and dash over to the back of the boat.

I climb the ladder taking me to the deck of the boat and as I get to the railing at the top of the ship. All I see is water surrounding the boat from all sides, miles wide.

Dropping to the floor in disbelief I just stare at the endless ocean.

"What's wrong Justin"? Ava shouts as she comes over to comfort me.

Justin Avery

I throw my hand back.

"Jacqui is out there somewhere, most likely dead or becoming a public example. I hate you. You let this happen to our friend." I shout out into the deep oceanic waters.

More thoughts run through my head, and I imagine that she's being tortured for information.

"I know that the Light will eventually break her and get some type of information on us. Everyone has their limit. No matter how stubborn she is, nobody can hold out forever." I mutter grimly.

Ava freezes, not knowing what to do with herself.

"I'm sorry Justin, I don't know what to say. I thought you'd forget after hitting your head on that ladder." She responds pathetically.

My eyes dart around, I spot Jade make his way over to me. As he holds his hand out for me to grab, hoping I'll take it to stand up.

I smack his hand away and stand up quickly before yelling in his face.

"And this is all your fault too"! I shout, shoving him towards the floor.

Jade picks himself up from the floor and raises his hands innocently, claiming he did nothing wrong.

Runaways

"Honestly, Justin, we both know that was the best decision for the group and I would do it all over again if I could." He comments calmly.

I cut my eyes at him and walk back to my bed slowly.

"You both are disgraceful. Leave me alone." I growl as I storm off.

Trying to contemplate the situation, I lock my door and start to create a plan to go save Jacqui on my own. I see in my room there is a map on the wall. I snatch it off and unlock the door before slithering over to the wheel where our digital map is.

"Now let's see how accurate this thing is." I think out loud.

I find our destination and I retrace it back on my paper map.

"I shouldn't be surprised. This paper map is garbage. There's nothing about the outside world on this map like the one Jade's dad created." I growl disgusted with the inconvenience.

After a couple minutes of planning things out I make an educated guess where I could find transportation back to Jacqui.

"We left Nero and not one of us on this boat know what the outside world looks like. Hopefully, some of these outside nations have a similar infrastructure as Nero. What if it's all just a bunch of small communities struggling to survive"? I think to myself nervously as I drag myself back to my room and plop down on the bed.

I consider many possibilities and slim down my options between stealing the boat and heading back once we get to our destination or finding another way back that will be a quick trip across the ocean.

"If I steal this boat right now, I'll have to handle these three by myself. It's probably best if I wait and just hope we make it to a thriving city". I debate, crossing my arms while pondering the best option.

Nothing comes to me though. I sit there focusing on what the possibilities would even be, considering I had a boat.

"There is no way I could make it back in less than the 2 days it has taken for us to travel this far. Jacqui is just going to have to hold out until I figure something out."

I pound my fist into the table, irritated with my inability to control the situation.

"Every second counts and I'm stuck on this stupid boat with a bunch of cowards and traitors"! I scream internally.

My turquoise Sathon aura flashes wildly and once I notice it, I do my best to calm down. As the light fades back into my body, I focus on what's ahead.

I finish bickering with the negative thoughts filling my head and take a seat, feeling defeated.

Taking a gander up to the ceiling almost in tears, all feels lost.

Runaways

I gradually come to the realization that there is a slim, if any chance that I could find a boat and even smaller of a chance that it would get me to Comely in under two days.

"I just want to make it back instantly! I can't believe I've been out cold for two whole days. There's no way I can make that time up. I don't even know if I could find Jacqui even if everything goes perfectly." I cry into my arms.

The frustration builds up inside my head. As it begins to bubble over, I swing as hard as I can, punching the wall. A turquoise flash ripples throughout the wall and it almost collapses on itself!

Instantly, I regret my decision. My hand begins to swell, and I curse under my breath as I go to kick the wall in a blind fury.

Suddenly the door to my room opens and Ava steps in.

I freeze and move back towards my bed. Grabbing the map, I created, I stealthily slide it under the pillow beside me.

Ava looks around, then finally to me.

"Listen. I know you don't want to talk to me, but I'm just worried about you. Are you doing okay in here"? She questions.

I cover my swollen hand slowly with my arm and nod without making eye contact with her.

"Well, we have some food prepared if you are hungry." She continues.

Before I can nod again, she exits closing the door behind her.

Waiting to ensure she doesn't return. I get up after a couple minutes and lock the door before wrapping my hand.

My stomach growls violently, hearing there is food awaiting my arrival.

"I'm starving! I was out for two days for sure." I chirp.

After heading out to the deck where everyone is, I notice what came out from the food pods.

"Enchiladas. My mom really made my favorite and stored it in a pod for us." I lament.

As I think about how much I miss my mother's home cooking, I frown. I scoop a plate and stack it with four enchiladas before quickly leaving.

"I refuse to eat with these three." I growl under my breath.

As I get back into my room, I retreat onto my forgiving bed.

Before I have a chance to get comfortable, Don walks in and sits down next to me after closing the door.

"Listen man, I know you probably hate all of us and I don't expect you to even answer me. I just want to say that I was totally on board with going back to save Jacqui. Obviously not as much as you were, but I wouldn't mind risking my life and going back to save her with you."

I cut him off.

Runaways

"I got it, I just wish she were here, she risked her own life for us, but we couldn't do it for her? The feeling that she could be gone forever makes me feel sick."

Don glances at my hand and looks back towards me with an expression of worry.

We make eye contact, but I refuse to acknowledge it, and continue talking.

"It's honestly stupid that we didn't go back for her! All of you are scum. I can't even believe that we abandoned her to die. This group is an abomination"! I shout angrily, my focus now on him.

Donshay frowns and holds my shoulder.

"Maybe she escaped buddy, we never know what other tricks she had up her sleeve." He states calmly.

Neither of us says anything for a couple seconds and he tells me everything will be alright as he heads out.

I lay on my back and look up to the ceiling.

Thinking of how my mother is probably being questioned about our disappearance and what could be going on back home, I begin to lose my appetite.

Before it's gone completely, I sweep these thoughts under my mental rug as I finish my food.

My imagination starts to run wild, and I try to take a nap to avoid it. With almost zero effort, I drift off to sleep.

As I run around in my dreams everything feels as if it's reality.

Lucid dreaming has always come easy to me. The only issue is remembering what occurred in the dream.

I feel restless as my body isn't exhausted and I toss and turn for a few hours.

As I wake up, I struggle to recall certain events that happened in my dream. Only broken fragments stick out, here and there, but nothing solid.

Annoyed, I hop up and head to the ship deck.

Finally, I spot a landmass before us. Within minutes, we're at the beach. Not knowing what life, if any, lives on the shores. I step off the boat cautiously.

As I trudge around, I get a bit more comfortable with my surroundings as my body loosens up.

It's nighttime and a multitude of eerie noises come from the surrounding trees and bushes. The trees seem to scrape the sky and there are so many of them I can't even spot the ending of their height!

Jade jumps down from the boat and stands beside me, both of us in awe at the size of these monsters.

As the wind begins to blow harder, the trees wave to us.

Runaways

"What? Have you guys never seen a tree before? Get over it."
Ava spouts.

I glare back at Ava, who shoots me a look back. Ava then
falters when I turn entirely around.

"Can you not be negative or condescending for five minutes? Is
that so hard"? I bark, annoyed.

"Sorry, I was just joking." She comments as she tiptoes down
the steps from the boat.

Minutes later, we clean the boat out. Grabbing our supplies and
heading into the forest, following our glowing map.

After a couple minutes of walking, I start to hear birds and
look to Don. He is looking around and just smiling as hard as he
usually does when he's lost in his thoughts.

The wind picks up and for the first time in my life, I start to
get uncomfortably cold.

"I can't believe I'm saying this. But I miss Nero. It's never cold
back home. I can't stand this." I mutter to myself.

We continue walking for a short time before we come across a
ravine. I look across and frown, knowing it's too far to jump and
too deep to take a risk even if we were comfortable leaping across.

"Hey guys, there used to be a bridge, but it must have fallen."
Donshay points out.

Justin Avery

I creep over to the edge and peek down into the ravine.

"Geez, that's a long drop. Yeah, Don's right, there was a bridge. Unfortunately, it looks as if it may have snapped at the far end. Also, most of it now hangs off our side of the ravine. Maybe if we had some rope, we could repair it though." I comment.

Ava runs along the edge with the map shouting and frantically pointing at something.

"There are people down there! Hey, could you guys show us how to get across this ravine"? She pleads desperately.

No response comes up from the figures at the bottom of the ravine.

Almost as if Ava is possessed, she screams and keeps pointing down into the ravine. As I look closer, I see there is a small break in the rocks down below, and a glowing light in what appears to be a small cave.

Ava hands Donshay the map and backs up as if she's going to jump towards the cave.

I run over and yank her back away from the edge.

"Are you insane?! A fall from this height would kill you instantly. We'll find another path to the cave." I roar.

Jade meanders over and stares down into the ravine and calls me over. I let go of Ava's arm and follow his eyes as he points down to a thin ledge.

Runaways

"If we balance on that ledge, it could be a pathway to the cave, and we could see what's in there." He suggests casually.

I take a glance down the thin pathway before shivering.

"You know I hate heights, and not to be pessimistic, but that thin ledge looks questionable at best. But I guess if the map says we have to cross, then maybe there is an opening on the other side of this cave". I mutter apprehensive about his idea.

Ava sprints down towards the ledge first and starts to shuffle her way towards the cave. Her back, tightly pressed against the rocky wall behind her.

"Yo, slow down Ava! We don't know how sturdy this ledge is." I shout.

Donshay follows her, ignoring me entirely. To avoid being last I hop in front of Jade, shuffling my way, not too far behind them.

I keep my eyes up, knowing how tense my body gets in these situations.

Everything seems to be going smoothly and I avoid any potentially fatal hiccups until Jade decides that he wants to be a comedian.

"Hey, is that Jacqui down there"!? He shouts.

Instantly my eyes shoot down before realizing my mistake. I abruptly stop on the ledge frozen by fear.

"Why would you do that"! I shout.

Justin Avery

My knees chatter uncontrollably like teeth in subzero weather.

I gaze upwards, trying to shuffle towards the end of the ledge. I notice that the ledge slants diagonally towards the ground on the opposite side of the ravine where the bridge ends.

I smile thinking to myself.

"I just need to get across and I won't have to deal with this anymore." I chuckle to myself encouragingly.

As I return from my mind, I step on a slippery clutch of pebbles and my feet begin to slide! After stabilizing my footing, I slowly take a few steps forward. My knees keep rattling like maracas, but I keep moving forward.

Suddenly a piece of the ledge cracks underneath me! I freak out and try to speed up. The ledge beneath me crumbles and I fall through swiftly!

I quickly put my hands out and create a Sathon forcefield encasing my body. As I rapidly plummet towards the earth below, I realize that I am having more of a conscious influence over my ability.

When I crash into the dark caverns below, I stand up and dust myself off.

Before glancing up, I look dismally towards each side of me as there is nothing but endless dark caves.

"Justin"! Ava screams out to me.

Runaways

As I direct my attention to her voice it takes me a second to register how far I fell. My mood deteriorates instantly as a soul crushing chill ripples over my body.

My heart sinks and my eyes widen at the sight, a couple hundred feet above me.

My friends, remarkably calm considering my current situation, sit a few hundred feet above me.

"Wow, if I didn't have that Sathon shield, I wouldn't have survived." I think to myself.

This soothes me for mere moments before I hear the aggressive barks of a carnivorous troop! Their cries, shattering my tranquil mindset.

"Are you serious!? Now I have starving monkeys to look out for." I growl to myself.

There is no way I could get back up towards my friends. As they all cross the ledge safely. They yell down to me asking if I can make my way through the ravine and out the other side of the cave. Don yells that they'll meet me when they get through their own path.

"There must be multiple openings to the cave, I hope their cavern and mine both lead to the opposite side so we can all meet up again." I ponder.

I give them a thumbs up and start walking towards the disgusting looking path. As I enter, it is too dark for my eyes to pick up anything. Once I shuffle deeper inside, the light from the surface dwindles until it becomes non-existent.

After shuffling my way around and tripping over some stalagmites. I get an idea and attempt to be clever by using my Sathon ability to make my fist a light source!

After a few moments of focusing, my hand lights aflame. The turquoise flames are mesmerizing and before I know it, they spread all over my body! I shriek for a moment startled by it. However, the flames do not harm me, and the fire transforms into a dull light.

I stick my hand out to gain a better view of the sight. Each finger on my hands is wrapped tightly in a turquoise glow.

The entirety of my body shines with this color. I grin warmly and continue down the caves muddy path.

It begins to get chilly the deeper I go into the cave. I focus more and the turquoise light starts to give off heat. A few minutes go by, and I end up strolling into a completely frozen section of the cave.

I gasp, surprised that such a beautiful place could have such a treacherous tundra.

"OOH OOH"!

My head whips around to a Sph, (SpottedHowlerMonkey). As I attempt to dash away, the Howler monkeys pursue after me!

I peer back to see my turquoise light glint off their terrifying fangs.

Runaways

Panting heavily, I make it to the end of the pathway. Turning to my right, I see a narrow opening in the wall where I can scoot between heavy stone walls to escape the vicious troop.

A few howler monkeys cut me off before I reach the wall and I slide to an abrupt stop. The howling, barking, and screeching, begins to get louder as all the primates circle me slowly.

The ones in front of me belligerently gnash their teeth and before I know it, a stone zips by my head!

The Howler monkeys from my left side start launching rocks in my direction! I spot more primates crawling and they all inch closer to me. I start to get anxious, putting up a shield to block the incoming rocks. However, a Howler monkey bares its teeth at me and jumps for my throat!

Without hesitation, I swiftly kick it into the ground. As it slides backwards on the ice, five more enraged primates charge me, alongside the original one.

I take a step back as fear and rage take over my body. My Sathon swirls around me and I levitate off the ground as a sharp energy builds up.

"Y'all want something to eat, huh? Well munch on this! Back off"! I scream loudly!

The turquoise energy spreads out in all directions, launching the monkeys and ice backwards! My attack begins uprooting stalagmites and blasts a gaping hole in the cave wall.

Justin Avery

I slowly descend from the air and collapse on the ground. Noticing there is mud on my hands, I look around to see all the ice has either been destroyed in the explosion or melted from the heat of my Sathon.

Standing up slowly, I make my way out the cave through the giant hole I created.

"How did I even do that"? I think to myself.

I ponder for a while as I exit the ravine, slowly strolling up a dusty hill, I eventually climb to the top. My eyes widen as I gasp at my surroundings.

The grass is unbelievably green and soft. After walking around for a bit, I start to fall in love with the scenery. The beautiful sky encapsulates everything nature has to offer and the wildlife that roam the environment look so peaceful.

As I make my way around the corner there is the most majestic waterfall I have ever seen. I jog over quickly and notice that the waterfall feeds into a sleek lake.

Deciding that it couldn't hurt to skip some rocks or even take a dip, I skip down a small hill as I search for some flat stones to use to skip over the water.

I quickly come across some exotic purple flowers, I choose to pick one up and place it behind my ear. Exhausted from the struggle in the cave I take a seat on the rocks, just enjoying the view.

Runaways

"I guess I can wait here until the group gets across and meets me at this lake. There's no way they could miss this beauty." I spout aloud, proud of my great find.

A few minutes into my nap, a large branch snaps nearby and I hop up instantly to go investigate the noise.

Making my hand a turquoise blade, I creep up a small hill nervously.

"I can't even lie, I'm honestly afraid of what I may find on the other side of this hill." I murmur to myself anxiously. My mind starts to flood with thoughts.

As I near the top of the hill my creative imagination runs wild.

"What if Lumin guards have tracked my friends and I to this place. They'll destroy everything here and I'm not sure how many I could take on my own." I stress.

Once I make it to the summit, I peer down to see there are people! Debating with myself if they are friendly, I walk towards them slowly but intentionally make noise. As I go, I crunch leaves and make my Sathon blade dissipate.

I want them to know of my presence, so they aren't surprised that I am approaching.

Once I get into earshot, they all turn and look at me. They freeze, eyeing me. I do my best to read all their facial expressions.

Justin Avery

The only word that comes to my mind that could explain their reactions, is stunned. Three teenagers, somewhere around my age. One looking older and the other two looking younger than me.

My eyes move over towards the girl, she has light blue eyes with bright red hair. The silence becomes deafening before I break the tension, stepping forward and saying hello.

The older looking of the two boys, steps towards me smiling, returning my greeting.

"Where are you from"? He questions with an inviting grin on his face.

I study the boy before responding.

He has bushy dark eyebrows, neat dark brown dreads, and a deep voice. He looks to be the same age or even older than I am, and for some reason is standing on an apple box.

I put my fist out for him to bump it and reply.

"A couple friends and I came from Joviality and escaped Nero on a boat." I state calmly.

Runaways

Again, they all look at me, eyes widened.

Immediately, I am filled with regret.

"Why did I say that? What if they are apart of the Lumin civilization? No… but if I lie, saying I'm from here and they catch me in my lie. Then I could potentially be putting myself and my friends in more danger." I argue with my own logic.

However, before my negative thoughts rush in, the boy bumps my fist with his own, and proceeds to introduce himself.

"I'm Bryan. This is my little brother Dwight and our childhood best friend Hailey." He states proudly as he wraps his arm around Dwight.

I shake Dwight's hand and as I do so I examine him as well.

His eyebrows aren't bushy like his older brother's and he's sporting one earring. His hair, which has smaller twists instead of dreads like his brother, are neatly done as well.

We look each other in the eyes, and I feel a mutual respect floating in the air.

"It's nice to meet you… what was your name again"? Dwight questions.

"My name is Justin, sorry about that." I stutter for a moment, spitting my name out fretfully.

Runaways

As I walk towards Hailey, she seems chipper and takes me into an aggressive hug, holding me tightly.

I laugh as I start small conversations with all of them and we chat for about five minutes, before being interrupted by a loud boom of thunder.

"Wow, I didn't even notice the sky got dark. That happened so fast." I think to myself as I anticipate the incoming rain.

Bryan quickly motions for everyone to follow him. We jog through the waterfall. Trailing the group through this dark tunnel, I arrive on the other side. Once we splash through the waterfall, there is a huge hill we must climb.

After making it to the top, I spot a tent I assume they have been staying in. Bryan opens the long zipper, and we all pour into the tent, fleeing the rain.

The outside of this tent would deceive anyone into believing that it could fit no more than two people and even that many would be a bit of a squeeze. However, when I step inside, there is enough space to support five adults. We sit in the tent for about an hour, and I explain to them the entire story of what my team and I have been through over the last couple days but wisely decide to leave out details about the Perdu pills and my Sathon ability. They all sit around closely and attentively admiring my story.

Once comfortable, I finally drop my suspicions.

"So, you've got a pretty unique Ki energy." Bryan comments.

I look around, and they all eye me, awaiting my response.

"Don't worry Justin, we aren't your enemy." Dwight assures me.

I relax before cracking a smile.

"Yeah, I guess you could say that." I smirk.

Dwight asks multiple questions and Hailey seems quiet now.

This becomes extremely obvious that she's uncomfortable, when I arrive at the portion of the story where my group and I ended up leaving Jacqui back in Nero. Hailey is so upset she begins to beg Bryan that we make it our responsibility to head back and save her.

Bryan, who is sitting down and staring at the floor, doesn't look up to respond.

"We can't do that Hailey. You know that if we head into Nero after what Justin just explained to us, we won't make it back out alive. Not to mention that it is forbidden to try and enter that country. The guards would be on us like white on rice."

He turns to me, looking up and making eye contact before chuckling.

"Sorry if she got your hopes up Justin. She has a habit to become over emotional and leave out logic. Solely making decisions based on her current feelings." He comments.

Bryan pauses for a moment before continuing.

"But back to your friend. I'm not sure if this'll help you feel better. But I have been captured by the Lumin guards when I was out with my father and the other men. They don't like to make unnecessary messes and most likely will try to intimidate Jacqui into conformity. Just like they attempted to do with me." He states confidently.

I jump up, filled with a mix of emotions.

"What do you mean!? They killed almost all the men in Joviality for a revolt a few years ago. If anything, they love to spill unnecessary blood. Those guys live for it." I shout, unaware of my volume.

Once I realize that I'm screaming at some people I've just met, I calm down.

"Sorry about that. I lost my father, and my friends lost a lot of loved ones back then. I wish I could believe you, but these guys are a different breed of evil. I can guarantee that much." I murmur disheartened.

Bryan frowns.

"I'm sure you know much better than I. My perspective is that if the Lumin officials don't have to make a big story then they won't. Unless the story is in the public's eye, then they'll obviously set an example. At that point, bloodshed is unavoidable." Bryan attempts to assure me.

My mind races as I think about how huge of a story we are right now.

"We're probably the talk of the nation if I'm gonna be honest with you guys. There's no way she won't be shaped into an example. I just hope I can make it back before…." I can't finish the sentence. It hurts too much to think about, much less to voice openly.

I sigh, worriedly thinking about what could be happening to her right now.

Turning to Dwight.

"Do you know of any way I could make it back to Nero to make an attempt at saving Jacqui"? I plead desperately.

Dwight shakes his head but smiles.

"There is a rumor that the Port ruby, located on this island, possesses the ability to give an individual super speed, flight, or teleportation." He claims.

"Oh great, not this stupid rock again." Bryan groans as he gets up and leaves the tent.

Dwight rolls his eyes and clears his throat before he continues.

"Unfortunately, the user would have to collect all the rubies and be a master of the Sathon ability. Only then, could they unlock the secrets to the rubies, which would fuse to the user's soul, making them unstoppable." He finishes.

Bryan rushes back in.

"Don't believe him, that story is straight garbage and is probably a legend made up by our people to give us hope. Nero hardly knows of our existence and considers us to be Lustronese people. If they found this settlement again, they would wipe out everything. Our people want to encourage us to never give up and fight back. Knowing the young would crumble without some stupid, overpowered fairytale. It's just a story to motivate the weak and simple minded." He barks aggressively.

Dwight frowns.

"Bryan don't say that." Hailey says softly, as she clutches her hands.

Bryan snaps at his younger brother, grabbing him by the shirt tightly.

"Don't tell me you actually believe in that foolishness, Dwight? There are five kings down in Nero with a powerful military and most of the supplies. The public are sheep, they follow whatever orders they are given. All the people that were Sathon users were either killed or brainwashed into thinking that we're the enemy"!

Dwight rips himself free from his brother and looks towards the ground before he kicks the floor.

"I know that someone will rise from the ashes of this broken world and stand up to those tyrants down in Nero! Someone has to! I swear I'll fight with my dying breath when that day comes. I'll never give up hope because I promised mom that." He shouts.

Bryan hesitates, taken back by his brother's words and shakes his head with a stoic facial expression.

Putting his hand on Dwight's shoulder he calmly hugs him.

"I… miss her too Dwight, I miss her too." He chokes out, holding back tears.

A few moments of silence take us over before I ask Bryan if he would know where the ruby could be.

He quickly cuts me off.

"Come on man, not to be rude or anything, but do you actually think that the Port ruby exists? Also, even if it did, you think that we have any clue on where it could be? That we wouldn't have already gone searching for it"? Bryan scoffs.

He shakes his head in disappointment.

"Weren't you listening? You'd have to have the other rubies to unlock their power and on top of that, you would have to be a master of wielding Sathon. Which no offense, but we all know you're not." He comments while rolling his eyes.

I sit back down realizing how foolish I sounded, thinking I could string together a rescue mission, with or without that ruby.

Hailey looks towards me and frowns.

I stand up and head for the exit.

"Hey, I'll be right back. I just need a breath of fresh air." I mutter, saddened by the hard and unforgiving truth.

Dwight gives me a concerned look.

Runaways

"You shouldn't walk out into the rain without an umbrella. You'll get sick." He warns.

I hesitate for a moment before creating a Sathon umbrella and proceeding to head out into the rain without responding. I can hear the gasps of disbelief, but I don't stop walking.

When I get outside, it is more of a light sprinkle instead of rain. I find a dry spot under a tree and sit down to think.

Chapter 6:
New faces

Around twenty minutes pass before I hear the tent unzip. Stepping out of the tent is Bryan, who makes his way towards me with something hidden in his hand.

I start to stand but he motions towards the ground, encouraging me to sit down.

As he plops down beside me, he starts talking about how he wishes we could do something to change the past and his rant continues for some time.

"I get how you feel man. But you and I both know we can't change the past. Fortunately, we can change the future with what we do right now." He states.

I cut in.

"Hey Bryan? No offense, but where is all this sentimental stuff coming from? You were so against everything we talked about earlier, so what's with the change of heart now"? I question him.

Bryan sighs before looking up at me.

"Listen Justin, I don't really know you, but you seem like you're a genuine person and I have no use for this thing anyway." He admits queasily.

As he opens his hand, a thriving green gem sits there glistening. My heart drops and I slowly take the Port ruby from him.

"You're the only person I've known to have the ability." Bryan continues.

"My mother, she was a Sathon user. But, one day Lumin soldiers raided many places, wiping out everyone who could stand against them. I wish the ability were passed on to me so I could have saved her." He gets choked up for a moment before he breaks down.

Bryan sobs beside me and I try and comfort him, but he holds his hand up, stopping me.

"No, I need to finish. If I were born with that ability you have, I would have run away a long time ago to collect these gems and avenge my mother. I can't lie to you, I have no intentions to save the world, I just have revenge on my mind. For so long I wanted it to be me, I wanted to be able to fight back like many of my people did before me. Even now, it hurts to accept that I just wasn't born to live out that destiny." He looks at me and smiles while wiping his face.

"It was your destiny all along, and I am going to be here to help you save the world! I lost hope, so long ago, but, now that you're here, maybe we have a shot at freedom and peace in this world"! He shouts as confidence leaks off every word.

I nod while grinning at him and pocket the gem in my backpack, before helping him up.

"Come on bro, we all should head back to camp." I state, calmed by his heroic and emotional speech.

"We should head back to grab some food." Bryan nods his head agreeing.

"Finally! You agree with me"! Dwight screams at the top of his lungs, running around the tent.

I chuckle and jog back over to the tent, helping Hailey pack up.

Soon we're on our way through the trees and back towards the end of the ravine. I look around and then it hits me.

"Where are my friends? I've been gone with these three for the past couple hours. Jade and company probably think I got lost or died in that cave"! I think nervously.

After a few moments I realize how they ignored Jacqui and I quickly shrug off any worry building in my mind.

"They didn't care if Jacqui died, so they'll be fine without me." I think to myself.

Bryan glances towards me and looks to be pondering something. I just give him a fake warm smile before changing the subject.

"How far away is this camp"? I ask.

"About a ten-minute walk from here. But that's nothing to a living legend"! Hailey replies with a huge smile on her face.

"Living legend, huh? I like the sound of that." I think to myself.

As we're enjoying the view, time seems to skip by. Before I know it, we arrive at the camp. As we walk past tents and small stone houses, I notice that my new friends have a small thriving community. Many members walk in from the mountains with huge jugs, full of clean river water and others carry baskets holding a plethora of fruit.

I sweep my eyes around the entire village and notice that everyone shares almost everything that is brought in. Unlike Joviality, there was no currency here, no need to search for a job to provide for your family. No need to pay bills. Here, the village was your family, and your job is to find your niche and use it for the good of everyone. I like that about this place.

Bryan's community gives off a very comforting vibe and just makes me feel as if I was apart of their home. We continue to walk around until we arrive at this small building with a fence around it.

As we head inside, I can hear Hailey joyfully exclaiming about how excited she is to see Billy.

I look to Dwight who just chuckles under his breath and whispers to me.

"Just wait for it."

Hailey rushes around and makes a turn, leaving us in the dust.

Once we head around the corner, Bryan stops at a wooden and dirty barn.

Justin Avery

I hear Hailey scream Billy's name louder and she wails.

"I missed you so much Billy! It's been two days since I could hug you." She muffles.

Not yet at the area where Hailey and Billy are, my brain begins to imagine that Billy is her boyfriend. If not, maybe he could be her older brother or even a close friend.

However, when I finally lay my eyes on who Hailey's hugging, Bryan and Dwight explode with laughter at my facial reaction.

I just smirk and softly laugh with them as Hailey squeezes a young calf. They both roll around in the dirt and hay.

"I thought Hailey was a little too excited to see a cow for the first time as well. Trust me bro, Dwight and I have experienced this too. It's weird." Bryan chuckles while facepalming.

"This is Billy? Why is she rolling around in the mud with a cow? Oh, please let that be just mud. Never mind, I don't wanna know anymore." I worry internally as I gaze upon Hailey and Billy.

Bryan wraps his arm around my shoulder and shakes his head disappointed.

"Okay Hailey, get off the ground. You know nobody wants to wait with you while you wash your clothes." Bryan comments, this time more serious.

"Oh, come on please! I love animals and I haven't seen him in a while. I only get scared when I have to wash my clothes at night". She pleads while staring up at Bryan with huge puppy eyes.

Runaways

"No. I'm not repeating myself. Get up, you're getting dirty." Bryan barks with undeniable authority.

As Hailey scrambles to her feet, Dwight bites his lip and holds back laughter before Hailey leads us out of the barn.

Before we have the chance to exit, three adults burst into the room screaming that we should head towards the river. I look at everyone perplexed on the situation. Bryan makes some odd hand gesture before nodding at the three men.

He quickly turns to us and tells us not to say a word to any of the people we see and to follow him.

We all nod in unison and follow Bryan out of the barn after the three men.

As we trail the men for some time, Dwight eventually gets bored of not being able to talk and starts doing anything to make noise.

Humming, forcibly burping, or even clapping.

It even gets so bad, that he starts fake yawning, just to contribute to some sound. As we walk farther, Bryan's patience wears thin, and he turns around snapping on Dwight.

Bryan grabs his younger brother and slams his back into a nearby tree while shouting at him.

"Listen! When I say shut up and follow me, I want you to do just that. Nothing more, nothing less! I don't want to hear another noise from you until we reach camp again. Do you hear me"? Bryan grits his teeth as he stares into his brother's soul.

Terrified Dwight nods his head quickly and his older brother drops him to the ground before continuing our walk.

A couple of the men enjoy the spectacle and chuckle at Dwight's expense.

I help Dwight to his feet, brushing the bark and dirt off his clothes. Without a word he promptly gives me a thumbs up and starts to follow the three men. Everything seems fine, until I begin getting a familiar feeling about the area we are hiking through.

However, when we turn the corner, I freeze.

"I know exactly where we are now." I mutter to myself.

Almost thirty or more people are around the boat that my friends and I had arrived on. Most of them have knives or swords and the three men we followed up here, are speaking in some language I can't understand.

It's blatantly clear, by their body language, they are not pleased with their find.

As I try to assess the situation, Bryan makes his way over to me with six angry men behind him.

"Do you know where that boat came from? Listen man, I personally don't care, but my father is extremely protective about our home, so please tell me you have nothing to do with this. We can't have Lumin citizens on our land." He shouts angrily.

I stand frozen, now worrying about what could happen if their community pins this to me or even worse, finds my friends. As my mental stability erodes, I notice something that immediately calms my nerves.

Bryan winks at me, easing my worrisome thoughts.

With the straightest face I can muster, I lie through my teeth and tell them I have never seen that boat in my life.

"I'm from a different village on this island. Even if I were a traveler, I wouldn't leave the boat out in the open." I announce confidently.

Bryan smiles and turns around to translate to his father and the rest of the men. More men climb the boat and start to search for life or anything that might answer their questions.

Hailey and Dwight pull me to the side stealthily.

"Justin. Did you know that there's a wonderful hot spring we could sneak off too while everyone else is super tense"? Dwight whispers with a devilish grin painted on his face.

"Oh, a hot spring you say"? I sneer excitedly.

Without another word we all skulk off back towards the camp. With newfound energy from our excitement, Hailey, Dwight, and I make it back to camp before Bryan or anyone else.

Justin Avery

As I glance over to my newly made friends. Hailey and Dwight sprint over to their house gasping for air.

"This would be a perfect time to switch my lightweight armor from clothes, back into my beach outfit." I think quickly, tapping my thigh.

As I begin watching the armor melt away into red swimming trunks, I smile, remembering Jacqui.

"What a handy gift." I think to myself.

As my two friends stumble inside and grab their clothes, they race back out the house full of energy again.

"Whoa, how did you switch clothes so fast Justin"? Dwight exclaims, full of shock.

"No time for that! Let's go to the hot spring." I shout nervously as I turn away from them both.

Laughing and leading the way, Hailey shows Dwight and I a shortcut. We head up a couple hills. Finally arriving, we all walk towards this giant hill that hangs over the hot spring.

"Well, who's first? We gotta enjoy our time while we still have it." Hailey states.

Arrogantly, I push my way between them both and stand proud at the bottom of the hill.

"Don't worry, I got this." I boast.

Runaways

Dropping my backpack off at the bottom of the hill, I turn around and give them both a smile. I begin racing towards the edge of the hilltop and do a backflip into the water.

As I plunge into the smooth water, bubbles rise to the surface, and they tickle my skin as they pass by.

I open my eyes to get a glimpse at my surroundings, the water is crystal clear. The gorgeous and transparent water looks so good, I debate for a moment, if I even want to come up.

Eventually reality hits and I am forced to swim back to the surface for air.

Hailey is cheering as I resurface. After briefly catching my breath, I give them both a bow, dunking my head into the water each time.

Noticing that Dwight is about to jump next, I swim over to the edge and return to the top of the hill. He turns to both of us as he skyrockets off the edge into a cannon ball!

When he hits the water, he sends a crippling ripple through out the hot spring. Hailey and I applaud his show, and to continue our joke we both act as if we're lifting scorecards.

When he returns to the surface, he starts laughing and thanks us for allowing him to be a small part in our salubrious event.

"A ten?! I've always wanted to win gold since I was four years old. I want to think my competitor, Justin, you put up a good battle tonight. His team has trained him well. I also wanna thank everyone for coming out tonight." Dwight starts his fake victory speech.

"Get out the water already! You're so extra for no reason. I swear I can't stand you"! Hailey shouts at him, laughing uncontrollably.

"Then sit down." Dwight gurgles as he treads in the hot spring.

After a couple moments, Dwight makes his way back to the top of the hill as he and I await Hailey's turn.

She wastes no time and dives off the hill, spinning like a top as she pierces the water.

Dwight taps my arm and pulls me down the hill with him into the trees. When Hailey comes up for air, awaiting her score, she looks around confused as we are nowhere to be found. Immediately, she springs out the water and runs up the hill. Hailey gazes around to see if we are still there, but, when she finds nothing, a look of bewilderment takes her over.

"Yo, this is too good"! Dwight starts to burst out with laughter.

"Shut up, she's gonna find us, loudmouth." I snicker back, struggling to control my own laughter.

Hailey hears our snickering and turns towards our direction!

"We have the cover of the trees, split up and hide." I whisper to Dwight.

I hide behind a tree and Dwight climbs up higher in the same one. Dwight bites his tongue to restrain himself from laughing while I lay against the trunk hoping she does not find us so soon.

Runaways

"Guys! Where are you? I really don't like being alone out here! Hello? This isn't funny Dwight"! Hailey begins to cry out.

I look up to Dwight who laughs so hard, he falls out of the tree! He twists in the air and crashes to the ground causing a lot of commotion.

Hailey turns toward us and starts chasing Dwight with her hand now in a fist.

"Come here you jerk! You know how much I hate being alone"! She hisses wildly.

I start laughing hysterically but head up the tree for safety and Dwight scampers away from Hailey.

I look down on the two as she chases him for a couple seconds before giving up and yelling at him.

"You're so annoying, I swear I can't stand you"! She cries.

"Then sit down." Dwight snickers as he repeats his joke from earlier.

Dwight begins chuckling as he climbs the tree and sits on the branch next to me, visibly out of breath.

Eventually Hailey grabs my bag and joins us in the tree. We all get comfortable in our respected sections and chat.

Only minutes into it I spot Jade, Ava, and Donshay walking in our direction!

Justin Avery

I whisper to Hailey and Dwight as we all peer down on the group. None of them seem to notice us and continue their approach towards our position.

"Stay behind me, I'm going to handle this." I growl as they spectate from behind.

I begin to glow turquoise as my energy spikes. Dropping down from the trees rapidly, I stand in front of Jade oozing with Sathon energy.

"You three need to head back the way you came." I warn.

Ava rushes forward attempting to hug me before Donshay yanks her back by her arm.

"Don't approach him, he's not the same." Don comments.

"Let me go Don, he needs us right now." She pleads desperately.

Dwight and Hailey drop out of the tree, standing by my side with their eyes fixated on our new enemies.

"Just leave like Justin said, we don't have to fight if you comply." Hailey states boldly.

"Fight? Justin we're friends. Why would we fight? We have a plan to save our people. Remember"? Jade questions.

140

Runaways

"I have new friends. We're going back to save Jacqui and then we're going to find others to help our people rise up. We will fight back." I growl.

"Then let's work together"! Ava wails.

"Never, I'd rather die than work with traitors like you again." I bark.

"Well then let's fight. Justin, we're not leaving without you." Jade assures.

I zip forward, hitting Jade in his chest with a sweet crushing elbow! He crumbles to the ground breathing heavily.

"Don't make me tell you again, I'm not afraid to fight you all by myself." I growl angrily.

Ava steps back.

"You've changed Justin. What made you like this? You used to be so understanding and sweet, and now because of a stupid girl, you're switching up on your true friends"! She shouts.

"My true friends wouldn't abandon someone who risked their life for us. Jacqui is a Lustro just like we are! You all just gave her up to the Lumin forces as if she weren't going to be chewed up and spit out like bubble gum"! I argue.

My energy rises gradually and my fist clenches.

"Real friends wouldn't become selfish suddenly. You guys aren't my friends. All of you could've stopped that boat and you chose not to." I scream.

Jade pulls himself to his feet, he attempts to convince me to ditch Dwight and Hailey.

"Justin, please bro… remember what we always talked about as kids? I'd carry on my family's name, and you'd always be my best friend. Don't drop all of our history for these people you just met. Please, come back to us. Just forget about Jacqui." He comments, gripping his chest tightly as he is still heavily winded.

Everything slows for a moment, and I think back on our childhood together.

Chapter 7:
Eye of the Biger

As the memories flow into view, it feels as if reality has stopped for a moment.

I look around noticing that my surroundings have changed, and I am much younger.

"Am I back home"? I ponder to myself.

As I peek around, everything begins to dull to a grey color before turning into a scarce turquoise.

"Is this my ability again? Why does reality distort like this"? I ponder to myself.

"Hey Justin. Are we going to be okay"? Jade questions.

I take a gander around again. The city is trashed and looks eerily familiar.

It only takes a few seconds before I realize that this is when the revolt occurred, back when we were eleven years old. I drop my head knowing what the future holds for Jade and his parents.

Still trying to process my new reality, I freeze and stutter for a few moments before responding.

"I don't know man. I honestly wish I could say we will." I mutter as debris floats around the air.

Justin Avery

I lead him back to my house and as we open the door, my father slams a Lumin guard into the tile floor! As they wrestle my mother dumps boiling water onto another soldier. Jade and I stare anxiously as we watch the brawl.

My father turns to us and shouts for us to hide.

We snap free from our fear, holding us in bondage. Jade and I dash into the closet in the back of the house. As I enter first, Jade slams the door behind us. Quickly we find different spots and try to conceal ourselves under unused blankets and boxes of junk in the closet.

The loud grunts from the fighting in the living room cease. As Jade and I listen intently for what could be happening next, we hear a loud explosion and multiple heavy footsteps flood into the living room.

"Get on the ground"! A Lumin official orders.

Multiple men begin to shout inaudibly, and I hear heavy blows land multiple times before the screaming stops.

"Search the house and find any traitors. Leave the woman. We'll make her children pay for her actions since she's Lustro filth." A Lumin guard barks.

"We can't kill her anyway, some new order from the kings." Another official responds.

"We should kill her and claim it was an accident." A younger voice suggests.

Runaways

I grit my teeth and begin to pull myself from my hiding spot.

"Nobody is killing my mom"! I shout internally.

As I shuffle from under the blanket, Jade warns me not to move.

"We can't take them on. Justin, we're just kids." He whispers.

As words almost leak from my mouth to argue with him, the door to the closet is torn off completely! The Lumin guards instantly spot Jade and drag him out the closet. I freeze, still well hidden under the blanket.

Jade kicks an officer in the groin and bites another's hand.

"You can't do this! This is evil and wrong." He pleads.

I hesitate to jump in and stop them when a bone shattering kick, bashes Jade's skull. Instantly, he crumbles to the floor and falls unconscious.

"Stupid brat, Lustro maggots like him, must be vicious from birth." A tall man comments as he stands over Jade's limp body.

Without a second thought he tosses my best friend over his shoulder and trudges out the house.

A visceral emotion ripples throughout my body but for some reason, my limbs won't follow my commands. I helplessly watch the group of Lumin officers take my friend away as my mother cries on the floor.

Minutes later, I can move again. I rush over to her.

Mommy, are you okay"!? I shout, nervously.

She looks up at me. Her face and body badly battered and bruised. Without any response she grabs me and pulls me into a tight hug. We don't move or say anything for hours as she sobs violently into my arms.

Everything whirls around and as the color fades back into view. I see Jade sitting in front of me. I look around and see Dwight and Hailey to my sides.

"I guess I'm back again." I mutter to myself.

"Jade, because of our past friendship, I'll leave you all be, but don't follow us. Find your way outta here alone." I order, calmed from the shell shocking memories.

I walk over and snatch the map from Donshay.

It glows from white to turquoise and splits off into a copy of the electrical map.

"We'll be needing this to save the world. You three just need to save your own skin and live in solidarity from this day forward. You're no help to me now." I spout.

Everyone looks at me with utter bewilderment painted across their faces.

"Let's go guys." I mutter as I walk away from the group.

Runaways

Dwight and Hailey turn and follow me begrudgingly.

We decide to head back to camp, when we arrive, Dwight leads us into his home and to the kitchen.

I take a seat next to Hailey as Dwight leaves the room. He returns shortly, with a giant plate of fruit, cheeses, and some unrecognizable meat that looks like roasted pork.

I reach out to grab a piece of fruit and Hailey swats my hand away. I give her a death stare and she stretches her hand out towards mine.

"Prayer first Justin." She replies with a piercing smile on her face.

I raise an eyebrow, perplexed by her request.

You guys still pray even with no adults around to watch"? I question them both.

Dwight chuckles.

Boy, do you have a lot to learn." He smirks.

Hailey and Dwight, both instruct me to close my eyes as we all join hands. Dwight prays for a few minutes and at last, we can eat.

"So, I'm assuming you all don't have prayer in Nero"? Hailey asks as she continues to eat, her eyes glued to her plate.

With more food in my mouth than necessary, I attempt to choke out a response.

"I mean we do have it. My mother usually prays for the both of us, we are forbidden to pray. Unless it's to the Lumin kings, but nobody cares." I admit as I bite into an unusually sweet strawberry.

Hailey smiles, and as we chat over the food. The topics seem sporadic. None of them really sticking.

"So, what's up with your brother Dwight? Why does he seem so closed off"? I question.

"Don't mind him. He's just healing. Ever since our village was raided for Sathon guides, he hasn't trusted anyone. But I think he's warming up to you." Dwight smiles.

I think back on the situation at the boat.

"That's true, he could have said I was Lumin. He trusted me and even covered for me. Not to mention he also gave me that ruby. Maybe I should cut him some slack". I ponder.

Over some time, the conversation continues to flip like television channels. With our stomachs full, we all talk about some humorous moments in our past. As we are all laughing loudly, our conversation is interrupted by a knock soft at the front door.

Dwight hops up quickly.

"I'll get it." He offers, as he allows us to sit comfortably.

Runaways

Hailey and I are silent, awaiting to see who will walk through the door.

As Dwight swiftly opens the door without checking who it could be, Bryan walks in and takes his seat by us at the table.

"So, you guys started your meal without me I see." He groans.

Dwight takes his seat once again and snickers.

"Of course, we had no other choice bro, I was dying. All that maturity stuff and village responsibility isn't for me. I'm just glad you handled the boat situation". He admits loudly.

Bryan chuckles with us and begins to stack his plate before digging into the pork and fruit as the conversation progresses.

"So, Bryan, I noticed that you and Dwight both wear earrings on opposite ears. But both of you just wear one. Why is that"?

Bryan sips some liquid out of a black, red, and gold bottle. He stares at the table gloomily and begins to talk.

"These earrings were our mothers. Remember when I told you that our village was raided by the Lumin forces? Well, I guess I can go into more detail, for your sake."

"Bryan, you shouldn't be drinking that." Hailey mutters.

Bryan eyes Hailey, before he takes another sip and continues.

"That fateful day, when a fleet of Lumin ships landed on our shores, was a painful one for everyone. Especially me. No one feels pain worse than mine. I was always around my mother. Sometimes my father and the elders of the village would call me 'shadow' because I was constantly attached to her hip. We did everything together. Once my father realized that I didn't have the combustion type Sathon within my vessel, he ignored me. Many of my people called me a failure and rejected me, assuming that I couldn't lead this village and succeed my father. The combustion type of Sathon had always skipped a generation. So, since my father didn't possess its glow, my people were disappointed that I wasn't born with that tenacious ability. So disgusted in fact, that I was picked on and beat up as a kid. My father knew but he never cared. For a while, I wanted his approval. The validation from him might fill the void in my heart. My mother however, taught me how to fight, how to defend myself. She taught me all different types of martial arts, and along with that, many life lessons. I was a quick learner and even without external Sathon, I was a formidable opponent to the other kids in my village". Bryan states.

"Combustion Sathon? What's that"? I question.

"Basically, there different types or qualities of Sathon. Combustion, being the strongest. Each type holds its own abilities, not one quality can recreate an ability of another type, unless they also possess that Sathon type. Almost like different dialects of a language, each quality of Sathon was a characteristic of the people that used it. With the history of Sathon aside, sorry. I'm rambling. Regardless of not having any external Sathon, my mother always stayed by my side." Bryan replies as he then takes a few more sips from his bottle.

"However, when our village was raided… those demons took everything from us! They knew our patterns, somehow, they had inside information on what we did and when we did it. While all the men and my father were out of the village on a mission, the Lumin fleet extinguished all Sathon guides in our land." Bryan begins getting choked up, tears, now streaming down his face.

"I was on my way back from school when I walked in on it. A hooded soldier, holding my mother up by her shirt. Her body bloodied and battered. I'll never forget the insignia on his cloak. That bird… he was apart of the 'Silent Canaries.' When I stumbled in on the brawl, my mother looked to me and screamed for me to run, but I couldn't. The man sneered as he beheaded my mother, the only person to ever accept me. She was the umbrella to shield me from the rain and she was gone. Without a second to process the tragedy, the fleet was called off. The man dropped my mother's head and they all just retreated! They murdered countless Lustros and just fled! I held her and cried until my father and the other men returned. To this day, I still blame myself. I could've stopped that monster if I had that ability that you possess. These earrings are from the day that she was taken from me." Bryan laments.

As I stare at Bryan and Dwight in horror, they both eye the floor. The depressed expressions fade slowly as Hailey comforts both of the brothers.

Another hour passes and we all decide to leave the house. I take the lead this time and we all start exploring the woods again.

"Where are we headed"? Bryan questions me.

I lift the electronic map I have. Everyone crowds around me curiously.

Bryan questions where I got the map from, and what is its purpose.

"Oh, you missed a lot while you were off with your father and the other men. But basically, I fought my friends that abandoned Jacqui and afterwards made my hands glow turquoise, creating this copy of the original map".

"Where did you find the original"? Bryan inquires.

"Ripped it from Don and used my Sathon to manifest our own copy. Like I just said." I repeat, slightly annoyed.

He nods and looks off into the starry sky.

"Hey, can we take a break here"? Hailey requests.

We all agree and take a seat down on this small hill.

I run everything that my friends and I have been through, over in my mind. Continuing to replay it constantly, I hear someone mutter something to me.

I don't reply. Still caught up in my mind before Bryan taps my shoulder.

"Hey man, you good"? He questions.

I freeze and glance around to everyone.

"Oh, sorry about that, just worried about Jacqui and thinking about everything that's happened recently.

The group stares at me, their eyes sympathetic.

Runaways

Bryan's voice breaks as he attempts to question me.

"Did... Did the Lumin elites actually kill your friend's parents"? He inquires as he stares into the dirt, unable to face me.

"Bryan! Why would you bring that up right now"? Hailey shrieks.

"No, it's alright. I don't mind." I assure her as I explain my story.

"They did. The Lumin forces are ruthless. Things definitely haven't gotten better over the last few years". I state.

I begin to talk about how the Light took my father and both of Jade's parent's lives. How they executed them without a second thought. I explain how the Lumin elites hid their lies and smothered our people. I talk about the countless murders of innocent Lustronese people who attempted to escape the country. The brutal work in the treacherous mines, the enslavement, and how the Light take all of our income to starve most of our people. I lament how the Lumin force took many heroes and had them extinguished in front of our community to make an example.

"It's been a tumultuous journey, but we're going to free ourselves from this life. I swear we won't be runaways forever"! I shout.

"That's terrible. I'm surprised your culture still has survived throughout all of that. How your people haven't been completely snuffed out. You are truly resilient. I'm so sorry to hear about your father." Hailey responds.

"Well, honestly. I don't know where my dad is. His name was never in the reports that came out after the revolt. They named everyone they murdered and no matter what news outlet I went to, I never found his name." I mutter.

"Maybe, they forgot about him"? Dwight suggests.

"No, they're definitely proud of every casualty. They wouldn't forget him. My father was a strong Sathon guide. Someone definitely would boast if they killed him". I respond.

"So, he could be alive"? Dwight optimistically asks.

I shake my head bitterly.

"It's possible, but I doubt it. It's easier for me to believe that he's gone. Otherwise, I don't see why he never came back for my mother and I." I spout, heartbroken.

"Justin don't think like that. The Lumin forces were probably all over him, maybe he's out there but he couldn't come back to you guys without endangering you both and obviously himself". Hailey encourages.

"That may be true, but to me he's gone. I don't want to get my hopes up and then he never reappears in my life." I mutter.

As I continue to speak, tears wrestle, fighting to pour from my eyes. I do my best keep them inside and continue to describe what my life was like, back in Joviality.

I begin to fumble over my words, and I start to see how the weight of what I am saying, carries onto my friends.

Runaways

Dwight looks towards the ground and grits his teeth in frustration, he then quickly gets up and walks towards a tree. Without warning, he punches the tree as hard as he can and a massive chunk of wood, sheds off the trunk!

I walk over to Dwight, speaking softly, in hopes of calming him down.

"Yeah, what was it that Bryan called them earlier? Demons? That's fitting." I state.

"It's just not fair! They ruined so many lives. So many people have been affected because of the Light! We can't sit around and just take it." Dwight shouts, his face buried in his arms.

After minutes of trying to keep him corralled, Dwight wipes off the splinters of wood and blood from his hand and hugs me.

Dwight holds me tightly, sobbing a little in my arms before letting go.

"Bro let's go get revenge on these demons. First, they took our family's home and kicked us out here! They killed countless others including my mother and now they are blaming our people for a war we didn't start! I still can't get over how they almost exterminate an entire continent full of innocent people and that's still not enough? How blood-thirsty are these dogs? They treat your family and friends just the same as they did ours. Well, no more! It's about time we got them back"! Dwight encouragingly shouts.

I smile as I feel a deeper emotional connection with him. I think to myself as he smiles at me.

"This is so sad. Dwight has been through so much. But he's so strong. Dwight is only fifth teen. He's too young to be dealing with this planetary curse.

"You know, I've never had a little brother or any siblings for that matter, but I feel like you guys are my family. I comment as tears of joy stream down my face majestically.

Hailey walks towards Dwight and I for a group hug.

"Bryan, get in here." Dwight chirps, a huge smile plastered across his face.

"Alright, fine, fine." He agrees.

We all hug for a while before releasing each other.

Dwight hesitates as he clears his throat.

"Hey Justin? Is it cool if we join you on your mission to save the world? I'm willing to follow you until the bitter end if it comes to it". He comments cheerfully.

I am exhilarated to hear this news but then ponder for a moment.

"What about your dad and the village? Won't they miss you all? I know Bryan especially, carries out a multitude of duties." I comment.

Bryan turns to us and begins speaking.

Runaways

"If I tell my dad that we're just going to explore the land and will be back soon, I'm sure he won't mind." Bryan claims.

"Oh yeah, their dad is super chill with us, he allows us to disappear for weeks at a time. As long as we bring the village something back, he doesn't care". Hailey chimes in.

"Awesome! That's perfect guys"! I cheer excitedly.

Dwight stops us for a moment.

"I don't think we should lie to dad though. If something does happen to us. I don't want him thinking we're on our way back." He comments as he rubs his head, twisting his hair.

"Alright, alright. I guess that's fair, I'll let him know. I don't think he would hate us for avenging mom." Bryan replies.

"This is about saving our people, Bryan, this is not for revenge." Dwight says.

"Maybe for you. I'm going to avenge mom, no matter what lengths I have to go to. Mother's vengeance is my priority, even over the liberation of our race. Don't forget that." Bryan growls at Dwight.

Bryan leads the group back to the camp and they quickly pack a few bags before coming back out.

I sit in the corner of the room awaiting the big question, but Bryan attempts to slink out the house without informing his father of our plans.

"Bryan. Come here son." His father's voice booms throughout the house.

Bryan freezes.

"I know you're leaving son. I don't mind. Just promise me you'll be careful. Remember to keep that temper under control." He assures his son calmly.

Bryan turns to his father, and they stare at each other for a while.

"I'll do my best dad. I figured you wouldn't let us leave if I asked permission." Bryan admits.

"No son. I'm proud of you and your brother for honoring our people and doing everything in your power to change the future."

Bryan sucks his teeth at the comment while his father continues his speech.

"Your mother would have loved that. She also would have loved the fact that you are bringing your childhood friend along as well. Make sure Hailey stays safe. I know it's dangerous, but the youth of this world are our only hope. I promise we will get together an army and support you in any way you need." He claims.

"Don't worry about it, we don't need your help." Bryan growls, trying to keep his cool.

As I watch them converse, I sit back pondering to myself.

Runaways

"Wow. Bryan really despises his father, I can see that he wants to say something, but he's holding it back."

Dwight runs back through the front door and hugs his father. They both enjoy a moment for a while before finally, he allows everyone to head outside.

"Oh, and Justin"? Their father calls out.

I turn to him.

"You better lead them well. I'm entrusting you with the last two members of my family." Their father states.

"Right." I nod and continue my way down the dirt path.

As we make our way into the walk, I turn to Dwight and question him.

"So, your dad can speak English"?

"Yeah, he just acts as if he couldn't, to see how you would respond. He does that with new people occasionally." Dwight laughs.

As we follow the map, we laugh while working our way through the country on foot.

"Our village scouts said your friends took their boat and left, so we'll have to find our own way back to Joviality. There's an abandoned country up north if we head that way. We'll just have to cross this bridge." Bryan informs me.

The group questions me more about what our plan is, to overthrow the Lumin kings.

"All the notes in the box that Jade received from his parents, say to collect the rubies. Unfortunately, that's all they instruct us to do. I'm assuming this green one, Bryan gave me, is one of them." I spout, shrugging.

Bryan eyes me, perplexed by my answer.

"What do you mean you don't know? You're telling me that you and your friends ran away from Nero just because a box of notes and a stupid electronic map told you to collect some rocks"? He barks angrily.

"That's rich, coming from the guy who was carrying one of those so-called rocks around in his pocket." I growl, rolling my eyes.

"That's just stupid and irresponsible, why didn't anyone plan anything out prior to leaving"? Bryan shouts, desperately awaiting an answer.

"Honestly, yeah. We thought that we would figure it out on the way, especially with my Sathon ability. We honestly were going to follow the rubies until we figured something out. Although Jade found some ring in the box as well. Something called the 'ring of power.' I think that's what he said." I admit.

"Give me that stupid map. I'll create a plan, this is ridiculous"! Bryan shouts as he snatches it from my hands.

"So, you and your friends aren't really sure what the rubies could do"? Dwight inquires.

Folding my arms and taking a deep breath, I sigh loudly.

"Nope. We really didn't have an option though, sitting around in Nero with that box and map wasn't doing us any justice either. Kinda like you said, maybe if I can become the best Sathon guide to ever live, the rubies could fuse with me, and I'll be powerful enough to stop the five kings." I comment, shrugging again.

"Sounds like a long shot, but also the best option. This sucks! We have limited information since everyone that knew about this map is now...." Hailey's words trail off.

"Dead. It isn't a hard word to pronounce." Bryan comments sarcastically.

"Don't be insensitive Bryan. It still could hit close to home for Justin so she's tiptoeing around the topic." Dwight comments, defending her.

"I'm fine. Let's just move on." I claim, hoping to defuse the situation.

"Even if the rubies don't fuse with you, you won't have to fight the five kings alone." She nods.

Bryan looks up from the map for a moment.

"Hey Justin. There is an abandoned city up ahead, once we pass this bridge it should be right there." He assures us.

"Alright bet, we can check it out as we cross this shaky bridge. Let's hurry up before it collapses"! I exclaim.

Once we arrive at the city, we stop and take a slow look around.

"We should stop here for the night. My feet are killing me. Besides, today has been a long day and I'm exhausted." I groan.

The others agree and we look for a building to stay in for the night. The gloomy surroundings give me an empty and ominous feeling.

"Everything okay with you Justin? I know we ask a lot, but I just want to ensure everyone is doing alright." Hailey comments.

I respond quickly. Poorly attempting to hide any sense of weakness.

"Yeah! I'm okay, only tired." I state as I scratch my head nervously.

I shake myself out of my funk and keep trotting forward as if nothing was bothering me. We decide that the first building we want to enter is the hospital.

As I get to the door, I notice there is shattered glass from the doors all over the floor, there is even glass sitting in the street.

Hailey points out that there is orange looking fur on some of the glass in the doorway. The fur is also scattered across the floor as well.

"There's blood. This glass already has claimed a victim." She comments.

"It's probably from some of the monkeys searching around for food." Bryan states nonchalantly.

We all step around it, careful not to cut ourselves on the glass, jetting outwards. Almost inviting our sensitive skin to graze it.

As we head down a dark hallway, there seems to be a dim light flickering in the waiting room. Hailey stops abruptly and questions.

"Why do we have to check this scary and dark hospital first? We couldn't have chosen anything else? Like uh, instead of a dim lighted hospital, maybe we should've picked something like a candy store". She lectures.

"Hailey, quit being a wuss. There isn't anything vital to our mission in a candy store. I'm sure there are some items scattered about this hospital, that we could utilize. Heck, they may even become imperative to saving someone's life in the future." Bryan scowls.

I laugh nervously.

"I can't lie, this place seems to chisel at my nerves, but I'm sure that there isn't anything to worry about." I admit as a chill runs down my spine.

The wind howls ominously as we all continue walking through the hall.

As we turn the corner and enter the waiting room, we all hear some heavy footsteps pounding on the floor!

But there's something off about these footsteps. It almost sounds as if they're not even human, as they pick up speed. Before anyone can register what, it is, the sound jumps all over the room.

Terrified, we scatter and find a place to hide in the small waiting room. I hop behind a couch, trembling with fear. Bryan and Dwight hop the counter where the receptionist would usually sit, while Hailey freezes and darts her head around franticly, looking for a spot to conceal herself.

Bryan yells at her to wake up and covers his mouth realizing what he's done.

Finally, she breaks free from her paralyzed state and rushes under the pool table in the far corner of the room. The pounding footsteps stop, and we all sit extremely still, hoping to not make a sound.

Suddenly, I hear a low growl and then I see the creature as I tremble behind the couch.

A Bull fused Tiger meanders around the room, searching for what was the source of the noise. I bite my lip and slide out of sight behind the couch.

"That feline is huge"! I scream internally.

The big cat growls and starts making its way towards my corner, sniffing the air. I know I am no match for the fully grown feline, and I prepare myself to fight for my life.

Runaways

Now soaking with sweat and trembling with fear, I begin pressing my back against the couch, bracing for whenever the beast pounces and I grit my teeth anxiously.

Just before I spring up, I make my arm a turquoise blade and breathe out one last time before hopping up.

"Clank"!

Something large slams to the floor on the opposite side of the room.

The tiger's attention moves to the knife that hit the floor. I settle back in, behind the couch, hidden from the beasts' sight. Now that the Biger's horns are pointed away from me, I take a deep breath, running a huge risk.

Instantly jumping off the arm of the couch onto the tigers back, I reach around with my turquoise arm-blade and slash wildly for its throat. I miss, slashing the tiger's arm instead. Blood spews onto the floor and the tiger tosses me off its back towards the table in the center if the room.

The feline lunges at me and I roll to my left quickly. Once it smashes against the table it turns towards me, rushing faster than I can react.

The tiger goes for my throat, but I luckily fall backwards avoiding its mighty jaws. Unfortunately, its horn impales my shoulder! Wailing in agony, I twist and turn, trying to escape the big cats' horn. The monster digs deeper, and she lifts me up before slamming me into the floor savagely!

Bryan hops the counter and stabs the beast in its back and rips the knife down hard. However, his dagger gets stuck, and his momentum pulls him to the floor. Dwight rushes over and pushes a bookshelf onto the Biger's backside!

The beasts' eyes light up with fury and she scrambles to get from under the wooden shelf to claw Dwight. Fearlessly, he then climbs onto the bookshelf to try and weigh the tiger down more than before. I reach for my shoulder, but it stings so badly I am forced to use my right arm only.

Quickly making another blade with my right arm, I clumsily stumble to my feet before getting off the floor. Without hesitation, I begin racing over to help Dwight and Bryan. Hailey crawls out from her hiding spot with a metal drawer that she pulled from the table and brings it down again and again on the Biger's skull! She repeatedly bashes the metal drawer onto the ferocious cat, until the metal is severely dented.

Bryan retrieves his dagger from the backside of the animal and as he threatens to kill the beast, she slows her movements, heeding his warning. Eventually the big cat gives up and stops fighting back.

Chapter 8:
Zero

We all sit down, exhausted, and bloodied, on the floor. Hailey opens her backpack and pulls out sports tape and bandages.

"Wait Hailey, you have to clean his wound first or it'll get infected." Bryan informs her.

She pauses for a moment and then gets up, taking Dwight with her down the hall.

After a few minutes they both return with their arms full. Dwight has a handful of medical supplies and drops them at our feet while Hailey cleans my shoulder. She then wraps it, so it will stay clean.

Dwight hands me an arm sling, reluctantly, I put it on, and they all help me to my feet. I pause for a second and remember that I was healed by my Sathon energy once before!

"I have an idea"! I shout excitedly.

"What is it"? Hailey questions, intrigue written all over her face.

I imagine a swirling liquid, my hand glows turquoise and the light slowly spins, resembling something like a whirlpool. I sit back mesmerized as it slowly spins and glistens.

The spectacle captivates everyone, almost as if time were slowing down. Speechless, they all watch me as I lightly press the glowing whirlpool onto my shoulder. Slowly it starts to heal my injury.

It's even therapeutic to watch. The gash begins to shrink until it disappears, it then starts scabbing over. Finally, even the scabs fade into beautiful unblemished skin.

"Wow, color me surprised! That was weeks of healing done in a few minutes"! Bryan exclaims.

Once the moment is over, we start to head for the door after packing our bags with more medical items. Suddenly, a soft meow breaks the silence.

Bryan whips around and stares at Dwight, asking if he heard that. They both nod and block off the staircase from where the noise originated from. Hailey rushes towards the stairs simultaneously and attempts to squeeze past them both.

They push her back and warn her about what the consequences could be if she sees the cat.

"You know how you get when you see animals! Remember Billy"? They shout.

"So! Billy is different, he's my baby! What could possibly go wrong with just letting me see the poor kitty". Hailey screeches.

She finally manages to split her two friends.

As she heads up the stairs, the defeated looking brothers trudge up after her. I look over to the injured tiger sitting on the floor and slowly make my way towards her.

Runaways

"Hey mama, I'm just going to try something okay? Please don't freak out." I state nervously.

"This is stupid and unnecessarily risky." I think to myself as I press my hands onto the tiger's wounds.

I create some swirling whirlpools with both hands and the tiger gives me a puzzled expression as I begin to heal her.

After a few minutes, her dried blood-stained coat is clean, and her flesh wounds are completely healed.

"There you go. You should be all healed up now." I smile as I rub her sides.

I beam, proud of myself. Suddenly, after I pull my hands away from the big cat, she pounces onto me!

She stares down at me for a moment, and I lay under her enormous paws, vulnerable to whatever she decides to do.

I close my eyes, unable to bear the suspense. Suddenly her giant tongue hits my face, and she licks me repeatedly! Afterwards, the big cat lets me up from the floor and without any warning she bounds out the back door.

"Wait, is she not going to take her cub"? I ponder to myself.

From the bottom of the staircase, I hear Hailey's loud cry of joy and she runs down the stairs with a Biger cub in her arms.

Justin Avery

"Justin! Look at him! Isn't he just the cutest thing you've ever seen"?

I rub his tiny head and agree with her.

"He is incredibly adorable. I can't lie." I smirk.

The kitten purrs and licks my thumb before rolling over on his side and going back to sleep. Hailey's eyes start to water, and she begs Bryan to allow her to keep the cub.

"He doesn't even have horns yet, pleaseee"? She pleads.

Bryan shakes his head and begins to complain but his argument quickly crumbles, and he gives in.

"Fine, I guess we could keep him as a pet and when he grows older, hopefully he'll protect us." He sighs.

"Okay, yep. I'm gonna pass out now. Goodnight, guys"! Dwight cheers.

We all find a spot in the chairs and the couch, to fall asleep in the waiting room.

When everyone finally wakes up, I reach in my backpack and toss a storage pod onto the ground. It bursts open and the group is astonished by the technology the Lumin civilization possesses.

"Yo, what was that? And look at all that food! Is this magic"? Dwight exclaims, his face full of excitement.

Dwight and the others stuff their faces and Bryan blurts out.

170

Runaways

"If this is the technology you had readily available then what do the Lumin civilians have"?

I pause for a moment, swallowing my food.

"I think my mother stole pods full of food, tents, water packages, and a few other items. She works in a factory where they build amazing things for the government." I reply.

Hailey nods her head approving of my statement.

"Your mother was an amazing woman for that. I don't think we'd last on the minuscule amount of food we brought." She states, joyfully snacking on the scrambled WaterChicken eggs.

Once everyone finishes breakfast, we pack our bags with items to keep a Biger cub entertained. After we finish, we all exit back through the shattered doors. Making our way around the abandoned town, we begin looting whatever is available. As we come to a stop outside the fence separating us from what looks like a small warehouse, I make my hand a blade once again and slash the fence twice.

As we all begin to step through the opening cautiously, Hailey shrieks in pain.

"Ow"! She winces.

"What happened? Are you hurt"? Dwight questions.

"I'm fine. Just nicked my arm on the gate is all." Hailey assures the group, and she presses forward.

Justin Avery

We all slide through the thin gap I created and search for something useful to get us on the water. As we enter the warehouse, some motion sensor lights turn on and a heater lightly hums in the background.

Bryan trots ahead and screams excitedly! When we find him around the corner, there are a dozen trucks and two boats.

We all spring as high as we can, ecstatic about our find and we pile into the truck! I jump into the driver's seat and mess around with everything. The boys hop into the backseat and latch the boat on the rear of vehicle. As they click their seatbelts I smile at my friends, as everyone vibrates in their seats, full of energy.

Hailey gets comfortable in the front, and we take off, exiting the facility as fast as we can! Wildly out of control we crash through the fence I had previously slashed and continue going in whatever direction the map leads us.

Hours later the visible excitement on our faces has drifted and has taken a long road trip of its own.

"I wonder how long this silence's itinerary says it'll be here for. This eerie feeling is giving me anxiety." I wonder to myself.

As I take a quick glance back, the backseat is now as quiet as a mouse. Bryan stares blankly outside the window and Dwight snores in the seat beside him, out cold.

Finally, the electronic map flashes softly, notifying us that we have arrived. I gently pull over next to a filthy sign, reading "Cavo" and something else in a foreign language I do not understand.

Runaways

We all slink out the car slowly. As we stretch our legs, the tiger cub stretches and hops out the truck right behind us. Everyone pauses staring at our new pet.

"What are we going to name this thing." Bryan inquires.

The Biger cub purrs and rubs itself around my legs, shedding everywhere.

"Stripes"? Hailey suggests.

Dwight does his best choking impression at the cliché name choice.

"We should name him 'Carrot.' No wait we should name him 'Tony.' That's a perfect name." Dwight states confidently.

Bryan and I stare at each other and then to Dwight before shaking our heads and laughing.

"Let me guess, because he's a tiger"? Bryan clamors, as he folds over with laughter.

"He's kinda red if you ask me." I butt in.

"That's the worst name suggestion for a pet if I've ever heard one." Hailey chuckles.

"Okay then! Justin! You come up with a name, since you're so smart"! Dwight shouts as he crosses his arms and rolls his eyes, clearly annoyed with my statement.

I suggest we name the cat 'Zero' and everyone looks at each other before nodding in agreement.

"I actually like that. It fits the cute ring he has around his eye." Bryan admits as he rubs Zero's adorable head.

"Then it's settled, welcome to the family Zero"! I cheer.

I lead the way into the giant city and the others follow closely behind. Amazingly, our pet tiger cub follows us.

"I think Zero imprinted on us"! Hailey stammers as she bounds and skips around excitedly.

"Ain't it weird how fast this thing is growing? Yesterday he couldn't even walk on his own, needing protection from his mother, now he's following us." Dwight murmurs.

"Speaking of which, where did his mother go? She wasn't in the waiting room when we got back downstairs to you." Bryan comments.

"Oh yeah, I figured I should heal her, no need for a beautiful animal like that to meet her maker so soon." I smile nervously, rubbing my head.

"Guys, isn't it weird how empty this town is? Nothing even looks to be ransacked. I feel like if there was a doomsday here, then people would have taken everything in these stores. But this city looks as if it was full and teaming with life one day and empty the next." Dwight suggests as he shakes, a shiver running down his spine.

Runaways

"Yeah, that's true, this place gives me some awful vibes. I can feel it, something terrible happened here." Hailey agrees.

After a few minutes of searching, we come across this abandoned grocery store. We run through all the isles, grabbing as many cans of food as possible. We load our bags and fill the extra room of the boat up to the ceiling.

Anything non-perishable is also shoved in the boat along with as many cases of water that were available. I start to worry, wondering if we can find anything to feed this tiger cub. However, when we head towards the back of the store, there are around ten giant meat slabs stashed in the freezer.

We pack the slabs into a mini freezer which wouldn't fit at first. I use my signature Sathon arm blade, slicing the slabs quickly. Each piece fits perfectly. The mini freezer is quickly rolled onto the boat beside the plethora of cans of food and our water cases.

After we finish packing, we hop back in the truck, and I begin our drive to the nearest body of water.

"Well, well, well. Look who we have here." A piercingly familiar voice scoffs.

My head darts around and as the group spins, we face our enemies.

Julien and Adrian float above us, smirking.

"Are- are they flying"? Hailey shrieks.

"It's simple. Not like you worthless roaches could accomplish it. However, you fill the soles of your feet with your Sathon energy. Once you balance it in the middle of your foot, it'll push you upwards and you'll be able to levitate. But there's a catch, focus too hard and you'll fall forward, don't focus enough energy and you'll collapse backwards. It's all about balance and Ki control." Adrian informs us.

I grit my teeth furiously, raising my power exponentially, a switch seems to flip.

"You two! Why are you here? How did you even find us."? I demand.

"Well, you see. These bloodhounds were able to track your scent. Although we did lose the trail when it rained the other day. However, when your friend there, began bleeding from her cut on the fence. The hounds were rejuvenated and led us right to you." Julien sneers as he glares at us.

"Where did you get my scent? I don't understand how you found…." I begin to question.

"That should be self-explanatory. We got the scent from your house. Your mother attempted to fight for you but had to submit when our Lumin soldiers arrived. It's a shame we weren't authorized to kill…." Julien attempts to spout.

"Don't you dare! Don't you say another word! I swear if you hurt my mother in anyway… I'll… I'll kill you"! I shout, cutting him off.

Adrian butts in.

Runaways

"Calm down. We weren't authorized to kill anyone. Your mother is safe. For now." He snarls.

"You think you're funny"? I growl as my turquoise energy swirls wildly.

"Justin, you take on Julien. Dwight and I will take on Adrian. Hailey, you get Zero and yourself to safety." Bryan instructs.

"I don't care what y'all do… just stay out my way. I growl."

I spring at Julien, screaming my head off. We both throw a crushing punch, and they collide violently. I feel electricity radiating off his hand as we clash.

"You're so bold Justin. It's crazy to me how a Lustro could have so much confidence. You're an outcast! Your race is pathetic, and you don't deserve to exist in our world"! Julien smirks.

"I'm not scared of you! I'll fight until my time on earth has come to an end." I spout.

Julien punches me three times in my chest and spins before kicking me back into the ground.

"Ironic how that day is today. You're nothing but a failure! A runaway. You and your friends will die here, then my kings can rest easy, knowing you're dead and gone"! He scolds.

"Wow, the kings authorized this? They must believe we're a serious issue"! I ponder to myself as I pull my body up from the ground.

Julien lands and attempts to crush my shoulder with his golden glowing heel. However, I dissipate into turquoise smoke and appear a few feet away from the attack.

I create more Sathon. Focusing harder, I make a pike out of my turquoise light.

"Bring it on Julien, I'm not dying here. My people need me, and they need my friends." I spout heroically.

Now rushing onto the offensive, I rip the pike upwards and nearly land a devastating blow.

I watch as Julien flips backwards to avoid the strike. Not wasting any time, I keep applying pressure with my onslaught. I spin the pike, passing it between my hands, before slashing from Julien's ear, down at his feet. Julien twists to his left, scantily avoiding the tip of the weapon, and I smirk. Now with his body stuck in midair, I know he can't dodge. I spin the pike and shove my Sathon weapon into Julien's stomach.

"Gotcha"! I cheer loudly.

Suddenly Julien's body evaporates into small golden particles. As his body drifts away in the wind, I feel as if something is off. Glancing upwards, I instantly realize what's going on. Julien has both his palms touching as he slashes down, a golden glittered aura around them. I turn the pike upwards and block the attack, but it cracks my Sathon weapon!

"An afterimage technique… Julien is a lot more clever than I gave him credit for." I groan internally.

"Well, well. You actually caught on in time, I seriously thought you'd be in two pieces right now". Julien smirks.

I struggle to hold off his attack. As his golden aura glows brighter, my turquoise pike cracks again. This time almost shattering!

"Julien's golden flare burns brighter, and he begins screaming as his power skyrockets.

"It's over! Perish"!!

Suddenly a kunai pierces his shoulder. Julien howls in agony as the blood streams down his arm. His power drops like a stone in a lake. As his aura rapidly fades, two more kunai hit his back and Julien drops to the ground. Heavily winded and barely clinging to his life.

"You... you wretch! How dare you attack my blindside. I'll have your head for this." Julien mutters as he coughs up blood.

"Oh, can it! I'm not here to kill you. I'm here to collect my reward.

The girl turns towards me, a huge grin plastered on her face.

"There's a bounty on your head Justin. No matter what you do, I'll find you, and I'll kill you. Your death will feed my family for a long time." She states.

"Who are you"? I question.

"I am Brooke, of the assassin community. We take jobs from the rich Lumin society and are sent out to accomplish our missions. I have been ordered to take you in, dead or alive. I swear I will accomplish my mission no matter what it costs me"! She announces confidently, her hands on her hips and her eyes in the sky.

Another assassin lands beside me.

"You're familiar to me." She comments.

As I turn to her, she smiles and then eyes me weirdly.

"I'm going to help your friends now. Sorry about having to turn you in, maybe we could've worked together in another lifetime. Oh, and also... let me know if this statement resonates with you. Different from the kings in control now." She comments.

"Wait... what? Who told you about that"? I inquire.

Without hesitation the girl bounds off towards Bryan and Dwight. The duo are in trouble against Adrian who seems to be handling both brothers thanks to his Sathon ability.

"Hold it Breanna. I wanna see what Justin's friends can do first. If they put on a show, we'll let them get a head start before we hunt them down. It'll make the chase more fun." Brooke sneers.

Breanna stops in her tracks and takes a knee, a few feet away from the battle.

"Right. As you wish." Breanna responds.

"Alright then. Well, let's see it. I wanna see a good battle."
Brooke growls with a huge grin on her face.

"That Breanna girl, she knew the phrase my mother always
spouted to me as a kid. Why? How does she know about that?
There's something off here. And to make things more ominous, she
gave me a lamenting glance earlier. Almost as if she were sad that
she's my opposition. Who is this girl"? I mutter to myself.

As I think to myself, the battle rages on.

Bryan flips and kicks Adrian in the head. As Adrian flails
backwards Dwight grabs him and smashes him into the dirt. Bryan
comes down with his dagger and impales Adrian's thigh.

They both begin wailing on his vulnerable body with punches
and kicks.

"Fight back Lumin! Fight back! Fight back"! Bryan and Dwight
scold, gritting their teeth in anger.

Everything looks to be under control until Adrian dissipates
into purple smoke and reappears in the sky! With a purple Sathon
ball in hand he shouts at them.

"You two think you can defeat me?! With no powers?! I'll kill
all of you"! He screeches as he laughs maniacally.

The Sathon ball grows to the size of a building! His power
rages wildly, shaking the ground we stand on!

"So, how about it Justin? Do you envy the power that Lumin
elites like us possess? Our latent ability greatly eclipses your maggot

race's power ceiling! There's no way a Lustro like you can keep up with us"!

"He's definitely gotten stronger. The air stings." I murmur as Adrian continues to power up.

"How did he move so fast? I thought you were being beaten to a pulp"! Bryan growls.

"It's an afterimage technique. That wasn't his real body." Brooke informs my friends.

"She's right, and here's another lesson for you worthless maggots"!! Adrian howls demonstratively as blood leaks from his mouth.

"I'll educate you two on this attack before you're wiped away. I call this the 'purple people eater.' You see, my Sathon is infused with Scepin. Yes, the acidic chemical that eviscerated many inhabitants of this world and ruined the ecosystem, is embedded into my very DNA. When I first discovered this, I wanted to test it out and vaporized a Lumin soldier. As a child I had a terrible temper. So, when I didn't get my way, someone had to die. Fortunately for me, there were plenty of Lustronese scum and no consequences for wiping you roaches away." Adrian snarls.

He continues.

"Unlike most Sathon guides, I can force Sathon out through different parts of my body. The average user can only utilize one limb at a time, or they can only utilize their hands, limiting how they can weaponize their Sathon and rendering them predictable in battle. However, with me." Adrian stops and launches a purple Sathon blast out from his foot!

The attack hits one of his bloodhounds and the canine is eaten away by the Scepin!

"I can multi-task." Adrian sneers.

"But now that story-time is up. I'll just have to put the kiddies to bed!! Killing a few malcontents is always fun! Night night"! He screams.

Adrian leans back and just before he launches his devastating attack, I feel a twinge in my soul. The turquoise flame that entered my body, rattles violently, hungry for blood. I spring into action! Worried for the safety of my friends, I take the blast head on!

"Foolish Lustro! You can't stop my attack! It'll feed off your Ki and consume you"! Adrian chants confidently.

As his enormous ball of death closes in, I shatter the Sathon bomb with a thunderous punch! A silver light consumes the purple blast, and it explodes into a pungent smoke!

The explosion sends Adrian, Brooke, and Breanna, flying in opposite directions. As they cry out from the rumbling explosion of the blast, the flame within my body dances barbarically. More Sathon energy courses throughout me and I feel rejuvenated. Wasting no time, I spin, taking advantage of the silver smoke. Using it as a cover. I fire Sathon out of the bottoms of my feet like a jet, and rocket towards Bryan and Dwight.

"Let's go. Now"! I shout as I yank them both up by their arms.

Soaring away from the two assassins and Adrian, I drop my friends off at the truck.

"I'm going back for Hailey, get everything packed into the boat now! The water's edge is right there, I need both of you to push the boat into the water! We must go before they catch us." I order.

Pivoting off my foot, I turn back and fly as quickly as possible to rescue Hailey. Fortunately, she's already scurrying in our direction. As I grab her with both hands, I put the brakes on to soar back towards the boat. Just before we arrive, I hear Brooke scathingly hissing.

"Where are you? I'll kill you, Justin. I will turn you in, I swear"!

"Man, she really wants that reward, I can't believe she tracked us down without bloodhounds"! I exclaim inside my mind.

I spot the boat out on the water and descend towards it. Suddenly, the flame dances again and my body locks up! Hailey and I go tumbling from the sky and slam onto the boat's deck.

"What just happened to my body"!? I ponder as I no longer control its power.

"Are you two okay"? Dwight worries.

"I'm fine! Just get us out of here." I mutter, my body consumed by an indescribable pain.

Without another word he jumps on the wheel, and we promptly set sail towards Comely.

"Justin, what happened back there"? Bryan questions as he and his brother sit me down on the cushioned seats.

"Yeah, your eyes man. They were glowing a silver color, and your aura too. Everything about you seemed different. Your energy literally ate Adrian's attack." Dwight squeals excitedly.

"I… I don't know. Something took over my body and I just reacted. Whatever that power was though, its multiplication of my Sathon reserves is incredible." I state.

"However, its energy boost comes at a cost. Your body pays a toll so severe. The anguish and pain paralyzes you after its use." Bryan interjects.

"Yeah, Bryan's right Justin. If you can, you should avoid using that technique. It's too dangerous. If that paralysis had occurred moments earlier, you and I would have been sitting ducks." Hailey agrees.

"Are you two insane?! Justin said he couldn't help himself! It just happened. Besides, if you didn't notice Hailey. Bryan and I were goners if he hadn't stepped in! Maybe if you weren't so useless, you wouldn't always need saving. That technique is way too cool to ignore. What Justin needs right now, is some rest. We have a mission to accomplish whenever we reach Comely. Everyone else too, get some rest." Dwight comments

"Useless, huh? Why I oughta…." Hailey growls as she punches Dwight in his arm.

After their momentary tussle, Dwight is pinned face down. He squeals 'mercy' repeatedly as Hailey twists his arm behind his back.

"I can't believe I'm saying this, but, you're right little brother. Well, at least about the resting part. We can discuss everything else tomorrow." Bryan responds.

It doesn't take long at all before everyone can get comfortable. Hailey begins to fall asleep as Bryan sets the coordinates in the boat for Comely. Dwight helps his brother finish up by setting the electronic map by the wheel.

They both quickly lay down in vacant beds and fall fast asleep.

"Man, this flame. Its power is incredible." I think to myself as I finally pass out.

What feels like five consecutive days of rest blurs past. I only recall eating for brief moments and sleeping. After my body fully recovers, I finally get up and see that it is now dark outside.

I stretch my recuperated limbs and meander around the boat. Slowly stomping around while wiping the sleep crust from my eyes, I spot a beautiful patch of stars in the sky.

Taking a long gander over the railing, I see nothing but ocean for miles. Finally done inspecting the waters, I turn around. Zero pounces from behind a chair and tackles me. My adorable pet continues, playfully biting my arms and face.

"How did you even jump that high? You little rascal"! I cry, as he aggressively play-fights back, shedding his red fur on my face.

Runaways

After wrestling Zero off, I notice his horns are starting to grow in.

"Geez, these things grow faster than I thought. Just a week ago he didn't have anything on his head." I exclaim, puzzled by his hasty growth spurt.

I soon head back over towards the railing and stare up at the stars. I ponder on our new enemies.

"So, we have two assassins with the Sathon ability pursuing us because of the huge bounty on my head. And we have Julien and Adrian, attempting to clean up their father's mess by killing off the runaways. Perhaps their father's position of power is at risk since my friends originated from the city he rules over". I ponder to myself.

Briefly, I think about Jacqui, how her treatment must be hell right now. How my mother is probably being subjected to daily interrogations. As the thoughts float around, my mind settles on my friends Donshay, Jade, and Ava. How they must be feeling.

As I reflect on past events, I regret how things soured before I departed.

"I wish they were here with me." I lament.

However, the thoughts of their betrayal return to my mind and I sweep all wishful thinking aside.

"They weren't going to help me rescue Jacqui in the end. They wouldn't be here with me because they don't care." I mutter annoyed by the thought.

I remember how they were okay with abandoning Jacqui, leaving her with the people who enslaved us. Furious with the realization, I run back to the wheel to check the electronic map. Thankfully, we only have a few hours left until we arrive in Comely. Seeing this gets me even more hyped to save Jacqui and to get my revenge on anyone who harmed her.

"Finally! Let's get her back! It's been too long. Hold on Jacqui. We're coming"! I shout internally.

"Don't stress yourself out, Justin, we're going to save her. I know you're just as eager as the rest of us. Probably more than that, if I'm being honest with myself. We're going to be by your side every step of the way. I promise." Dwight vows stoically.

"I know. You have no idea how much I love and appreciate you guys for doing this with me. I honestly couldn't have gotten this far alone." I admit, now looking up from the map to Dwight.

"Same goes for you, bro. We have our own reasons for why we need to avenge our people. Now don't be up too late, get some rest homie." Dwight states as he smiles and walks back down to his room.

I nod, after he disappears. I think about what Hailey and Dwight discussed with me back when we were in their home.

"Maybe a small prayer could help us." I ponder to myself.

I just stand there staring up at the stars and think to myself.

Runaways

"Hey, sorry for doubting you. I know we don't talk often, or really at all since dad disappeared... but, if you help my friends and I save Jacqui."

I begin to get choked up as all my memories of the riot and losing Jacqui flood back.

"If you help us, I would be forever grateful." I cry out loud.

I wipe my face and trudge back to my bed. I smile as I begin rolling up in my blanket and passing out.

Chapter 9:
The Katun Ripple

Hearing the map go off, snaps me from my slumber faster than usual. I begin to roll out of bed, eager to get going.

Excited and slightly nervous of the unknown future, I decide to walk over to the sink and splash my face with cold water, to really shock myself out of my groggy phase. After trotting out to the deck, I see everyone else is already awake and awaiting my presence. We all sit down at the table as Hailey discusses her dream to Dwight and Bryan from last night. Once her story finishes, Bryan turns to me.

"What do you have in mind for today? We can go for a stealthy approach or rush in." He questions.

Calmly, I start explaining to the group the layout of the city from my limited knowledge and memory. After coming up with the best escape routes available, we decide to split up in groups of two.

"Don't forget where the boat is, we're coming back here. It's a good thing this fog is covering us, we would have to abandon the boat and swim to shore if it weren't present." I chirp happily.

Over the next few minutes Dwight turns the boat engine off completely and we let our momentum carry us to shore. Our boat begins to slowly come to a stop and before it slowly collides with the dock, I place a puffy Sathon cushion between us and the solid dock.

Runaways

Dwight returns to the table, and we all review and repeat every step in our plan before we agree it's time to head out.

"Wait. You'll need this if you get into trouble." Bryan offers generously.

Bryan eyes his dagger for a moment, he sighs quietly before he slides the knife across the table to Dwight.

They both nod at one another and smile softly.

"We meet back at the grocery store in an hour. That is, if you can't find anything that'll bring us closer to locating Jacqui." I state firmly.

"Stay stealthy, we're teenagers so blend in and relax"! Hailey reminds everyone.

Bryan pauses for a moment and glances over to Hailey.

"Hailey, I consider you family, please take care of Dwight, I need you both to be safe." He assures her.

Bryan hugs them both tightly and we split up, exiting the boat and begin walking into the city from the dock crowded with other ships.

Bryan and I head towards the town hall while Dwight and Hailey trail us before peeling off and heading towards the local arcade. When Bryan and I arrive in the town hall's living room, it's not very full. We easily move around while avoiding direct eye contact with too many adults.

Justin Avery

"What are we even looking for Justin"? Bryan inquires.

I look at Bryan sighing indifferently.

"I'm not entirely sure, but I'll know what it is when we find it." I comment confident, as I run my hand through a magazine, attempting to look intrigued.

"Well, let me know if you see anything, and stop shaking so much! You look nervous. Someone's gonna think you stole something out of here." He growls silently.

"Right. My bad." I mutter, nervous of getting caught.

We keep pressing through the small crowd and find a group of teenagers relaxing in a computer room upstairs.

The group of teens look to be around our age.

Bryan, being more of the extrovert, easily gets us included in their conversation. After a little while, the oldest guy asks us if we heard about the escapees from a week ago.

"Oh yeah, that was wild"! One of the girl's yell.

I act completely oblivious, and they all go crazy on me.

"How have you not heard of the story"!? They all shout.

After I laugh it off, they go into detail about what all happened and one of the girls starts "fangirling" over the characters in the story with the Sathon abilities.

Runaways

"I know he's Lustronese but, oh my god. That bravery to have the idea to escape Nero, and not only that… but he actually pulled it off"! She fawns over the mysterious boy for a few moments.

Her friend chimes in.

"You would really get in trouble with the Lumin authorities just to get your hands on that boy, wouldn't you? You already know that a relationship with this guy is way out of the question." She states with disgust in her eyes.

"But what if he converted into a Lumin citizen like some of the wealthier Lustronese people do? Then we could legally have a shot at love"! She persists.

Her friend responds again, even more spite rolling off her tongue than before.

"Relax, he's just a troublesome Lustro. Girl, your future husband is out there somewhere. Besides, he's a runaway. Even if he came back and surrendered, the Light would probably have him, and his friends executed. Face it, he wants to live freely, and we don't need their kind around. Your two goals in life are diametrically opposed." She scoffs.

The girl that was a huge fan of my bravery now drops her head.

"I know, I just was being optimistic." She mutters.

They continue the story while Bryan and I give each other a look of concern.

I don't allow the group to see my facial expressions as I turn to them to laugh. I stay neutral, adding small comments here and there, as they tell their story.

Some parts are obviously exaggerated, but I keep my mouth shut, loving every moment.

One of the quiet girls in the back of the group shakes her head saying.

"It's sad that one of the girls got caught. I get it, we're supposed to hate the Lustronese, but what they did seemed way too far."

I look at the girl, trying to keep my composure and ask her what happened to the Lustro that got caught.

A hush falls over the group and they refuse to say anything for a moment. Nervously I ask again. The oldest guy just pulls up a video on one of the computers. As he types 'Comely.' 'Public punishment' auto-fills into the search-bar and my heart drops like a rock.

"If you can't watch, I totally understand, it's pretty brutal." He comments gloomily.

"Why didn't she just say who all was with her. I swear Lustros are stupid too, they would've let her go easy if she snitched." One of the guys blurt out.

When the video starts, a chill ripples violently down my spine.

Runaways

Struggling to hold my emotions back as I read the subtitles at the bottom, I start to shake.

Bryan frowns and puts his hand on my back sympathetically. Visibly upset to everyone in the room, I try to calm down.

"I'm supposed to hate Lustronese people, I can't be this visibly upset." I tell myself internally.

Five guards, tie Jacqui to a tall metal pole with everyone in the city watching. The bleachers are packed to capacity as everyone cheers on the Lumin guards or covers their eyes, knowing what's coming won't be easy to stomach.

The Lumin officers walk around Jacqui very slowly, as they badger her with multiple questions, she keeps her eyes closed, not even acknowledging them.

When Jacqui refuses to answer the question, one of the guards loses his cool and swings wildly, bashing her ribs with a baton!

The crowd roars violently and many familiar faces in the crowd look away, a bleak look in their eyes.

The other three officers just watch, chuckling and enjoying the show. A little girl rushes out from the crowd screaming loudly.

"Stop! You're killing her"!

The Lumin leader pauses for a moment and snatches the little girl up by her shirt. He then headbutts her and tosses her back towards the bleachers.

"Shut up brat, we're just getting started. Matter of fact, who's kid is this? Bring her family down into the circle next! We're gonna teach the entire family some manners." He barks.

Lumin guards in the crowd swarm over, dragging the family down the steps and toss them over the railing. The children and parents, lay bruised in the arena where Jacqui lies.

I stand back, completely disgusted at the atrocities occurring on the computer screen.

As if he had not done enough to a helpless child, the officer proceeds to spit on the little girl!

This enrages some members in the crowd, and they start a ruckus. Many people begin to try and hop the fence to defend their loved ones. It seems all hell is moments away from breaking loose.

More officers rush in, and as everyone seems to be on edge, some individuals becoming rowdier than others start fighting the Lumin officers! The Lumin civilians begin to stop cheering a look to help their police force.

Merely moments before a fight between the Lumin citizens and the Lustronese people starts, gun shots ring out!

BANG BANG!

Everyone starts screaming and then a man in polished white armor, hops the railing and saunters out into the middle of the circle.

"Everyone shut up"! He barks.

Instantly a hush covers the crowd, and they watch him, nervously anticipating his next words.

"Maybe you worms forgot who owns you, but we run this city. Hell, we run this entire nation"!

As I glance around the room some of the girls have very visceral reactions to the way the man treats our people. Even some of the guy's faces are full of disgust.

"Wow, so I guess all Lumin citizens aren't evil. Even these teenagers don't agree with what's going on. Maybe there are some good Lumin folks after all". I debate internally.

I peek back to the screen and the abuse from the Lumin soldiers continues.

This goes on for minutes and Jacqui refuses to answer, she just keeps taking the beating. Jacqui slumps down in agony but her hands are tied above her head, so she just hangs there, weeping. Her glossy white hair, stained with her own blood.

A guard hits her in her ribcage and she spits up blood onto the floor. At one point the guard asks her something, but the subtitle pops up on the screen as 'inaudible' and she spits blood into his face.

Furious, he punches her, and all the guards just start swinging wildly. Eventually they tire themselves out and she drops to the floor broken and bloody. Bryan steps in between the screen and I, shaking me and demanding.

Justin Avery

"Justin are you okay man"?! He cries.

I look around and notice I've begun to shine a bright silver and the room around us is in a wreck.

"Did I black out? What just happened"? I wonder to myself.

I look back to Bryan and the group. But everyone just stares at me afraid for their lives.

"Please don't kill us, one of the girls beg.

"We know it's wrong but it's all we've been taught." She pleads.

Bryan grabs my shoulders.

"Bro, are you okay"? He shouts again.

Unable to give him a response, Bryan resorts to repeating his question again. I attempt to answer but my voice breaks. Before I can even complete my response, Bryan just hugs me tightly and I struggle to get my words out.

"Where is she now"? I finally choke out.

"She's in the hospital down the road and she's still alive. Her room is being guarded though." The quiet girl says.

I let go of Bryan.

"I am going to eviscerate… everyone. Every guard that had some connection to that is going to perish." I state.

Runaways

"You're not going anywhere you scum." An adult screams as he and two others charge me.

Without thoughts slowing my movements, I turn to them and blitz the adults!

Sliding through the first man's legs, I pop up behind him and land a brutal spinning kick to the back of his neck.

The man goes limp and falls to the ground unconscious.

I dash at the second and third man with my entire body flashing brilliantly. I rip through the air and kick one man underneath his chin, shattering his jaw and the other man attempts to grab me.

My body reacts on its own and I dissipate. Moments later I re-appear behind him. Unannounced to the man, he attempts to grab an afterimage of my body and falls to the ground.

"What the"! He shouts as he picks himself up and looks at me petrified for his life.

I spring at him landing a devastating flying knee and he crumbles to the floor. I grab his hair and lift him up.
Now with him staring me in the eyes I smirk.

"The only scum are Lumin citizens like you." I growl furiously.

I then headbutt him and toss him to the floor.

"Get up and fight"! I scream.

"You Lumin are so proud of your heritage! Stand up and fight back"! I order.

The man stands up to his feet before quickly stumbling to the ground again.

"Please, have mercy." He groans.

His failure irritates me, and I blitz him, landing a frenzy of punches and a spinning elbow which sends him rocketing through the floor! Once the debris clears, he lays back in the lobby, far below us.

I slowly breathe in and out, my silver glow fades back within my body.

I promptly walk back down the stairs and out the door.

"Justin! We should think this through, the room is guarded. We gotta at least go get Dwight and Hailey"! Bryan suggests, apprehensive of my next decision.

I don't break stride as I keep walking in the direction to the hospital.

"It's already been decided. I'm going to give this city an insurrection they won't ever forget. As for Dwight and Hailey, get them on the boat and get ready to depart." I calmly state.

Without glancing back, I know he nods and takes off towards the arcade.

Runaways

"This day will always be remembered. I'm going to pay them back for what they did to Jacqui, and all those Lustronese people that were beaten that day. If anyone steps in my way, I'll waste them"! I determine in my mind.

I walk through the front door of the hospital and past the receptionist at the front counter. My hearing fades in and out, I'm so enraged I can't even think straight.

My vision blurs from the tears in my eyes and a ringing begins in my ears, but I press forward.

I make my way up the stairs and see a couple of guards in front of the door down the hall. When I see the guards, I just take off. I don't even think of what to do. Everything just becomes a blur.

As they train their weapons on me and scream for me to stop. I just sprint faster, and they look stunned as an unarmed teenager charges them.

My lightweight armor turns from a normal outfit, back to its original state. My identity mentally clicks for both the guards, and they open fire. I quickly create a transparent silver colored shield with my right hand! The bullets ricochet off it and fall harmlessly to the ground.

"This... kid!? Why are his eyes silver? Is that the Katun ripple." The men clamor.

With my left hand a long blade grows and as I launch myself into the air, the guards fall to the ground while trying to retreat.

Nothing but a disrupted wail leaves them both. I slash down as hard as I possibly can, severing anything vital.

I turn and punch through the steel door using the energy as a cover for my fist. When I slide through and enter the room, I see Jacqui laying in a bed hooked up to a machine.

"I'm surprised they actually kept you alive." I think to myself before making both my hands healing whirlpools.

Unconscious, she has no reaction to anything that's occurring. After a few minutes, her dried blood and bruises vanish but unsurprisingly she's still out cold.

Suddenly, I hear multiple sets of footsteps storming up the stairs. I know it's time to dip out, and I grab Jacqui. I imagine the heaviest thing that comes to mind and a silver boulder blocks the door.

Shattering the window with a lethal kick, I create a bunch of huge pillows at the bottom of the building. However, focusing on the pillows makes the boulder dissipate from the door and the guards start breaking the door down, squeezing their way in!

Instantly I jump from the building, and we land in the pillows below. As we crash, I hear the men storm into the room.

Carrying Jacqui to the side of the building where we can conceal ourselves from enemy eyes, I attempt to shake her awake.

"Geez, all this dead weight isn't really helpful Jacqui." I chuckle to myself.

Runaways

Without a second to catch my breath, I hear the guards begin to rappel down the side of the building!

I begin to bound away from the building to the foggy dock where I remember the boat is located.

The flame inside my body dances wildly and I feel my body attempt to lock up!

"No! Not now! Don't you quit on me right now." I growl.

A bullet zips past my face, cutting my cheek and I get an adrenaline rush.

"No way! I didn't get this far just to die now"! I shout as I pick up my speed.

Racing to the nearest spot to hide, I stumble behind another building, falling forward onto my face. Jacqui hits the ground and wakes up, but she's still dazed.

I try to slide over to her but another bullet breaks through the brick wall and I get down as fast as possible.

I hear one of the Lumin Officers scream.

"Keep up the fire, they're trapped"!

Now attempting to worm my way over to Jacqui, I am instantly disconnected from her as the bullets have such a steady flow that I can't even see!

"The debris from the bricks is too much." I mutter.

Justin Avery

Before I can even try something else, there is debris everywhere and the guards are on top of us!

They all surround us, guns aimed at my head, daring me to flinch.

With things looking grim I get one last-ditch idea! Closing my eyes slowly, I begin focusing hard and a sparkle begins to form. It's so small that no one seems to notice it. I do my best to keep it as small as possible. As I'm focusing on my Sathon sparkle, the leader walks up to me and lifts his weapon into the air, ready to strike me.

"Open your eyes and look at me boy"! He barks.

I open my eyes smiling and the sparkle explodes, sending everyone flying!

I dust myself off and get up quickly. I spot guards scattered everywhere, while some are plastered into the surrounding buildings, others are piled up on the ground. As I take a step, my body feels as if it was struck by a lightning bolt, and I collapse to the ground.

"No! The effects of this silver light have started taking effect"! I wail.

Before I can no longer move, I toss a fist sized Sathon blast onto a building nearby and hope to detonate it but as it sticks, my body stops moving completely.

Runaways

As I look around, I can see some officers survived my sparkle explosion and they begin to limp towards me. I start to worry and try forcing myself up, but, to no avail.

"Jacqui, I'm sorry. I wish I could have saved you. I got cocky and now my body is frozen". I lament as I grit my teeth.

The leader with the white polished armor, approaches my body. He takes a knee right in front of me and smirks. His armor is busted, and he looks battered.

"Well, it seems you couldn't escape, boy. You really thought that you could just run into Nero, the stronghold of the earth. Take your friend over there, and then just leave? We own you, kid. Once a slave, always a slave. I'll make sure we work you in those mines until you collapse. You'll be starved and then beaten to death… right in front of your mother." He sneers at me.

"I'll kill you! Don't you dare mention my mother. You're nothing but talk and I'll prove it"! I screech as I struggle, just to push myself off the ground.

The man's smirks at me again and a few soldiers scoop up Jacqui before making their way back to a truck.

"Well, we're gonna take your friend back to the hospital where she'll succumb to some… uhh medical mistake." He comments sarcastically.

He kicks me in my ribs, and I cough up blood!

"You and I though. We're gonna have a lot of fun until that truck comes back to pick you up, boy." The Lumin officer grins.

Suddenly the two men hop in the back of the truck, carrying Jacqui with them. Two more soldiers from the truck begin to walk towards me. I glance up at the soldier in white armor, when suddenly, a lime blade pierces him from behind, and sticks out through his stomach!

"So, tell me again who was gonna kill who… boy"? The guard states arrogantly.

The leader tumbles lifelessly to the ground and the Lumin guard behind him smiles at me with his ring flashing.

"Jade"! I shout excitedly.

"Aren't you glad I didn't stay away now"? Jade grins as the other guard moves his mask, revealing his identity.

It's Donshay! Both Jade and Don begin to lift me up. They carry me and lay me down on the inside of the truck. The first two Lumin guards gaze at my friends for a split second and are quickly corralled. Jade and Don pin them down and detain both guards with the electric bands as handcuffs. I gaze over to Jacqui who sleeps safely beside me.

Don begins to drive us over to the dock and Jade explains everything.

"So, I know you're super confused. Do me a favor and just listen. Don and I have been out on some missions, and we decided that we needed to right our wrongs. I'm terribly sorry about how I acted when it came to saving Jacqui. If it were me in her position, I would hope you all came back for me. And I couldn't miss an opportunity to help you. It seems you've attained a new power and one of the rubies as well too"! Jade chirps exhilarated by all the recent events.

"Wait, but that lime sword that extended from your ring? How did you do that? I thought you said you didn't have the Sathon ability, so the ring was just an accessory." I spout.

"I don't have the ability. Although, I sorta lied. So, the ring of power actually pulls Sathon energy from the sun and I can use that energy to wield something similar to the ability you possess. The ring doesn't have an energy reserve cap like the human body though, so the ring has zero limitations." Jade smirks.

"Ohh, I see. That's dope, I'm glad your father left that behind for you, it's fitting." I respond.

Don glances back and holds out a dark blue crystal. The gem dances with the light particles that shine through the window, and he smirks.

"We found this a little after we split up, so that means we have two of the gems now. We'll have to check the map and instructions inside but we're one step closer to saving our people." Don smiles.

"That's great guys! Thank you so much for saving me. This new ability emerges when my anger is aroused and seems uncontrollable. What makes it scary to use, is that the transformation eats through my Sathon like crazy and even leaves me paralyzed afterwards"! I reply as I chuckle to my friends.

Don glances back again, this time with a concerned expression on his face.

"How many times have you activated this transformation"? He questions.

"This is the second time. Wait, where is Ava? Wasn't she with you both when I left"? I inquire.

Jade beams so brightly, the crystals pale in comparison.

"That's the best part, she said there was another gem east of where we found this blue one. The map said it was in some volcanic areas, so, she went to grab it while we came to rescue you." Jade responds.

"Right. So, we should have three stones altogether"? I ask.

"Correct. We're gonna drop you off at the boat and go help Ava. We don't want her getting hurt. We said to wait until we got back but you know how she is. But keep up the good work Justin, we need you to help us liberate our people. We'll meet up again, okay"? Donshay spouts.

Once we arrive, the others greet us with glee. As Jade and Don carry us both to the boat, Jacqui becomes more cognizant and does her best to not be dead weight. However, it only makes things worse. Jade and Donshay don't stick around long and are speeding off in their truck as soon as Bryan and Dwight trade off with them.

Bryan helps me slide Jacqui into bed while Dwight zips away from the docks, as we depart from Joviality.

Hailey shuffles over to me whispering. "I see why you wanted to come back for her, she's so pretty."

Runaways

I smile warmly before kissing Jacqui on her forehead.

"We should head back home and just lay low for a while." Hailey suggests.

I consider the idea momentarily and agree that things would be best if we stayed out of Nero for a while.

Bryan takes a seat beside us and says something that makes my heart drop.

"The map is blank." He queasily mutters.

I stare at him awaiting laughter, but he never breaks character.

"What did you say? What do you mean the map is blank"? I stutter heavily, struggling to respond.

Bryan's eyes don't leave the floor as he mumbles the same heart wrenching phrase again.

"The map is blank." He cries bleakly.

Dwight helps me to my feet, and we impatiently rush over to Bryan, demanding a response.

"What do you mean the map is blank? Why do you keep saying that"?!

He looks me in the eyes, lost for words and just shakes his head. I walk over to the map to see that not only is it blank, but the electronic paper has turned black and even the previous directions that we already accomplished, have also disappeared.

Staring into the blank dark abyss that used to be our map, everyone stares at me in shock.

Not knowing how to respond, I just drop the blacked-out map and limp with Dwight's help, towards the front of the boat puzzled by this.

Multiple thoughts run through my head all at once.

"Where do we go from here"?

"How do we get back to their home"?

"How are Jade and the others doing? Is their map blacked out too"? I fret.

As the seconds pass, I become more stressed, and I attempt to clear my mind. A hand rests on my shoulder, as I turn, I see its Dwight, doing his best to comfort me.

"Hey man, don't stress, we'll figure everything out." He softly states.

Even with his best attempts to reassure me. My mind sits fried as I shake myself free from the pessimistic mindset.

I turn around and hug him, Hailey and Bryan join in, and we all just sit there for a moment.

Runaways

"The most important part is that we got Jacqui out safely and nobody got hurt." Hailey comments, highlighting the situation.

"She's right, I'm just glad we didn't get split up." Dwight admits.

As I smile and inspect all of them cheerfully, we gaze out to the ocean.

Mere moments pass and something whistles loudly before connecting with the ship!

Exploding on impact, the front half of the boat is ripped to shreds and Dwight tumbles off into the raging water! Everything seems to be happening in slow motion and then it mentally registers to me what is going on.

"We're under attack! Get down"! I scream desperately.

Bryan races over to the ledge of the boat attempting to find his brother, lost in the waves. Before I can even get another word out, the boats behind us fire off shots and Bryan gets blasted down!

I tackle Hailey and we both lay down as bullets whiz over our heads. The onslaught completely obliterates the top half of the boat. I look over to Bryan and instantly freeze as I watch his lifeless body slide off the damaged boat into the water. My eyes begin to water uncontrollably. I can't even begin to fathom the situation. It hurts to even process what I just witnessed. My friend, with holes through his body, slipping off the boat to die alone at the bottom of the sea floor. His brother, somewhere lost in the water with no idea of the threat that surrounds him.

Justin Avery

I get up from covering a quivering Hailey, I climb to the top of the shattered boat, and I stare at the four boats trailing us, enraged. I feel the flame within my body twinge in my soul again.

"No Justin! Don't use that technique again! You'll die if you get paralyzed fighting against the Lumin forces"! Hailey cries.

I scream, engulfed in my rage and a huge silver flame encapsulates my body. The glowing silver flame is embedded in my Sathon, my eyes, and my aura. The power fluctuates and finally overflows. The ocean below me begins to create waves, just off my aura flaring alone.

I feel myself begin to levitate in the air before I raise a massive transparent silver colored wall. One of the boats slam into it and the other three zip around, quickly staying hot on our tail.

More boats follow in pursuit and before I can react, there is an entire aquatic army on our tail. Hundreds of boats chase after my friends and me. The power deep within me roars. I float higher into the sky while simultaneously flying backwards to keep up with Hailey and Jacqui on our boat.

I lift both arms behind myself and begin charging an attack. The lightning from the gloomy clouds strikes me, and I feel as if I could explode from all the energy flowing within my body! As both of my hands begin to glow silver, loud electricity crackles. The electricity hits a few boats, and they explode!

"Dying before my attack is even ready? Don't ruin the fun"! I shout.

Runaways

Thunder booms and my aura pulsates violently. Reality seems to distort as a turquoise orb appears above each hand. The center of each orb is a silver flame.

"You killed my friends… and now I'm mad. You all will pay… prepare yourself! Your expiration date is today! Oceanic Hellfire"!! I roar as I slam both arms together.

Justin Avery

Runaways

Seven arching beams rocket out from my palms and consume hundreds of boats! As the beams hit the ocean, the water changes to a bright turquoise color. Silver razor sharp rocks jet out from underneath the surface and the boats in the area explode.

"The water is now a minefield and you've fallen into my trap." I scowl.

I lift a hand and move it to the side. Suddenly, lightning in the sky turns silver and wipes out a dozen battleships. As I dismantle the Lumin fleet I feel the flame twinge inside my body again.

Now returning fire, the Lumin aquatic forces don't back down and a plethora of missiles are launched at me!

"I put out my index finger and begin to shoot down the missiles one by one. However, the number of projectiles launched at me is too much.

I attempt to create a shield to protect myself from the flurry. When the missile collides with my shield something shatters and before I know it, I'm blind. Everything goes white. I can't hear anything. I feel myself plummeting towards the unforgiving waters below.

As I crash into the water my sight returns, I feel my lungs expand, quickly filling with salt water. I try and move. However, nothing happens. My limbs won't obey my commands and I slowly drift to the bottom of the ocean like a leaf floats in the wind, powerless to change its course.

Justin Avery

When I hit the bottom, I see my entire life flash before my eyes as my vision blurs. Things go dark and I can't hold my breath anymore.

I wait patiently for my existence to fade away. Moments pass as I lay at the seafloor, hoping the end comes soon. But it doesn't. I open my eyes and flinch back in shock as I finally see my surroundings. I'm floating a couple feet above the ground and my body is transparent.

"Am I dead"? I think to myself.

I see my mother bawling her eyes out at my grave. The sight breaks my heart, I feel so torn watching her suffer.

I float down to her, crying out that I'm right in front of her but it's as if she can't see me.

She blames herself and mumbles that it's all her fault.

Attempting to reach out and grab her, I long to shake her to her senses when my hand phases through her shoulder!

I look at her and it all starts to make sense. I must be dead, and my mother is suffering the loss of her only child.

I scream and beat my head with my fists, fervor building up inside my mind.

"I failed you! I'm sorry mama"! I cry out, heartbroken.

Runaways

As I return to the earth inches from her, I shatter the ground with a punch in frustration. I punch again and again until my fists are bloody.

I scream even louder when I think about all the things that are gone. I'll never get to experience all the things that life has to offer, I won't be able to fix things and expose the truth to Nero and its people.

"How did this happen, it's not fair! It all happened so fast"! I shriek.

A wild tornado forms, spinning and consuming everything I knew as a child. When it subsides, I hear my friend's voices calling out to me. Jade, Donshay, and Ava search for me back where I ditched them. Another tornado appears and wipes them away.

They reappear again, as my surroundings change. This time at my house with my mother looking sickly.

I desperately try and float over to them, but I can't get up from the ground where I punched the earth. My fists glow turquoise and I'm constrained to this spot.

My mother tells Don, Jade, and Ava that I didn't make it and I died with four others in a terrible accident.

"Accident"? I roar bewildered.

"Mom, they ambushed us! It wasn't an accident"! I scream to no avail.

She continues to tell them that I had kidnapped the other four individuals and had injected a lethal drug, 'Angel Dust,' into my system.

"Mom, please don't tell me you believe that flagrantly disrespectful lie. You know me, I'm not what the Light tells you I am"! I shout.

Still struggling with whatever unnatural force that keeps me constrained to the ground, I flex my Sathon powers but it's no use. Nobody can hear me. I can't move.

I savagely fight against the force, now throwing knees into the ground and ramming my shoulders as well. In a desperate attempt to free myself, I slam my head down into the dirt and the earth cracks!

My fists glow brighter, and I keep slamming my head into the dirt. I focus harder on the crack in the ground and keep fighting but after a few minutes I'm exhausted with little to no progress. I look up and see a tornado barreling towards my friends and my mother, but I'm powerless to stop it. The tornado grows tremendously and is making a beeline for all of us now!

I yank harder from the force and still can't get loose. An ominous feeling comes over me. I pull with both hands and stand up screaming as loud as I can, attempting to tear myself away from the earth as something inside my brain snaps.

"I have to save them! I can't let my friends die"! I scream.

Runaways

Rushing now, I create a force field to stop the tornado. As it collides with my energy, something ruptures, and everything just disappears.

When I awaken, I'm sitting on a floor in an abyss of nothing but darkness. I stand up and walk around, there is no sound when I speak or walk.

I only see myself and the abyss, there is nothing for miles. Taking a gander at my surroundings, I decide to meander around the area for a few minutes.

Before I know it, there is an empty podium sitting before me. It looks identical to the one where I found the flame after I had chased Jade into the burning house.

But this time there is no flame. There is nothing for me to do. A turquoise silhouette of a man begins to form in front of me. As he takes his steps closer to me my body freezes.

"Why do you keep summoning me, boy? Do you need my power's once again"?

The man stops and presses his hand onto my head. We sit in silence for a few moments before he speaks again.

"Oh, I see. You all were caught in a firestorm of an ambush. And now you need me to bail you out once again. Listen kid, you and I have the same goals but by no means does that make us friends. You embody the freedom that my people deserve. However, when you clean up my mess, I will return and have vengeance on this world. Every being will bow to Lord Lustro. I will engulf this earth in a fire so deep, it will tatter the fabric of history itself. I'll finally be able to rest once this world is placed back in its archaic period."

Lustro smiles at me.

"So, for now… you and I are on equal standing. The only reason I'm telling you this is because I despise you so greatly and maybe your fear of my existence will fuel your power. I need your vessel to become sturdy. The stronger you become, the stronger I become, I will break free from this prison. So, strengthen yourself and free my disciples. Each time you enter my domain, by using my form, you are empowering me. I can't wait to be freed. This world shall fear me. Oh, and you should probably dump those 'Rubies of Legend'. I don't think you wanna keep those so close to you." Lustro sneers as he begins to fade back into the darkness.

"Tell me where to go! You can't just pop up, spill some garbage, and then leave like this. Who has the answers"? I demand.

"Follow the white haired one but beware of when she's out of your sight. In her soul, dark and light fight for the control." Lustro smirks.

As he slinks back off into the darkness, I am released from his grip and can move once again.

"Why did he want me to ditch the rubies? And 'beware of the white haired one.' Is he talking about Jacqui? No, he must be bluffing, he's just trying to split the group up." I convince myself.

As the situation simmers on my mind, a tsunami rushes in, overtaking me. When the water washes away, I stand up, choking on the liquid in my lungs. Now finally able to open my eyes, I see that the black abyss has transformed into an endless white plane.

"Oh no. Not this again." I fret.

Nervous if what happens next, I turn to see the podium has vanished and a paper is rolled up neatly in its absence.

The white plain starts to shake furiously, and I stumble, before falling onto the paper. I cover it quickly by curling up in the fetal position. As I do so, a giant wave wipes me off the plain and I wake up on the boat in bed.

Terrified for my life, I wake everyone as I scream, not yet realizing where I am.

Jacqui rolls over before holding me tightly and the others run into the room. Dwight and Bryan question if I'm okay and as I see everyone standing around me, I break down in tears.

Hailey scampers over, begging me to tell them what's wrong. I grab everyone and pull them into a tight hug. I don't say anything for a while, before finally explaining what had happened and inform the group that the situation with Lord Lustro.

"So, he's alive? He's actually plotting against us"? Hailey wails.

"Somewhat. He told me that he's going to help us along the way to free his disciples. But it seems once we've finally gathered world peace, he has plans that differ from our own. Problem is, the strength I gain through his form, also feeds his flame. I think it's called the Katun ripple." I groan.

Struck with fear they all just stare at me fretfully.

"So, to mitigate his growth, don't use that form anymore." Jacqui states.

"It's not that simple. Every time I've been forced to use it, there was no other way to resolve the problem. This form is aroused by my anger. I can't use rage to fuel my Sathon. Raw emotion is the main pathway to powering up." I complain.

"Well, it's nighttime now, let's just figure this out tomorrow morning. Thankfully, we didn't run into any boats besides a couple fishers." Bryan comments.

"Try not to stress about things, we're here to fight alongside you. We'll help you keep that power under control." Jacqui assures me.

I smile and just sit there staring at each person. As they all return my warm grin, my train of thought slows to a stop and my worries evaporate.

"I love you guys. I hope you all know that." I state softly.

"We love you too"!! Hailey shouts as she hugs me again.

"Hey man, we're not going anywhere, I promise." Dwight smiles cheerfully.

After reassuring me of that, Dwight leaves and pulls his beanbag chair into the corner of the room.

Bryan does the same, coming back with his air-mattress. He struggles to fit it through the door, before finally sliding it through and laying it on the floor next to his brother.

Hailey ignores their idea and decides to plop down on the air-mattress with Bryan.

"We're staying right here until the morning." Dwight comments, doing his best to convince me.

I give him a comforting smile and he continues.

"I promise that we won't fail! We'll show everyone what the Light has done"! He growls.

I smile again and thank everyone for being here. Soon after, I peacefully drift back to sleep.

When I reawaken in the morning, everyone is still passed out in my room. I tip toe around each of my friends and slip out the doorway.

As I make it to the table, I hear a soothing voice.

"Where are you going so early in the morning, loser"? A feminine voice questions.

I turn around, coming face to face with Jacqui.

She strolls over and hugs me tightly. Unable to hold my beaming grin back, I lift her up, hugging her back. Eventually I release her.

Jacqui smiles back at me and looks towards the ground shyly.

"Thank you for coming back to save me, loser. I honestly thought I was a goner." She mutters.

"It's no problem. I owed you the attempt at the very least. You saved my life." I smile blissfully.

Stretching and yawning, I take a seat at the table and pat the cushion beside me, motioning for her to sit next to me. Jacqui takes a seat beside me, leaning her head on my shoulder.

"Hey Justin"? Jacqui inquires.

"Yeah, what's up." I answer softly.

"I know where we can go since the map doesn't work anymore." She says with a huge grin on her face.

As I await her next sentence, Lustro's voice rattles inside my head.

"Don't forget what I said kid. Beware of the white haired one." His voice chuckles harshly.

Doing my best to ignore him, I turn to Jacqui, intrigued.

There's this country my brother used to talk about, he claimed it had the largest trees, freshest fruit, the cleanest water, and the most exotic animals." Jacqui continues.

I sit up, now fully engaged in this idea of hers.

Runaways

"There's just one thing though, it's very dangerous, the animals haven't been around people very often and most are extremely territorial." She warns.

Jacqui comes to a stop and hesitates before starting again.

"I've always wanted to go, and since we're lost, we should go relax there until we can figure out how to fix our map." She finishes.

I pause, contemplating it briefly, before I agree that we should head in that direction.

"Only problem is, where is this place Jacqui"? I chuckle.

She stands up and whips the boat one hundred and eighty degrees before turning back to me grinning from ear to ear.

"Oh Justin, nobody taught you how to read the stars, huh"? She boasts arrogantly.

Without a word from me, she smirks and walks away.

"We're headed to Mirra"! She bellows excitedly.

Hours roll by and slowly, the ship comes to life as everyone else wakes up. Throughout the day we all make up games to play and bond until we hear shouting.

"Land hooooo"! Dwight screams.

Bryan looks at him disappointed.

"Don't be that guy... that hurt my head." Bryan comments.

"What? I have always wanted to scream that. Now that we're on a boat it only seemed fitting." Dwight explains as he scratches his head, embarrassed.

I turn my head away from the brothers, eager to lay my eyes on this foreign land. As we edge closer to making contact, Jacqui starts to load all our food in storage pods.

After everyone helps empty the boat, we follow Jacqui until we find an area that looks abandoned. We pick the biggest house in the area and start cleaning.

"What's with all the abandoned houses in the area"? Dwight inquires.

"This place has a small village from what I heard, but the rumors are that the Lumin special forces, ran through this area a few years ago. They didn't hesitate when it came to murder and wiped out all the Sathon guides." She shares with the group.

"So, probably the same thing that happened in Cavo. That place was abandoned but I'm glad we found Zero there." I respond.

On cue, our small pet tiger hops from Hailey's shoulder to mine.

"You've been with Hailey a whole lot, haven't you buddy"? I say to the cat, almost using baby talk to communicate.

No more than a half hour into the hygienic makeover of the house, I hear Hailey and Jacqui screaming in the backyard.

Runaways

I bolt towards their cries franticly.

"Didn't she warn us about those wild animals"!? I grit my teeth nervously.

When I make it to the girls, I slide abruptly to a stop. Glancing up, I spot a rare Ziraffe, towering over the girls and I. Nervously, I take a few steps back. However, the girls scream with glee and rush over towards it rubbing the beast's legs.

"No! Are you guys insane? What are you two doing"? I shout hysterically.

Thankfully, the Ziraffe doesn't pay the girls any mind. Even as baby Zero trots out there, it keeps peacefully eating the leaves from the surrounding trees.

I shake my head slowly and laugh to myself as I head back inside. Bryan and Dwight are in the living room trying to slide the old freezer out the door since we have our own. I notice they are struggling and before rushing over to push with them I get an idea.

Standing behind them, I back up and focus for a moment. I pinpoint my glare onto the freezer, and a turquoise glow begins to encase it. As Dwight and Bryan take a step back, I attempt to launch it out the door! The freezer grazes the doorframe and obliterates the corner!

The boys look at me with the straightest face. Both disappointed and impressed simultaneously. Dwight tries to close the door to see there is a small gap at the top left corner from the collision, even with the door completely closed.

"I didn't see nothing." Bryan comments as he tosses his hands up, leaving the room.

"You mean you didn't see anything." Dwight corrects him.

Without a word said to me, they both disappear upstairs, carrying their bags behind them. Almost as if on cue, the girls come in through the back door and Hailey notices instantly.

"What happened to the door"!? She scolds me harshly.

I try to avoid the question, but Jacqui presses me next.

"What did you idiots do down here"? Jacqui demands.

"We left you three alone for five minutes and you already started tearing things up"! Hailey growls, clearly annoyed as she facepalms.

Zero trots into the room and yawns before sitting on the floor.

"See what happened was. Uhhh, Zero did it"! I shriek as I race up the stairs, attempting to escape their wrath.

The day seems uneventful as nightfall comes quickly.

Jacqui calls everyone into the kitchen and briefs us on all she knows about this place.

"Mirra is a very gorgeous but dangerous place guys. I need everyone to keep an eye out for one another, nobody leaves the house after 9pm. It becomes extremely dark outside and we're not here to become Lion food. Okay"? Jacqui coaches.

We all nod and Dwight chuckles.

"What if I wanted to be lion food, huh? Did you think about my dreams Jacqui"? He mutters sarcastically.

Bryan, Dwight, and I all start snickering. Now, each of us cracking jokes.

"She acts like we don't know that. No need to state the obvious." Dwight chuckles.

"Don't become lion food." Bryan mocks her.

"Dwight, get out of the lion's mouth! Did you know that its teeth are made out of teeth"!? I join in, making my best impression of Jacqui.

Jacqui shoots us a cold glare and we quickly stop laughing.

"Y'all are peak comedy, I hope you know that." Hailey growls sarcastically.

"They're all a bunch of idiots." Jacqui adds.

Rolling her eyes, Jacqui then tells Dwight and Bryan that they will share the room upstairs, while Hailey and herself get the other room downstairs.

I attempt to object about getting stuck with the couch, but quickly realize nobody is going to budge, so I keep my mouth shut. Everyone grabs some food and heads to their rooms. Zero and I, cuddle on the couch downstairs a couple feet from the front door.

Justin Avery

It does not take long for my eyes to get heavy and as sleep takes over, I hear some irritating buzzing by my ear.

I swat at it, and it fades off in the distance. As I start to fall back into my slumber, I hear it by my face again and I start swinging wildly at it, but it just seems to keep returning to my ears. Zero gets annoyed with my constant fidgeting and he hops off the couch before heading upstairs. I sit up deeply enraged with the constant buzzing when I feel something sharp prick my neck. I smack the pesky insect and wipe the mosquito on the rug before finally passing out.

Chapter 10:
Silence is Golden

The next morning, I wake up to everyone chatting in the kitchen. As I sit up, my foot lands in a warm puddle.

I freeze as I realize what the liquid is.

"No way, you have got to be joking with me. I swear on my life if this is what I think it is…"! I shout frustrated.

I look at Zero and he scampers off, as if knowing he is in the wrong. Shaking my head in disgust, I hop on my left leg and do my best to use the stair railing to get towards the bathroom.

Finally, I reach the top of the stairs and I settle in the bathroom.

"I guess I should just get a shower while I'm up here." I think to myself.

I get undressed and tap the door closed with my knee. A few minutes later, the water finally warms up. Moments before I step into the shower, the door swings open! I whip around clutching the towel around my waist tightly and Jacqui walks in, smirking fondly.

"So, before you say anything, I just wanted to help you relax because you're about to get really mad." She giggles.

I glance at her, puzzled. Jacqui proceeds to say nothing else and now, more bewildered than before, I turn back to the mirror.

Justin Avery

She walks up behind me and pokes my neck, as I begin to turn towards her, I feel a throbbing fire in the surrounding area.

"Ow! Yo what the heck was that? That hurt so much"! I shout as I stumble back in agony.

Instinctually, I push her away and look at the bump in the mirror.

"I'm sorry Justin, it isn't funny, but it is." She snickers hysterically, she stumbles backwards and then comes forward towards my neck.

Jacqui analyzes it before stating that I was probably bit by a Redtoed Mosquito.

"Why don't you just heal it, silly." Jacqui inquires.

I facepalm and make my finger glow before pressing it to the bump on my neck.

"You know, sometimes I forget I can do that." I chuckle, pressing my finger to the bite.

On impact, I seize up and fall to the floor. I can see everything around me, but I have no control of my limbs. A flashback of my body sinking in the water comes to mind and I freak out, struggling to move even an inch. Jacqui starts screaming and rushes out the bathroom and downstairs.

When she returns, Bryan is with her. He has a concerned expression painted across his face.

Runaways

Bryan quickly dismisses Jacqui, and he leaves momentarily. When he returns, Bryan has some new clothes in hand.

Once he sits my limp body up, Bryan struggles to dress me.

Laughing to himself, he then tries to prop me up against the wall as if I was a child's favorite stick. Without the ability to speak or move, I am useless and spectate patiently as Bryan finally dresses me and stands me up. Leaning my body against his own, he walks me to the staircase before pausing.

"Can you use the Sathon ability still"? Bryan questions.

I attempt to shake my head, but I stay frozen.

Attempting to grunt aggressively, I desperately try to signal that I can't do anything.

"What the heck is wrong with me? That mosquito must be venomous"! I ponder fretfully.

Dwight races around the corner and up the stairs to our aid. Cautiously he grabs my arm and they both walk me down towards the couch. After sitting me down gently, they both leave, heading towards the girls in the kitchen. After a while, everyone returns, and Bryan is carrying his backpack, which looks fully packed.

The group sits down with me and attempts to explain the plan. Hailey talks to me as if I were some sort of wild animal they plan to corral.

Justin Avery

"Justin... WE ARE YOUR FRIENDS... OKAY"? She states as she belittles my intelligence.

"Hailey, he's paralyzed, not stupid. He still understands English." Bryan laughs before cutting her off.

Bryan then turns, joyfully questioning me.

"Ain't that right Justin"? He questions.

I roll my eyes at all of them and focus on sending the flowerpot above their heads, crashing down onto them.

Fortunately, for their sake, the pot refuses to budge.

"Man, I really can't even use my Sathon while like this." I cry to myself.

Internally I sigh and let them ramble on and on about some options for where medicine could be located. Attempting to ignore them, I do my best to zone out, but they keep talking before finally, Bryan stops.

In my absence they must have asked something because when I focus in on their conversation again, nobody is speaking.

My friends stare at me, awaiting a response. I just stare back, wondering when the reality of the situation will click for them.

"Awww, you must be shy." Jacqui giggles.

Dwight butts in, irked by the lackadaisical concern my friends show.

Runaways

"Could you guys just shut up for five minutes? Everything doesn't have to be a joke, we're not even sure if he'll regain activity of his limbs. I swear for being the youngest one in the group, I have to parent y'all so much". He laments.

Everyone pauses, really letting his words sink in.

Bryan speaks up first.

"You're right, I need to step up and see if we can find something that'll help Justin." He comments.

Jacqui informs us that after seventy-two hours the effects will be permanent.

"You mean I could be stuck like this and you're just sitting there cracking stupid jokes"!!? I roar inside my head.

Lord Lustro begins to speak again.

"I'm telling you to be careful who you trust, you should just ditch everyone and save our people alone." He harshly comments.

"Shut up! Get out of my head"! I growl.

Jacqui continues talking.

"That is if he was bitten by the Redtoed mosquito. Most times they're harmless though. Honestly, I'm so scared and surprised that Justin happened to be this unlucky." She comments.

Bryan nods. "Well, I guess I should get going then." He states calmly.

Bryan picks me up and Hailey rolls out a wheelchair from the kitchen.

"I guess there was an elderly couple living here previously. This should come in handy." Hailey cheers, a huge smile concealing her worry.

As they settle me into the chair, Bryan starts to push me out the door. The others cheer for us to be safe and wish us good luck on our trip.

When we arrive outside, the heat hits us instantly. Bryan pushes us down a dirt path towards the nearest settlement. On our way down the path, I feel as if I am regaining the feeling in my neck. Excited by this progression, I begin smiling slowly. Bryan and I spot some wild Warthogs, Antelope, and wild Buffalo over by a rushing river, eating the long grass.

"I don't think there's a city nearby, so I'd say that if there was a small village around here, the members would build it along the path of this river. A continuous clean source of water is imperative to a village's survival. Good news Justin, we may be close"! Bryan exclaims.

"Oh, thank God! I can't stand this anymore." I cheer happily inside my head.

Surprisingly, we avoid any potential confrontations with the hostile wildlife as we arrive at a flourishing community. Bryan rolls us past a group of small markets on our way into the center of the village.

Suddenly a woman calls out to us.

"Hey, you two young handsome men! Don't tell me you would pass up an opportunity to get a great deal on some gold." She offers.

I try to warn Bryan to ignore her, but I am still unable to speak.

"There is no way Bryan is falling for this obvious scam. This lady is... Bryan? Where are you going? No! Don't trust her." I shout, but my words stay trapped inside my head.

Bryan turns and takes a few steps towards the woman before stopping again. I assume he's cautious of the woman's intentions.

"This lady seems like she's nothing but trouble. I can sense her deception from here. How can Bryan not see that"? I ponder internally.

As Bryan looks as if he's going to turn away, a girl around our age walks out of the shop wearing a gold necklace. She smiles and waves at Bryan.

"I hope you're considering buying something at my mother's shop. It would make those gorgeous earrings standout." She insists.

"Oh no. She played the mother card. He's definitely going to crumble if he thinks his mother's earrings will stand out. We're doomed." I growl to myself.

Bryan hesitates and turns us towards her shop.

"Wow. Handsome and smart"! The older woman compliments him, luring Bryan closer.

"Thank you." Bryan replies, almost blushing.

"Bryan no! She's obviously marinating you! She's probably going to scam us or rob us if we're not careful! Watch your surroundings"! I attempt to shout.

She sneers devilishly as we come to a stop in front of her.

Without a single thread of fear, she confidently walks up to Bryan and puts a golden tennis chain around his neck.

"Oh my God! Come with me to the mirror so you can see how good you look"! She exclaims as she runs her hands up and down Bryan's arms.

Bryan blushes and follows her around the corner to the dressing stall. I roll my eyes thinking to myself.

"Why was it so easy to grab his attention"?

"Well look who's finally here." I hear a raspy voice chuckle.

A fearful death grip clenches my throat as I want to scream. My head whips to the left where an old man meets me. Our eyes lock, and he smiles.

Runaways

"This guy looks super weird, why is he staring at me"? I worry internally.

"You know, it's a bit rude to speak to your elders like that, kid." He comments.

"Did he just read my mind"?! I scream inside my head.

The man dissipates into thin air for a moment, and I lose sight of where he transported to!

A dark bag comes over my head and I am ripped from the wheelchair!

I hear a high-pitched humming sound, and even through the bag over my head, I see a bright red flash.

Before I have the chance to register what happened, the bag comes off my head and I am sitting on the ground. As I glance around, I notice that I am in the mountains!

How did we get up here? We must be miles up from the ground. There's no way we traveled this far so quickly"! I shout nervously.

The area we have arrived to is a flat top environment, engulfed by mountains and trees! We would need a helicopter to make it to this location and even with that, I do not see how we could have landed here. There are too many trees around for there to be a safe landing spot.

I glare at the old man as he approaches me with a mosquito swirling around his fingertip. I stare back at him, baffled. Without a word, the insect lands on his index finger and glows red! It then flies down towards me and bites my neck again!

This time I hop up angry and eager to fight when I realize I am standing with my own power.

The old man finally speaks. "I think you are starting to understand now, Justin."

I freeze, longing to interject and question how he knows my name. Instead, I stutter and attempt to ask him the multitude of questions swirling in my head.

"Stop Justin. Just relax for a moment." He advises, still staring off into the sky.

I cut him off, demanding.

"Did you use that mosquito to restrict my movement? How did you even do that? Did you use magic"?! I shout.

The old man becomes visibly irritated and glides across the ground smoothly, with his knuckles glowing red. As I try to back away, he quickly hits my pressure points with the glowing aura.

Before I tumble backwards to the ground, the red aura ripples across my body. Once I am immobile, he continues to speak, animosity tightly blanketing each word.

"Yes, I paused your ability to move, but there was no magic involved." He admits.

I give him a puzzled gaze. However, the man continues.

"If you train your Sathon ability, you can fuse it with your life energy, called Ki." He continues.

"Excuse me, not to cut you off again, but what is Ki"? I question him.

This time he smiles softly.

"Ki is your life force. It is everywhere. Ki unites everything, whether you can see it on this physical plane, or not. Combining your Sathon ability with this life energy, even for mere minutes, makes you immensely stronger than before." He states.

I stop him again.

"Wait, how do you know I have the Sathon ability"? I demand curiously.

Roen smiles before helping me off the ground.

"My name is Roen. I stayed here when the Scepin war ended. The Nero government that calls themselves, 'The Light,' kept your nation in the dark, about the truth of the outside world."

My eyes widen.

"So, there must be many other settlements outside Nero. Villages like Bryan's must be the norm and not an anomaly. I think to myself.

As Roen continues, everything starts to make sense.

"Justin, everything you know is a lie. Even the animals becoming fused due to the Scepin fallout from the war. Well... that's partly true." Roen admits as he scratches his head tentatively.

"Dang, this is going to be a mouthful to explain. Sit down so I can get started, kid." He orders.

"So, to get started, each nation's leaders injected a plethora of animals with Scepin and forced them to mate with other creatures to create the wildest combinations. These demons also did the same with the environment and ruined their own ecosystem to control the narrative. The truth is the world leaders of the past countries wanted these three relics. These items have the potential to become absolutely devastating, their power can boost the Sathon user's abilities exponentially. With even one of these relics, any one of the nations could dominate the world and destroy the balance that holds everything together." Roen explains.

I butt in with a question.

"Oh geez! So, I'm guessing Lustro was safeguarding these items for a good reason then." I spout out loud.

"Yes, unfortunately your people couldn't keep these enemies at bay for long." Roen laments.

"Over time, the outside nations scoured the planet for these relics. Even traveling to the moon a few times in a desperate attempt to find them. When rumors spread that the relics were scattered in Lustro, a divisive plan was created, and the outside countries had these needless wars." He explains.

I cut in again.

"Wait, what? So, these items can give a user, great Sathon power"? I question, desperately attempting to understand every detail.

"Yes, you're a prime example, your Sathon ability keeps growing exponentially. As you fight and continue to utilize this gift, it becomes stronger. Each item was created by the strongest of our people. Lord Lustro, a deity, put his remaining lifeforce into that flame which burns brightly inside you. Anyway, let me finish." He comments.

"Not only were these needless wars built by the nation's leaders, now known as the kings of Nero. But the kings also spread lies about some rubies being the relics, attempting to throw many people off course. There are three relics, a shadow blade, a gleaming gem, and a turquoise flame. No more, no less." Roen informs me.

"Wow, so that map we were following was wrong from the start then." I ponder to myself.

Roen continues his tale.

"Stay vigilant of what people tell you, think of their true intentions." He warns.

"After realizing that as separated nations, they could not defeat Lustro alone, the leaders of each country convinced their people that the Lustronese people were the enemy. It didn't take long for the people to become blood thirsty tyrants once an explosion occurred in a few cities. After claiming these explosions were attacks from Lustro, the outside nation's armies grew exponentially, and it became effortless to play each of their populations for fools. The combined leading officials created a treaty to attack Lustro and take their land. After the war was over, they killed off or enslaved members of our race. As they still search for the items today, the threat of all balance has been lost. If the kings get their hands on these relics, our people will be no more". He groans quietly.

I drop my head saddened to hear the truth about my countries past. Stuttering, as I choke out my disappointment.

"It's even worse than the reality I believed I was living." I state as I look towards the sky, trying to distract myself from this situation.

Roen puts his hand on my shoulder.

"Don't worry. I am going to teach you how to use your Sathon abilities to the fullest and I will join you and your friends."

That map you had, only became useless because I blacked it out. I needed you guys to find your way to a landmass so I could finally meet you". He claims.

I glance back at him puzzled once again.

"None of this is making sense. How did you know any of this"?

Roen chuckles as he leads me into his house.

"Let's take a seat before I explain all of this to you." He smiles.

When we sit down, he brings out a bowl of ramen and sets it in front of me. As we chat over the food, Roen explains how he sensed my energy from Nero! He also claims that he could sense my emotions.

Roen, then proves this, by explaining my roller coaster of emotions. Ranging from betrayal, all the way through the point where I rescued Jacqui, and I was feeling elated.

"I will admit though, it took me years to master this ability. Even still, your lifeforce had vanished completely, almost as if you had died". Roen explains as he digs into his bowl of noodles.

I think back to when I had first discovered the turquoise flame, and then when I was in a room with those two hot pink figures, and lastly when I sank to the bottom of the ocean, fearing I was dead.

Once the memory of the tornado ripping through my friends and mother appears in my mind, I snap out of my daydream.

"So, did I die? If my energy completely vanished from this world, did I perish and then resurrect myself with my Sathon ability? Or maybe it's this legendary flame inside me that Roen speaks of. Maybe Lord Lustro refuses failure, thus why I keep finding ways out of these predicaments". I ponder to myself.

"When you and your friends were close enough, I used animals or birds to spy on you." Roen states.

"What do you mean? You can take over other beings with your Sathon ability? What else can you do"? I shout, excited and scared of all the possibilities my mind creates.

"The way I controlled the mosquito was with my Sathon ability, not Ki. However, without first harnessing your Ki, you will not be able to accomplish this technique. By bending the light particles, you can first shock the creature. Then, while the being is disoriented. You may be able to fuse your Ki with your victim." Roen explains, slurping his noodles down.

"Everything has Ki, it is life energy. However, every being does not have Sathon. So, if you are successful in disorienting the animal, then you will have one hundred percent control over it. Your will should override the being's. However, if you fail to combine your Ki and Sathon first, or your energy is not strong enough to outweigh whatever you attempt to control, you will become disoriented. This failure will leave you twice as vulnerable as your prey was." He continues.

Roen also tells me how I can use my Sathon to shield myself from attacks.

"When fusing said life energy with your Sathon ability you can control the light particles themselves."

Roen stands up and concentrates for a moment. The sunlight that had crept its way into the room retreats instantly, becoming a ball in his hands.

"Whoa! That's so cool! I think I've done that a few times"! I exclaim loudly.

"No, you were using more Ki energy than Sathon. When using Ki as a primary source, your abilities are limited and much weaker, as you are pulling from your own strength. However, when using Sathon as a primary and using your own Ki as a reserve, your energy comes from the sun or any light particles in the surrounding area. You still use your Ki, but only fractions of it. Lord Lustro's powers have become a crutch for you. Which is why your stamina burns out so quickly." Roen informs me.

"So, if I train to combine my inner strength with my Sathon ability, I could surpass Julien and Adrian. I could even control that Katun ripple transformation better." I think to myself.

"Ohhhh, I get it now. So, using my own life energy should be a last resort, not my main source of power. I need to utilize the sun for my power then." I respond.

"Right, some techniques require Ki and can't be replicated with Sathon, but I'll get to that later. You can also change the hue of the light particles." Roen spouts.

As Roen open his hands the room glows red and slowly changes into every color of the rainbow.

Roen, then lets the ball float back into the air and it dissolves into nothing. As he takes a seat, the light goes back to its form and the original colors fade back into their place.

"That was absolutely amazing! You have to teach me that"! I scream, standing up enthused, a huge smile stretching widely across my face.

Roen smiles.

"In time I will, but first you must learn the basics. Once you master fusing your Sathon with your life energy, I will teach you how to use it. But first, I need you to realize how Ki feels before you are able to utilize it as a reserve". He comments, as he begins to stand up from the table.

"Alright, that sounds awesome"! I shout excitedly.

I follow Roen outside, giddy to learn so much about my talents.

"Sit down, I want you to close your eyes. Now focus on something broad. Like the trees, or the animals, I want you to tell me what you feel." He orders.

Settling into the idea of feeling out other being's life energy, I close my eyes slowly.

Almost as if I had another set of eyes, I see the bird's energy zipping around the sky. Startled by this, I lose focus and open my eyes, losing track of the birds Ki.

"Justin don't lose focus! You had it right in your grasp. Close your eyes and focus again." Roen barks, stomping the ground in frustration.

"Geez, this guy has zero patience." I growl to myself.

"I can still read your mind." Roen chuckles.

I spot an ant, crawling about on my leg.

"He must be using that technique again, the same one he used with the mosquito. I wonder what'll happen if I hit the ant." I think.

As I flick the ant off, Roen holds his face, startled by the small flick he felt on his forehead.

Runaways

"Get out of my head, Roen." I snicker.

"Now, let's see if he can still hear me. Testing, testing, one, two"? I think to myself.

As I sit there doing nothing, Roen grits his teeth impatiently.

"The technique! Master it! Now"! Sensei Roen shouts, now on the verge of losing is cool.

"Right! Sorry." I nod to Roen and continue to focus again.

A pair of squirrels scamper past me. They settle by a tree and tussle over an acorn before the winner scurries up the tree with her prize.

"Look around with your mind. Justin, you must separate the physical from your mental." Roen coaches me encouragingly.

Without moving my head to search for Ki, I notice some ants carrying wood, drizzled with sweet sap.

"Now open your eyes and tell me what you feel." He questions.

I open my eyes and almost shout in disbelief.

"I can still see them! But not with my eyes. It is so weird because I know the ants are there, even without looking at them. I don't know how to explain it." I shout, amazed by the ability.

Roen smiles.

"You're a quick learner, I want you to continue practicing this in your spare time so you can improve. He comments.

"Once you practice it enough, this will become as effortless as breathing." Roen states confidently.

"Also, as a sign of respect, you will refer to me as your Sensei and bow to show your gratitude."

I bow, smiling at Roen.

"Yes, thank you Sensei." I respond respectfully.

As he bows back, we both continue to go over the basics for combining my Ki with my Sathon ability.

Unfortunately, I keep struggling with the last step. Fusing the two together. Each time I attempt to create an object, the fuel is always my Ki.

"I don't know why combining the two is so hard. The sun is a huge ball of light. Why can't I pull from that, instead of my own strength"?! I shout, frustrated with my continuous failures.

"That is peculiar, usually my students struggle to pull from their inner being, since that energy is so much smaller than the sun's. Well, I'm going inside, you got this. Whether that physical form is a ball, a spear, or anything you choose, if you can create a physical object, you've accomplished the first step." Sensei encourages.

As he walks back inside with his back turned, I attempt something.

Runaways

I create my favorite thing, my signature Sathon arm blade. It comes out normally and I hear Sensei shouting at me.

"No, no! Do it again! You're just being lazy and trying to use your Ki first. Fuse the two, then create a blade"! He shouts annoyed.

"Ki inside the body, is soothing and brings tranquility. However, when outside its original vessel, Ki fused with Sathonic elements can become extremely destructive. I want you to fuse these two and create a purely Sathonic orb. I don't want you relying on that blade every time. You'll become predictable in battle. So, gather up both energies in your chest, which is the highest build of Ki. Then make it travel through your limbs. Once at the tips of your fingers and toes, you should be able to finish the first step"! Sensei Roen barks.

"Work on this and don't come inside until you've mastered it! I don't care how long it takes. This should be simple, considering the other feats you've already accomplished." Sensei Roen then walks inside.

As the days roll by. I stay up all night, practicing the same trick. My energy begins to fade, even though I haven't made any real progress. Each day is a new adventure, as I take periodic breaks to hunt for food. Most times I find myself failing in finding that. Instead, I end up relying on familiar nuts and berries in the area. As I return to my spot next to the tree, I become more frustrated with each setback. If I've learned anything, it's how to fend for myself without a bed, copious amounts of food, and how to fight without my teammates. This mountain holds its own pests. Enormous bugs that hunt for easy prey, are scattered around the area. Every night, survival is my only task. Eventually, I begin to adjust to my new lifestyle. There's clean water at the running river a few miles down the mountain, a plethora of nuts and berries that are safe to consume, not too far from my resting place, and I have even built a safe haven up in the trees to avoid all the creatures that rule the night. As I gaze up at the sky, it's nearing the end of the evening. Many days later, still no progress with my technique, but I keep trying. I begin gathering Ki and Sathon in my chest and force it to travel through my arms. Once it reaches my hands, I do my best to create an orb. However, every time I get something physical to form, the object explodes in my face!

"Forget this! I'll do this my way! I need to mold Ki in my left hand. Then harness Sathon from the sun in my right hand. When I place them together, and I should be able to create a purely Sathonic orb." I growl.

Doing things my way begins to show results immediately. A turquoise sphere begins to form, and I beam brightly. Losing my concentration for just a split second is all it takes though. The Sathonic sphere detonates, and I slam into a tree behind me.

"Alright, let me take another break. Maybe I can figure it out tomorrow evening". I think to myself.

Sleep feels nonexistent as I become restless. I'm completely obsessed with mastering this technique of energy manipulation. It doesn't help that the air up here on the mountain is so thin. I'm still not fully adjusted to the altitude. Regardless, I get up and train for the rest of the night and into the next day. My eyes, now heavy from lack of sleeping, doesn't help my focus, but I press on.

Runaways

As the day rolls by, the sun begins to set once again. I gaze behind my shoulder to see Sensei Roen watching from the building's window.

"Alright, this time I'm gonna get it! Collect Ki in my left hand! Mold Sathonic particles in my right! Press both hands together! Come onnnn! I can do this"! I roar.

A bright beam flashes from in between my hands, into the sky! The turquoise light can be seen far and wide. It radiates and the Sathonic particles feel like bubbles in a pool. Even Sensei Roen sits up, intrigued by my newfound progress. Startled by the feeling, I fall back onto my tailbone.

"Owww! Dang it! I had it there. What was that light though? I've never created something so bright." I exclaim.

After struggling with the technique many times, I throw my hands up, shouting in frustration.

"I just can't do this! I can't hold it, it either dissipates into nothing or explodes in my face! This… is… so… stupid"!! I scream.

Sensei Roen shouts at me while I'm throwing a temper tantrum.

"I swear, kids are so annoying! Justin, you can't guide the Sathon! You must take control of it, forcefully make it conform to your will. You're too soft! It isn't like you're gonna hurt the energy"! Sensei mocks me.

"Then, why do they call us Sathon Guides"! I chirp back at him, irritated.

As my rage begins to boil over, I feel the Katun ripple form, awakening inside me.

"I'm too soft, huh? Okay, then what about this"! I roar furiously.

Filled with fury, I turn to the trees creating a giant Sathon ball!

As it glistens brightly, I fire it and it rips through the air, hurtling into the trees! It explodes on impact, sending shockwaves rippling through out the surrounding area. When the smoke clears, many trees are on fire or completely obliterated.

"Whoa! I can't believe I just did that"! I exclaim, bewildered by my own powers.

Sensei Roen hops down from his window and places a hand on my shoulder.

"You are too stoic. You should use your pain to embolden your power. What hurts you the most"? Roen inquires.

I freeze, fleeting thoughts of my father appear in my mind. However, I push them away before my brain can focus on them.

"No… I can't… it's too painful. Besides, that pain would lead to rage. I can't use that to get stronger." I spew out.

Roen eyes me curiously.

Runaways

"Why not? Rage will elevate your ability to great heights, I can already sense it. Your power will be tremendous." My sensei grins felicitously.

I cut his idea down quickly.

"No! You're wrong! There's something wrong with me. This flame, at first, I thought it was a blessing. That I could use it as a gift to free our people. But, after recent events, I'm convinced that it's a curse. Death follows me whenever I fuel my power through rage. I fear that my vessel is just a gateway back into the real world for Lord Lustro. His interests seem to be with redemption. I'm not sure what for, however, it terrifies me. If he plans on coming back with vengeance, then I won't allow him to resurface." I comment.

Sensei Roen nods at me and looks up towards the clouds.

"At the detriment to your own strength? If you're not strong enough, you won't be able to stop the Lumin kings. And if what you say is true, that you possess Lord Lustro's power. Then you must be the one to take back our place at the top. Liberate our people, Justin, you must get stronger."

As the wind blows, he takes a deep breath and looks back to me.

"Well, I guess that's all for today." Sensei Roen grins.

"Oh, and I know you're hiding behind that tree. I can feel your energy." Roen boasts.

I turn around, now aware of the bleak presence of another human being.

"How did Sensei sense this Ki? It's almost like the person's suppressing their life force.

I prepare myself for an attack. Searching for any other life energy in the area, I am surprised to find that the individual is alone.

"Come out coward"! I order.

As the individual steps out from behind the tree, I drop my hands, smiling.

"You really wanna attack your best friend"? Bryan spouts facetiously.

"I mean if you want smoke, then pull up bro." I laugh at him jokingly.

We both laugh and bump elbows.

I turn around and Roen is watching us with his hand on his chin, he looks as if he is pondering something serious.

"A light type, and hmm… I can't tell what that kid is. Maybe he needs some help to find his powers". He murmurs.

I question what is on his mind, but he brushes off my statement.

Roen steps forward and smiles.

Runaways

"Bryan, I want you to train with us. I see potential in you too. As a fighting duo, both your energy types could be unstoppable. Now both of you get inside." Sensei adds.

"How did you even find me"? I inquire of Bryan, who eyes me with a mysterious gaze.

"Ohhh… you know. Just that super bright turquoise beacon. The one that was visible for miles and lasted for a few seconds. Maybe it was that bright light that kinda helped". He spouts sarcastically.

"Hurry up! We don't have all day! You'll both be up early to start sparring." Sensei barks impatiently.

"Earlyyy? Sensei! I'm so tired though… can I please sleep in"? I beg as I jog inside.

"No! You should've mastered the technique I gave you a lot faster than you did. It took you two whole days and nights to do it. And you only pulled it off just once, right after I made you livid."

As we head to our separate rooms, I sit down on my cot, exhausted. As soon as I lay my head to the pillow, I pass out.

Over the course of the next few hours, I drift in and out of sleep, due to nightmares.

I wake up in the middle of the night to the sound of something being torn through viciously. I hop off the cot, anxiously awaiting the next noise. A moment of eerie silence passes, but nothing happens.

Justin Avery

I slip out of my room and search around to find Sensei Roen and Bryan.

As I crack Bryan's door open, a massive dark figure peers at me from the dimly lit corner of the room. It has six thin eyes and before I can say anything, it glares at me angrily before baring its fangs.

"What the hell is that thing"?!! I shout inside my head.

The beast towers over me, coming from all fours, to standing on its muscular hind legs. Even a muscular tail uncoils from behind it's back. The creature's ears perk up and it snarls at me hungrily.

"I'm coming for you Justin. I'm going to take your life… very… very… soon." The monstrosity murmurs.

"What… what are… you"? I question as I step back, cautiously avoiding the figure.

"Not what, but who." The mysterious figure corrects me.

I shudder as it growls again. The low rumble from the demon's gut, sends a chill down my spine! The beast roars loudly and slams its disgusting tail on the floor. As it repeats this again and again, its tail opens at the tip like a rotten banana. Suddenly, an infestation of baby spiders rocket out from its tail and begin to surround me! As my attention is taken off the beast, and to the lurching spiders, it makes its move. Instantly, the creature shrieks and charges me! Rampaging barbarically, it shoves its horn into my arm, and we slam through the door! As we take a tumble towards the ground, the horn jets upwards, taking a chunk out of my arm!

258

Runaways

I make my arm a blade and sink it into the demon's head! It disappears into a dark mist, and I tumble towards the unforgiving floor. The demon's shadows reform and the figure stands in front of me once again.

"You're gonna pay for that, boy. Just you wait... I'm gonna make. The creature starts.

I wake up in a cold sweat, shaking violently. Turning over in the cot to find the clock across the room, I see it has just barely hit 5 am. Begrudgingly I force myself out of my comfort, as my eyes adjust to the growing sunlight. Something about my nightmare won't shake loose from my mind.

"What was that thing." I ponder tentatively to myself.

Chapter 11:
Uninvited guests

"Well, I guess it's time to get back to reality." I spout, trying to convince myself that my nightmare was just that.

As I synch my breathing and my focus on finding Ki, it becomes easier to practice searching for energy.

Bryan walks out of the small building and trots over to me. In his attempt to spook me, he forgets I can sense him approaching.

I quickly whirl around, startling him instead. Bryan flies back screaming.

"Yo chill, you scared me man." He shouts petrified.

I begin chuckling to myself before taking notice of Sensei Roen exiting the building.

"All right, you both will be sparring against each other today"! Roen calls out to us.

Bryan vehemently objects as I burst out in laughter.

"Oh, and Justin. You won't be using your Sathon ability." Sensei snickers as he watches my confidence dwindle.

My smile evaporates along with my advantage. They both cheerfully ride off into the sunset.

"Yes sensei." I mutter, annoyed.

Bryan mocks me and I punch him in his arm. Bryan then shoves me, and we butt heads, gritting our teeth angrily.

"Knock it off"! Sensei yells at us.

Once we back off and get set to spar, Bryan eyes me, irritated.

"I want you two to spar, fight as if your life depended on it. Don't hold anything back. Do you understand"? Sensei Roen barks.

"Right"! Bryan and I both agree.

"Alright, now you both can start." Sensei commands.

As Bryan and I stare each other down, the tension builds. We both don't budge for a few moments as we attempt to spectate every movement.

I spring at Bryan, quickly attempting a spinning back fist. With no hesitation, Bryan blocks it and fires a flurry of punches at me. Nervously, I begin backing up, dodging every single strike. I twist and fake a spinning back fist again, before reversing my spin and sending a kick thundering into his ribcage.

Bryan grunts and looks as if he is going to crumble, but then he clutches my ankle with his right arm before I can bring my leg back down.

As he raises his elbow, my eyes widen, realizing what he's going to do. Bryan slams his elbow into my quad, and I reel back in pain. He does this repeatedly before I hop up and kick him in the chest, freeing myself from his grasp.

We both fall to the ground in pain.

Rolling over to pop up before he does, I am met with a punch to the gut and Bryan sends me back to the dirt with a kick.

"Get up Justin. You're not so good without your powers to save you, huh"? He barks at me.

I grit my teeth and hop up eagerly. Before Bryan can register my next move, I am in his face with my fists glowing turquoise.

Almost as if time has slowed to a stop, he looks down at me with distraught in his eyes. With three quick strikes, Bryan grunts and falls to his knees. He quickly crumbles to the floor in front of me.

I make the Sathon glow dissipate and stand over him laughing.

"What's the problem Bryan? Just three simple blows and you're face down in the dirt. Guess I am stronger than you." I chuckle.

"No, you're not. You're pathetic, using that relic as a crutch won't get you anywhere. You'd be dirt compared to me if I had the Sathon ability." Bryan growls.

I can hear a disappointed sigh from Sensei Roen.

"Justin, if you cheat the training, you won't become any better at close combat." He groans.

Runaways

Sensei Roen moves over to us both, handing us a small piece of the insides of a mango. I eye it cautiously, the insides are ruby red.

"Bryan, get up, this is for you. I want you both to eat it." He instructs.

I inspect the fruit cautiously, pondering on why Sensei wants us to eat it. As I trust the food, I decide to consume it. When the fruit juice hits my taste buds, I smile and enjoy the sweet flavor.

"What is this"? Bryan mutters, his face still in the dirt.

Our Sensei responds bluntly.

"Just eat it, you two must have been the pickiest eaters as children." He barks impatiently.

Bryan lifts his head and tosses the fruit in his mouth before dropping his face back down slowly.

"See, that wasn't so hard, now, was it? What you both ate is called SuperFruiit. It has extremely great healing qualities, not only that, but it will boost your mental focus, recharge your stamina, and elevate your natural physical abilities. It comes from our Lustronese ancestors, one of the powerful deities created this as a reward for brave mortals. The Miyazaki mango is the." is the loftiest of fruit. Mostly known as the 'egg of the sun,' this fruit excels with the task of molding Sathon."

Bryan stands up, dusting himself off.

"Wow, he wasn't lying. I feel a lot better. The pain is still lingering, but it is slowly fading." He exclaims.

Sensei Roen smiles.

"Correct, the effects are not instantaneous unfortunately. However, you will heal completely. The only downsides are that the SuperFruiit won't do anything spectacular, like regrow lost limbs or cure sicknesses. It may also make you exceptionally hungry. Speaking of which, we should head inside and grab some breakfast, you both have worked pretty hard." Sensei Roen smiles as he leads us inside.

Bryan and I turn towards the door, excited to grab something to eat. As we race to see who will make it inside first, we are cut off by a kunai hitting the doorframe! I shout as I am petrified, the kunai nearly hitting my head!

I whip around and everyone is apprehensive.

"I don't see anyone, where are they"? Bryan whispers.

I scour the area for their life energy, but I sense no Ki whatsoever. Terrified, I focus harder but still come up with nothing.

"They're suppressing their energy, Justin. You won't be able to sense their presence. Unfortunately, ninja like these, are trained to hide their life force." Roen states.

Sensei forms several red Sathon balls and launches them in all directions. One of the Sathonic blasts rocket at the boulder off to our left. Brooke, dressed in all black, has one pant leg down at her ankle and the other cut short, skyrockets from behind the rock throwing more kunai at us. Instinctively, I roll away from the attack and respond by launching my own Sathon blast at her.

Runaways

Brooke reflects the attack back towards me and I do a backflip, kicking the blast straight into her chest!

It explodes and I cheer, excited with my direct hit. As the smoke in the air clears, I feel something moving around in the shadows.

"She's still here." I think to myself.

"You two need to get inside now"! Sensei Roen screams at us.

Bryan denies his command.

"No sensei, we are going to stay and fight"! He argues.

Still feeling sore from the sparring match with Bryan, I do my best to ignore the pain and press forward. As Brooke slides out from the smoke, she sneers devilishly at us.

"You again? Get out of here"! Bryan demands.

Her smile grows wider, and she finally speaks.

"You two must be quite troublesome if the kings of Nero want you dead." She claims with an impressed look in her eyes.

Shock from her statement freezes Bryan in his tracks. I shake my head, furiously boiling with rage.

"You're pretty arrogant to attack us altogether Brooke! We got you outnumbered, three to one." I smirk confidently.

"Actually, you might want to recount." Breanna sneers as she drops down from the trees.

"No matter, you're both still outnumbered"! I begin laughing at her loudly. I then charge her with my hands glowing.

"Bring it on"! I shout as my energy spikes.

"No Justin, stay back"! Sensei Roen orders.

I ignore him and launch myself at Brooke, landing a spinning kick to her stomach!

She grunts for a moment and as I go to kick her again, her smile returns. Without hesitation, she slashes at my leg!

"Sorry kid, but I eat those." She boasts.

I spring back at the last moment and the kunai nearly catches my flesh!

I back up, still in my defensive stance.

"What kinda body armor does she have on? That kick basically tickled her"! I think to myself.

Before a moment passes, Brooke's onslaught continues, as she begins slashing wildly! I have no choice to stay solely defensive.

"Why do you keep running! Fight back Justin." She laughs maniacally.

Bryan attempts to jump in, but Breanna cuts him off.

"Sorry, but your fight is with me." She snarls.

As I glance over to them, I worry for Bryan's safety. Sensei Roen appears frozen, spectating both fights simultaneously.

"You should keep your eyes on me"!! Brooke roars, and my attention clicks back to her, adrenaline rushing throughout my body.

Quickly backing up as I dodge, Sensei jumps in, kicking Brooke away from me.

Sensei Roen then crosses his arms and a red glow wraps around her, restricting her movement.

"Hey! Let me go right now you old bastard"! She screams furiously.

"You were running out of space to dodge." Roen comments calmly as he turns to me.

"I had it under control, I didn't need your help." I cut him off, annoyed.

"I know that, but you are vital to the future of our people. We need you to lead your friends to change the world. If I'm being totally honest. I don't think I can beat her." He admits, his tone somber.

I look at him, perplexed.

"What do you mean Sensei"? I demand.

Roen inspects me momentarily before finally he begins smiling softly.

Runaways

"Oh Justin. Unfortunately, I am not a fighter, I only know how to manipulate my Sathon. Even in my youth, fighting has never been my forte. Now with old age, I'm not as quick as I used to be. I have my small tricks but she's a trained assassin. Those tricks won't help me here."

"But Sensei! You're not saying that you could." I start.

If I must, I will sacrifice myself to ensure you both escape with your friends. It's clear that you're a brawler Justin, and your friend Bryan has some type of experience with martial arts. You both could really change the world together. You just need the right teacher. Yes, combustion with light, those qualities of Sathon could save our race." He responds stoically.

"Don't say that!! Sensei, you are our teacher! Let us fight alongside of you." I blurt out at Roen.

Sensei Roen smiles briefly.

"I'm sorry, but we both know that would be a grave error." He laments as he stares into the dirt.

Bryan, still fighting with Breanna, slides back on the dirt but somehow, he keeps his footing. As Bryan reels backwards he grabs his dagger and brandishes his weapon.

"You're dead"! He shouts as he lunges forward to stab our enemy and Breanna smirks.

"You just fell right into my trap"! She snickers.

As we all attempt to process what trap Bryan could have walked into, Breanna dissolves into a red dust. She then is blown into the air and the red sparkles glimmer in the sunlight.

"I don't understand. Where did she go"? Bryan inquires inquisitively.

"Like I said. You fell right into my trap." Her voice echoes from all sides and begins to get louder.

Confused by the trick, I freeze in my tracks.

"Where is she? I can sense her energy everywhere"! I shout fretfully to myself.

Suddenly her red dust particles split into two beings! Both copies of her. One of them race towards Bryan with a Sathon kunai in hand as the other jumps into the air with a katana aimed for my head!

"Now choose old man! Who will you save"? Breanna roars.

Time slows as I glance up and see Breanna tumbling down from the sky! As she crashes into the dirt her body twinges with pain. Our sensei is also on the opposite side of me, attacking the other copy of Breanna! He drops from the sky, smashing Breanna with a crushing elbow.

Sensei Roen lands beside me and then dissipates into a red smoke, floating away.

"How did he get over here so fast! There's no way anyone could move that quick"! I shout, nervous but filled with excitement.

Runaways

"They're just afterimages. I took her technique, at least part of it. The way she split her energy into dust particles was utterly amazing. It takes a master of Sathon and Ki control to split your body up like that. Even still, her physical body isn't here. Keep your guard up." Sensei warns us.

Suddenly Breanna rips out from the earth and attacks Sensei himself!

Her bone crushing kick scantily misses as Sensei ducks beneath it. However, as he is forced to evade the blow, his red barrier is shattered, and Brooke is now free!

"Bryan! Justin! Both of you leave! Now"! He shouts desperately as he turns to us.

"Sensei, please don't go, let us help you." Bryan cries out, fiercely attempting to convince our teacher to trust us.

Sensei Roen shakes his head.

"I want you both to run, she and her friend here are articulate ninjas. I don't care how well you two think you can fight. They are on a completely different level. Now I will not repeat myself again, leave"! He mandates.

Brooke lurks towards us with two kunai in her hands.

"Thanks Breanna. I needed that, now I can finish all three of these malcontents off." Brooke snarls as she turns to us.

"Now you're dead"! She grits her teeth, blood thirsty.

Sensei pushes us behind him.

"Go now"! He shouts.

Bryan and I dash for the door to grab our stuff. Almost instantly, before we reach the front door, Brooke teleports in front of Bryan and I, smirking.

We freeze trying to stop on a dime, as she springs at us, slashing wildly for my throat! I block her kunai with my turquoise light, the shielding glow wrapped around my wrist.

She presses it forward and as I lean back fighting hard, my feet come out from under me.

I look up from the ground, laying on my back. Thinking to myself.

"Did she sweep me? What just happened? That was so fast."

With no hesitation, she brings the kunai down at my chest with both hands!

I slam my hands together using my Sathon powers, creating a shield and pushing back against her.

She howls loudly while pressing harder, cracking my shield.

"You're dead, I am going to kill you and collect all that gold as my righteous reward"!

Runaways

Maniacally laughing now, she starts forcing the kunai through the Sathon barrier.

I freak out as she starts progressively moving the kunai towards my chest. Fortunately, it does not shatter the Sathon light, it only cracks through.

Bryan drop kicks Brooke off and helps me up from the ground.

"Come on, let's go"! He shouts as he rips me up from the earth.

We dash past her and into the building. Huge explosions rattle off as I assume Breanna is firing Sathonic blasts at the building.

"Get back here you two"! Brooke wails toward us.

I turn and see our Sensei step in front of her, his arms out wide and glowing red. I keep running, grabbing my bag with Bryan and we rush out the back door into the woods.

After a few minutes of running, we stop by this tree with a hole in the trunk. Winded, Bryan chokes out.

"Okay bro, I think we can rest here for just a moment. Do you think Sensei can win against them"? He inquires.

I drop my head saddened as sensei Roen's words ring in my head.

"I... I don't think he can beat them, Bryan. I am not sure he knows much of anything when it comes to combat."

Bryan nods.

"I didn't think so either, he just seemed like he wanted to get us to safety more than anything." He admits.

Silence falls upon both of us.

Attempting to break the silence, Bryan suggests we move forward to keep distance from the ninjas.

I inquire how we are going to find our way back to Hailey, Dwight, and Jacqui.

"Once we're sure that this killer is off our trail then I would be happy to make it back towards them, but until I'm sure she's gone, I don't want to inadvertently put our friends in danger." Bryan comments bravely.

I agree and keep my responses short.

"We should try and mark trees leading away from us, so we aren't tailed."

Before Bryan answers, I sense something in our presence and dart around. The sight makes my jaw drop in horror.

Standing there is the assassin, with a red aura around her! Brooke is covered in blood and snarls at us.

"What did you do to our Sensei"?! Bryan demands, his voice cracks as we both assume the worst.

Runaways

She sneers, saying nothing as she slowly approaches us, a trickle of blood coming from her mouth.

Bryan snaps, and flies at her, swinging wildly.

She leans back and slashes upwards, her kunai ripping through Bryan's left shoulder!

As Bryan tumbles to the ground, he tries to throw sand in Brooke's eyes but his arm flops around like wet spaghetti.

"Yep, my left arms done for." Bryan chuckles nervously.

After smiling at him Brooke sweeps his legs and springs up in the air with the kunai glowing red.

"This again? Thanks for telegraphing your attack." I think to myself.

I shoot a turquoise finger beam and it launches the weapon from her grasp into the trees. She lands empty handed, eyeing me angrily. Once her smile disappears, I raise my power and make my hands glow turquoise.

"You do know that you both are going to die here. Right"? She hisses slyly.

My ego kicks in, and I laugh at her comment.

"Is that disrespect? I'll take your breath." I growl.

Her eyes tighten and she races at me, her red aura flaming hotter than before.

I press both hands to the ground and fire a Sathon burst, it launches my body sky high, and her sloppy punch misses badly. I shoot another finger beam, but she deflects it into the ground.

"You won't land another one of those, just accept your fate and die, it'll help you avoid the suffering you're bound to endure if you hit me again." She warns belligerently.

Slowly descending, I come up with an amazing idea. Without saying a word, I create a small spark of Sathon on the backside of my left hand and on the knuckles of my right hand. To distract Brooke, I kick another Sathonic blast at her feet and she jumps up to avoid the explosion!

"You're going to have to try much harder if you want to hit me"! She spouts arrogantly.

"Perfect. You fell for it like I thought." I think to myself.

Quickly, I spring into the air and meet her with a crushing punch to her jaw, leaving the Sathon spark on her face. With the sparkle being as small as glitter, she never notices the danger she's in.

Instantly, I use my right hand to launch out turquoise fire and propel myself behind her. As she uncontrollably flies into me, I turn away from her, facing the opposite direction.

Now confident in my new technique, I slam the backside of my fist into her face, leaving the second Sathon sparkle attached to her forehead.

Runaways

As she zips away from me again, I prepare to finish my attack.

"Detonate." I whisper.

Simultaneously, the two Sathon sparkles explode!

BOOM!!!

I land slowly and Bryan stares at me in shock.

"How did you do that!? Is she dead? Justin, that was amazing"!

I look at him and smile.

"Honestly, I've used small Sathon sparkles in the past to save myself from the Lumin guards. Nobody really focuses on minor details in the heat of battle." I inform him.

"Hey man, we got it handled. Let's head back and try to find Sensei." Bryan comments.

I agree and we start walking back to the building when something nicks my face.

I turn to see that the battered assassin is still standing!

"Come on, you two couldn't have thought you'd get rid of me that easily"? She smiles and dusts herself off.

"Since I'm cut up and bloody now, someone's going to wish they were never born." She hisses.

Bryan and I back up, staring in awe. Almost as if I'm frozen, my body refuses to move. She creates a plethora of small blazing red cubes with both hands.

"She survived that attack at point-blank range?! How durable is she"? Bryan screams.

"That was a nice attack you had earlier Justin, it's unfortunate you couldn't finish the job. But don't worry, I won't return the favor." She growls.

As she launches the wave of death at us, I create a giant Sathon orb. My Sathonic orb, shields Bryan and me. The waves of the cubes hit the shield with such force that it cracks it on impact. However, I keep my ground and try to strengthen my fortress.

Brooke laughs at us as her lacerations begin to reopen and bleed profusely.

"I can do this all day! But, on the other hand, who knows how long your barrier will hold up." She laughs.

Bryan looks to me, awaiting my next move.

"Justin, what are you going to do now. Get us out of this mess"!? He states, staring at me with a poker face.

I stare back at him, so rattled, I struggle to answer.

"I don't know man. I think I can block that wave a few more times. But, after that, I'll have no energy. If only I mastered that energy fusion technique! I admit dismally.

Runaways

Another wave hits the shield harder than the first and I almost crumble, attempting to hold the orb up. Now down on one knee I flex my strength.

"Are you both ready? This one is going to end it! Once that troublesome safeguard comes down, you both will perish"! She screeches excitedly at us.

I stand up, using the rest of my energy to strengthen the shield again.

"Say goodbye"! She shouts.

I look to Bryan as his lips move. However, I hear nothing as the blazing cubes shatter my Sathonic barrier as if it were glass!

I crash to the ground, helpless. Brooke's cubes rip through Bryan and I viciously. As the devastating flood of Sathonic cubes ends, I roll over onto my side and see Brooke standing over Bryan. She yanks him up by his shirt.

Bryan leans back, almost unconscious.

I murmur with what little strength I have left in my reservoir.

"Leave… you better leave him alone." I struggle to utter.

No response.

Brooke does not even acknowledge my words and makes a red blazing blade out of her hand. I watch helplessly from the ground, just a few feet away from my best friend.

Justin Avery

"Bryan! No! Please fight back, don't die. You have to… fight back". I choke up blood as I plead.

As Brooke makes her hand a radiating blade, she sneers and demonstratively shouts.

"Finally! I'll be acknowledged in my community! I'll be known as the greatest assassin around! Once I get Bryan out of the way, it'll just be the leader left.

Out of nowhere, Sensei Roen zooms down kicking her away!

"You will not murder my students! I won't allow it to end like this"! He shouts.

Forcing my eyes to stay open, I smile knowing that our Sensei has fought his way back to save us.

"Brooke, you should know what I'm capable of. Remember when we first sparred? You were such a moldable kid back then. I'm sorry it's come to this. You're not the only one with the combustion quality of Sathon." Sensei Roen smirks confidently.

Brooke's smile fades. As her demeanor shifts into a serious one, she growls at Roen.

"Stop talking to me as if I was your student! Those days are over. I was sure Breanna could handle you alone, but I guess I was wrong. You're not all bad, old man." She comments.

"She was once your student too"!? I roar.

Runaways

As I look at my sensei, appalled by this news, he doesn't respond. He and Brooke do not break eye contact.

Sensei Roen even laughs at her, as if he was withholding some secret. Both individuals stare at each other for a few moments when Brooke stops frowning. She then smirks as well.

"So, you have one last trick up your sleeve old man? So be it, bring it on, I will even let you prepare. However, if it doesn't end me, you will regret it." Brooke snickers.

"Are you a woman of your word"? Our sensei questions.

Brooke nods her head and takes a few steps backwards, dropping her hands.

I drop my jaw in shock as Roen sits down meditating.

"She's just going to let him charge his attack"? I freak out in my mind.

I try and yell at my Sensei, but nothing comes out, just a soft toned yelp leaves my body.

"Wow, my body really has no Sathon left. I can't even speak." I groan.

Suddenly, my teacher begins whispering towards Bryan. His eyes still closed.

"Bryan, long ago, your combustion quality of Sathon was sealed. It's faint, but I can sense that it's still there. If I do this right now, with the Sathon level I'm currently at, I'll probably die. But, if

I can completely attach our life forces, your curse shall be lifted. My Ki will fuse with your Sathon. This is the ultimate energy fusion technique." Sensei Roen mutters.

"Quit murmuring over there, old man! What are you saying? I'm starting to get impatient." Brooke scoffs coldly.

"What are you doing? Attack her. Charge up a giant Sathon ball and launch it at her. Why are you meditating right now of all moments"? I worry.

My Sensei does not respond.

I start to get an eerie feeling from the silence. I sense life energy dissipating for some reason, but I can't pinpoint where from though.

I gaze over to Bryan, hoping he might have the answer. However, he is unconscious, and I can feel his life essence retreating from his body.

I become more perplexed after looking to Bryan though. His body starts shaking slowly. For a moment, it looks as if he's about to stand up, when the shaking comes to a stop. Shortly after that, he begins shaking violently! His limbs flail around, and his pores erupt with blood. The entire sight is so graphic that I begin screaming.

"Sensei! Something is wrong with Bryan! I think he's having a seizure." I begin pleading.

As I look towards my Sensei, he is still sitting on the ground, meditating. Infuriated with his lack of responses, I feel my energy begin to spike. Sathon from the sun begins to collect inside my chest. However, with lack of proficiency in the fusion technique, my body struggles to harness the energy. My turquoise aura flashes on and off as my energy fluctuates.

"Sensei!! Save him! Please Sensei, save Bryan"!

Still no response from Sensei Roen.

I glance back over to Bryan who is still shaking fiercely, before abruptly stopping completely. I can no longer sense the Ki dissipating and now realizing what's happened, I punch the ground. Filled with rage, I scream at my Sensei.

"I hate you! Why didn't you save him? Why are you just sitting there"? My voice breaks as I start sobbing.

"Bryan, you can't be gone." I sob, as my head feels as if it'll explode.

My vision blurs from my tears and as I look over to Brooke who is laughing to herself, I force myself to stand up.

"Where is this energy coming from? How can you even stand"? Brooke gawks in horror.

I hobble towards Sensei Roen.

"I swear you'll pay for this! You were supposed to protect us." I shout furiously.

As I attempt to wrap my hands around Roen and yank him up from the ground, I phase through his body and fall forward!

I fight to stand back up. As I turn around to find that Roen's body is gone, I turn to Brooke. Her smile is nowhere to be found.

"Wait… what!? Where did he go? I still sense that power coming from somewhere." I think to myself.

"I'm sorry Justin. I wish I was stronger. But you and Bryan will have to carry this burden for me." I hear Sensei's voice speaking softly.

"Ahh… yes. A Light and Combustion type. Fighting side by side." He chuckles as his voice begins to fade away.

Instantly after, I feel a spike in Ki. Now with a bittersweet demeanor, I look to Bryan.

His body still laying on the ground, is now glowing a bright red and the color flashes hot, turning white. The spectacle blinds me, and I close my eyes.

"Ow!! What is that light"? Brooke questions from behind me.

When the flash fades, Bryan is floating with a disgusted glare in his eyes.

"You're alive"! I stand in shock, staring at him.

Bryan rubs my head, rustling my hair.

"Of course, now I'm going to handle this threat." With no hesitation, Bryan teleports in front of Brooke!

Her eyes widen as she stares at him, perplexed.

Runaways

"How are you alive? I thought I killed you." She stammers.

Bryan hits Brooke with a flying knee in her stomach, and she spits blood onto the ground.

No words exchanged, he quickly uppercuts her. As her body rises from the blow, Bryan soars into the air, his fists blazing red.

As he brings both hands down, his blazing red fists, clenched together, hurtle Brooke towards the ground. His strike sends her skipping like the perfect flat stone in a cold lake. When her body skids to a stop, Bryan continues his assault.

Bryan stretches his fingers out. A red electric Sathonic whip emerges.

"Bryan has the Sathon ability"?! I think to myself confused.

As I process what is occurring, Bryan lashes the whip forward and it shears Brooke's back. Almost as if it provided no resistance, her lightweight body armor peels like an onions skin.

She howls in agony and turns over onto her back firing three Sathon blasts at Bryan.

His head movement is impeccable as he evades all three projectiles with no effort. His neat dreads sway back and forth as he smirks confidently. Even his single earring gleams brilliantly in the sunlight. Now walking forward towards Brooke, he lashes the Sathon whip again. This time, latching onto her left ankle. Bryan grasps the whip with both hands and his red aura flashes wildly.

Justin Avery

The Sathon whip grows thorns around her ankle and pierces flesh! The attack puts Brooke in agony.

Bryan spins rapidly like a top and this brings Brooke off the ground. As he spins faster, she slams through the surrounding hollow trees and bushes!

I stumble back and fall onto the ground, covering my head, avoiding the destruction completely. Eagerly wanting to see the action, I peek through my hands as Bryan stops on a dime. The Sathonic thorns jet downwards and rip anything in its path. Brooke's foot is bloody, and she passes out. All Bryan's momentum launches Brooke through the sky. Just as we're both sure a plummet from that height will kill Brooke, Breanna springs up and catches her comrade. The pesky ninja turns to me specifically and says one thing that terrifies me.

"Different than the kings in control now." She comments.

As she descends to the earth, they both teleport away.

"Again!? That phrase, how does she know it? My mother says that all the time." I question to myself.

Once again, I find my body toiling just to push myself off the ground. Bryan rushes over and sits me down.

"Do you think you can make it until I can get you to a hospital or whatever the medical facility this small village has"? Bryan inquires.

I shake my head.

"No, but I think I can teach you how to heal me. Put both hands slightly above my chest and focus your energy into swirling pools."

Bryan gives me a puzzled look but obliges.

"Like this"? He asks.

"Yeah, you got it, now just keep focusing on it, I think it should start soon." I chuckle before instantly seizing up from the intense pain.

As Bryan attempts to start the healing process, he looks at me confused.

"Bro, nothing is happening. I'm not sure that I can replicate your technique. Remember what Sensei said about different qualities of Sathon having different abilities? Maybe it's linked to that. By the way, how did you even figure out that you could do that"? Bryan comments.

I frown.

"To be honest, I saw that this Sathon ability could pretty much do whatever I imagined it to, so I was curious if I could heal myself and it worked. There hasn't been anything I have been able to accomplish with this ability. Although it does take a little while to get the healing process finished up, leaving me vulnerable. So, I doubt I'd be able to pull it off in the midst of combat".

Bryan nods his head, agreeing.

Justin Avery

"Oh yeah, for sure! I wish you could though. It definitely could become useful"! He exclaims.

I cut him off.

"Wait! Do you think Sensei had some extra Superfruiit hidden somewhere"? I shout.

Bryan reaches into his back pocket, pulling out a piece of the bright red mango.

"I'm not gonna lie to you, I got hungry and stole some the night before. I'm glad I did. It really came in handy just now. Lesson learned, always steal"! Bryan smirks.

I shake my head at him disappointed.

"You really stole from our teacher? And you were going to keep that in your pocket while I sat here suffering? Dude what's your problem? Seriously, where are your priorities"? I complain.

Chapter 12:
A New Power

Bryan shrugs his shoulders.

"I'm sure that Sensei would have shared the fruit anyway. Wait, what happened to Sensei"? He questions.

"I saw him meditating and then when I rushed to grab Sensei Roen, he was gone. He floated away like he was made of smoke. But he seemed proud, it's bittersweet. I'm just glad he's happy that you and I will be fighting together". I explain as I gaze up at the sky.

As I consume the fruit my body feels as if a giant weight has been lifted off it.

"This fruit is so rejuvenating"!! I moan.

Bryan inspects me closely.

"I don't want to sound crazy, but I think he fused his life force with mine. I really don't know how to explain it, he was with me. He smiled and turned into a bright white light. When the flash ended, he was gone, and I felt a raging power within myself." Bryan states calmly.

I stand up staring at him, stunned.

"So, do you think"? Bryan begins to question.

I cut him off again.

"Yeah, I can't sense Sensei's energy anywhere. It is almost like he never existed".

Bryan looks to the sky wistfully.

"So, he really is gone. He gave up his life to save me. I can't even get over the fact that I have this ability now. I swear Sensei, I will not fail my mother, and you. I will avenge you and fix everything I failed to do as a child." Bryan exclaims loudly.

I place my hand on Bryan's shoulder.

"We are going to accomplish everything. Together, with the others we can save our people." I state candidly.

"Yeah... sure. After my vengeance. Roen gave me a second chance at my ambition. So, because of that, I'll fulfill his dream. Just after I figure out who sealed my combustion Sathonic quality! I was robbed of my birthright! And my mother was robbed of her life! We've been over this." Bryan shouts.

He then calms down and continues.

"But I guess we should probably get rid of this map too." Bryan comments, handing the blacked-out map towards me.

As I take the map from him, I create a small Sathon flame in the center. The flame wastes no time and spreads out towards the edges of the paper. The map crumbles into a burnt mess before dissipating into a light blue smoke.

Runaways

Bryan smiles and leads us back down the trail towards the building and we start on our way back to the group. The trip does not take too much time and we make it back to the house.

As I creak the door open slightly, Zero pokes his fluffy head through the space, doing his best to get to me. I smile and crouch down, pushing his little head back.

"Hold on buddy, let me come inside the house first."

When the door finally opens all the way up, Zero pounces onto my leg.

Eagerly, he climbs up my leg and into my arms. When I hug him and walk around the house looking for the others, I find the beautiful sight of my three friends sitting in the living room watching television.

"Hey guys." I spout softly, suppressing my joy.

Hailey looks up from the floor first. Her eyes widen and she rolls over, escaping her blanket before rushing over to hug me.

Zero sees the aggressive excitement and bails from my arms, scampering under the couch.

Hailey jumps up and hugs me tightly.

"We missed you!! I am so glad you are okay. Why were you guys gone for so long? We tried to come find you both, however, there was a red Sathonic cage around the building. It stayed there since the third day you both were gone and lasted for about a week. It faded away about two hours ago."

"Yeah! We couldn't even leave the house! And then some transparent old man appeared and said you both would be home soon. We decided not to move from that point. I'm just glad you both are safe. Your clothes are so tattered"! Dwight also chimes in.

I begin pondering to myself.

"So, Sensei had enough energy to hold up a protective shield for an entire week! Then, on top of that, he could telepathically communicate with our friends from many miles away! He wasn't a fighter but, he definitely had many esoteric abilities".

I chuckle and try to explain the story but decide Bryan would be better suited for the job.

"Well guys, why don't you ask Bryan." I respond.

As I say this, I step off to the side, tossing both hands towards Bryan.

Doing my best "Jacqui the car saleswoman" impression, I laugh, recalling the memory.

Jacqui giggles and hops up from the couch, heading over towards me. I smile and we hug.

"I missed your big head." She claims cheerfully.

As we hug, Dwight begins squealing obnoxiously. We both let go of each other and stare at him.

Runaways

"Wait, so Bryan has Sathon powers too? Why couldn't I go instead"? He pouts for a moment but hugs Bryan.

"Nah, but for real, I missed you bro. I just wish I could've gotten my hands on those amazing abilities"! Dwight admits to his brother.

Bryan smiles, delighted to be with his brother again.

"I'm glad Sensei had you guys stay put. Things could have been hectic if you lot showed up."

"Oh Dwight! I got you a gift." Bryan comments as he hands Dwight a katana from the battlefield.

"Whoa! Where did you get this? This quality is stupendous"! Dwight exclaims.

"Oh, look at toilet boy, he's using big words now." Hailey chirps.

"Toilet boy? What is she talking about"? I question curiously.

"DO NOT CALL ME THAT!! You will not speak of that"! Dwight demands, his voice booming throughout the house.

"Alright, alright. Your secret is safe with me, you weirdo." Hailey obliges.

I inform everyone that there is a new plan from this point forward, but, let them know that we will discuss it in the morning.

Once everyone settles in, we all split up and go relax. Jacqui and I go and cuddle on the couch, watching television together. As she falls asleep in my arms, I smile colorfully, knowing that everything is great again.

Thinking out loud, I murmur to myself.

"We finally saved Jacqui. Bryan and I have the ability to guide Sathon. Dwight and Hailey are doing well, and we have a tiger mix as a pet. We're unstoppable! Kings of Nero! We're coming for you"!

I think back on Sensei Roen and frown. Thoughts of the troublesome assassin duo, flood back and I shudder, wondering how she even found us to begin with.

"Maybe she could sense our Ki as well"? She was concealing her energy after all. Anyone that can manipulate their life force like that, is going to be a problem in the future." I assume.

As more pessimistic thoughts bubble up inside my head, I begin to worry.

"The fact that the kings of Nero would hire two assassins, while simultaneously sending Julien and Adrian, is terrifying. What if Brooke went after Jacqui and the others instead? In that case, I have no doubts that Brooke would have made it through Sensei's barrier. Nobody here could contest those two in strength. Breanna and Brooke would have… yeah." I trail off, to avoid the horrid thought.

Now attempting to evade the nightmares, I roll over and try to fall asleep. However, in the process I accidentally wake Jacqui. She looks up at me inquiringly.

Runaways

"Hey loser, is there something wrong? You look upset. Is there something you want to talk about"? She questions.

I almost lie to protect her from the grim truth but stop myself.

"What is it? You can tell me anything." Jacqui sits up, looking concerned for me.

I explain the story in full detail, from beginning to end, not leaving out the parts of Roen's demise or the murderous assassins.

"So why did you and Bryan leave that part out when he told the story earlier"? Jacqui gawks at me hesitantly.

I drop my head, ashamed.

"I don't know, I just didn't want you all to worry." I lament.

Jacqui inspects me bewildered.

"Justin, do you think that not informing us about a pair of psychotic killers was a better idea"? She questions.

"Bryan handled Brooke, so I didn't think it needed to be said."

The television catches our attention, and we stop arguing.

"The kings of Nero are now accepting all occupants who are willing to train, in order to hunt down and kill these enemies." The announcement states.

My brow furrows as a picture of my friends and I pop up on the screen. I yell, livid and appalled at the fact that they have photos of us.

The news report continues.

"These seven individuals are armed and dangerous. One of their individuals, presumably their leader. Wields Sathon."

I calm down, thinking for a second.

"Seven? What does he mean? Ava was involved with us, and he is referring to us as the group that escaped. Why is he leaving her out"?

A video pops up of me shielding bullets with my powers. The next clip is Jade, and Donshay fighting against Lumin officers. I stand up bewildered at what I am witnessing.

"These teenagers are unpredictable and must be stopped at any cost. Look at this footage, captured by our loyal Lumin guard body cam." The reporter states lethargically.

Again, a video appears of me attacking the two Lumin officers guarding Jacqui's hospital room. There is screaming as I rush aggressively, then the video cuts to black as I slash. The next clip is a video of the Lumin guards chasing me out the window. As I escape the group, carrying Jacqui out the building, the video jump cuts, but stays with the same situation. The clip continues to the point where I have all the Lumin guards surrounding me, and I detonate my Sathonic sparkle.

Runaways

My Sathonic blast, launches all the officers a great distance, some of them hitting the building and then the video cuts again. The reporter is back now, with a black eye! She begins shuddering with fear. She stands in front of the camera with a governor from each city in the country of Nero.

"Look Jacqui, the governor from Comely, it's a different guy than before. Do you think that the king actually killed the original one and his council like he threatened"? I comment.

Jacqui doesn't respond and the broadcast continues.

"We must put these fugitives away for good! If anyone… in our proud Nation of Nero, has anything… they can offer, whether it be information on the criminal's location, or providing services to help us kill- I mean capture these fugitives, it would be greatly appreciated." She states wearily, as she tiptoes over every word.

"Did they punch her for saying the word 'kill' on national television"? Jacqui inquires, petrified of the truth.

One of the Governors step forward. It takes me a moment, but I recognize him and yell for the others to pile into the room. They rush in, ready to watch the news cast with us.

"Walk in a room, with a purpose." Dwight sings to himself.

"What is it." Bryan questions as he enters the room.

Jacqui shushes everyone, instructing them to just watch the television.

The governor begins speaking.

"I, proud governor of the city Joviality, take an oath on my position as leader of the city. To put forth my best effort in finding these criminals as not only the leader of those fugitives came from my city, but a few of his despicable friends also escaped. I will take full responsibility for whatever happens from this point forward, and I will not fail our kings. As a gift to the kings of Nero, to right my wrongs. I have decided to bless this mission with my gift from God"! He shouts triumphantly.

"Gift from God? What is he even blabbering about"? Bryan questions.

"Be quiet, he's about to explain." Jacqui shushes him loudly.

The governor steps back and his two sons take a step forward. Their golden and royal purple aura's dancing wildly.

"My twin sons! Both possessing the rare and sacred ability! They will be leading the operation to hunt down, and take these fugitives in. At any cost, our goal is to arrest these individuals. However, if ending their life is in the best interest of the nation or the kings, then it will be done. Right boys"? He questions, confidently awaiting a response.

Julien, shining golden, sneers devilishly and starts spouting nonsensical patriotic garbage. He knows that the people of Nero will eat it up and love him for it.

At this point I reach for the remote to turn off the television, but Hailey stops me.

"Wait a second, I want to see what his brother has to say." She informs me.

I recoil, allowing everyone to continue watching.

"Adrian looks nervous." I mutter.

Bryan nods his head in agreement.

"Yeah, he does not look like he wants to be involved with any of this." He comments.

As Adrian murmurs the Nero national song. I begin to think back on how he stepped in, between his brother Julien and me.

Now pondering back on that situation, I watch him struggle to find something crowd pleasing to say. I stare at the screen, feeling somewhat sympathetic for Adrian. Before anyone says anything about his embarrassing performance, the television cuts off abruptly.

"Turn it back on, Justin"! They all scream in an uproar.

"I didn't touch the remote!! I promise." I throw both hands up innocently.

Dwight turns towards his brother, seeing the remote is closest to him.

"Bryan, turn the television back on"! He barks.

"Don't tell me what to do kid, I had enough of watching that asinine garbage." Bryan spouts.

Dwight shoves him, reaching for the remote.

"Then leave! Just let us watch it, this could be important." Dwight shouts, animosity building between the two.

Bryan's nose wrinkles, and the two butt heads, pushing each other.

"Hey guys, do you see those clouds"? Hailey hesitantly questions while staring outside the window at the sky.

Nobody responds and the two keep arguing over the remote.

I look to Jacqui who is trying to settle the sibling rivalry.

"Guys"? Hailey whimpers again.

No response from anyone as the bickering continues.

"Hey! Pay attention"! Hailey bellows at all of us, frustrated at our lack of care.

We all stop and turn to her, giving her our undivided attention.

"Look, there is a bad storm outside"! She barks.

Bryan pushes past everyone, looking outside, inspecting the sky.

"You seriously yelled at us because you saw some dark clouds"? Bryan inquires.

Runaways

"I know, it sounds stupid, but just hear me out. There is something about this storm that just feels… I guess the word I'm looking for, is ominous." Hailey replies.

Bryan eyes her cautiously. "You sure you didn't hit your head while Justin and I were gone"? He spouts facetiously.

Hailey whines, pushing Bryan playfully.

"No! Seriously! I just feel like we need to leave or find better shelter." She worries more than before.

"I agree, at first, I was questioning whether or not Hailey was being timid as usual, but now that I look at the storm. I get this eerie feeling as well." Dwight chimes in.

"Shut up! You only want to leave because there's no more food in the fridge." Bryan comments.

Dwight clenches his fist.

We all gaze out at the storm together.

"Maybe we should leave. That assassin Brooke somehow tracked us here. What if there are more enemies on their way"? I comment, my eyes locked on the storm clouds.

Dwight and Hailey turn simultaneously. "I'm sorry, could you run that message by me one more time"? Dwight requests.

I nervously look at them both. I notice the heavy glares from both Dwight and Hailey, who share the same facial expression of mad, perplexed, and curious, all at once.

"I'll explain later. Let's just try to settle in and weather the storm for now. Once it passes, we can leave tomorrow morning." I state, doing my best to reflect their curiosity away.

My comments are followed by murmurs of disgruntled complaints. It stays as such, up until Hailey speaks up.

"Hey, Justin. I don't really feel safe sleeping here tonight. Now thinking about that assassin, you mentioned earlier, I feel like we're sitting ducks if we stay here. That news report hasn't helped either. Everyone wants us dead." She whimpers queasily.

Everyone agrees. I look around at my friends, their faces struck with worry.

"Alright then guys, lets pack up and leave then. I don't want to get caught in that storm, so please hurry." I comment wearily.

Hailey smiles and hugs me.

"Thank you, Justin. I really appreciate you being considerate." She responds warmly.

"Yeah man. We are all so proud to have you leading us." Dwight comments candidly.

"Wow, I never really thought about it like that." I chuckle, thinking to myself.

Everyone but Bryan gets in close for a brief group hug. Hailey does her best to convince him to join us, however, he doesn't budge. Bryan stays by the window, glaring outside at the clouds.

Runaways

Before everyone splits off to pack their stuff, Dwight stands on top of the table and claps to gain our attention.

"Hey guys"? Dwight questions.

Everyone looks to him, curious of his next statement.

"When life gets you down, it's like a box of chocolates, you just gotta get back on that horse." He comments, brightly grinning.

"What the heck does that even mean Dwight"? Everyone bursts out laughing uncontrollably.

"Uhh, I really don't know. I just wanted to be motivational, and it didn't sound as good as it did in my head." He comments candidly.

Jacqui falls to the floor in laughter and Hailey crumbles to her knees, laughing just as hard.

"Just chocolate your way back onto that horse." Hailey mocks, now rolling on the floor, sobbing with laughter.

"I didn't say that! It was better than that"! Dwight objects, embarrassed by his attempt to rally us on.

"Whatever. I'm only glad I can be y'all's entertainment." He smiles.

"Dwight, you killed me with that. You gotta chill bro." I chuckle.

Justin Avery

"Give us another quote man. Please, these are gold"! Jacqui hiccups as she can't stop laughing.

"Alright, lemme think." Dwight fondles the twists in his hair as he thinks to himself.

"Just like Justin's flame burns hot… you can stop forest fires when you recycle." Dwight chants confidently.

The room is filled with silence. As everyone stares at Dwight, we even hear crickets chirping outside the front door.

"You ruined it… you ruined it and I'm leaving." Bryan growls as he walks out of the living room.

"Dwight, I know the quote was supposed to be awful, but that was terrible." Jacqui comments.

"Well, I'll be calling you toilet boy and chocolate horse from now on." Hailey giggles.

"Don't you dare"!! Dwight shrieks as he chases her out the living room.

Chapter 13:
Power Trip

Once everyone finishes packing our items, we meet back in the living room. I have everyone sit down and I explain to them what happened with the map and why we ditched it.

I continue the story by catching them up on how the rubies are fake and a distraction set up by the kings.

After finishing with the details, I gaze at everyone.

"We need to find the three relics. Bryan and I could boost our abilities exponentially if we could get these items in our grasp." I state.

"What if we destroy the relics instead"? Jacqui suggests.

The room goes silent as I stare at her, stunned from the idea. Stuttering for a moment, I finally spit the words out.

"What do you mean? Why would we find these sacred items and destroy them"?

Jacqui considers her idea for a moment and then she begins to explain it to us.

"Listen, if we get these relics and the Elite twins steal them from us, or the Lumin kings get two out of the three, then we're screwed. Plain and simple. Our enemies are already stronger than us, they have much more manpower too. Don't even get me started on the pair of ninjas that now want the bounty on our head. What we

need to do is even the playing field as much as possible. Destroying
the items seals the fact that they can't be abused. I know that if we
can get back to the country with proof of outside life. Then we
could show our people that the Light lied. The people would rebel,
and we might just."

Bryan cuts her off.

"We would all die. Justin and I have just recently gotten these
Sathon powers, also with no teacher to show us how to use them,
we don't stand a chance against that Lumin army. The Lumin kings
have their own two teenage prodigies, who have been trained since
they were kids. On top of that, just because we prove there is
outside life, doesn't mean anyone will believe us. Much less revolt
against the kings themselves." He grunts, bluntly shooting down her
idea.

"Quit rambling, what are you trying to say"? Jacqui grills him.

Bryan stands up, looking down at us.

"It means without those relics, we will fail. We simply do not
have the strength to compete with the military might of the Lumin
forces. We need those relics to even give Justin and I a chance.
Once we break in and take control of the nation, all havoc will
break loose. If the kings can't deceive the people into submission,
they'll force them to fight against us. There is no way of avoiding
death, so stop trying. We can't convince the people with facts. We
have to force them to see the truth, to rebel against this way of life"!
Bryan shouts.

I stand up, stepping between the two.

Runaways

"What about the Lustronese people? They are our people, Bryan. Surely, they will hear the news and fight alongside us. They already know that the Lumin forces are corrupt and lied to conceal the truth. They just don't know to what extent." I spout, desperately trying to calm my friends.

Bryan shakes his head.

"I just don't think we should leave it to chance. Destroying the relics? That's so arrogant! You really think we can stop them by handicapping ourselves!? If we get these relics, we could become unstoppable and change the world"!

Jacqui eyes Bryan curiously.

"Bryan, we don't need that power to change the world. We can save everyone with love and truth. If anything, you just sound power hungry." Jacqui groans.

Bryan is taken aback by her comment and seems offended.

Instantly he gets in her face.

"Maybe I am! They took my mother away when I was just a child! What do you know of my pain? Huh!? Tell me that! You had a family your entire life, so of course you want to be all soft and dainty! Love isn't going to get us anywhere! It'll just get you killed! Death is coming Jacqui. I smell it in the air." He roars.

Jacqui has tears swelling up in her eyes and she looks towards Bryan. Sympathy written all over her face.

"There is no avoiding this war. I prayed to God, my entire life I've longed for this ability. And now that I have it, I truly feel invincible! I'll do anything to gain more power! I won't let anything stand in my way now, and I refuse to ever feel like that powerless kid ever again"!

I push him back, holding onto his shirt tightly. Staring them both down I shout.

"That's enough! Could you both clear your head and calm down? We don't have any relics as you can see. We have zero power to make either of these decisions right now, so how about we just take things slowly and eventually figure out what is the best course of action. We will cross that bridge when we get there. Everyone got it"? I bellow, annoyed by their petty squabble.

Bryan yanks himself free from my grip.

"Sure, whatever. I got it." He mutters.

Bryan quickly storms out into the rain, slamming the door on his way out. The door, slams so hard, it reopens. Dwight stands up and heads over to the front door, closing it softly. Hailey hops up, attempting to mend the wounds of the argument.

"You guys, Justin is right. These relics have been searched for by everyone for centuries. Who knows if we will even find them and run into this situation? Maybe we'll avoid this problem entirely"? She beckons Jacqui in for a hug.

Jacqui nods smiling. "You're right Hailey, thank you. I just want everyone to find their family again. There doesn't need to be anymore unnecessary pain." She states.

308

Runaways

Hailey and Jacqui hug. Afterwards, they both smile. Jacqui has a small stream of tears running down her face.

"Oh no! Are you okay? Tell me what's wrong." Hailey wails.

Jacqui tries to hide the sadness in her voice, but it is clear for everyone to see that she's mildly upset.

"When Bryan said the Light took his mother, I understood how he felt. His rage and frustration are justified. I hurt with him. I miss my entire family and I just want these relics destroyed because with all that power, there is bound to be more fighting, more pain, and more children losing family members. It isn't fair to anyone, and I just want to help Bryan heal."

Dwight walks over and hugs Jacqui.

"I'm sorry for what happened to your family. When Bryan hurts, I don't know what to say or how to feel. I was too young to really know my mother, but the way Bryan talks about her. It makes me feel as if she was always there. All Bryan longs for now, is vengeance. I'm afraid what he'd do to get the power to avenge mom. In a way, you are my mother figure Jacqui. You always have been there for us, and I was so excited to go with Justin on our mission to rescue you. We haven't known each other long but all of you have been the closest thing to family I've ever had. I would give each one of you my dying breath if I had to." Dwight sobs quietly.

We all hug, and for a brief second it feels as if there are no worries in the world.

Justin Avery

As each second passes I shudder internally, knowing that this moment has to end eventually.

"Alright, alright, enough crying." Dwight chokes out while laughing.

"Let's go find my crazy brother." He cheers.

After everyone detaches from our close-knit hug. We turn off the lights and close the door to this house for the final time. As we pile outside into the rain, Zero climbs in Hailey's backpack to avoid the savage downpour. I look around and see nothing in the surrounding area.

"Where could Bryan have gone"? I think to myself.

"Do you think we should split up"? Jacqui inquires.

We all look to each other for a moment. Dwight speaks up first.

"I'll go with Jacqui, and we'll head into that small town, maybe Bryan just wanted to get out of the rain. You and Hailey should go out further into the jungle and desert area, to see if you can spot him. If we can't locate Bryan, we'll meet back here in an hour. If we do find him, bring Bryan back here and we will wait for each other. I don't want to get lost and be apart from everyone again. Please be safe alright"? Dwight admits candidly.

Everyone agrees.

Runaways

The wind, now howling at us, picks up, almost taking Hailey to the ground. I quickly grab her arm, helping Hailey regain her footing.

"Thank you." She mutters cheerfully, her teeth chattering wildly.

Once the group divides, Hailey and I head into the jungle area. Hopefully, Bryan attempted to avoid the rain in the underbrush.

I keep Hailey close by my side and seek out possible threats as we trek through the muddy jungle grounds.

"I know there are plenty of predators in these woods. But I don't feel scared. I feel safe when you're with me." Hailey comments.

I smile at her warmly and we continue searching through the trees. I spot what looks like a troop of Orange gorillas.

"Are those… Oranges"? I think to myself, slightly petrified.

One of the males makes direct eye contact with me and I almost melt in fear. I quickly grab Hailey's hand. Pulling her back towards me, I take us both behind a giant tree, fleeing the troop's overprotective eyes.

"What are those things. They're huge and look super scary." Hailey questions.

Trying my best to keep my voice down and stay calm, I answer slowly.

Justin Avery

"I think those are gorillas, whatever happened to them with the Scepin fallout, must have made them huge and turned their fur coat orange. If I have learned anything from my time training with Sensei, that means they probably are extremely aggressive. I hate that all the new animals are so blood thirsty." I admit.

Hailey and I hear a large branch snap and she shrieks in fear. I quickly clasp a hand over her mouth as we both shudder in silence. We begin to fret about what is behind the tree, lurking towards us. I take a glance and two huge Oranges stare back at me. I recall from my time in the mountains that this great ape's vision is poor in the daytime but is multiplied twice in the darkness.

I shudder at the thought. Looking around to inspect the area, Hailey notices that with this weather, it may as well be nighttime. The clouds and rain block out all sunlight. My eyes widen when I register how massive the gorillas are. Both bulked out in muscle, each ape looking to be at least five hundred pounds.

I whip my head back around, staring at the trees. Hailey glances at me and starts trembling uncontrollably. She then grips my arm tightly, trying to keep her calm. We hear more twigs creaking or snapping as one of the beasts approaches our position. I create a miniature Sathon blast and launch it over my shoulder without looking.

Using my ability to sense life energy, I can tell that the Sathon blast attached itself somewhere in the trees. I detonate it and the Oranges all look in that direction instead of continuing towards us. In that split second, I grab Hailey and race off to escape the gorillas.

Runaways

In the middle of my desperate dash, I slip on a wet tree root and fall face first into the mud. Hailey flails onto the ground and we both scramble into the hollow part of a tree and hold our breath.

Without making a sound, we both sit in a hollowed-out tree, staring each other in the face. I feel cramped and fight the urge to readjust my legs. As we lay there crumpled together like a pathetic piece of origami, the massive Orange walks around our area. He finally halts at our tree, sniffing like crazy.

"He must know we're here; their sense of smell is impeccable." I worry.

Hailey starts hyperventilating and I shake my head fiercely at her. Begging her with my gestures to find whatever restraint she has left and to stretch it out. Hailey finds her happy place, closing her eyes and holding her mouth shut, we both sit in silence.

"Please stop fidgeting Hailey." I plead desperately inside my mind.

It looks as if the ape is about to depart from our tree. Suddenly, Zero pokes his head out of the top pocket of the backpack and begins to hiss at the gorilla! Instantly the beast growls back and punches through the hollowed-out tree. His enormous fist mere inches above our heads! Hailey screeches and the enormous ape reels back with both hands to crush us! Hailey screams at Zero and I spring out the log with both of my feet glowing turquoise. I kick the Orange in its jaw and spin, kicking it again.

It stumbles backwards and then comes charging at me like a raging bull. With no time to process the situation, I fire out some

Sathonic bursts from my hands. The forceful energy propels me to the left, like nitro boosts a car.

I slide on the sloppy ground but keep my footing. The downpour continues and the compacted dirt slowly turns into mud.

Enraged with adrenaline rushing through my veins, I scream at the beast.

"I won't back down to you"!

The Orange beats his chest, baring its gleaming canines at me. I make my entire body glow ferociously and I throw some Sathonic blasts at it. The beast is hit, but only seems to become more agitated from the blows. He charges me and I point my hands down towards the earth, using another Sathon burst to launch me above the danger.

As I ascend above the Orange, I get an idea.

Now returning to the earth, I shoot Sathonic bursts from my feet. Launching myself at the gorilla faster than it can react. I spin and punch as hard as I can! When my fist connects, the ape cries out and stumbles backwards, dazed by the attack. Two more Oranges rush in, and I return to the skies.

Once I launch myself high enough, I sit in a tree, attempting to devise a strategy that'll get rid of the monsters. Then something clicks.

"Where is Hailey"? I ponder, frantically inspecting the area as I attempt to spot her.

Runaways

I look down and see her fleeing with Zero in her arms. Instantly I notice a few female Oranges pursuing after her and I jump from the tree to fight them off.

Landing sloppily on the mud, I almost bust my tailbone. As I catch myself, I pop up quickly, sliding in front of the apes. As their eyes turn from Hailey, towards me, I drop down, sweeping at their ankles. A turquoise ring spreads outward like a ripple in a pond.

It wipes out many trees and forces the gorillas to retreat. I stand back up, smirking.

"Yeah, that's what I thought"! I boast arrogantly.

A bad vibe overtakes my body and instantly, I see it.

An Orange does a few leaps and bounds before seeking to crush me! As he smashes into the ground, I hop backwards, evading his landing spot. I rise slightly, attempting to flee backwards, but the gorilla backhands me with his unrestrained and reckless strength! I smash into Hailey, and we slide to a stop, scraping against the jungle floor. For a few moments I feel broken, but eventually I pull myself to my feet, fearing for our safety.

"Justin are you okay"? Hailey wails worriedly.

"This Gorilla is huge! I'm honestly not sure if I can take another shot like that." I admit as I laugh the pain away.

The Orange charges wildly and I zip behind him, leaving an afterimage in my wake.

Justin Avery

Hailey dives out the way as the ape punches through the gigantic tree, snapping it as if it were a twig!

I stand behind it, now wondering what I could possibly do to stop this monster. As I debate a plan in my head, the gorilla spins around, swinging its massive fist towards my head!

I catch his arm and spring over his head with great athleticism, catching his other arm and yanking both backwards.

"I'm going to break you"! I scream as I pull with all my might.

My turquoise aura flashes violently and I heat my hands up vastly, burning the ape's hands as I struggle to pull his arms back behind him.

The beast cries out loudly and starts pulling back. Now losing grip on the ape, I focus and my Sathon becomes stronger. I begin pulling harder, hoping that something will give, when suddenly, the gorilla finds new energy and flips me over his head!

The new surging energy allows him to effortlessly slam my body into the ground! As I collide with the unforgiving earth, my breath leaves my body momentarily.

With the wind is knocked out from my lungs, the ape wastes no time and begins to spin me rapidly in circles before launching me into the busted rubble from the tree he attacked earlier.

"Justin! Oh my god, are you okay"? Hailey cries, pulling me out of the broken wood.

Runaways

I weakly lift my head up, staring at the Orange, fearing for Hailey's safety I raise my hand to fire a Sathonic blast.

BOOM!

A red explosion detonates, searing the area.

Even the mud that was launched up from the ground is so hot from the attack, that it scalds the ape! I look back at my hand confused at what just occurred.

"That wasn't you, Justin, you're too soft to intentionally kill something." Bryan shouts as he lands in front of Hailey and me.

"Bryan, what do you mean? The gorilla is still." Hailey begins to comment.

Bryan dissipates and appears in front of the Orange in the air. His leg scorching, Bryan kicks with all his force and all I see is a massive red Sathonic flash.

The attack resembles my turquoise Sathon bursts. I used those to avoid the heavy thunderous blows of the gorilla. However, Bryan uses his for offense instead of defense.

Bryan slowly begins to descend to the ground and his red glow fades away. I look to him and then back to the great ape who was beheaded by the kick! Bryan lands in front of the body, his back turned towards us. I stand up, confused, and filled with mixed emotions.

"You didn't have to kill it, Bryan! There was no reason to go that far." I shout, angered by his nonchalant demeanor.

"What in the world is wrong with you? Why did you do that? Bryan, you could have scared it off! There was no logical reason to kill it. What could you have possibly gained from that"? Hailey screams frustrated with Bryan's actions.

Bryan turns his head, rolling his eyes at us. "I eliminated a threat, you're welcome. Let's just go find Dwight and Jacqui so we can leave this wretched place". He comments, annoyed.

"No, that wasn't cool, we just needed a distraction to get away, you really didn't need to go that far." I begin to state.

Bryan cuts me off sharply.

"Shut up Justin. The reason why your Sathon is so weak, is because you never fuel it with emotion. Isn't that what Sensei was trying to teach you? You won't be able to keep up with me because you're a disgrace! You have a legendary relic inside you, and you continue to waste its power. Give in, feed into it. Use your emotion. Let it be your motivation. That ape had no business touching you! You need to start going for the kill, Julien isn't going to play nice, and neither are the Lumin kings! I can promise you that." He scolds scathingly.

"I can't give in to that power, you just don't understand this flame like I do. There would be devastating consequences if I let this energy run wild. I can feel it." I argue back.

Hailey, now fed up with Bryan, rushes over, shoving him towards the ground! Bryan smashes his face into the mud.

Runaways

"Listen Bryan, I don't care for whatever power trip you're going on right now, but I'm not here for it! You need to figure your life out right now because we have more important things to worry about than your midlife crisis. We all lost someone close to us, okay?! You need to get it together and help us find these relics so we can save our people, isn't that what's most important"? Hailey shouts.

I stare at them both, staggered by this sudden eruption of emotion from Hailey.

"She's usually so timid and sweet. But she's really had enough." I think to myself.

Bryan stands up and flashes his Sathon aura, which launches the mud and dirt off his clothes and face.

"What's most important, is avenging my mother. Truly, if I could do that, I couldn't care less what happened to our people. Oh, and Hailey, learn your place. I may be struggling right now, but at least I'm not a useless pacifist always in the need of saving. What are you? A child"? Bryan spouts and takes off like a jet, flying through the rain.

"Bryan can fly"? Hailey questions.

"I wonder when he learned how to do that. What's even more scary is that he doesn't have this relic inside him. This flame releases my untapped potential." I state.

Hailey goes off on a tangent now that Bryan is gone.

"Yeah, you're right Hailey. I honestly need to apologize for how I've been acting. Let's go find the others and get out of here. This storm is progressively getting worse. Was that so hard to say? And what's worse is that he just flies off"! Hailey roars.

Hailey stops and looks dispirited.

"Although… he's right. I am useless… I can't even protect myself and I get in the way no matter what I do. It's my fault that we even got into this mess. I swear, Justin. I won't be a burden from now on." Hailey growls annoyed with her own failures.

As we both trudge through the wind and heavy rain, the storm picks up. Once arriving back at the house, I can see Jacqui and Dwight huddled under the out stretching roof.

I race over and greet them eagerly. As I catch them both up on the wild story that occurred while we were separated, they stare at Hailey and I in awe.

"You guys survived that insane attack?! I hate that I always miss the hectic action." Dwight whines.

I laugh, reminding him that we have plenty more ahead of us.

Jacqui hugs me as she begins to worry.

"I swear, I'm gonna have to stay by your side to make sure that you don't get yourself killed. It seems like you're a magnet for danger." She states anxiously.

"Noo!! I want to be around Justin! I never get to do any of the fun stuff. I wanna test this katana." Dwight cries.

Runaways

I smile cheerfully, embracing the warm hug.

"You act as if I have a problem with you always being by my side Jacqui." I reply slyly.

We both laugh while staring into each other's eyes. Getting lost for a moment I forget the storm continues to worsen around us.

"They aren't listening to you, chocolate horse." Hailey snickers.

Dwight rolls his eyes.

"Maybe I should test this katana on you then"? He grins.

As he's about to start chasing Hailey, I glance up to see an enormous tornado barreling towards the village!

"Wait a tornado? Like the one in my nightmares"!? I fretfully shout.

The tornado looks to be far enough out where we have a chance to warn the citizens before escaping.

"Alright, everyone come here! We need to get these people out of this village before that thing hits. Bryan and I will try and slow the tornado down, and you three need to go door to door, warning everyone." I order promptly.

We all nod and take off to our jobs. Bryan sprints beside me and looks over, questioning.

"So, what's your idea on stopping this monster"?

Justin Avery

I yell back, competing with the howling wind.

"If we can use our Sathon abilities to speed around the tornado in the opposite direction of the airflow, we could slow it down. Although we're gonna have to be moving at breakneck speed". I suggest.

Bryan gives me a doubtful look, but obliges, admitting that he doesn't have a better idea.

Once we get close enough to feel the tornado's pull, we both slide to a stop.

"Alright Justin, it looks as if it's spinning counterclockwise, so we have to rotate around it going the opposite direction if we want to disrupt its spin." Bryan comments.

We nod in unison and start racing around it, using our powers, we fire a Sathonic burst from our feet. Mere moments pass as we circle the tornado. The color from our auras glow around the tornado and the base looks to be a bright purple color. However, I can feel the cyclone dragging me in towards the center of death and I quickly bail on the plan.

Bryan and I move further away from the danger. We take a seat on a small hill, exhausted from our attempt.

"Justin, no offense but that idea was atrocious! We didn't even affect it. Using Sathon to blitz around the tornado, drained my energy faster than I anticipated. And with-it being nighttime, there's not enough sun to replenish our Sathon. We'll be working on an empty tank soon. Even if we were making a difference on the tornado's spin, we wouldn't be able to keep that pace up long enough to stop it." Bryan scowls.

I look to Bryan, desperate for an idea to save the village.

"I know, I know. I don't have anything else in mind to stop this thing though. It'll destroy the community here and all those people will have nothing to go back to if we fail! We have to try something". I shout anxiously.

"We're running out of time Justin. We need to come up with something quickly". Bryan comments.

I glance over and see a small whirlpool in the middle of a lake. As a duck takes flight and lands in the lake. The duck sends ripples that affect the whirlpools speed. It's not until the waterfowl itself, begins to get pulled into the whirlpool's grasp, and hits the dead center, that I get an idea.

"I got it Bryan! If I can get into the dead center of this tornado and have enough of a force to stop it. Then we could save the village and all the people"! I exclaim.

Bryan neglects making eye contact with me.

"You're crazy dude. Why would you risk your life for these pathetic people? What if your farfetched plan doesn't work and you toss yourself into the center of that for nothing"? He replies disparagingly.

I turn back, looking at the village. I notice Jacqui holding two little girl's hands and escorting them to safety. I turn back to Bryan, smiling.

"It's worth the risk, these people will die out here if their community is destroyed by this tornado. There are so many individuals that would be negatively impacted by this. I can't just sit idly by and watch everything they worked for, be wiped out. Besides, if I can't save this village, then I don't deserve to call myself a hero. These are our people, and this is their home." I chant heroically.

Bryan shakes his head, puzzled by my logic.

"I have no idea what makes you tick, but the world definitely needs more people like you." He comments.

I thank Bryan and start to explain the plan.

"Just hear me out, I want you to give me almost all of your Sathon energy. Just enough so I can disrupt this tornado and hopefully disperse the threat." I order.

"You do know that if too much of my energy leaks out of your body while you attempt to destroy this tornado, you could implode from all the power"? Bryan warns me.

"What do you mean"? I question.

Bryan rolls his eyes.

"Are you stupid or what? I'll have to explain it to you, huh"? Bryan scolds again.

Your body has certain points where it can store Sathon. Your head, hands, feet, and chest. As you train and gain more experience with the energy, your body rapidly grows to accommodate the amount of Sathon being stored in your body. However, if someone like you were holding too much energy, then the Sathonic reserves inside your body would begin to flood and overload. The energy would begin to leak out of you as if you were a busted faucet, and soon after you could detonate. You should understand that, since your Sathon would no longer have a stable vessel to reside in. Obviously, this would kill you instantly. Are you sure you want to do this"? Bryan informs me.

I nod, acknowledging the risk.

"I got it. These people need a hero. And they're our people Bryan, they're Lustronese just like us." I spout.

"God, you are just incorrigible." Bryan growls.

With no hesitation Bryan creates a red light in his hand and it grows into a decently sized Sathonic ball.

"Don't die Justin, Jacqui will send me right to you if she figures out, I let you do something so dangerous." He anxiously admits.

He tosses it over to me and I absorb the Sathon, multiplying my power. For a moment, the red Sathon surges and my body shudders, attempting to handle the energy.

"Oh, this was definitely a terrible idea"! I groan as I feel shockwaves throughout my body.

I snicker, grinning at his concern of Jacqui's anger over my own health.

"No promises." As I spout a final joke before taking off into the sky, Bryan stares at me, concerned.

Weighing my chances at succeeding, my smile fades when Bryan can no longer see my facial expression.

"Even if I don't die or get torn apart by this tornado, if it pushes through this energy blast, then the town will be demolished, and everyone here will be doomed." I think to myself.

On my way up, the winds pick up and I struggle to stay up right. My head aches and I heat up exponentially. The relentless downpour continues, and it becomes extremely hard to see where I'm going.

"I'm fine… ow. This pain… oww.! Is manageable, I just have to take my time and go slow. That way only a minuscule amount of energy will travel through my body." I wince, as I float higher into the sky.

I glance up and see something glint in the clouds. Without any thought my body moves on its own! Twisting to the side almost as if I were seeking to shimmy down a narrow pathway.

A lightning bolt rips through the sky, nearly connecting with my right arm! The bolt hits the ground, and an explosion widens, the damage causes a spark in the jungle and a fire ensues. I look down at the jungle, watching the rain combat the flames.

"There's no way I just dodged a bolt of lightning! My body just reacted too. I didn't have time to process that." I think.

My body heat spews energy again and I continue ascending to the sky.

I stop and begin choking. I gag, and my head feels as if it'll explode. I vomit, but only pure energy leaves my body! It's clear and explodes as it leaves my mouth! As I struggle to keep pushing, more energy flows down my face in the form of tears. My body feels like a marshmallow that was just left out over the fire. My mind begins to go blank, and I feel as if my body is melting!

"I have to hurry, I feel the Sathon leaking out"! I scream internally.

As I reach the apex of the tornado, my mind wanders. Second thoughts flood in along with doubt. I look back towards the town and see masses of people leaving behind everything they know, in an attempt to survive.

"Wow, they really have no other options either. I can't back out. These are our people." I roar.

Attempting to end my suffering, I use my full Sathon power to launch myself towards the center of the tornado! The whirling winds catch my body and send me rocketing around wildly in circles.

The blast from the cyclone grips me tightly and seems to start pulling me in multiple directions. I scream in agony, fighting to keep my body intact!

I seal my body in a turquoise Sathon and pull my limbs close towards myself. After gaining energy control over my power, I fire a turquoise burst from my feet, forcing myself further into the center of the tornado. Before the tornado's strength can force me back into its fatal fury, I release all my Sathon fused with Bryan's, in a giant energy bomb.

"AHHHHHHHHHHHH"!!!!!! I scream as the energy tears my limbs. It surges, unrestrained by anything to escape my body.

Like the outstretching blast I used against the cave monkeys. The Sathon flash is a bright violet and once I release all this energy, I can't process sound. I can't see anything but bright violet everywhere.

Before I know it, my battered body drops from the sky like a rock. My eyes clash with the urge to close. However, before slamming into the ground, I am caught by something.

I glance up and see that Jacqui has extended her Bo staff. The very end of my shirt caught onto the staff and because of the incredible strength of the fabric armor, I was able to latch on!

My senses somewhat return, and I gaze up to Jacqui, smiling. She lets me down slowly and rushes over to hug me.

"I can't even lie with you Justin, that was really stupid. But it was really brave too. These people needed a hero, and you came through. I had no clue that you could even hold that much Sathon energy at once." She sobs into my arms.

"I couldn't in all honesty. Bryan gave me almost all his energy. I just flew up there to release the explosion that could destroy the tornado. I felt as if I was going to explode with every breath I took. There was just so much energy in my body. It's just like Sensei said. Once the Sathon doesn't have a vessel to keep it stable it becomes destructive. That energy was definitely leaking out as I made it up to the top of that storm. I just hope I never have to do anything that risky again." I chuckle nervously.

"So, if you have too much Sathon you would explode?! That sounds terrifying." Hailey chimes in loudly.

"Yeah, I think the more I train though, the more acclimated my body will become to the Sathon energy, allowing me to harbor more in my body. The more I practice, the more I can hold and that just means I'll get stronger as time passes." I reply, doing my best to keep my mind cognizant.

Suddenly, Bryan slams into the ground beside the group! Everyone stares at his battered body. Nobody says a word until Bryan sticks his head up, enraged.

"Ouch! Where was my catcher? Nobody cares about me, huh? That's fine guys, I'm only the guy with the assist. It's not like I gave him my energy or anything." Bryan mutters.

"Sorry Bryan! I didn't know you were up there. We didn't see you." Jacqui replies.

"But you're telling me you saw Justin at the top of a tornado and through that giant violet explosion! All of you are terrible friends"!! He yells.

Bryan slow stands over to me and starts to move his hands to heal me. Unfortunately, when the red whirlpools start spinning, he gets a jolt of electricity and falls to the ground.

"Ouch"! He yelps and Dwight helps his brother to his feet.

"I guess I still can't heal you." He comments.

Everyone looks at me nervously now.

"Are you okay? We thought you could just get healed and would be fine. Maybe we really took your abilities for granted". Jacqui admits.

"Come on guys, let's get Justin out of here. We need to find that hospital." Dwight comments.

A tall man approaches us with a sizable crowd behind him.

"Wait, you teenagers are nothing like the Light's description of you. Not like we would trust their words regardless. But we thought you five would be a threat to our peaceful way of life. We didn't think you would risk your lives to save a community you knew hardly anything about." The man admits, admiration spilling from his smile.

Jacqui smiles and visibly lowers her guard.

"Oh of course! You guys were asleep and had no idea of the incoming danger, we had to do our part. Besides, we're all the same, you all are Lustronese just like us." She cheers.

"The Light has damaged our people. If we don't stick together then we're doomed." Hailey comments, grinning almost as big as the tall man.

Runaways

The man steps forward with his hand outstretched to Jacqui. A group of their members rush towards us with a gurney. They lift me up and lead all of us towards the town.

"We're proud to share Lustronese blood with you all. Make Mirra your home for as long as you feel necessary." The tall man offers.

As I look around at the smiling faces, I notice there are a lot of children. Once we arrive at the hospital the members lay me down in a comfortable bed. They rush out and come back in with a huge platter of various foods that I have never seen!

As the table of foods roll in, I spot a dark blue hog in the middle of the table, surrounded by other meats and cheeses. I curiously inspect the new fruits towards the end of the table. After approving of our meal options, I notice all my friend's mouths are watering just as bad as mine.

"When was the last time we actually had a real meal"? I ponder to myself.

I'm snapped from my thoughts as a woman calls my name.

"Justin, we are forever grateful for what you and your friends did for us. We will nurse you back to full health and house you all. Please accept this as a token of our gratitude. My name is Alismet, but you kids can call me Alis." She smiles, her warm grin brings vibes of tranquility to the room.

"Thank you for all of this." I reply.

Dwight quickly fills his mouth full of blue hog. As he tries to speak, cheese spills out.

"It's amazing that you guys had this cooked up so fast! What even is some of this stuff"! He chokes out as he gobbles down the meal.

Everyone stares at Dwight, either embarrassed for him or laughing at him silently. However, the woman keeps her straight face and thanks him for the compliments on the food.

"Hey Dwight"? Hailey questions, a devilish smile appearing on her face.

"What's up"? Dwight replies.

"You gonna chocolate your way onto the horse"? She giggles.

Jacqui spits her drink into her lap, and we all start laughing hysterically.

Alismet stares at us bewildered for a moment but smiles again.

Before she even gets any words out, Dwight holds back his laughter and attempts to act annoyed.

"I...hate... all of you." Dwight rolls his eyes, struggling to hold back a laugh of his own.

Chapter 14:
History of a people

"Well to answer the young boy's question, Dwight, this is the most important meal of our people. We already had everything cooked, in preparation of our annual celebration. That's why we didn't have any lookouts for trouble. That, and we've had a shortage of adults. You kids don't know about Moonlit paradise day"?

We all look at each other, confused.

"No Ma'am, I don't think my friends and I have heard about that." I respond.

"Well, we have a lot to show you all while you are with us." Alis grins ear to ear.

She grabs a chair and begins to teach us about the history of our people. She then yawns as she takes a seat.

"Centuries ago, a small group of the Lustronese people were gifted this energy. The original story has so many different views and the details have long been polluted with exaggerations or just blatant lies. So, I won't get into that part of the tale. The name of this energy over the years changed but now has settled on Sathon. When this energy was first introduced into the world, it was one with the user's life energy or Ki. Over time this ability was used to surpass our human limitations. The ability, to create anything with one's mind was a unique and extremely useful technique. Obviously when other nations of people discovered our ability, jealousy quickly set in." Alis informs us.

"So, the Sathon ability was just exclusive to the Lustronese people"? Dwight questions.

"That's literally what she just said dude. Pay attention." Bryan scoffs.

"Sorry, this food is just so good." Dwight smiles, almost in tears.

Alismet continues.

"These individuals were the only ones in history with this ability, they were instructed to only procreate with other Lustronese people." She states.

"Why? That sounds extremely selfish, hoarding all the power to ourselves"? Jacqui inquires.

"We have a good reason, Jacqui. Our people were created by the deities Lustro and Mirra. Our biology is meant to wield this power. However, there is something inside humans that accelerates the strength of the Sathonic ability and negatively affects the chemicals inside their brain. A fatal flaw in their design I'm afraid. With this flaw, humans have developed extreme emotions, along with anxiety, depression, self-loathing, and a negativity bias." Alis states solemnly.

"Oh, so we're built differently and won't experience those symptoms"? Bryan inquires.

"Not necessarily, we can develop these experiences as well, but something in our genetic makeup allows us to overcome these issues and become more mentally stable as we grow. It seems with humans, the stronger their Sathon ability is, the more demented, unhinged, and despicable they become. Most humans are ruthless and lack empathy. Once they become power hungry, it consumes them." She sighs, scratching her head.

"Good thing we're all Lustros." Hailey darts her head at Bryan and cuts her eyes.

Alis continues her tale once more.

"If the other deities had followed instructions, we would have kept the Sathon ability within our community and it would only be infused with our bloodline. Unfortunately, four of the seven individuals with this ability, did not heed this warning. Lustro and Mirra were the only two that followed instructions. Yintago, Syuble, Hypor, and Matiya went on to create families outside of our nation and eventually left everything behind. For this egregious act, they were punished. Each one of the former deities would be the last to wield their godly form. They were turned into mortals." Alis laments.

"Wait"! Jacqui blurts.

"Those are the names of the other nations around the world! Also, what does this have to do with the Moonlit day? And what happened to Roi? You didn't mention that name." Jacqui shouts.

Alis smiles.

"Don't worry sweetie, it'll all make sense soon. You see, those deities abandoned our people and left all customs behind. After telling their new loved ones about their ability, they hoped to gain admiration, love, and power from this. Which they did, their nations adored them but there were individuals that had deep envy for their ability. Eventually each of those three gods were either seduced or had willingly settled down to create their own families. Each deity had a different quality of energy. I'll explain each quality later, but just know that the Sathon ability was passed along to the humans. Along with the plethora of problems it carried."

Alis clears her throat and takes a sip of water before continuing.

"After some time, these deities passed away and moved into the Chroma realm. Each respected nation honored their gods by naming the country after them, solidifying these individuals as legends. Roi, on the other hand, he was nothing like his siblings in the beginning but ended up becoming worse than all of them in the end. Roi went out of his way to teach his children how to use their ability for their selfish desires and clouded his nation's judgement. They were raised to believe that Sathon was strongest when used through rage." She comments.

"That's because it is. I was taught that from my former Sensei"! Bryan shouts, unaware of his volume.

"Knock it off! We're trying to understand what's going on." I scowl at Bryan.

"Your sensei must have been from the nation of Roi. In a way, he wasn't wrong. But for humans, training them to feed off their hatred and rage for power would immensely accelerate the deterioration of their minds. Even for us Lustros, feeding off rage is dangerous." Alismet sighs

"Right." Sorry about Bryan, he's an idiot. Could you please continue Alismet? Jacqui pleads.

Alis nods.

"After Roi passed onto the Chroma realm as well, his nation ended up leading the way. They started the Scepin war and flipped the script on our people. The other nations followed suit and you know the rest unfortunately. Moonlit paradise day is the celebration of when our people were blessed with the Sathon ability. Sorry about getting sidetracked there, I have a habit of rambling." Alismet admits hesitantly.

As everyone in the room stares at Alis in disbelief, Jacqui stands up.

"Tell us about the three relics." She demands, determined to understand the truth.

Alis looks shocked, but, then smiles softly and ushers everyone besides my friends out of the room. On her way back, Alismet tumbles, crashing onto the floor! She knocks a few chairs over and almost flips the table in the process.

It feels like an eternity as no one says a word or even moves. Alis pulls herself off the ground and sits back down to continue her story.

"Silly me, sometimes I'm just a little clumsy. Now back to the tale of the three relics. When Lustro and Mirra passed into the Chroma realm, they knew that the other nations would revolt against our people. The outside nations wanted to put us down, they had vengeance on their mind, since we had kept the ability to ourselves for centuries. Lustro funneled his power into a flame before he passed. This turquoise flame is rumored to have his Sathon ability within the fire. It would make sense since Lord Lustro possessed the solar quality of Sathon. Mirra possessed the elemental quality of Sathon and left her life force inside a gem. All would have been well, but it seems that Roi knew of this. He repeated their actions before he passed, creating the shadow blade. Roi possessed the shade quality of Sathon. Right now, these relics are hidden where no mortal can travel." She calmly states.

My eyes widen as I look at Alis.

"So, based off the relic, a human could gain these qualities of power? What if the other deities created relics as well? What if there are more dangers left behind than we are aware of"? I ask.

"Yes, I guess that is a possibility. Perhaps a small explanation of the seven gods' powers could help you spot a relic if there were such an atrocity". Alismet replies.

"As you know, Lustro utilized the solar quality of Sathon, sometimes referred to as the light quality. This allowed him to fly and accomplish a variety of feats that other qualities of Sathon cannot replicate. As the siblings worked to create earth, Lustro was responsible for the creation of the sun. Secondly, Mirra possessed the elemental quality, allowing her to control water, earth, air, and fire. Mirra created the planet and shaped all the landmasses you know of today. As wild as those feats are, it only gets crazier. Roi contained the shade quality. Where the light shine during the day, the darkness rules at night. This quality allows the user to enter an almost magical state, shade Sathon users can control others and even summon life forms to do their bidding. Guides of this quality have aura that is always black." Alismet states before stopping and taking a few more gulps of water.

"Sorry, this is just a lot to explain. Anyways, Syuble was a master of the marine quality of Sathon. He created the oceans and all sea-life on earth. However, his strength was so great that the waves became uncontrollable. With the earth in critical condition, he disappeared to avoid the shame. Unlike elemental Sathon. Individuals with the marine quality, chiefly control water particles with their energy. They can also summon past and present sea creatures. Next is Hypor, he was a different child, being the youngest, he was looked down upon. So, he trained alone, at night. Over time, he was able to avenge Syuble by controlling the waves on earth by creating the moon. Hypor can even change the color of the moon and to this day, he alters the patterns of our lunar friend." Alis smiles.

"It's a lot to take in, but we're almost finished. Matiya was the strongest out of the siblings, her combustion quality of Sathon was the most powerful. Although, it was the hardest to control. Matiya could bend fire to her will, along with that, she weaponized all heat, pulling it from the most mind-blowing of climates. With just an iota of heat from her body, Matiya created volcanic eruptions all over the planet!! Singlehandedly ending the earth's ice-age. Lastly, we move on to Yintago, he was an odd child, mostly a bookworm and never really left his introverted stage. However, he learned much about the anatomy of every life-form. It's stated that every land creature was designed by Yintago himself. He knew all. Yintago could hit countless pressure points or Sathon spots on his enemies' body and leave them immobile. He was a master of energy manipulation. His intelligence alone made him a great leader. His IQ was rumored to be immeasurable. He could solve any problem with just a few moments of concentration." Alis comments.

"So much for a small explanation." Bryan grumbles.

I look down at my hands, making a bright turquoise glow.

"So, I found the first relic back when I tried to save Jade from that house fire"? I think to myself.

"It seems your leader has already found the first relic, haven't you Justin." Alis grins, clamoring with excitement.

I look up, laughing nervously.

"Oh yeah, I guess I did a while back, I had found the flame after attempting to save my best friend." I state.

"Once you gain enough energy you should be able to heal yourself back to full strength. Lustro was the only one that could rapidly heal himself and others. It seems that ability has been passed on to you". Alis states as she shuffles over towards me.

Jacqui holds my hand gently.

"Yeah, Justin healed me out of a coma and saved me from an army of Lumin soldiers"! She cheers.

"Then his abilities should only grow with time, the more you use your Sathon, the stronger you will become. Guides with the relic get stronger by just utilizing their energy." Alis shrieks excitedly.

"What about me"? Bryan questions, disdain dripping from each word.

Alis turns to Bryan, still smiling.

"Even without the sacred relic to boost your ability. You should still get better as you become more comfortable with the power." Alis comments with a hefty grin painted on her face.

"Wait, how does Justin's boost benefit himself compared to a natural Sathon user, like Bryan. Or even a human Sathon guide"? Hailey inquires.

"Justin and anyone else that can get their hands on one of the relics will have their power greatly improved after each use. Even if it is something small like creating a flame to warm some soup. This effect is called the Katun ripple. The relic enhances your Sathon. If you're alive, you'll improve no matter what you do. For Bryan however, his ability should improve much slower, but he has a higher peak power in combat. Again, it depends on his type of Sathon. But, if he has the combustion quality, his power will be unrivaled as long as he trains. For a normal human, their Sathon has a nice medium between the two. Their power grows quickly as they use the ability, and it has a high peak power in combat. The issue with their Sathon as I have previously stated, is that it starts to affect their brain and they slowly become unstable." Alis stands up and makes her way for the door.

"I think I've taken up enough of your time, you children should rest. It's late." Alis comments with a warming grin.

"Goodbye"! Hailey and Dwight shout happily.

"Thank you for everything." I smile.

Without another word, she disappears out the door, closing it behind her.

Over the next few days, I rest in the bed. Hot meals, warm showers, and company from the town's teenagers keep us busy.

For a moment I consider the thought of staying a bit longer, but I know we should get moving soon.

I lightly limp over to my bed and sit down. As the television is playing, I decide to turn the volume up and listen in. Jacqui walks in after me, offering assistance.

"You know that I would have helped you back to the room. I don't want you to hurt yourself trying to be one hundred percent healthy when we both know you aren't." Jacqui sternly warns.

"That's a pretty bird." I comment, staring at the television, as I do my best to ignore her.

"What are you in here watching anyway"? Jacqui questions.

As she plops down on the bed beside me, we both focus on the Nero update show.

The entitled wannabe reporter sounds off with his opinions of what's going on in the world and in Nero.

"Good morning, everyone! My name is Joshua and welcome back to the newest episode of NUS! The Nero update show! I have some news that I may have gotten from a little birdy. Now to make sure the government doesn't come after me. My content is simply for entertainment purposes and is completely satire. My show is also full of conspiracy theories, so take all this information with a grain of salt. Now let's get started! I have a strong reason to believe that there is life outside of Nero! Look at what my team was able to find"!

A video of the sky pops up and the ocean is flowing smoothly. Suddenly, the water starts getting rowdy and an ungodly vivid purple light flashes for fifteen seconds before slowly fading back into the normal sky.

The over eager reporter screeches like a giddy school kid.

"Guys did you see that? A bright flash lit up the sky like a firework! But what could that have been? Well, I'll tell you whatever that was, it was a human life that caused it! I'm telling you all, the kings of Nero have been lying to us. Even if you want to say that this video has been edited. Right? I'll go with you just for the sake of argument. There is no way that a bunch of Lustros have survived this long, out in that 'toxic environment.' Those kids aren't even old enough to graduate from high school! The kings are stupid for putting out that advertisement to hunt down the teens. It proves my theory. How could they have survived? If the environment outside of Nero is so 'uninhabitable,' then why don't we just let the children die off? There is no way that they fought off Nero's elite twin duo and have found consistent food and shelter! There is someone out there helping them."

Josh stops for a moment, pushing his glasses back up onto his face.

"There has to be something out there that we don't know about, otherwise why would it be highly illegal to leave the country"?

The comment section lights up with thousands of self-made comedians and scientists. Each giving their opinion about what is really going on.

Josh continues, pushing his glasses up again.

"The Light has been lying to us about the outside world, and we need to discover the truth for ourselves"!

Suddenly, we can hear shouting and banging from behind Josh's door.

"LBI! OPEN UP"! The voices shout.

As the door gets kicked down, the livestream abruptly cuts out.

Jacqui looks at me inquisitively.

"So, what do you think we should do? If this guy who has a sizable online audience, thinks there is life outside of Nero. Then it is only a matter of time before that cavalry of presumed 'heroes' with Sathon powers come searching for us." She comments as she does the air-quotes.

I pause, considering everything.

"Yeah, you're right, we need to leave before we get ambushed again, I don't want anyone else getting hurt because of us. Or worse." I reply dauntingly.

Thinking back to the situation where we lost Sensei Roen.

"I can't believe we lost him over something he wasn't involved with. He really laid down his life for us. I can't have this village hurt because of us." I think to myself.

The pain stings and I brush it off. Pushing myself off the bed I land awkwardly on my leg and hop for a moment before walking out the door.

Jacqui, rushing close behind me, does her best to convince me that I need help walking. Being too proud to accept it, I keep pushing forward. Once reaching the lounge, everyone hops up from the couch to greet me.

"Hey! It's Justin"! My friends shout.

Cheerfully, Hailey and Dwight hug me. Bryan at first is entranced with something on the computer screen but eventually notices my presence.

He walks over and questions my strength on the leg.

"I'm fine, right now we have to leave. I don't want to put this community at risk, the longer we stay here, the more we do just that." I reply.

"What do you mean"? Bryan questions me.

I catch everyone up on what Jacqui and I just watched in the other room. Bryan still looks unfazed.

"It's fine, unlike Roen I'm not a failure. Did you see what I did once I gained his Sathon? He had all that power and Ki control, but no combat experience. What a waste of ability! In a way, it's good he's gone. Now I can realize his true strength." Bryan scowls.

"What did you say!? You better watch your mouth"! I begin to yell.

"Oh please, you're still injured and I'm stronger than you are now. Don't waste our time." Bryan smirks.

"Yeah! Bryan is the strongest now"! The girls around Bryan clamor like parrots and repeat his every word.

"Wow. Is there an echo in here? I keep hearing the same lie over and over." I growl.

"The Lumin forces can't find us here anyway. Roen was the only one who could sense Ki from across the planet and he's dead." He looks back to the girls, hoping to get a reaction.

The girls hanging around Bryan giggle.

I cut my eyes at him.

"Sensei... Roen." I growl, correcting Bryan.

I facepalm and shake my head annoyed.

"Besides, even with that, we should leave regardless. I don't want an army of Sathon guides or ruthless Lumin soldiers on us, especially with all the children in this town. They would devour this place." I lament.

Runaways

Bryan continues to put on a show. Rubbing a little boy's head, rustling his hair.

"I'm sure that we could take them. Isn't that right JJ"?

I look down at the kid, he could be no older than twelve.

The kid flexes his miniature arms.

"Yeah! They don't want problems with any of us"! He shouts, extremely confident.

"I appreciate the offer but nobody in this town is a Sathon guide. There isn't much you all could do, and I don't want anyone getting hurt." I smile before addressing all the teenagers in the room.

A painstakingly long sigh leaves multiple children all at once.

I look back up to Bryan.

"We're going... now! I insist.

"Nah, I don't really feel like it. Besides, who put you in charge? You have no right to bark orders." Bryan bucks back.

"I put myself in charge. You joined me, so you're gonna do what I say! And I'm saying we're leaving"! I bark.

"Let's take this outside then"! Bryan shouts as we butt heads.

As the kids cheer for Bryan, we both head outside. Its dark and it's raining pretty decently.

Jacqui follows us outside.

"I know I can't stop you both from fighting, so, how about this? You can fight for who is the leader, but, not in a Sathonic battle. No powers, and first blood is the loser." She suggests.

"First to bleed is the loser? Sounds good to me." Bryan smirks.

"Let's get started then." I state.

As the rain falls, Bryan and I stare each other down. We both grit our teeth and slowly circle each other. Each step on the muddy earth, puts us an inch closer to the battle. We both spring at each other, throwing a punch. Both our fists collide, and we continue to clash with brutal strikes. Knees, elbows, punches, and kicks all clash. We spring back and Bryan begins laughing at me.

"You're weak Justin. Just looking at you makes me want to gag." He bellows.

"You're jealous of me Bryan. It's clear that you envy me. Even after gaining your Sathonic ability back, you still feel empty." I chuckle.

"I ain't ever needed a false deity to give me power or do a damn thing for me"! Bryan shouts, boiling over with rage.

We both rocket at each other and spin, kicking each other in the chest. As we hurtle back, Bryan springs forward again. He throws a quick jab and I sidestep to my right. I then sweep at his feet, and he tumbles. Before I even think of what to do next, I slam my heel down, hoping to connect with Bryan's chest. Unfortunately,

Bryan rolls and pops up, this time on his hands and he kicks at me relentlessly. His stance throws me off as he is completely upside-down and throws rapid kicks in my direction. One kick lands on my chin and I bite my tongue accidentally. I wince at the pain but do my best to keep a straight face.

"Darn! I can taste blood. I can't let Jacqui see or I'll lose." I think to myself as I catch both his feet, stopping the incoming kicks.

I swing back and lift Bryan. As I go to slam him, I feel a tweak in my ankle and drop his body. Bryan then tumbles on top of me and lands on my elbow. This busts his lip and I begin laughing hysterically. His blood runs down my arm and Bryan attempts to wipe his face quickly.

"No! No! That's so weak! I'm fine! I can go on"! He shouts.

"Nope! That's it. Justin wins. We're packing our stuff, Bryan." Jacqui announces.

"Awwww no." The kids watching begin to whine.

Bryan looks defeated but follows Jacqui back inside the building. My friends smile and do the same. As we pack up everything, I notice we are missing something. As soon as I go to call out his name, Zero pounces onto my back! I grab him, slinging him over my shoulder and hold him up in the air.

"Heyyy! I missed you buddy! Where have you been! Wow. you definitely have grown since we arrived here. Yeah, you're even growing larger horns out your head"! I cheer.

As Zero wriggles about in my arms, I feel them burning.

Justin Avery

"Alright you're getting heavy. I'm gonna put you down now." I smile.

I let Zero down and he scampers over to Hailey. Once she lifts him up, Zero crawls into her backpack. Only peeking his eyes out, the bag.

"I'm surprised you can fit in that bag Zero." Dwight sings.

Dwight shuffles over to her bag rubbing Zero's soft face. As he continues to babytalk him, Alis and a couple adults approach us.

The people behind her have these woven baskets and they look heavy. As she comes to a stop, Alis wastes no time thanking us and the people behind her come forward placing the baskets at our feet.

In a quick exchange, they back out and everyone gives their goodbyes. A young girl runs up and hugs Bryan sobbing.

"Bryan why do you guys have to go! I don't want you all to leave! I'll miss you."

"It's alright, after we save Nero we'll come back, and we can play games all day." Bryan hugs her softly.

The little girl smiles.

We depart from the building and head outside towards our boat, which has been worked on by the people of Mirra!

Chapter 15:
Fuchsia bubbles

We thank them and quickly load everything onto the boat. Wasting no time, Dwight and Hailey take the ship controls and we set sail for another place to settle in at.

As we finally slow down and relax. Thinking back to what Alis told us, I realize we're going to have to change our appearance just a bit too fit in.

"I'll tell everyone later. We still have plenty of hours to burn today." I think to myself.

I glance around and see Dwight laying down on the cushions towards the front of the boat. Zero is fast asleep on his chest. Assuming Bryan is taking a nap as well, I decide to lay my head back, knowing we have a long way until we reach our destination.

As I slouch down, I get an amazing idea.

"I should create some new attacks while we have nothing to do, then at least I can make use of this time. I could even surprise Julien and Adrian if they do find us again." I shout cheerfully.

Zero's ears perk up as he is awoken from his slumber. I raise my hands innocently, almost as if he could understand I didn't mean to disturb him.

Zero purrs, drops his head, and passes out again.

Justin Avery

"He's so adorable." I grin warmly as I ponder.

As I enter my mind and imagine Adrian and Julien cornering my friends.

I gaze around, there are at least one hundred Lumin officers. I turn to see all my friends, armed with various weaponry and staring back with a stoic expression. Each person ready to fight until the bitter end.

Now turning back to see Julien standing on a rooftop with his brother Adrian, no longer looking lost.

"Well, it's about time we met again Justin. You and your pathetic friends have been runaways for far too long! It's time you face your fate." Julien barks.

Bryan loses his patience and launches himself directly at Adrian.

"You'll both die where you stand." He screams, connecting a devastating punch to Adrian's jaw.

As his fist slides off Adrian's jaw, a red flash emits, and everyone charges the opposition, ready to fight.

I turn to Julien, our eyes lock. He wastes no time, Julien sparks golden and zips through the air at me! I hop up and he crashes through the ground beneath me. I look down with only seconds to process his next move. Julien flies up through the smoke he created from shattering the ground and kicks me in the stomach!

I grunt and try to block his next attack but he's too fast and his glowing fist slams into my chest. I disappear in a bright turquoise flash and look up at him from the ground.

"Hey! I'm down here Julien"! I scream arrogantly.

Julien smirks and raises both hands above his head.

My confidence evaporates as I notice a massive golden ball of destruction floating above him.

"What's wrong Justin? All that bravado was so entertaining. Have you finally realized that my power eclipses your own"? Julien laughs maniacally.

With no warning he throws it down as hard as he can. The enormous bomb of Sathon rockets down faster than I expect, especially considering the attack's size.

I hop backwards and brace myself for the explosion. When the Sathon ball collides with the earth, it detonates violently, sending me spiraling backwards.

The explosion slams me into a building and an ungodly shockwave rips up and down my body. I struggle to stand up and notice Julien has taken full advantage of his opportunity.

Giving up his guard completely, he charges with his hand glowing golden. I create a turquoise ring with my fingers and launch it at Julien. He dodges it, still flying towards me at breakneck speed!

I open the ring, pull it back and lock it around his torso. I smile and bring both my hands together. This forces the ring to squeeze him tightly and his hand fades back to normal as he cries out in agony.

"Get this thing off me! Julien writhes.

He grabs the ring, which burns his hands, but he continues pulling it from his waist! I stare at him, appalled, but snap out of it, thinking quickly. I make Sathon bursts jet from the bottom of my feet and punch him as hard as I can. The attack lifts us both back into the air. His face turns turquoise for a moment as he looks extremely disoriented. I start glowing brighter and start my barrage of devastating attacks. Slamming my glowing knees, elbows, feet, and fists into his body!

I create a giant Sathon ball to finish him off. As I charge it up to end my combination, Julien stretches his limbs outward, shattering my turquoise ring.

"That's enough"! He screams loudly, now livid.

I launch my Sathonic ball, but he deflects it without a second thought.

Disappearing into thin air, Julien appears in front of me, punching wildly. I block his blows with my hands. Golden and turquoise sparks flash everywhere, and we take our fight to the earth.

I block a punch and counter by swinging back. To no avail, he blocks my attack, sweeps me, and meets my chest with a crushing punch! Laying on the ground choking and gasping for air, I frantically attempt to spring up before he hits me again.

Runaways

I bounce up with a Sathonic pike and begin slashing everywhere. The pike is razor sharp and you can hear it cutting the air with each slash. I do my best to hit Julien with the pike, but he's too fast. I slash upwards and spin, hoping to catch him off guard. I launch a turquoise tether around Julien's waist with my free hand. I yank him back for a devastating pierce, however, Julien withers away into a golden dust.

Suddenly, he's above me again. This time a golden Sathonic sword in hand. He attempts to pierce me, but I evade his strike.

Julien kicks me back to the ground and extends his hand. I stare at him, petrified for my life.

"You know Justin, the look in your eyes is so worth all the work, all the training I had to put in to get to this point. I'm so glad that I was born a Lumin royal! Goodbye Justin. You put up a good fight." He boasts.

I cross my arms in a 'X' and create a Sathonic orb to shield myself.

Right before he launches a Sathon blast, Julien locks up and falls onto his face!

I freeze for a moment, confused by Julien suddenly stopping. I gaze up to see Dwight behind him with a katana. Julien curses Dwight as Hailey rushes over to help me to my feet.

"They finished all the Lumin officers by themselves"? I think to myself as I freeze, so bewildered by their accomplishment.

Justin Avery

"Justin, finish off Julien while we still can"! They shout, demanding me to act quickly.

I stare down at him and create my signature Sathon blade.

Raising it above my head to finish the job, everything starts to get blurry!

"Do you really think it'll be that easy? Your friends are weak. You all will die if you fight the kings." Lustro chuckles.

"Shut up! Get out of my head"! I demand.

I hear someone calling my name repeatedly and I snap out of my daydream.

"Justin, hey. Are you okay? You were asleep for a while." The voice murmurs in a concerned tone.

I glance up to see Jacqui and the others smiling at me. The sky is now dark and there are trees all around as well.

"Are we in Hypor already"? I question and Jacqui pulls me to my feet.

"No silly, we made a stop for the night since we came across this peculiar looking place." Jacqui laughs.

Still rubbing my eyes, I follow the group off the boat. When I hop off the staircase my body fully awakens.

"Where are we? Is the ground made of... a leaf? A giant singular leaf"? I stutter, puzzled.

Runaways

Bryan and Dwight laugh and take off their shirts before taking a dip in the eerily clear water. As they splash around playfully, Jacqui starts to explain what I missed while I was asleep.

"So, we sailed for a while but decided that we should rest here for the night. But this place seems almost like it was hidden in the middle of nowhere. It's hard to explain but I think the Scepin might have affected this area more than other places." She states.

I gaze around, now registering that this environment looks like a giant leaf but in the center is a huge lake.

"It's almost as if we're ants and this is just a normal fallen leaf with a rain droplet in the center. It's hard to comprehend what I'm looking at." I ponder to myself.

Hailey rushes past us and cannonballs into the lake. Jacqui grins devilishly before she proceeds to drag me towards the water.

"Come on loser, we have to take a dip! This place looks so amazing"! She urges relentlessly.

I toss caution into the wind and take off my shirt before diving into the water. As I swim around, I notice there are giant pink bubbles scattered everywhere!

"What are those things." I think to myself.

Accidentally swimming into one, the bubble gets lodged onto my head. I keep swimming, now being able to breathe with the bubble providing oxygen.

Justin Avery

"This bubble produces oxygen?! What is this place"?! I exclaim.

I gaze upon Bryan and the others swimming around. When they notice what I've accomplished, they grab a bubble and join in on the fun.

We all continue to swim around, exploring the water. There are abnormally sized crustaceans crawling at the bottom and even the fish here are our size!

Once we return to the surface the strong scent of foliage hits our nostrils. The bubbles pop and we pull ourselves back onto the giant leaf. We all laugh and talk about our individual perspective on what we experienced while underwater.

"Hey guys, Bryan and I found this glowing light in the water down there. Don't call me crazy, but it was almost like there was life in that cavern". Dwight chokes out between gasps.

"If there is any life here whatsoever, Zero wants nothing to do with it." Hailey laughs.

Zero peeps his head above the boat's rail at the mention of his name but quickly dips behind it again.

We relax for a few moments, exhausted from all the swimming, when a loud rattling noise breaks the silence.

I toss my shirt back on and it forms into a hoodie, sensing my body heat dropping. Soon after I sense a sizable amount of Ki energy. It doesn't look human, what is the form of this creature"? I ponder.

Runaways

"Is that a snake"?! Hailey shrieks, startled by the noise.

"No, it definitely isn't a snake, it's got multiple legs." I respond.

"You can see it?! How"? Jacqui inquires.

"I can sense its life energy. It's still kinda fuzzy because I'm new to this, but it's not a snake." I answer.

The mysterious being jets away and I settle down. The group starts to relax for a moment when an unsettling screech slaps us from behind.

Our heads whip around as another sound emits from behind us. Nothing happens for a moment, but I keep staring diligently. My patience pays off, but not in the way I would expect.

A giant cockroach with bright pink glinting eyes, scurries towards the edge chasing us aggressively!

We scatter, diving back into the water! Everyone escapes whatever threat that insect could have posed. Grabbing another bubble, I spot the rest of my friends following Dwight and Bryan towards the eerie light at the bottom of the lakebed.

I roll my eyes, annoyed, but decide to follow everyone else. As I'm on my way down, I get the feeling as if I am being watched.

"I hate the vibe I'm getting from these waters. That stupid roach has got me on edge now." I whimper in my head.

Moments later, a giant Koi fish rams into me!

Justin Avery

The bubble on my head pops and I rush towards the light at the bottom faster than before! Gazing up, I know I won't make it back to the surface before drowning. I make a big push for the bottom of the lake! Another fish hits me again and as I attempt to push forward, I am hit again.

"I didn't take a deep breath before that stupid fish hit me! I'm not prepared for this." I growl in my mind.

I feel as if my lungs are on fire, and I do my best to swim faster. I see another incoming fish racing towards me, his eyes glowing bright fuchsia!

"Where have I seen this color before, it's so familiar for some reason." I think.

Runaways

I stop swimming and point my hand at it, blasting the Koi fish where it stands. The fried and lifeless fish sinks to the lake floor.

Others scatter away from me or after the dead fish and begin to feed. Wasting no time, I swim towards the light feeling everything burning in my body!

As I finally make it to the cavern, I fall out of the water slamming onto a hard surface. I cough out some water and look around. Struggling to catch my breath, I lay down for a moment. After glancing around, I see that I am in some sort of hidden pit.

After inspecting the walls and floor, which are made up of some unknown materials, I turn around, seeing that the water doesn't enter the room.

Perplexed by this, I walk back towards the entrance pushing my hand through the water and pulling it back. Still, no water protrudes through such an obvious opening.

"Justin"! Hailey calls out.

"Follow us, Dwight found something"! She shouts, her voice echoing down the vacant halls.

I cough up some lingering water and follow Hailey's voice down the poorly lit hall. As I finally catch up with the group, they seem to be transfixed on something ahead.

I push past Bryan and Hailey to see a huge door. The outline is glowing an ominous pink and the door looks to be made of a different material than the floors and walls. Still, I can't identify what it could be.

"What is this"? Jacqui questions as she presses her hand against the door.

"It looks so... ancient, but the metal and lights give off such a high-tech new age vibe."

Nothing happens for a moment and Dwight takes a step back. His foot sinks in on a pressure plate causing the doors to rise. As we all watch the doors rise, Hailey points out that they are disappearing into the ceiling.

We all walk through the inviting opening looking around cautiously. There are three tunnels ahead and we stare at each other puzzled on what move to make next.

"Every time we split up something bad happens, so let's avoid disaster just this once." Dwight chuckles.

He leads the way down the far-left tunnel, and we all shrug our shoulders at each other, following his lead. A solid door with a pink encrusted message into it, slams down behind us once we all enter the tunnel.

"Well, I guess there's no going back now." Dwight jokes.

Nobody laughs and he presses forward trying to keep up his cheerful mood. I turn towards the stone, making my Sathon energy spike.

Justin Avery

"No way we're getting stuck in here"! I yell reeling back and punching the stone wall as hard as I can.

A violent shockwave ripples throughout my arm and reflects the energy I sent right back, launching me towards the ground! As I stand up dusting myself off, I notice the rock wall isn't even slightly chipped from my attack.

"Well, I guess we're not leaving through that way." Bryan sighs in disappointment.

Dwight just smiles harder.

Don't worry guys! We will find our way out. Let's just stay positive." He insists.

Bryan and I give each other an annoyed expression before simultaneously giving Dwight a glare.

Almost as if I could read his mind. I hear Bryan's voice in my head.

"How long is he going to keep up this charade"?

I bite my lip to avoid laughing and trail Dwight down these winding tunnels. It isn't long before Jacqui notices that Hailey's teeth are chattering rapidly.

"Hey, are you okay? You make a surprisingly good beaver impression." Jacqui laughs.

"Yeah, I'm doing okay, it's just freezing for some reason, and I think I'm claustrophobic." Hailey smiles and responds quietly.

Jacqui's eyes widen and she pulls off her jacket, giving it to Hailey.

"Here, we can't have you getting sick down here." Jacqui replies cheerfully.

Smiling softly, Hailey accepts the jacket and throws it on quickly.

I gaze around inspecting small critters crawling up the walls.

"This place doesn't seem to have been touched in decades." I think to myself.

Hailey runs back up to the front with Dwight and they both skip merrily down the eerie hall.

"How can those two be happy in a place like this. I honestly have to stop my skin from crawling just from the ideas this place gives my mind". Bryan scoffs.

Before I can respond, a thick fluorescent pink door slams down splitting Bryan from the group! I turn and see another door cut Jacqui and I off from Dwight and Hailey. The floor opens below us, and we free-fall towards the bottom.

Plunging into the water below, Jacqui quickly pulls herself onto the solid landmass floating near us. She helps me out the water and we both attempt to dry off.

"Hey Justin, is it just me or is the water down here a lot warmer"? Jacqui questions.

"No, it definitely was considerably warmer for some reason. I also feel like there's a deeper meaning to everything we find here." I comment, taking my soaked hoodie off and wringing all the water out.

Jacqui nods her head, looking back up to the pink stained stone above.

"Wow, we fell from a long distance." She frowns, disheartened, but continues.

"I just hope our friends are okay, especially Bryan, he got separated from everyone." Jacqui laments.

Longing to reassure her, my mouth opens but I stop myself.

"There's not really anything I can say to make her feel better. I can't guarantee anything right now." I remind myself.

Jacqui turns around and we both see a pathway ahead, almost begging for us to trail down it. I turn back admiring the calm water and glowing fuchsia crystals.

"Just look at this place, it's amazing what nature can create." I state.

I pause for a moment, really taking in the scenery.

"This place is gorgeous. It seems whatever is happening, that we should move on, I just feel something in my gut insinuating that we should leave this area". I murmur cautiously scanning the area.

Runaways

As Jacqui and I turn our back to the lights, the pathway begins to appear more inviting. Once we make our way far down the path, another door drops down, denying us the option to retreat.

We decide to look around for another exit, but, once we find nothing, Jacqui sits down on a rock.

"Let's just take a break here for now." She says into her hands.

Out of nowhere, I get courageous and think to myself.

"Well, the others aren't around, maybe now is my time to talk with Jacqui alone."

Smirking, I slide down onto the rock next to her and smoothly rub my shoulder against Jacqui. I slyly convey my hidden thoughts.

"Jacqui, I have a question." I pause, giving my comments some weight as she awaits my next response.

"So, we're close right"? I ask.

"Yeah, of course we are loser, what would make you think differently." She questions, puzzled.

"No, no, I was just thinking about our relationship and uh. How we could be closer than we are now." I respond.

Jacqui looks off into the distance, squinting at something. I ignore that and try to push myself past the awkward moment and just ask her how she feels about me.

Justin Avery

"Well, I mean it's no secret that I have feelings for you, and I was wondering." I pause for a moment, now nervously waiting for her to give me the green light to continue.

Nothing comes from her side, and I decide that I've already pushed this far, so I have to finish.

"So uh, do you like me too"? I question nervously.

Jacqui, still squinting at something off in the distance, now stands up.

"Hey, hold that thought Justin." She hesitates and walks off for a moment.

I look to the floor, my face burning from embarrassment.

"Did I just get curved? Did she just ignore the entire conversation and then change the subject like that? Ugh, I'm so stupid!! Did I rush that"? I think to myself.

I glance up to see Jacqui is still keeping up the act. I roll my eyes, looking back to the ground.

"I totally rushed that. I wish she didn't ignore me though." I admit candidly.

Jacqui chases some small pink sparkle around the cave and crashes into me! We both tumble behind the rock, twisted like a pretzel.

I see the pink sparkle float down and land on her nose and everything goes white.

Runaways

Almost as if I were hit with a Lumin guard's flash bang, my eyes sting from the bright light. I shield them and when the brightness fades, I drop my hands. Looking up, I see a tall pink figure standing above Jacqui and me. We both lay crumbled upon the ground.

As we both rush to our feet quickly, my eyes meet with the figure's. She's tall, and her eyes glisten, almost inviting me to say something to her, but my mind can't form any thoughts. Much less, convey them into a response.

Neither I, nor Jacqui, say anything for a few moments and then the déjà vu hits me. I think back to when I saw these bright pink figures running around and having fun before I had saved Jacqui.

Immense heat radiates from the woman as she steps towards us.

"Don't be afraid, I am not your enemy. It is nice to see you both together after all you have been through".

I smile, thinking about how Jacqui's safe now. All the effort my friends and I put in paid off, because now she's standing beside me. The woman stretches her hand touching Jacqui's nose.

"You have a great amount of hidden potential. Your power will be vital to saving our people. I beg of you, work together, and redeem my failure. You and your friends have a long journey ahead of you, please stop the kings. It pains me greatly to witness the enslavement my people endure every day.

She sticks out her hand, holding a small silk bag. I reach out and take it from her.

"In there, are five pieces of the divine fruit. Don't waste them please. I won't be able to replenish this gift again." She smiles.

"Is this SuperFruiit"? I think to myself.

Her soothing voice interrupts my thoughts.

"Yes, what other fruit would I bestow upon you child"? She grins warmly.

Taken aback, I stare at her.

"She can read my mind? Okay that's wild, noted though." I glance back up, noticing that she seems to be sporting a halo above her head.

After she hands me the bag, she drops her smile and continues.

"I want you both to spread the truth to the world, not just our people. Many may call you imposters or liars, some will attempt to take your life. However, this is inevitable. Gain many friends as you travel around the world, revealing the truth." Mirra states calmly as she lifts her finger and Jacqui ascends from the floor!

Mirra twirls Jacqui around and then presses her two fingers on her chest. A fuchsia glow appears briefly and slowly fades.

"Good luck! We're depending on you all"! The lady cries happily before disappearing.

Runaways

Before I know it, Jacqui and I are back in the area with the lake and fuchsia crystals. The rock we stand on begins to rise and a hole in the ceiling opens.

"Who do you think that was, Justin"? Jacqui questions.

I look at her, shrugging.

"I think that could've been Mirra but who knows. What did she do to you"? I question.

As we reach the top, Jacqui looks at me smiling.

"I'm the one lifting us, loser. She blessed me with her Sathon ability." She giggles.

I stare at her, in awe.

"That's incredible, Jacqui! Wow! So, you can do some of the things Bryan and I can"?

"Yeah, I guess so. My energy feels so different now. I don't understand how you two control this strength. It seems that with my ability, I can control any material the light particles encapsulate." Jacqui looks to the ground still smiling.

Once we reach the top the stone stops and its fuchsia glow fades.

I think to myself.

Justin Avery

"This fuchsia glow, where have I seen it before? The déjà vu is killing me"!

Suddenly it clicks.

"I saw this glow when we attempted to escape from Nero the first time! When I was looking up the ladder, I remember seeing flashes of that energy. But wait? Does that mean that Jacqui has always had this ability and she's just now showing it to me? And the Perdu pills... those are the same color too! Something here isn't making sense. Who is Jacqui really"? I worry inside my head.

"In her soul... dark and light fight for control." Lustro whispers in the back of my mind.

I freeze, petrified of the implications Lustro has been planting.

"Hello? Justin? Are you alright"? Jacqui inquires.

Concealing my fret, I turn to her, attempting to put on a façade.

"That's so cool! I love that you have these powers too"! I shout, exhilarated by Jacqui's new abilities.

"Now let's go save our friends." I beam, overcome with positive emotions. I begin to glow turquoise.

I get in my stance, ready to rush the stone wall and smash through it, when Jacqui puts her hand on my shoulder.

"Calm down hot-shot, I got this." She comments.

I look back, puzzled.

372

Runaways

"Oh, right, my bad Jacqui." I mutter as I power down.

Jacqui floats inches off the ground, glowing brightly. She closes her eyes and puts her hands together in front of her. The wall in front of us trembles and when she pulls her arms apart the boulder splits like paper!

My mouth gapes and I rush over to the remains, holding heavy stones of what is left.

"This boulder was a couple feet thick! How did you split it so easily"?!

She blushes, engrossed by the attention.

"I can see the molecules inside all elements if I focus on them. My Sathon quality allows me to manipulate those particles to my will. The more light that covers the element, the less Sathonic energy is needed. And just like that, solid rock splits like a banana! Actually, speaking of which, I'm starving. Let's get out of here." She suggests as she floats forward.

I grin brightly and follow her lead. Jacqui rips through the stone like a warm knife through butter. I chuckle to myself as we shatter through the rock.

We come to a stop when we find Bryan standing in a room all alone. He turns to us, jolted by our arrival.

"Did you two just walk-through solid stone"!! He stutters as he falls, backing up in fear.

Jacqui now flexes her new abilities just for fun and sinks into the earth! She pops out just inches in front of Bryan and lends him her helping hand.

"I have a lot to tell you and the group when we get back to the boat, but right now we just need to find the others." She grins widely.

Bryan hesitates but grabs Jacqui's hand. After he's on his feet, Jacqui is back underground again, I assume searching for Dwight and Hailey.

I follow the path of gaping holes in the walls and the quaking floor as she leaves us behind. Jacqui is clearly exhilarated by her new abilities.

Bryan lags behind, his hands in his pockets and his head drooped over, clearly still shaken by the encounter. I slow my pace and match his speed.

"You okay homie? You look depressed." I inquire, worrying about him.

Bryan responds, keeping his eyes on the floor.

"Yeah, I'll be fine. I can't even lie to you. I just really envy her powers. Like, that stone was rock solid and made of some mysterious material, and Jacqui just splashed in it like it was a kiddie pool." He mutters.

I smile at him.

Runaways

"Don't stress it man. Your Sathon seems to be better suited for attacks. My Solar quality is just more flexible. I can use my Sathonic ability for an array of problems compared to you. But your Combustion quality packed the power to beat that raging Orange a little while back. With just one kick too! We all have our strengths and that's what makes us a great team." I grin brightly.

Bryan looks up, smiling at me.

"You're right, I'm glad we all have different gifts. If you had my ability, then who would heal us when we needed it most? Sorry about that, being jealous is sort of childish." He admits, rubbing his head, embarrassed.

I fist bump him and laugh cheerfully.

"See, there you go. I'm glad you're feeling better. Let's go catch up with Jacqui now." I reply.

As we both race down the hallway, we end up following the destruction and warped or misplaced stones. After a while, we find everyone.

Dwight and Hailey look to be lost. I walk past Jacqui and help Dwight to his feet.

"What's wrong with you two"? I snicker.

Dwight shoves me off, stumbling around before catching himself.

"What do you meannnnn." He chokes out, slurring his words heavily.

Justin Avery

Dwight gets aggravated and starts throwing his heavy fists around. As he misses me with each swing, he becomes more irate.

"You don't think I'm drunk, or anything do you? Well do you"?! He demands belligerently.

I raise my hands, attempting to exonerate myself from his wrath.

"No! Not at all, just a little inebriated is all." I smirk, looking back at Jacqui and Bryan for help.

They both bite their lip or cover their mouth to avoid laughing.

"I don't know what that means, but it sounds tasty. Do you have some left over"? Dwight questions, leaning heavily.

"I'm surprised you can still stand, what did you two do"? I burst out in laughter.

Hailey stumbles away from me and dunks her head into a waterfall. Gurgling loudly, she attracts everyone's attention. Even Dwight looks over to her, confused for a moment.

Jacqui heads over and pulls Hailey's head out of the waterfall.

"Hailey, I know you're thirsty, but you can't just drink cave water"! She warns harshly.

Bryan bursts out, laughing uncontrollably.

Runaways

Dwight brushes me off and rushes over, dunking his head into the pool of water left behind from the waterfall.

When Jacqui manages to yank Hailey away from the pool, Dwight falls into the waterfall entirely! Bryan runs over and pulls him out.

"Alright that's enough! It was entertaining at first, but it's not anymore. You guys are gonna end up drowning yourself being stupid"! Bryan growls.

"You don't get it, that's not water! It's sugar free"! Dwight chokes out.

I sit back laughing at Bryan and Jacqui struggling with our friends.

"What is wrong with them"? I laugh to myself.

"Why are they even this strong! What's in that water?!! Steroids"!? Jacqui screeches, pulling with all her might to get Hailey out the liquid of joy.

"She's so small! Why is she so strong"?! Jacqui screams again.

I wipe my eyes, tears now streaming freely from my face.

"Okay that's enough." I state as I use my turquoise Sathon to create two chains.

I launch them out and they wrap around Hailey and Dwight. Forcefully yanking them both over towards me, they fly with no resistance.

Justin Avery

"Alright guys let's go back to the boat." I grin confidently.

378

Envious of my quick work with these two pesky kids, Bryan looks at me appalled.

"Clever girl." Bryan snickers quietly.

"I mean that's great Justin. But how are we gonna get them back to the boat? We got in here by swimming." Bryan then questions as he begins filling his black and red bottle up with the waterfall liquid.

"Bryan! You're seriously getting more of that"? I scream as the two lost sheep yank my Sathonic chains in opposite directions.

"I got this guys! Don't stress about that. Everyone get close, we're gonna group hug"! Jacqui butts in.

I drag the chains over to Jacqui.

"Why do you always want to have a group hug. I don't see how this can help, but, okay"? Bryan admits, lightly kicking up dirt from the ground.

The moment we all hug, the earth beneath us rockets us into the air! The ceiling opens and we ascend faster and faster, until we rip through the leaf at the surface.

We all look around, confused and breathing heavily. Bryan freaks out, screaming wildly as he rushes towards the boat.

"What was that!? I never imagined that we could move that fast"! He stares at Jacqui in horror.

Justin Avery

"If I'm being honest with you, I wasn't one hundred percent sure that would work. We would've crashed into the stone ceiling if I messed that up." She slips past me, whispering in my ear.

She keeps her smile plastered to her face as she carries a terrified Hailey to the boat.

Chapter 16: Super Nova

As I drag Dwight over to the boat, I notice everyone is crouched down by Zero.

I release Dwight from the Sathonic chain and trot over to the group.

Zero is hissing, clearly infuriated, and does his best impression of a roar.

Bryan and Jacqui attempt to calm him down, unfortunately they have no effect and Zero rushes around the boat, screeching at something.

"Is there something on the boat"? Hailey murmurs.

Suddenly, a massive beast rips through the giant leaf holding up this area! Just from a small glance, the monster looks to be twice the size of our boat and probably outweighs it and all of us by a couple thousand pounds!

We all stagger back, staring at the enormous monster emerging from the water beneath the leaf.

Time seems to slow down to a stop as I watch the monster swallow Zero whole and disappear back under the water!

"Hell no! Not my baby"! Bryan growls and dives after the monster.

Jacqui rushes to follow, but I grab her arm.

"No, you need to stay here and make sure those two don't drown themselves." I bark aggressively as I go to trail Bryan.

Jacqui looks as if she wants to argue, but, stops herself and rushes over to our friends.

I quickly plunge into the water after Bryan. Without hesitation, I fire Sathon out my hands and feet, forcing myself to go tearing through the water.

I spot Bryan's red aura flashing brightly in the water ahead of me. We continue the chase for a few moments when the beast peers back at us and hops out the water to defend itself.

I splash out the water, my turquoise aura glowing aggressively.

"You're going to die! Give him back"! Bryan screams angrily.

As the animosity builds sky high, I glance at the monster standing before us. Now getting a view of the entire animal, I realize I've never seen or heard about this thing.

"What is this beast? It's mixed with so many various lifeforms"! I growl annoyed.

The monstrosity, on all fours, towers above Bryan and me. It appears to be at least seven tons, and not only that, but its body is large and stout. On top of that, it looks to be built like a hippopotamus, but the animal's skin is rock solid.

Runaways

Just from my first glance I can tell its skin is tough, if anything, this monster could be compared to the old legends of Dinosaurs our parents ranted about.

"Hey Bryan, this thing reminds me of what an omnivore dinosaur could look like. Let's be careful here." I comment.

"I've seen the fossils of those things, but this animal just seems to be the living version of those monstrosities." Bryan responds, his fists balled tightly.

Pondering to myself, I try and piece together what animals were fused to create this life-form. As the beast turns, its weaponized tail drags behind it. Four razor sharp spikes, man the tip of the tail, pointing out in all directions.

Bryan and I step back hesitantly.

"Bryan, is it just me, or is that thing the size of a school bus"? I mutter anxiously.

Bryan doesn't break eye contact with the monster.

"I don't care, I'm getting Zero back or I'm killing this thing! Quit being scared Justin"! He demands.

Bryan aggressively launches himself at the creature's head swinging wildly. His red aura dancing like a flame.

The beast headbutts Bryan's fist and he winces in pain before springing back.

Justin Avery

"That thing's skull is made out of solid rock, man." He grunts as he grits his teeth viciously.

"Are… are you okay Bryan? Your entire hand is swelling up already"! I worry.

Bryan tries to open his hand and an agonizing pop resoundingly echoes.

"Oww!! What was that? My hand is purple"! Bryan cries out as he stumbles backwards.

I rush over to him creating healing whirlpools with my hands.

"Here let me help you." I reply.

"No, you idiot! Get away from me! You're gonna get us both killed"! Bryan screeches.

As I take a step to him, the creature spins, and its tail smashes into my stomach! I go flying and skid to a stop, getting a nasty grass burn from the trip.

I spit up and struggle to pull myself back to my feet. As my hands explore my chest, they reach for my stomach. A quick inspection ensues, and I breathe a sigh of relief.

"If I had been a couple steps back, it's spikes would have pierced my stomach. Thank God that just the tail hit me, I am sure I wouldn't have survived." I fret to myself, shaken by the near-death experience.

Runaways

I finally manage to get back on one knee, still winded from the attack. As my head finally gazes up to see a terrifying sight, I freeze from fear.

The monster paws the ground as it is locked in a death stare, his sights set on Bryan. This monster is in fight or flight mode, and it looks too aggressive to back down.

Bryan, still down on the ground, suffering from the excruciating pain exploding in his hand, doesn't notice the freight train in front of him.

"Bryan, move out of the way! That monster is gonna crush you"! I shout desperately.

Bryan slowly gazes up and his eyes widen.

The beast charges at him! Even for its size, the animal moves incredibly fast. It seems as if everything is happening slowly. All I can imagine is the aftermath once the beast crushes Bryan. Tears swell up in my eyes as I recall everything that happened.

"What could I have done to change this outcome"? I cry out in my mind.

I close my eyes and turn my head, knowing that Bryan has met his end.

CRACK!

I look back and see another giant has barreled into the fray, knocking the monster backwards! As they collide, the enemy beast's mouth opens and Zero flies out! His soft body splashes into the water!

With no hesitation, I quickly dive in after Zero! I search for his bright fur coat in the murky waters. Things only seem to get darker underwater when I finally spot him. A giant hungry fish makes its way towards Zero and I spin, launching a turquoise burst from my foot!

The burst shreds the fish, viciously mutilating its body and I scoop Zero up before pulling us both back to dry land. I lay him down and look to help the new monster that jumped in to save Bryan.

I pause, watching in awe as this beast seems to have it all handled without my assistance.

The new monster has a massive head, which jets outwards, along with sizable horns attached to its skull, keeping its enemies at bay.

Instead of attacking, I rush behind the two, grabbing Bryan and dragging him to safety. After pulling him a safe distance away, I immediately start to heal him and slowly but surely, his bloated and purple hand shrinks back to its normal size while regaining its original color.

As I finish up, we both look back to the battle ground where the new monster flips the other and spins, relentlessly hitting the other with its spiked tail. Eventually the smaller beast retreats into the water.

Bryan and I stare at the victor anxiously.

"Justin, that thing is bigger than the first one! What do these things eat"? Bryan whispers, careful not to startle our friend, for the moment.

The beast turns its head towards us, and we flinch, afraid we'll trigger its temper.

However, the animal trots over to us, it licks Zero with its massive tongue. Zero purrs and shakes himself wildly, spraying saliva everywhere!

"Ewww! Oh, come on." I shout annoyed.

I anxiously turn to the beast and approach it slowly.

"Hey, uh. We don't want any problems, simply curious what you are. Don't attack me, okay? I'm just gonna pet you, alright"? I whisper tentatively.

"Justin no! Are you insane"? Bryan shouts in a whispered but terrified tone.

This somehow works, and I gracefully stroke the beasts face.

This time Bryan gets aggressive, shouting wildly.

"Are you crazy! Get away from that thing or he will destroy you Justin"! He warns.

The monster turns its head and growls at Bryan.

"Uh, I mean, she… will destroy you. Bryan corrects himself.

"Haha yeah, uhh. I'm just gonna wait back here." He mumbles, walking away.

I rub her soft, fluffy head and she smiles at me, licking my face.

The female creature looks totally different from the male. She has a soft fur coat instead of tough skin. In fact, she's much bigger than the male was, and she has four horns on her head instead of the two that manned the male's head.

"Yo Bryan, I think this thing's motherly instinct is what saved us. Do you think she protected us because we attempted to save Zero"?

Bryan gives me a look.

"What are you on, dude? Did you hit your head? Or did you sip on whatever liquid that has Dwight loopy right now? That thing is potentially dangerous and I'm not sure why it saved us, but let's just ditch it and head back to the boat." He scoffs.

I smile, beginning to climb onto her back. Zero follows me up the creature's snout. As he makes his way onto her back, Zero purrs, cuddling my arm.

"I think she's taken a liking to me and Zero. Come on Bryan, she can lead us back to the boat." I laugh cheerfully.

"Dude, are you even sure that thing knows where the boat is? Can we not take this behemoth with us? It makes me feel nauseous." Bryan comments tentatively.

Runaways

The monster growls at Bryan, but I quickly rub her head and she stops.

"Bryan, just get on her back so we can go to the boat." I comment.

"Why God? What did I do? Why does this always happen to me"? He mumbles as he heads our way, slowly.

Bryan shuffles to the side and eventually pulls himself onto the beast. She slowly trots over to the water and starts swimming. Even with her head and majority of her body underwater, we all sit atop her, dry as a bone.

Once we make it back to the boat, Jacqui rushes out screaming.

"Our boat's been destroyed! I think that monster did it." She exclaims loudly.

As she lays her eyes upon us, she freezes in her tracks.

"What the hell are you two riding"? She asks, her face colored with bewilderment.

I snicker and boast arrogantly.

"Well as you can see, we found ourselves a new friend and she saved us from that previous… uhh. What do we call these things by the way? I can't come up with a name". I comment.

"An infestation on my life." Bryan coughs out so the beast won't hear him.

It doesn't work and our new friend slaps her tail on the water. The waves splashes sky high and, on its way, back down, only hits Bryan.

"I… hate… my… life." Bryan murmurs, sopping wet from the splash.

"Well, we were saved by her, and she can be our way of travel now, since the boat is destroyed." Bryan surrenders a reply to Jacqui.

"Oh, now you love her so much, since we no longer can use the boat, huh"? I smirk, eyeing Bryan.

"Don't push it." Bryan growls as he wrings out his shirt.

Jacqui just stares at us with a blank expression.

"I'm not even gonna ask. I'm just gonna grab the others and drag them onto her back. Seems you two have this figured out." She murmurs.

After a few minutes we put everything, we own inside the few storage pods we have left and then everyone walks out towards the water.

Zero is perched atop his new friend's back, fast asleep, and then Jacqui squeals excitedly.

"I have the perfect idea now! Zero falling asleep made me think of how uncomfortable it'll be sleeping on this creature's back. I'll create a huge saddle for her"! Jacqui drops her bags and runs over to the water's edge.

Runaways

She takes a deep breath and brings water out of the lake with one hand and the particles from the leaf come up meshing with it. She continues pulling particles from the surrounding area. Including soft clay and even pulling sap from the trees! The soon to be saddle begins to glow, and a slight fuchsia tint is added.

"Justin, come here and make a blade. I want you to cut this into a saddle."

I'm taken aback at first but make my hand a turquoise blade and get to carving the material. After some time, a huge saddle for our creature is finished. I sit down on the ground, exhausted, and Jacqui levitates the saddle with her Sathon before she slowly places it on the animal's back.

We all climb up into it and lay down.

"Wow, there's a lot of space up here and this ma- material is surprisingly soft. Great work guys". Dwight slurs, still slightly drunk.

"It isn't a boat, but I guess it's alright." Bryan scowls, still annoyed at our predicament.

Hailey, lying face down glances up for a moment. "We should name her." She murmurs sluggishly.

"What did she say"? Bryan comments, his arms still crossed as he stares into the sky.

Justin Avery

"She said. We should name our newest member to the group." I state beaming brightly.

"The fact that you even understand a word she said is amazing. That's gotta be some kinda talent. While you two were gone, I was so confused on what they wanted." Jacqui complains as she rolls her eyes.

Dwight perks up, hearing some disrespect being thrown his way.

"Jacqui got mad at me for losing half of our storage pods in the water. But, what she... she didn't realize, was that I was making myself breakfast"! Dwight rolls over and begins lamenting his pain.

"Dwight, you were blending Zero's food and our juices. What were you expecting me to do? Why did you grab his biger food anyway"? Jacqui rolls her eyes.

"Protein is why! I was hungry and thirsty at the same time! You can't blame me for wanting the most important meal of the day. They're great"! Dwight argues back.

"It's one in the morning"! Jacqui scolds back.

I chuckle, pausing for a few moments.

"Well, Hailey's right. We should name her. I don't wanna call her a monster or beast anymore." I state.

"Name her whatever you feel like Justin. You're the only reason she's even here." Bryan scowls, staring off at the bright stars showered across the night sky.

"Bryan, stop acting so sadiddy. Sheesh, just lighten up for a little while." Dwight mutters, still sluggish from whatever drink he had earlier.

"Sadiddy? What does that mean"? Jacqui questions.

"Oh, you know... snobbish, arrogant, uppity. Basically, slang for people like Bryan who feel superior". I concur.

Surprisingly, Bryan unfolds his arms and smiles.

"Alright, you win, I know I've been pretty difficult recently." He admits.

I almost get lost in the view of the starry night myself. Then a name hits me.

"Nova, we should name her Nova"! I shout.

Hailey groans and covers her ears. "Shut up, shut up, shut up... you guys are so loud all the time." She mumbles, kicking her feet around like a child.

I burst out laughing and pull myself off the saddle, now sitting on Nova's massive head. I rub her fluffy mane and speak softly to her.

"You hear that girl? You have a name now! Welcome to the team." I cheer quietly.

Nova bellows in what I'll assume is joy, and I rub her head some more, before rolling back into the saddle.

"Alright guys I'm gonna pass out now." I comment.

Nobody responds as Dwight and Hailey are out cold.

I glance over to Jacqui, who is drifting off slowly, but fights to stay awake. Bryan stays silent as he continues staring towards the sky.

I smile and lay down before rolling up in my blanket and passing out.

When I wake up, Hailey is laying on Nova's head. My eyes struggle to open because of the bright sun, but it appears as if she's talking to Nova. I can understand a few words here and there, but Hailey is having an entire conversation with Nova.

I shake my head, rubbing as I rub the sleep out of my eyes.

"Hey man, we're close to Hypor. The map says we're only a few minutes out." Bryan helps me to my feet.

I nod, still trying to wake up.

"Wait, Bryan. How did Nova know where to go"?! I stare down at our massive friend.

"Is this thing a mind reader? This doesn't even make any sense." I gasp, thinking to myself.

Justin Avery

"No? What? Justin are you good, bro? Jacqui created some sturdy rope and I used it like a leash. It's just to guide Nova in the right direction. After a while she didn't need me to guide her, and Nova kept swimming straight." Bryan replies.

"Oh. Yeah, that makes a lot more sense." I chuckle, nervously rubbing my head.

Jacqui calls out to everyone, beckoning them to gather around.

"I'd say in about an hour we'll arrive at the shores of Hypor. Now, we must think about this, there are probably people here as well. If what Mirra told me is true. There will be people that will be willing to help us, but there will also be enemies. Many more out to harm us, than help us. We must blend in and figure out if there are any Sathon guides here that would join us, or maybe even a teacher that could train us to manipulate our energy better. I want everyone to stay vigilant. Nothing stupid, risky, or attention seeking. Be careful when you're out there." She preaches sternly.

Bryan rolls his eyes, clearly not taking her seriously.

"What if we end up getting exposed. Walking around the city as a group is just begging for attention. We need something that'll keep us concealed in the background." He comments.

Dwight's eyes light up.

"I got it, guys! We all should go to school like the other kids, and we could blend in there! We could find a bunch of disgruntled people at school too. Maybe enough to stand up when we make our return to Nero". He cheerfully states.

Runaways

"Then it's settled, we'll all attend the same school, so if we need to, we can help out. However, from the first day of class, we don't know each other in public. Hanging around in our group might make us easier to recognize." Jacqui spouts.

"Ooh, we should probably change our clothes for now too. I think they're a dead giveaway." Hailey laughs.

"Aww man. I'm gonna miss my lightweight armor hoodie." I whine.

Bryan elbows me in my arm.

"At least you have that. We never got anything from you or Jacqui." He growls.

"What's with the animosity, chill Bryan. I didn't even know you existed at that point in time." I argue back.

"Enough, we shouldn't need anything like that right now anyway. Stay out of trouble and I'll get you guys some lightweight armor after we figure out what we need to do"! Jacqui shouts, frustrated.

"I call keeping Zero and Nova with me"! Hailey shrieks.

"They're going to be my pets while we do this mission and I'll make sure to keep them out of trouble." She claims.

Bryan and Jacqui give her a look.

"Uh, Hailey. I can understand you keeping Zero with you, but how are you going to pull off keeping Nova from looking suspicious? She's a massive Hippo thing with fur." Jacqui comments.

Hailey's smile fades.

"I guess that's fair, okay. I'll just keep Zero with me. Sorry Nova." She sighs, folding her arms and kicking at the floor of the saddle in frustration.

Nova bellows.

"Also, Justin and Bryan. No using your Sathon abilities. It's too risky." Jacqui claims.

"Alright bet, then it's agreed, well I'll see you all when I see you. We come back to Nova to sleep at the end of the night just in case that wasn't obvious." I state.

I give everyone a glance, awaiting an agreeing nod before I move on.

"Okay, now let's switch these clothes out for new ones." I chuckle.

Nova looks back and slows to a stop before we reach the shore. Dwight hands out our clothes to us and slips behind Nova to get dressed.

"Man, I really do miss the privacy of having my own room to get dressed in." Hailey wails.

Bryan perks up to the sound of this.

"Oh, so you hate that we lost the boat too? Because I hate this tradeoff"!

I cut him off.

"It's not a tradeoff, Bryan. The boat was busted because of that monster. We're honestly lucky to have a way of travel and thanks to Nova you're still breathing to even say something so insensitive"! I scowl.

I step closer, getting into his face.

"And I'm getting really sick and tired of your pessimistic attitude all the time. It's getting old. Quit acting depressed since I'm stronger than you! Would your mother like this?!." I shout.

Bryan shoves me backwards.

"Get out of my face! Keep my mother and her expectations for me, out of your mouth! I'm not taking orders from you or anyone here! I'll do whatever I like and say whatever I feel! I do as I please. As for my strength, I think it's about time I did something to change where you and I rank"! Bryan grits his teeth irately while he clutches his clothes tightly.

He begins to glow red before shooting off like a rocket, disappearing off into the city.

"Wait! What happened to not using our Sathonic powers Bryan"? Jacqui cries out.

It's too late though. Bryan is long gone and completely out of earshot by the time she finishes her sentence.

Justin Avery

"That was reckless. Hopefully, nobody saw him." Hailey mutter.

"Well, everyone be safe and try to have fun." Jacqui whimpers, clearly disheartened by the quarrel between Bryan and me.

Everyone nods at her, smiling.

"We'll be safe Jacqui, we promise. This isn't some vacation." Dwight says, attempting to encourage her.

I disappear off the back side of Nova. Sliding down her tail, I balance on that, and switch my clothes.

"I should definitely keep this armor under my new clothes. If I need it, it'll still do its job." I think to myself.

When I finish getting dressed, I jump up and pull myself onto Nova's back.

"Okay guys! I'm gonna go now"! I shout as I glow turquoise before levitating and flying off like Bryan did.

As I'm zooming through the sky, my stomach growls loudly. I search around for something to feed my appetite. My eyes water with joy when I spot a breakfast spot, and I discreetly descend behind the building.

Promptly walking around the corner, I enter through the front door. As I clean my shoes off on the welcome mat, the bell on the front door rings.

Runaways

A group of upbeat cheerful employees greet me excitedly as I make eye contact with each of them.

"Hello there!" They shout.

A lady rushes over to me and quickly seats me at a table full of other teenagers who look to be around my age. Before I can get a word out, she disappears back behind the counter and the group chuckles.

I smile nervously.

"Sorry about that guys, I'll move since you're probably waiting on someone." I mumble nervously.

An older guy waves me off.

"No, you're all good. Please sit. Our friend probably isn't showing up anyway". He assures me.

I grin and sit down slowly, thanking him.

"So, what's your name"? The girl sitting beside him asks me pleasantly.

"I'm Justin." I state, smiling back.

Instant regret fills my body.

"Why did I tell them my real name"! I scream internally.

Nobody changes their expression, and the girl keeps smiling.

"That's a pretty name, my name is Sapphire. Where are you from"? She questions.

I freeze.

"I don't know anything about this place. I usually am a good liar, but I didn't plan anything out." I worry to myself.

"I'm actually new here, I don't really know the area just yet." I comment, scratching my head nervously.

"Justin is not a pretty name, it's pretty common if you ask me." A guy at the corner of the table spouts.

Sapphire quietly slams her fist down onto the table. She grits her teeth, growling in an angered whisper.

"Can it, Lewis! Do you always have to be rude"? She demands.

Completely changing character, she turns back to me.

"Sorry about that, Justin. Lewis is an only child, so he doesn't really know how to behave himself in public. His parents let him do whatever he wants. But this is Violette, you just met Lewis, and this is my boyfriend, Rj." She smiles brilliantly.

Everyone introduces themselves and we all make small talk as we await the arrival of our food.

The lady from before returns with a stack of plates. As she hands them out, my mouth waters and my stomach growls again.

Runaways

"You okay over there, Justin? Your stomach is growling as if you haven't had a real meal in a week or so. Rj laughs and tells everyone to dig in.

"Well, he's not wrong." I chuckle internally.

"I guess Ms. Sandra must've figured you were our friend Zakari. He never shows up, so she's never seen him before." Sapphire comments as a cheerful grin covers her face along with syrup and pancakes.

I stuff down some food, thinking for a moment before responding.

"You guys must come here often then. She didn't even take our orders before coming back with all this food." I laugh.

"We come here every Saturday. You should hang out with us, Justin. You seem like a cool person." Violette joins in.

Sapphire agrees loudly, communicating with obnoxious chewing.

She finally finishes and speaks.

"Definitely, you can just take Zakari's spot. It's not like he ever hangs out with us anymore". Sapphire laments.

Rj frowns for a moment.

"Yeah, I miss when we would all hang out. Feels like forever since I've even heard from him." He laments.

Rj flips his frown and smiles.

"But we have you now, so everything is looking up again." He states.

"Yeah, Zakari used to be here a lot, but once he got a girlfriend that was 'Goodnight Irene' to our hangout sessions." Violette complains.

"Hopefully, you're not Fugazi like him." Lewis mutters under his breath.

"I'm sorry what"? I question.

"Fake. You could also use the term on our friendship with him, broken." He replies.

"Riveting... I'll be sure to keep that in mind." I painfully state, forcing a smile.

"Don't listen to him, Lewis is a little odd, continually responding would only goad him to say something you'll disagree with. He likes to argue." Sapphire whispers to me.

"Oh, okay then." I nod my head.

I beam, gladly accepting their invitation of friendship. As we talk some more, I begin to learn a little about each one.

Rj is currently running for president of the student council, and pretty much has everything going well for him. Both parents living together, siblings doing well academically, and he even has a scholarship to a school in Nero!

Runaways

Violette is eerily quiet overall. Almost the opposite of Sapphire's outgoing nature. Both girls have similar aspiring goals to become students at universities in Nero. They want to either study children's psychology or sport's medicine.

Lewis on the other hand, he seems to be content with life, he has no goals to move out of Hypor. In fact, he even says he wants to relax until he can collect his parent's large inheritance.

"Tell us about yourself, Justin." Rj requests as he downs his coffee.

While mentally noting all the details about their lives, I tell a half lie about my own.

Chapter 17:
High school Shenanigans

"Well, my parents split when I was younger. I bounced around Nero before my father took me out on his business trip. I guess he has to study life-forms from the other nations". I reply.

"Whoa, that's super cool Justin! I thought nobody could leave Nero. Are the restrictions lifting"? Sapphire questions.

I lie again.

"Between me and you all, I'm not supposed to mention it, but we're here because the kings let him leave on a high-class security mission and we're supposed to keep quiet about it." I grin sinisterly.

"I shouldn't be this good at lying." I ponder to myself.

"So, the kings of Nero are finally letting people leave the country and explore the world? Last we heard, there were a few fugitives that escaped from the nation and are being hunted as we speak. Have you heard about them"? Sapphire questions.

I wipe my brow nervously.

"Oh yeah, those kids are way in over their heads. Nero wants to stomp them out because apparently, they found some information and want to expose the truth about the war to the Lustronese and Lumin people. Most people in Nero don't even think outside life exists, the kings are working on how to ease the news in. It's tricky because they have to do it without causing a panic or raising suspicion". I state.

They all laugh and continue eating.

Lewis speaks up.

"Even if those kids managed to expose the truth. Which they wouldn't because the Lumin military would crush them if they ever tried to return. But regardless, even if they did. The Light would just deny the war and any knowledge of the outside world. The kings would end up claiming to have wanted the safety of their citizens to be a top priority, and all panic would cease. And with that, so would the fugitive's hopes of a revolt. They would need both the Lumin and Lustronese people to stand together, and we all know that's never happening." He laughs maliciously before continuing.

"I'm not gonna lie, they make me sick, but the kings are hella clever, the way they plan to disguise and fix their mess is absolutely impeccable." Lewis chuckles.

"Wait, what do you mean"? I question anxiously.

"Oh, come on Justin, you don't know? In less than a year from now they're going to kill off the rest of the Lustronese people and use the sacred items to create some weapon that'll wipe out all life outside of Nero." He casually goes back to eating.

"Wait! A weapon? Mass genocide? Why aren't you guys worried about this!? The Light is going to kill off an entire race of people"! I shout queasily.

Rj laughs.

"Oh, relax Justin. After they're all killed off, we're moving in to take their place. All the nations know of each other's existence and know that it's just a matter of time before we can all reside in Nero together." He comments.

Rj takes a bite of his biscuit before continuing.

"Well, all of the nations except for Mirra know about the plan. That place has been abandoned for decades. My dad tells me." He turns to me with a menacing smile on his face.

"Don't you get it Justin? We aren't in danger. All humans of each nation will be spared, while the Lustronese slaves will be wiped out. They are starting to outnumber us, it's better to put a sleeping beast down before it can be awakened." He spouts confidently.

Violette breaks her silence.

"Why do you care about those worms anyway? They bombed and killed our people, then vehemently denied the idea of sharing their land after everyone signed a treaty. If it wasn't for our great leaders from each nation taking them down, we wouldn't even be sitting here". She states.

"The Lustronese people attacked us and poisoned the planet with Scepin, they were going to let us all die. They deserve to be extinguished." Lewis growls.

I begin to scream in my head.

"That war had nothing to do with my people, they really do despise us. They have no clue that each king played a role in attacking each other's nation and then flipped the blame onto us"! I erupt inside my head.

I lose my appetite and stare at my plate, wondering how much longer I can masquerade as one of them.

"We have to get moving now! There's no way we can stop them if they get their hands on the last two sacred items. They'll wipe out my entire heritage and we would have escaped Nero for nothing"! I think to myself.

"I'm surprised you didn't know all that, with your dad having top secret clearance and all." Sapphire eyes me oddly.

I struggle to put a smile on my face and respond quickly.

"Oh yeah, he doesn't really tell me a lot. Ya know... it's super important stuff." I nervously comment.

Sapphire's phone rings.

"Hey guys, we should head towards the school now. We're going to be late, and I'm not trying to hear Mrs. Jefferson's voice again". She groans.

We all quietly get up from the table and I watch Rj leave one hundred dollars under the cup as a tip!

"Geez, this guy must be made of money"! I think to myself.

I follow everyone outside. Sapphire unlocks her car, and everyone hops in. She looks over to me from the driver's seat.

Justin Avery

"So, I'm assuming the entire planet, outside of Mirra and the Lustronese population, hates us. It's a shame that the kings had the autonomy to convince entire nations of such pathetic lies. As fragile as they might be, it's going to take a lot to prove that these stories aren't truthful." I ponder to myself.

"Well? You gonna get in, silly"? Sapphire questions me.

I snap back from my thoughts and hop in the back seat.

"Oh right, thanks by the way." I answer tentatively.

As we settle in, some music blasts loudly from her speakers.

"Oh yeah! This is exactly what I needed before school today"! She screams loudly.

Rj rolls the volume all the way up and Sapphire presses the gas, sending us flying down the road.

I look out the window and do my best to focus on sensing Ki. The loud music makes it difficult to focus, but from what I can manage to capture, there aren't a lot of people in this city.

We drift into the parking-lot and Sapphire parks sideways before shutting the car off.

"Alright let's go! We have a meeting in the cafeteria and then I'll see you all at lunch, okay"? She shouts.

Everyone pours out the vehicle and we head towards the school. As I approach the building, I can't help but notice the exterior.

Runaways

The building looks nothing above average.

"After all the money that I can see they possess, why is their school so average? This looks no better than the town hall in Joviality." I think to myself.

On my way into the building, I follow a huge crowd into the cafeteria, where I notice Jacqui sitting up front. She's surrounded by a huge group of people.

The majority are guys, and they all look to have more money than my new friends! I turn to Rj.

"What's up with that group over there? They look like they could buy this school." I comment.

Rj shakes his head annoyed.

"I hate those guys. Bunch of rich pretty boys who think they run the school. They pretty much get whatever they want, there have been many drug allegations pinned to their names, but their parents have so much money that it doesn't matter. Not to mention that nobody challenges them because of the havoc they'd cause when they retaliate to ruin your life." Rj replies.

He scratches his head.

"I don't recognize that new girl with them though. I hope she knows about what most girls have been through, when hanging out with that shady group, it's not pretty." He spouts anxiously.

Justin Avery

I follow his eyes and realize he's talking about Jacqui! Something inside me makes me long to storm over there and yank her away from them, but I can't.

"Can't blow my cover, calm down Justin." I repeat to myself in my mind.

I just take a deep breath before I sit back in the seat next to Rj and a few of his friends. As I search around the cafeteria with my eyes, I spot Dwight, Hailey, and Jacqui, but fail to find Bryan. Suddenly, the lights go out and a tall and older looking woman walks out on stage.

A few people rush in and let down a projector and she smiles brightly as a video cues up on screen. As the video starts, a flag appears on screen, and everyone stands in unison.

I stand up quickly, trying not to bring any attention to myself and move my mouth, acting as if I know their national anthem.

I notice teachers and security are walking around the area making sure everyone is reciting it. Rj glances to me perplexed, and I make eye contact with a security guard! The huge, walking refrigerator of a man, gives me a cold glare and I freeze.

Now to avoid Rj and the security guard, I stare forward, hoping neither of the two recognize that I'm an outsider.

After the anthem ends, the security guard makes a beeline for me! He grabs me by the shirt and drags me off to the side.

"Where is your school uniform"!? He gives a nasty growl and angrily hisses.

Runaways

He looks so livid. I believe that he could bite his tongue off in the heat of the moment.

I look down at my clothes and then around to the other students before I realize everyone is wearing the same uniform.

"How did I not notice that before"?! I scream internally.

The guard tightens his grip and pulls me closer, his greasy head pressing onto mine.

"Well, boy! Where is it"? He repeats.

The security guard's breath stinks badly and his teeth are a plaque yellow color. In my head, I laugh to myself.

"Bro, do you eat rocks? What's wrong with your teeth"? I laugh to myself.

Rj rushes over, tapping the guard's shoulder rapidly before whispering in his ear.

"Justin here, is new, and he will have a uniform after the assembly is over with. I'll give him one of mine." Rj assures.

The guard drops me, and I hit my tailbone on the floor! I end up biting my lip, so I won't scream in the dead silence of the cafeteria and bring more unwanted attention.

Rj helps me to my feet, and I whimper, rubbing my rear end while limping back to my seat.

Justin Avery

"You doing okay, man? I'm sorry that happened to you. Just be thankful you got friends in high places." Rj smiles and chuckles.

I give him a thumbs up and keep my eyes on the lady on stage.

"By the way, Justin, that's Mrs. Jefferson. Stay out of her sight, you honestly don't want her to know your name. Even if it's for a good reason." He comments quietly.

I nod my head, keeping my eyes forward. I can feel the guard's eyes burning holes into the back of my head. I just know he's staring at me.

"Good morning school"! Mrs. Jefferson chirps excitedly to us.

Something about her smile just feels forced and makes me distance myself from the leadership in this school mentally.

"I'd rather take care of a drunk Dwight right now, than listen to this filth speak." I murmur to myself.

Mrs. Jefferson starts.

"We are so excited to share this information with you all! We knew you lot with more financially stable families have already heard, but it's official now. One of the three sacred relics have been found! The Lumin leadership are currently in the process of adding the item to the weapon that'll wipe out all of the Lustronese people and we will finally be welcomed back into our home"! She cheers.

A thunderous roar from the crowd of students rips through the air and her grin grows larger.

414

Runaways

I look to Dwight and his face drops. He spins his head around searching for me.

When our eyes lock, we both nod, knowing we have to meet up tonight after everything is over and I make the same mental agreement with Hailey when her eyes meet mine.

When I look up front to Jacqui, I see her giggling with her new friends, and they hop up from their seats and depart from the cafeteria!

I almost scream out in rage, shocked at what I just witnessed.

"How can they just walk out of a meeting so important to this school. I almost was choke slammed for not having a stupid school uniform, but them leaving whenever they feel like isn't considered disrespectful"?!! I think to myself.

Over the next few minutes, the students are shown statistics about my people having a lower income, a lower hiring rate, and leading in crime statistics. The students growl and many shout out about how we should be wiped out so they can go back to enjoy the homeland.

Many students start small chants about how we're the most disparaging race of people to ever exist.

Others throw things and Mrs. Jefferson grins sinisterly on stage, even encouraging some of the chants. At one point she hushes everyone.

"Now, my beloved students. The kings of Nero wanted me to share this with you all. Your parents should already be aware but if they aren't, please inform them. Unfortunately, the weapon has about a year left before being finished if the timetable we received is accurate. So, while we wait patiently for the extinction of the Lustros, I need you all to be aware of some things. There are some fugitives going around, apparently trying to find something that links the war and our nation's past. As you all know, our past relates to the other nations. If those kids use their Sathonic powers and convince their people that there is hope, they may cause another revolt." She pauses as many shocked gasps escape students in the crowd.

"We will not be allowed to join the homeland if they are successful. The kings of Nero may use their weapon on us if we fail to contain this issue. So, if you see anything suspicious, please report it to Lumin officials. It's highly unlikely that the fugitives are on Hypor right now, and they would be foolish to be in this very room. However, if those kids can spill the truth to their people, they have the numbers to take Hypor down." She admits candidly.

"Now to add some good news to wrap up this assembly, we have the weapons, and we also possess the rare Sathon wielding twins"! Mrs. Jefferson exclaims.

The crowd roars again as Julien and Adrian step onto the stage! I stare onto the stage in horror.

"No…No! How?! No! What are they doing here"! I fret terrified inside my head.

Mrs. Jefferson continues.

"These two fine boys are here to recruit any students that possess the Sathon ability. Anyone who joins will be given better food, their families will be moved into Nero, and they will have the honor of hunting down those criminals who dare defy the kings! Julien and Adrian will only be in the city for a few days, as they must move onto the next nation to continue their recruitment and search. So, please meet up with them after the assembly if you're interested! Everyone have a good day in class, and I hope you excel in all your studies"! Mrs. Jefferson finishes.

The lights flash back on without warning. Blinding everyone for a moment.

I grab Rj and rush him out the cafeteria doors.

"We need to go to your locker now! I have to get a uniform on". I shout.
Rj eyes me distrustfully.

"You okay? You seem nervous about something." He questions.

I escort him down the hall, doing my best to create distance between myself and Julien and Adrian who would easily recognize me if they spotted my face.

"I'm fine! I just don't want to get in trouble already. I just got here." I murmur as I stare over my shoulder worriedly.

Eventually, I convince Rj to lead me to his locker and I grab the uniform before quickly running into the bathroom to change clothes.

Justin Avery

As I slide into the second stall I relax and put the toilet lid down before taking a seat. I hook the hanger on the side of the stall and rest my hands on my head.

"Julien and Adrian can't really be here. This situation couldn't get any worse. Of course, the first civilization with a sizable population has to despise our people. I don't know how we're going to communicate with each other at night with all the people wanting to be outside and around Julien and his brother. This town is going to be bustling." I mutter annoyed, as I slip the uniform on. As I button everything up, suddenly, the door rattles and I hear Adrian's voice!

I pull my hand back from the lock and peek my eye through the door space.

Julien slams the door after a few moments.

They look around as if awaiting someone to speak up from the loud noise. When nobody says anything, Julien stares into the mirror. His patience thins and he kicks the trashcan across the bathroom!

Used paper towels fly everywhere and Adrian shouts at Julien.

They argue for a moment and Julien pulls away, staring back into the mirror.

"Why do we have to search for recruits all over this god-forsaken planet! You and I can take them by ourselves." Julien complains.

Runaways

"I don't know. I don't even want to do this. Why are we hunting down people our own age? This feels so wrong, we should be enjoying our summer right now like some normal teenagers." Adrian mutters.

Julien yanks Adrian up by his shirt aggressively. He slams him into a wall.

"We aren't normal teenagers though. Are we? I've been getting tired of your nonchalant attitude lately and if I hear any other comments like that, I'll deem them treacherous. Julien barks.

Adrian's eyes widen.

"No! I'm not thinking about leaving or abandoning our mission. I would never! I just wish we could relax sometimes." He whimpers.

A devilish smile plays along Julien's lips as he gazes down at his brother.

"Good. It'd be a shame if the kings heard you were being defiant." Julien smirks as he lowers Adrian to the floor.

"Relax bro, we can be normal teenagers when we get rid of the Lustronese vermin and stamp out these fugitives. They're the enemy. They're the only reason we can't be relaxing right now." Julien says softly, attempting to calm his brother.

"It just feels so wrong, killing off a race of people, just to be 'normal' again. I miss mom, Julien." Adrian states, his eyes pointed to the floor solemnly.

I brace, fearing for Adrian. However, Julien's outburst of rage never comes. Instead, he rubs his brother's head and rustles his hair.

"I know. Me too bro, me too." He whispers.

Julien hugs his brother and lifts Adrian to his feet.

"Now let's get out of here before someone walks in on us." Julien orders.

As they both exit, I peer through the door crack at the mirror, trying to gauge if the front door has closed yet. Once I hear it click, I step outside of my stall, breathing heavily.

"What the heck was that? There's so much I'm trying to process right now." I gasp.

"So, there's a weapon that could wipe out my entire race, it'll be prepared in a year. The Lumin forces have found a sacred item. It could be the gem or the shadow blade. Julien and Adrian are here in Hypor searching for recruits from each nation. Bryan is nowhere to be found after our fight and Jacqui is caught up in a group of guys with questionable character to say the least. Why does this all have to happen right now"!? I growl.

It takes me a few minutes to recover, and I stand up confidently.

"I can't just give up because I'm rattled. I have to find my friends and explain the situation". I grin.

As I exit the bathroom, I look both ways making sure my enemies are clear out of sight before I enter the hallway. As I am peering down the left side of the hallway, a familiar voice calls out to me.

"Justin, come sit with me in my next class. Pleaseee, it's super boring and I hate it."

I turn and see Sapphire looking cheerful as she begs for me to join her.

"It's my study hall class and there's nothing to ever do in here. Please come sit with me"? She pleads again.

A wave of relief flushes over me. I'm excited to see a familiar face around this bland school.

"Of course. Let's hurry up before we're late." I agree eagerly.

She smiles and we both head down the hall and enter a colorful looking classroom. The walls are painted red and have plenty of art from previous students over the last few years plastered on.

I follow Sapphire and we both sit down at a desk in the back of the classroom. As the bell rings, everyone pulls out their phones and begins intermingling amongst themselves.

The teacher doesn't pay the volume any mind, allowing all the students to do whatever they please. I look back to Sapphire who's beaming brightly.

"I'm glad you decided to come sit with me, I really appreciate it." She states.

"Oh, it's nothing really. I was sorta lost and ran into you so I'm glad you asked me to come with you." I comment with a huge smile on my face.

As we chat about things in the city and what we usually do for fun, the door swings open. Everyone in the class stops talking and looks towards the door.

It's the super-rich pretty boys' group that Rj told me about when we were in the assembly earlier. I roll my eyes and begin to look away when I notice Jacqui is walking in with them!

"She's still with them? And they actually came to class of their own volition? That's interesting, I wonder what made them wanna stay." I ponder, as I watch Jacqui.

Our eyes lock and I long to motion her beside me, but she quickly looks away.

"I have to warn her about what those guys do to women who trust them. She's in danger." I think to myself.

Sapphire leans forward, tapping her pencil on the desk.

"Hello? Earth to Justin? You okay"? Sapphire jokes.

I gaze back towards her.

"Oh, hey, sorry about that. I was just a little distracted. You can continue telling your story." I spout out anxiously.

"So, do you think she's pretty"? Sapphire questions, as she stares at me, rolling her pencil back and forth on her lower lip.

"Uh… no. What do you mean"? I nervously comment as I flee Sapphire's intimidating gaze.

"There's no reason to be afraid Justin. I can tell by the way you two looked at each other that there's some connection. A bump in the hall? Perhaps you both reached for something and touched hands? It's obvious you two have at least met before." She says, applying pressure.

I begin worrying internally.

"How could she tell? We just looked at each other for just a few moments! I can't let her make too many connections or we could be found out." I think to myself.

As I relax my face and stare back into her eyes. I slow my rapid breathing and lie through my teeth.

"Nope, I was just curious on who was coming in the door." I state smiling.

Sapphire smiles as well, and I drop mine. She calls my bluff.

"So, let's go talk to her." She suggests.

"Why is she so persistent"! I internally scream.

Turning around, I spot Jacqui and her clique sitting at the front of class. I get a sickening feeling in my gut.

"Nah, she looks like she has enough male attention already." I comment, annoyed by their presence.

"Ooh, was that a hint of jealousy I sense"? Sapphire squeals excitedly.

I think back to when I tried to ask Jacqui where we stood, back in the pink lit cavern and I cringe at the memory of the outcome. I even roll my eyes.

"No, not jealousy. I'm just not one for competing, especially for some girl." I state proudly as I cross my arms.

Not realizing my own volume, I look around to see most of the classroom is staring at Sapphire and me.

I brush it off until I lock eyes with Jacqui. Her facial expression confuses me. She doesn't look angry, or hurt, just a blank expression as she stares at me.

She whispers something to one of the guys next to her and they all start to snicker while staring at me.

I stand up aggravated, again unconsciously raising my voice.

"Something funny"? I demand while piercing their souls with a glare.

The guys at the table look surprised at first, but don't back down.

"Yeah, just looking at you makes me wanna laugh." One of the guys claim.

I ball my fist up and take a step closer to their table.

Runaways

Immediately, Sapphire reaches out and grabs my arm.

"Hey, let's take a water break." She suggests as she coerces me out the classroom.

"Yeah, listen to your little girlfriend, kid. You don't wanna get your arms broken in front of her." One of the members threaten.

I grit my teeth, longing to insinuate something towards his group, but Sapphire closes the door behind us.

"Hey what's up with you? I was just joking before, but you seem to have history with that girl. Is she your ex or something"? She questions.

I ponder for a few moments before responding.

"I really don't know how to explain it. There's just a lot going on and you'd hate me if I told you." I admit quietly.

Sapphire looks taken aback.

"Hate you? No, you're really sweet and you just seem troubled. I don't think there's anything you could say that would make me hate you, Justin." She says, doing her best to encourage me.

"If only you knew the half of it. Trust me, I know you would. Listen, I'll be fine. I appreciate you being here for me, but there's just so much you just wouldn't understand." I reply dismissively.

Sapphire looks as if she wants to reach out and hug me but doesn't move.

"I'm here for you. Whatever you need Justin." She claims, clearly dispirited.

"Thanks." I state, no energy in my voice.

I give her a painful smile and head back into the classroom.

As I pass by the teacher, I notice their head is still buried into a book. On my way back to my table one of the guys from Jacqui's table sticks his foot out and trips me.

As I hit the wall, I quickly push myself off the ground to swing back. Before I begin my attack, the bell for class dismissal rings and everyone quickly heads for the door. I want to give chase, but I let the group go.

"Bryan wouldn't have done that, Justin. Letting them go? You're acting like a child. Maybe we should go after them. You're not weak anymore. Why are you letting these rich nobodies punk you"? Lustro suggests in my head.

"I'm not going to expose myself as a fugitive to these people. You just want me to end up fighting half the school. I'll be forced to succumb to rage and use your stupid form again." I growl.

"You're not as naïve as before." Lustro chuckles.

"Get out of my head Lustro." I mutter.

Now trudging back to my table, disheartened, I grab my bag before flinging it around my shoulder. On my way out the door, I look around, wondering which class I'll settle into next. As I peer around the hallway, suddenly someone grabs me from behind! I hear a raspy voice whispering something into my ear.

"Move, and I'll kill you right now. You're coming with me you fugitive." They growl.

Fear fills my body as my blood runs cold.

"No way, they know." I struggle to move for a moment.

I spin, throwing them off my back. Ready to fight I get into my stance.

Dwight tosses his arms up.

"Yo chill! I was just playing with you, bro." He shouts.

I laugh loudly and quickly help him to his feet.

"My bad homie. I wasn't sure what was going on. You honestly play too much." I shake my head, attempting to recover from the scare.

As we both walk down the hall, we decide to take the route leading outside.

"So far, you're the only person that I know that's heard that crazy plan on stage from earlier this morning. I saw Jacqui but she was super distant. She's even with this new group of guys and I haven't heard anything good about them." I comment, tentatively scratching my head and looking towards the sky.

Justin Avery

"Oh wow, they sound like trouble. She shouldn't hang around them if what you've heard is true. They could be preying on her. Don't worry though, we'll explain everything to Jacqui tonight when we meet up by Nova." Dwight assures me.

"To make things worse, Adrian and Julien are here as well. It seems as if everything is imploding at once and I can't stop it." I worry.

"Don't stress yourself out, there is a reason that we are all here with you. You don't have to solve everything by yourself, Justin." Dwight chimes in.

"I hope so. I'm worried about her." I sigh.

As Dwight and I enter the second building, we casually walk up the stairs and enter the gymnasium.

We take a seat in the bleachers. As my eyes dart around the empty gym, I lock on a familiar face.

Chapter 18:
Lying in wait

"Is that… is that Jade"!? I think to myself.

Dwight notices the intrigue painted across my face and slides over towards me.

"What is it? You look worried." He questions.

I stand up and hop off the bleachers with nothing but curiosity in my mind.

Making a beeline for Jade, I weave through the small groups of students congregated on the basketball court.

I reach Jade and spin him around violently.

His face glows with joy when he sees me, and he tries to grip me in a hug. I make my fingertip glow with Sathon and poke his chest.

"Don't touch me. What are you doing here!? You need to leave right now." I demand in a hushed tone.

"Ow, that hurts." He yelps, backing away from me quickly.

He eyes me, clearly puzzled, he approaches again with his arms spread for a welcoming embrace.

"Justin, come on man. You know me. We're friends, don't tell me you forgot about your best friend."

Instantly, I sweep his legs and as he tumbles backwards, I catch his shirt. My fist is balled up, ready to strike.

"I didn't forget you at all. Why are you here? You're gonna mess up everything by being here. Julien and Adrian are here. None of you have Sathonic powers so you'll just get in the way." I bark as I drop him to the floor and lower my fist.

He looks up at me with shock, not moving from the floor.

"Okay, no hug… Justin, hear me out. Ava, Donshay, and I know some secret information about someone who's going to be here! If we can do this right, we can damage the Lumin totem pole." He says slyly with a stupid grin on his face.

"Alright, you have my attention, speak." I mutter.

"There is supposed to be a huge arrival of Comely troops coming in. Ava, Don, and I found the rest of the rubies and we're ready to execute our plan. Just sit back and watch what we can do." Jade grins.

Don comes up and takes the remaining rubies from my backpack and slides them into his bag.

"We figured out what the Ring of Power does when connected to the rubies. Just watch this." Don chirps excitedly.

Suddenly, the bell rings and we're all instructed to take our seats.

Runaways

"We'll explain later, Justin. Byeee." They whisper as they run off.

I take a seat beside Dwight, gazing down at our instructor.

"Okay, you gotta explain what's going on Justin. Who is that and what's going on"? He desperately questions as he scratches his head in confusion.

I spot his foot tapping rapidly on the bleacher seat and I chuckle.

"That's one of my old friends. Jade, he and two others are apparently in the city on a mission of their own. You met him briefly, after we saved Jacqui. I have no clue why they're here though." I mutter while staring over at their group.

"Oh, I remember him! They could potentially jeopardize our lives if we're found out. The Lumin public and everyone else knows about you and them. We can't be caught together, or things may get messy." Dwight responds.

"Exactly, I don't know what they are up to. I wish we had more time to listen to what they had to say, but I got too caught up in my emotions. I'm so stupid, we could have figured out what they are planning and helped them execute it"! I wail, hitting myself in the head gently.

"Hey, calm down Justin. Your emotions are valid, everything could go wrong if they mess this up for us. I'm not sure how you feel considering how they ditched Jacqui. I know they tried to make amends though. If you still have some ill feelings about them, I can understand that completely. I see how important Jacqui is to you, don't beat yourself up." Dwight highlights.

I give him an uplifting smile.

"Thanks man, you always know what to say. I just don't need anything else to go wrong. I refuse to lose anyone." I reply.

Dwight quickly cuts me off.

"We won't lose anyone. I promise." He assures cheerfully.

"Don't promise something you can't guarantee." I state calmly.

As we finish up our conversation, the coach walks in and stands by the instructor.

"It looks like we have more students than usual, or is that just me"? The coach asks, his voice rugged and scratchy.

The instructor looks down at a few papers on a clipboard and responds.

"Leadership has warned that we may have to hire more staff as Hypor's population steadily grows. It seems that most upper class Lumin citizens are departing from Nero as the weapons' completion nears. It won't be long before we have to upgrade the school to compensate for the steady influx of our student body". He comments.

The coach spits something into his water bottle. Eyeing him, I notice there's something poking out from under his lip.

Runaways

"What's that black stuff in his bottle"? Dwight whispers to me.

"Tobacco, at least that's what it looks like to me." I claim.

"Alright class, we're inside today. Basketballs are to the left and volleyballs are down at the end of the courts. Have fun, we have an hour before lunch, and a special visitor is also supposed to arrive sometime today." He barks before he waddles off to a nearby chair.

Everyone erupts, racing down the bleachers and grabbing the best basketballs out of the container. As Dwight and I slowly make our way down to the courts Ava steps in front of us.

"Hey Justin. It's nice to see you again. Have fun ditching your friends? Did you even plan on coming back for us"? She growls.

"Did you plan on coming back for Jacqui"? I question.

She hesitates and stutters for a moment.

"Exactly, there's your answer." I attempt to push past Ava and grab a ball, but she puts her hand on my chest and shoves me backwards.

I barely budge as I glare into her eyes.

"Listen, all I wanted to say, was to stay out of our way when we make our move. Once we execute our plan, we can assume power in this entire nation, crippling the Lumin forces." She boasts proudly, her hands rest on her hips as she smirks.

"Yeah, I don't remember asking. Get out of our way little girl." Dwight chuckles, moving her aside with no effort.

We grab a ball and head down to the bottom corner of the courts to shoot around.

The class quickly skips by, and once the bell rings we all head out for lunch. As Dwight and I walk down the hall, we enter the lunchroom along with a huge crowd of students.

We grab some chicken sandwiches, fries, fruit cups, and some water before heading out the side door towards the bus ramp to eat alone.

As we exit, I spot Jacqui and her group of friends. They all eye me eerily. Then the door closes behind me completely.

"Yo, what do we do until tonight. It seems like everything is just piling up right now. I honestly just feel so overwhelmed." I groan, tiresome of the constant arising problems.

"Let's just focus on one thing at a time, okay? So firstly, we need to get everyone together so we can all give our input. However, until that point, you and I got this." Dwight encourages me.

He wraps his arm around my shoulder and pulls me in for a side hug.

"I know we can do this bro, we have you on our side." Dwight grins.

I return his smile and we both eat our lunch as we recall every event that occurred within the last few hours.

Runaways

The bell goes off again, signaling the end of lunch and we see crowds of people heading towards the gym.

"Where are they going? I thought there was another class after lunch"? I question, confused.

"Remember what coach said. We apparently have another visitor". Dwight responds.

As we toss our boxes into the trash, we decide to trail everyone and chat while we take the long way down the gym.

Once entering the building, Dwight and I spot the group that hangs with Jacqui. Before they see us, I stick my hand out and we both stop behind a wall, listening in on their conversation.

"I'll be right back, I'm gonna go use the bathroom." Jacqui comments before heading off towards the restroom.

Once the doors close, the guys begin gossiping about something. I listen closely as one of the boys speaks up.

"So, when are we taking her to the party"? He inquires.

Another boy responds.

"We're going to set up a party after the game Friday night, and everyone will be there. It'll be easier to get rid of our... uhh accessories." He chuckles.

"But, what about Holly"? The first kid questions.

"Who"? Another voice responds.

"The new girl with the white hair." A deeper voice chimes in.

"Oh, we'll just keep her busy like we do with all the new girls. If she gets in the way, handle it." He says bluntly.

I whip my head back towards Dwight.

"Did you hear that? They're going to hurt Jacqui if she gets in their way"! I shout in a hushed tone.

Dwight nods.

"We have to tell her. They're not going to hurt anyone ever again." Dwight growls angrily.

As we listen in again, we hear the group all head into the gym and as we follow them in, Jacqui comes out the bathroom. To avoid her, I rush Dwight in the gymnasium and up the bleachers, away from her friend group.

Once we sit down, breathing heavily, we finally settle in, and the lights dim.

A bright light flashes and nasty green aura streams in from the air!

Suddenly a tall man stands in the middle of the gym with two others beside him. The light in the gymnasium fades green and I realize this isn't a special affect from the school. That man is creating the green hue!

Runaways

"It's the king of Hypor"! A boy cries out and everyone instantly bows down before him.

Caught between not wanting to stand out, and refusing to bow to this arrogant scum, I begrudgingly bow while eyeing him with disgust. His crown shines brightly and the king raises his right arm up in the air. Everyone in the school stands to their feet in unison as the king clears his throat to speak.

"I just want to speak highly on this nation. I'm so proud of every individual that has volunteered to join our new Lumin Sathon force. LSF for short." The king states.

My eyes dart around nervously as something in my soul screams for me to leave the building. I watch the men beside the king disappear into thin air and appear out in the crowd!

"Did- did they just teleport"! Dwight cries out nervously.

I sense a strong energy behind us and whip around quickly to see the Lumin sentinel towering over Dwight and me! He could easily be seven feet tall.

Without hesitation, he grabs me and yanks me up by my shirt.

The king continues to speak.

"It's honestly an honor to have such a guest in our city. The lowlife fugitives are in this room as we speak." He shouts, now turning towards Dwight and me.

I glow turquoise and kick the sentinel in his shin bone before headbutting him.

"Dwight, we have to go! This was a trap! I don't know how, but they knew we were here"! I shriek as I rip him from his seat.

The students around us, cut our path off, blocking the clear stairway down the bleachers.

"You're telling me that some Lustronese scum has been sitting right under our noses"?! A few students scream.

"Let's kill them"! Others shout.

"No, bring them to me"! The king commands, his voice booming throughout the gymnasium.

The students nod and converge around us.

"There's no way I'm going out like this. I'm taking as many of you bums down as I can"! Dwight shouts as he yanks his katana out and grits his teeth angrily.

Suddenly, I hear shouting from the opposite side of the gymnasium as I see a furious red aura being thrown around!

"Bryan! That's right, he's here too. I haven't seen him since we argued back on Nova, but, if we can fight together, we can win this." I think to myself optimistically.

We clash with the students, and for the most part it's a breeze. These kids don't have any fighting experience and with my Sathon ability, Dwight and I dispatch many of them without exerting too much effort.

Runaways

I rush a group of students and drop kick them! The room flashes with turquoise light as we fight for survival.

The king looks intrigued by my attacks. However, what he does next concerns me. The seven-foot giant sentinel attempts to subdue me, but the king commands him to halt.

"I want to see what these runaways can do." He mutters, smirking at me.

A deep cold glare pierces my psyche, and he allows us to continue fighting the student body.

"Let's go Lustros, I want to see what you worms can do"! The king barks.

I keep fighting as hard as I can, using everything I've ever thought about attempting in a fight and applying it. A huge student rushes me with a dagger in hand! He slashes wildly and I block it using Sathonic wrist guards. Each time the steel collides with my aura, there are turquoise sparks shattering and collapsing to the floor.

"How does this kid even have a dagger in school? That's got to be illegal"! I shout and the king chuckles.

The kid slashes upwards cutting my school uniform off and then he spins, bringing the blade down quickly!

I roll out of the way and look down to see my lightweight armor has now activated itself.

I glance up from my armor, back to my opponent, who's rushing me with his dagger, eager to draw blood.

Quickly, I slide through his legs before popping up, spinning around, and kicking him through a wall! I turn and see three more students charging me with their own Sathonic abilities.

"This must be the LSF." I growl.

With no hesitation I dust my hands together, leaving ten miniature Sathon sparkles strewn across the floor.

"Dwight, run! I sprinkled some sacred dust"! I shout, desperately trying to get his attention.

He hops off towards the side, simultaneously dodging a flurry of kicks from one of the Sathon wielding students.

I snap my fingers and a plethora of explosions go off ripping lots of the floor up and decimating the hateful student body.

I glance back over and see Bryan fighting for his life as well. He backflips over a kid before sending a thunderous kick into the student's head!

Bryan slides through another student's legs and hits her with fourteen lightning-fast jabs before round house kicking her to the floor.

"Yes! Yes! Keep fighting, you worms. A Lustro to a Lumin is like a cockroach to a human. You all are improving your worth the longer you hold off these students." The king claims.

Runaways

My eyes dart around searching for Jacqui, but I can't find her. Suddenly a golden Sathonic blast rockets towards me! I immediately press my hands to the floor using a destructive shockwave to launch myself out of harm's way!

The attack continues, ripping through the floor and exploding, sending hundreds of students into the wall and floor.

I glance up and see Julien giving his signature unmatched glare.

The king commands everyone to stop fighting and our enemies pause, obeying.

"It seems these criminals aren't just lucky high schoolers. They actually have some skill. But let's find out how much skill"! He shouts excitedly, rejuvenated from the spectacle of our battle.

"You're laying it on kinda thick with the criminal comments for a man who's planning on wiping out a race of people"! I bark.

With no warning the king snaps and a green light consumes the entire building. We are all transported outside to this empty wasteland. Somehow the day has skipped by, and a full moon is out.

"Did he change the time of day? How could he even manage that"? I scream to myself.

This time no students sit across from us as the opposition.

Just about fifty Lumin guards, the giant Lumin sentinels, Julien, Adrian, and the king himself.

The area is so wide open and almost looks to be built for a final fight like this.

There are enormous Bingo statues surrounding everyone in a massive circle.

These white and green statues make even our eight-ton friend Nova look like a small car. I run my hand on the material and notice its granite.

"I know you're a little perplexed on how we got here, but don't worry. It won't matter when you're dead. A Combustion and Solar quality user sitting right in front of me! This banquet is going to be divine." The king taunts.

Julien steps up onto a tall pillar made of stone and points down at me.

"I've had enough of your kind. You all make me sick. This world can't be purified until you and others just like you, are exterminated like the vermin you are." He shouts.

"Shut up! I've had enough of everyone's hate. My friends and I had nothing to do with that stupid war. We just want to live freely like everyone else does. We don't have to end things like this, you've been lied to, Julien. Ask the king what really happened." I respond coldly.

"I know what happened. It's time I put you down... mutt." He growls.

Julien bolts through the sky towards me faster than I can mentally register. When my eyes lock on his golden aura, they widen. It seems as if everything starts moving in slow motion as Julien's leg, now golden, rips through the air! I duck scantily, avoiding his thunderous strike.

When his leg connects with the enormous column behind me, it sends a vociferous crack throughout the entire Bingo statue!

As huge fragments larger than us, shed off, we dodge them, continuing to fight. Cleverly thinking on the fly, I do a backflip, sending turquoise ripples through the bus sized stone. Forcing it to zip towards Julien.

He anticipates this, and somehow, he punches through the granite! It breaks off into a plethora of pieces, zooming towards me in a barrage.

Swiftly, I surround myself in a Sathon orb to shield myself from harm.

"I can use the smoke as cover." I think to myself.

Once the attack subsides, I put my index fingers together. Resembling a gun, I fire a thin beam which tears through the remaining debris, piercing Julien's shoulder.

"Ahh! My arm! You'll pay for that Justin." He cries out.

I smirk and glance over to Bryan who is handling Adrian with not much of a contest.

"Come on Adrian. You're one of the elites, right? Fight back! Land a punch since you're apparently so special! You Lumin people are nothing compared to us"! He screams as he hits Adrian with a sweet mix of hooks and well-placed kicks.

A group of Lumin guards rush in to help Adrian but Bryan powers up. Now glowing brighter than before, his attacks hit heavier, and his strikes are quicker. Bryan rushes behind a guard and snaps his neck with no effort.

He quickly grabs one of the guards and hits him with two devastating left hooks. Bryan tosses the man into the air and springs up after him. He does a front flip and crushes the man's skull as his heel smashes through the helmet. As Bryan lands, another Lumin soldier rushes him with a long sword and Bryan tosses the deceased guard into the blade! He then dissipates into a red smoke, disappearing for a moment before reappearing above one of the other soldiers.

Everyone watches with great focus and Bryan comes down with a crushing knee, knocking the man out cold.

"You're sleeping"! Bryan stands above his opponent's limp body, screaming demonstratively.

Donshay rushes a few soldiers taking three on at once, he makes quick work of them as his Bo staff has blades at the ends and they tear through armor as if it provided no resistance.

He spins and keeps most soldiers off Bryan and their efforts become less of a threat. Don elbows a Lumin guard charging from behind him and a blade jets out from his armor! The man folds over like a piece of paper and Don smiles.

"It seems their armor provides little resistance to my new blades. Justin, after this, we have so much to catch up on." He chuckles.

I smile and turn back to Julien. I notice he is now accompanied by two Lumin guards. They both have their assault rifles trained on me.

Runaways

"These are Sathonic rifles, our bullets are built to pierce your shield. Don't even try to fight. Just surrender kid."

"About time we corralled you. You should be grateful that my king wants your energy. Otherwise, I'd smite you where you stand." Julien sneers as he wipes some blood from his mouth.

"That's enough! Get down kid." One of the guards order.

I raise my arms up in defeat, as I think of a new strategy.

The king sees this, and for some reason frowns. As the guards walk forward with their weapons trained on me, they slightly drop their guard. I smirk, firing a Sathon tether towards the earth. The tether latches onto a granite chunk from the Bingo statues.

I spin, launching it at the soldiers! The granite rock crushes the first one's helmet. Instantly, I spread my arms wide, creating a Sathon barrier and the bullets from the second soldier's assault rifle, ricochets off my shield.

"What? How is this possible? These weapons were created specifically to stop you"! The soldier cries.

Before he can react, I drop my hands and the shield dissipates slowly. As this happens, I spring into action and sweep at their legs three times! Huge turquoise waves wipe out a plethora of guards.

Julien rushes me, but, with only one functional arm, he's no match. I evade his punches and retaliate with my own.

Julien swings, his golden fist missing completely. I then uppercut him. As Julien rises from the strike, I zip up in the air and behind him. I land a knee in his back. Julien spits up blood and rockets into the ground! As his body bounces back off the hot sand, I teleport down and string a crushing punch to his jaw! A turquoise line of explosive energy pierces through his body.

Justin Avery

"Come on Julien, is this all you got"?! I taunt, arrogantly flaunting my skills.

I perform a spinning back fist and send Julien to the dusty earth.

The king sneers once again. I gaze at him, perplexed.

"Why is he smiling? His men and his two elite teenage prodigies are losing." I worry, terrified by what he could have up his sleeve.

"No, I can't lose. I won't lose"! Julien shouts as he powers up. His golden flame now flickering wildly.

I look over towards Hailey, Dwight, and Jade's group. I gaze around aimlessly, hoping to remember what's missing. My hope diminishes when I finally remember.

"Where's Jacqui." I think to myself before searching around nervously.

I glance up and hear her screaming as she slams both her hands, clenched together, down into the king's head! As he tumbles to the ground, Jacqui lands and transforms the sand into stone. She lifts the king up, as he is encapsulated inside the rock. Jacqui then sends more massive boulders from both sides into the king's body! Jacqui doesn't stop there. She begins to float and so do the boulders that crushed the king.

"Now you die, your reign of terror is over! Amethyst rain"!! She roars.

Suddenly, pink clouds form in the sky. A bright fuchsia lightning bolt hits Jacqui and she is given an immense boost in strength. Jacqui grins and brings both hands down from her head towards her toes. The rain floods in and as it saturates the leftover Lumin soldiers, it turns them into stone! The twins and giant sentinels spring on top of the Bingo statues, avoiding the rain. The remaining Lumin soldiers are turned into leaves and flutter to the ground and others are turned into a pink liquid. They all collapse to the sand. Jacqui exhales loudly, and as she blows air out, the wind picks up. The ensuing abrasion erodes the rock that held the king, into pebbles! Obliterating him entirely. Jacqui slowly drops down towards the earth, exhausted by her heroic work.

"She got him!! Good job Jacqui"! We all cheer, excited about her devastating flurry of attacks.

"Jacqui is sooo cool! I can't wait to get strong like her"! Hailey cheers.

I sit back, in awe.

"Where did she get all that power? I mean, it's a shame that Julien, Adrian, and the two giant sentinels avoided the attack, but we at least got the big fish out of the way"! I think to myself.

As we all take a deep sigh of relief, a green lightning bolt strikes the ground! As the smoke clears, the king smirks sinisterly.

"I'm back… did you miss me"? He questions mockingly.

He doesn't even seem to be phased by her attack! The king then flashes towards Jacqui and grabs her by the hair! The ruthless king slams her face into the sand!

"Well, your first mistake was assuming that I would just die from that"! He snarls.

"What! How did he survive that attack"? I screech.

"Your second mistake was not confirming your kill by searching for a body. Man… you guys have a lot to learn".

I bolt in Jacqui's direction, hoping to provide aid. However, Julien sucker punches me, and I hurtle into one of the statues.

"Ow… you have got to be joking right now." I mutter, pulling myself out of the granite statue rubble.

I attempt to stand up. I struggle heavily, finally making it to my feet.

"How does he have so much strength left? I damaged Julien so much." I think to myself.

I peer up to see the king slamming Jacqui into the group, knocking them to the ground!

"Oh yeah! That's gotta be a strike"! He chants excitedly.

As Hailey sidesteps the attack, the king frowns, but bounds away to continue his assault.

"Damn. I missed one"! He groans.

He then teleports from statue to statue, slamming Jacqui's battered body into the massive Bingo and converting that into a smooth combination of kicks.

The king howls with malicious laughter as he strings along his attack, striking her with a frenzy of kicks so fast, I struggle to follow his movements with my eyes. The king then takes Jacqui and rockets towards the ground! Jacqui wails, terrified.

"Ima plant me a Lustro tree"! He screeches as he slams Jacqui's head into the earth!

Runaways

When they connect, a green explosion ensues. Everyone stops fighting and peers over to the king. Covered in Jacqui's blood, the king plucks her from the earth by her leg and spins her right side up. He grips Jacqui by her hair and lays his hand right under her chin. As Jacqui's face drops down into his hand from fatigue and pain, he proceeds to blast her face countless times!

"How did he even do that? That attack hit her rapidly, and in just a few moments, he's shattered any hope we had of winning. We don't stand a chance against him. We never did. Worst of all, he doesn't even look like he's trying. There's supposed to be four more kings too! But here we are, unable to defeat just one! How are we supposed to liberate our people"! I cry out internally.

"Now that I've broken your hope. I think I'll be on my way. I have a dinner to attend." The tyrant snickers maniacally as he eyes our group.

After dropping Jacqui into the sand, his leg glows green and he turns his back on us.

"Oh, Uno and Bevo"? He calls out.

His seven-foot Lumin sentinels look to their king. I struggle to see their facial expressions through their masks, but they seem intrigued for the first time.

"Bring the Sathonic kids to the prison, north of Nero. You two should be knowledgeable on the prison on Larios Island. Oh, and for the others." He pauses for a moment.

"Kill them." The king smirks, clearly unhinged.

"No. This can't be happening. He doesn't have any use for my friends without the Sathonic ability, so he's just going to kill them"?! I think to myself as I watch the king turn away from us again.

Justin Avery

His leg still green, now rips backwards and his heel connects with Jacqui's ribcage!

She hurtles through the air and knocks Hailey down.

"Alright, I guess a spare will do. I was never any good at bowling." He scratches his head, clearly annoyed.

"Is this just a game to you"?! I scream, losing my cool.

"Why, of course child. I'm actually winning this one. I could never defeat my brother in bowling, so, you all will have to do." He says nonchalantly as he meanders away.

"There's no way I'm just gonna let you leave after doing that to Jacqui! You're gonna pay for that"! I scream.

My power skyrockets and I feel a silver aura take over my body. I blitz at the king and punch as hard as I can. Suddenly, a man dives in my way. My arm shatters a Lumin officers chest cavity. I rip my arm out the man's chest and look towards the king, who springs backwards.

"Careful kid, that strike might've done some damage." He sarcastically comments.

"Don't you run from me"!!! I bellow.

I fly at him and create two crescent shaped beams in my hands. I grip them tightly and slash, crossing my arms in a 'X.' The attack erases the rest of the Lumin forces. As they tumble to the floor, cut into countless pieces, I spring up into the sky, charging my strongest attack.

"Well, I was hoping to have some men left over from this encounter. But I guess you didn't like that idea too much. Alright,

Runaways

I'll accept your challenge kid. Give me everything you got in your final attack"! The Hyporian tyrant shrieks.

"You're gonna pay for what you did to Jacqui!! Oceanic Hellfire"!! I shout, blasting all my energy at the king.

Halfway through my attack, my Katun ripple ends, and my body fades back into my base form.

The king drops to a knee. I smile, knowing my attack will connect.

Suddenly, he springs up and kicks my blast into a Bingo statue! The energy eviscerates the massive statue, and it feels as if the earth itself, shakes violently from the explosion!

The force sends me flying even higher and I notice that the tyrant is smiling at me.

"That one actually stung quite a bit. This was fun, but I must go. You've already made me late to the summit with the other kings. They are gonna be so jealous that I got to fight you. Ciao." He waves to me.

As the king departs, our opposition is just the two sentinels and the twins.

The Hyporian king snaps and the sky turns green for a moment. When it fades back, he is finally gone.

"He left, just like that. He's so confident in his men, he teleported away." I think to myself as I descend from the sky.

"Man, I'm exhausted. Using up all that energy really has taken a toll on me." I mutter.

As I take a deep breath, Julien punches at me again. I block his strike before quickly countering with a swift leg kick.

We parry each other's blows and take considerable amounts of damage.

"I can't keep this up. I burned too much Sathon earlier." I grunt as I grit my teeth.

We trade strikes and both of us begin to slow down, fatigue settling in. Unfortunately, Julien's blows just have more strength to them, and with the others busy with the sentinels, I struggle to defend myself.

Dwight lunges at the Lumin sentinel, digging his katana deep into the man's left arm. He rips it down to shear flesh, but it shatters!

"What? I- I don't understand what just happened." Dwight stutters, clamoring for an answer.

"Sorry kid, but you and your friends just didn't make the cut"! Bevo answers.

"Please… no puns." Uno says to his brother.

Bevo ignores this and grabs Dwight. Bevo's body glows green and he slams Dwight into the ground and kicks him like a soccer ball! He then grabs the broken blade of the katana and pursues after Dwight to keep up his attack.

Bevo rushes towards Dwight after kicking him into the air and it seems like time stops again, when the effect fades, I see Dwight being hit with a vicious flurry. Heavy hooks, knees, and elbows hit his vulnerable body, and before anyone can react, he's blown away with a destructive blast. Bevo then finishes this up by slamming down from the sky and stabbing Dwight in the leg with his own katana.

"Guess you weren't a cut above the rest." Bevo chuckles.

Bryan springs into action, his body glowing red-hot.

"Unhand my brother"! He shouts.

Without looking backwards, Bevo swats Bryan like a fly and Uno vanishes completely. When he appears again, he's floating above Bryan. As Bryan flies upwards to Uno, Uno stomps Bryan into the ground mercilessly. He then lands, crushing Bryan's throat with his knee.

"How about you unhand my brother. I hate brats." Uno smirks.

"Noooo"! Donshay yells angrily and he charges Bevo.

Uno teleports in front of Don, punting him backwards! As Uno's leg connects with Donshay's head, a loud wail leaves Don's body as he lands onto the hot sand.

"I literally just said 'unhand my brother,' and then you target him. What's with these kids"? Uno questions.

Uno immediately jumps on top of Donshay and presses his weight into Don's chest. As the boot threatens to crush him, Donshay pushes back with his Bo staff. It looks as if he can power his way out of the predicament, when suddenly, his sturdy Bo staff, snaps in half! Uno's heel slams into Don's chest!

Justin Avery

Don spits up blood on himself and it's clear there is some serious internal bleeding occurring.

"No, please stop! We just want to live freely"! Hailey screams, bawling her eyes out.

Out of nowhere she rushes the sentinel and drop kicks him off Don.

She starts wailing on his face and for a moment, she seems to have the upper hand. Uno does an attack that looks like my own. Almost identical to when I widen my Sathonic energy outward as it explodes wildly.

As Hailey hits the sand, she tries to stand up, but the two guardians blitz her at once and crush her! They slam their shoulders into each other! The ruthless brothers sandwich her tiny body. Both of the sentinels chuckle as Hailey collapses to the ground, bloody, but still breathing. I worry about my friends, and as I turn to aid them, Julien screams at me, enraged.

"You're more worried about your friends than you are for your own health? Don't worry, I'll fix that"! He barks, now going all out on the offensive.

Julien starts punching faster and I flip backwards to create some distance between us. In the middle of my flip, he rockets his knee into my chest and a golden explosion overtakes me.

"Die! I want you dead"! Julien screams.

I lay desperately on the ground, winded from the attack. I feel my energy plummet rapidly.

When the smoke clears, I gaze over and see Jacqui out cold and the two massive sentinels now wailing on Dwight and Bryan mercilessly.

Runaways

Chapter 19:
Too little too late

"It's no question why the king left. These guys are too strong, we have to run". I murmur, dragging myself towards Jacqui.

Julien stomps on my leg as hard as he can, and I feel something crack! He doesn't stop there. He grinds his boot deeper, and I writhe in agony.

Adrian looks over at me but keeps his stoic expression.

Julien begins to kick my battered body. Over and over, his heavy kicks bruise me. I choke, as one kick feels as if it pierced my lung. Julien points his hand down, beginning to blast me with Sathon repeatedly.

"Hey Bevo and Uno, you can leave, Julien and I got this." Adrian claims.

"You brats are no fun, just let us finish one of these kids off"! They growl.

"Shut up and get going before I tell the king you gave us lip." Adrian hisses.

The two sentinels both nod and back off. Knowing as high up on the totem pole as they are, the twins rank higher. Uno and Bevo both teleport away and Julien glances up for a moment.

"Oh, I see, you wanted to do all of the killing yourself little bro. Well let's get to it. It's not like those pansies over there are going to be able to stop us now." Julien scoffs as he eyes Jade, and Ava.

Runaways

"Those two have been frozen in fear since the fight began and have done nothing to help us. I thought Jade had some cool attack that involved the rubies and the ring of power"?! I think to myself.

Julien stalks over to me.

"Well, it seems this is the end for you buddy. It was a fun fight while it lasted. Wouldn't it be ironic if I killed you with your signature attack? I think that would make for a fitting end." He smirks, creating a Sathon blade.

I lower my head, accepting whatever comes next.

"Well, this is the end." I mutter to myself.

Suddenly, Jacqui shoots her arm out, and a raging ravine rips open, almost sending Julien and I underneath!

Julien grabs my body and takes flight.

"That was cute, honestly it was probably the best acting I've seen all day. Pretending you were knocked out, awaiting the perfect moment. I applaud you." He chuckles sarcastically.

"Unfortunately for you Jacqui, it failed, and now you're going to pay with your life! I'll expunge your soul from existence"! Julien shouts resentfully.

"We're not killing Jacqui! You heard the king, Julien. We can't just disobey his authority like that. All of the Sathonic wielding ones stay". Adrian shouts.

Julien ignores every word that was said and points his finger at Jacqui. His fingers glow golden, and an electric current now seems to be roaming around his body! She lays there on the ground, helpless.

"Well, it wasn't really pretending. I don't even have the energy to defend myself." She chuckles solemnly.

"No! You better not touch her! I swear I'll kill you if you hurt Jacqui"! I grit my teeth, knowing I can't stop him.

"You honestly disappoint me. Just have fun for once, I doubt anyone is going to care. We can just say it was an accident." Julien growls as he spits onto the ground near Adrian.

"Now, go to hell"! Julien smirks, now eyeing Jacqui.

The golden lightning leaves his fingertips and I freeze, knowing that this is it. I reach out trying to make a shield for Jacqui, but nothing comes out my body as I am almost empty of Sathon.

Suddenly, Jade is in front of Jacqui! He kicks her body violently towards the side and as he turns to avoid the bolt, everything flashes.

"What? No! What's going on"? I scream internally.

As fast as it started, it's over. Jade's body eats the Sathon lightning. The bolt tears through his chest effortlessly, hitting multiple vital organs and smashes into huge boulders below in the ravine. I stare in shock as his body collapses to the unforgiving earth.

Adrian springs into action, attacking Julien and my body is dropped. As I slam into the earth I desperately crawl over to Jade.

Uncontrollably sobbing, I embrace Jade in a hug.

"Why would you do that!? Are you stupid"? I shout, the tears rushing down my face in streams now.

"Maybe a little, I did run into a burning building at one point." He chuckles.

His body begins to lose blood rapidly and I feel the warmth blanket my hands.

"This isn't the time for jokes Jade! Why would you do that knowing you would die"? I choke out.

"Call it some late karma. I had to pay back my debt for not saving her the first time. I couldn't watch the same thing happen twice." He chuckles as his body convulses from the lightning dancing around in is body.

"No Jade, you were supposed to live. After what happened to your parents. I stutter, still sniffling and weeping.

Jade cuts me off.

"Don't do that, I always loved you man. You've been my brother since day one, besides, you and I both know Julien would've killed me and the others regardless." He comments.

"Let me heal you! I can save you." I start.

"Don't waste your time, I've already lost too much blood at this point." Jade says.

Jade chokes on his own blood, suffering from his wound, he speaks slowly.

I need you to promise me something though. Before I go." Jade weakly murmurs.

"What is it? Whatever you need bro." I mumble as I feel his life force getting weaker. I begin to bawl harder.

Justin Avery

"Don't let my family name perish in vain. Free our people at any cost. You gotta stop being scared, alright? Promise me you'll stop letting your fear consume you. Our people need a leader... is that you"? Jade questions.

With so much raw emotion flowing throughout my body, I struggle to speak. My vision blurs from my constant flow of tears.

"Oh, and here. Take my ring. With all the rubies gathered, I could've resurrected my parents. It only would work if the user possesses all of the rubies and possesses my heritage's blood. I can't lie to you. I planned to sacrifice my own life to accomplish this. However, I couldn't do it here. My parents would just be killed again. I even attempted to resurrect your father while we were on the battlefield, but for some reason the ring wouldn't allow me. Perhaps he is alive Justin. Point is, I'm going to trap my essence inside the ring. I'll protect you no matter what problems you face."

As Jade's essence leaves his body, a lime-colored light swirls around me. It carries the ring off his hand and onto mine. When the ring locks onto my fingers I hear Jade say one last sentence.

"I love you, bro."

I nod and feel his body go completely empty. His life force disappears as I clutch his hollow body, weeping so hard I struggle to breathe.

Nothing happens for the next few minutes as I sit here next to my best friend. The rubies lay around me, all of them without their luster. Each ruby is now a dull grey and the ring is a bright lime.

Runaways

Justin Avery

I gaze behind me and see Adrian and Julien fighting.

Nothing seems to hold weight anymore as I care less and less of what happens to us. In fact, a small piece of me hopes Julien wins just so everything can be over.

I zone out, just staring at the dusty ground. My soul feels empty. My perception on time is lost and what feels like moments later, Adrian is tapping me on the shoulder.

"Hey, I'm so sorry about your friend. I knocked my brother out and we don't have a lot of time. I can get you and your friends out of here. I know I have no reason for you to trust me but." He states.

I cut him off.

"Leave. I don't want you here. You waited until my friend lost his life before you got the courage to stand up to your brother." I growl.

"I know and I'm sorry, but you all are in bad shape. I can get you to safety if you just let me help." He pleads.

Cutting him off again, I pull myself to my feet, attempting to shoot Sathonic blasts at Adrian. Nothing comes out my hands as my Sathonic reserves are completely dry. I tremble slowly as I recall what he said about Julien.

"Adrian, you failure! Julien escaped! Can you do anything right"? I groan, disdain and misery saturating each word.

"I...I swore he was." Adrian begins to fumble over his words.

"Leave!! I'll kill you"! I sob as I tumble back to my knees.

462

Runaways

Adrian frowns and slowly disappears into the night.

As fog begins to settle in, Ava approaches me and tries to help me to my feet.

"Get away from me! I swear as long as there's breath in my body. Ava, as long as I have life, I will literally do everything in my power to end yours". I shout as I attempt to shoot her down too.

No Sathon leaves my hands as my body has been completely depleted of energy. I am now just relying on reserves to keep me alive.

"You sat there and watched all of us get beaten to a pulp. And I realized now, that when we attempted to escape Nero, you helped the Lumin soldiers capture Jacqui! I heard you two fighting. You also weren't included in the fugitive listing that came on the news! What's up with that!? Answer me"! I scream.

"I- I'm sorry. My parents paid the Lumin government for my safety and in exchange for my freedom, I had to trade one of you in. I chose Jacqui because I was closer with Don, Jade, and you! I didn't ask for it, I just wanted us to be normal teenagers again." Ava weeps.

"You disgust me! You traded in a fellow comrade to save your own hide. You're the worst type of scum. Don't ever show your face again or I promise I'll end your life"! I weep angrily.

I can't really see Ava with all the tears and fog, but a blurry silhouette of her body, rushes off into the distance.

Over the next hour I sit around all my unconscious friends and begin digging Jade a grave. As I recover small amounts of my energy, I eventually finish it up.

Finally covering everything up, I start to feel numb. After a small amount of time passes, I bury my best friend and say a few words before patting the dirt down and backing away.

"Okay guys, I guess it's time we get out of here." I mutter to myself, knowing everyone is still out cold.

"Don't worry I'll help you move them." A feminine voice comments from behind me.

I turn around and something heavy bashes my head.

Chapter 20:
Loser

Everything goes dark and my head throbs violently.

When I come to, my surroundings resemble a prison. I notice that my body is extremely cold as well.

"Where… am … I? Hypor was everything but cold, and I know the prisons in Nero aren't this frigid either. Even up north, in Larios Island, it still couldn't be this cold." I murmur, shivering violently.

Suddenly, a woman dressed in heavy cold weather gear, enters my cell.

"Get up"! She commands.

"Who are you, and where am I"? I ponder to myself, feeling nauseous from standing too quickly.

"Here, eat this." She offers very hurriedly.

I slowly take the small red fruit and as I bite into it, things begin to clear up.

"Was that Superfruiit"? I wonder.

Before I can even get a word out, she barks another order at me in a hushed tone.

"Put this on and follow me. Don't ask any questions, just follow me." She states.

Justin Avery

I look around nervously and can't help but question her.

"Who are you? Where are we? What happened to my friends? How long have I been out? Where are we going"? I badger her, concerned, but firm.

I put on the cold weather gear she hands me and begin to warm up slowly.

"Man, this feels like the material my lightweight armor was made out of." I ponder.

She gives no response as she leads me out of my cell. We creep down the eerie hall and Lumin guards walk down a hall across from us!

"What in the world have I gotten myself into"? I think while my eyes dart around, skittishly surveying the area.

Something about this entire situation makes me feel extremely queasy. The lady leads me into this room, and she stops in her tracks before briefing me.

"Okay on the other side of this hallway is our freedom. There are cells in this hall so just keep moving forward until we get out the door. The other prisoners may act belligerent, but you must ignore them. It's imperative that we get outside and run as fast as we can." She preaches.

As she turns away from me, I reach out and grab her arm.

"You need to tell me what's going on first. I'm so lost on this entire situation." I growl, annoyed with being pushed around.

She turns back to me, unenthused, but she complies.

466

Runaways

"Listen, no more questions after this but, I found the second sacred relic. Well, found is a bit of a stretch, I more like… stole it. Regardless, we need to get far away from here before anyone notices it's gone." She whispers as what sounds like a boat's hull, creaks loudly.

I stare into her hand. The clear gem shines promisingly and before I can say anything, she pockets it again.

"Now can we please leave"? She pleads.

Nodding in agreement, we both slide down the hallway, ignoring the loud clamoring from the prisoners.

"Please let me out"!

"Don't leave us"!

"Am I going to die here"?

The prisoners shout at us as we pass. I turn to some of them, looking to be around my age.

"I'll be back for you all whenever I get this mission completed." I whisper.

As we dash towards the front door, the gem falls out of her pocket and bounces off the floor into a cell.

I screech to a halt and slide my hand through the bars trying to pick it up. I strain, but, to no avail. The gem is too far out of my reach. Suddenly, a small child in the cell picks up the item and hands it to me.

"Go now Mr. Justin. Save us when you can come back." The child chirps with a smile on their face.

Justin Avery

I nimbly race after my new acquaintance and catch back up to the hooded woman.

After following her out the front door, we make a dash once we're outside.

I then realize that we're in the dead center of a blizzard and appreciate the cold-weather gear and boots she provided me earlier.

The hooded woman keeps running and for a few moments I struggle to keep up with her.

"Why are we running so fast? Nobody's chasing us. I think we've put enough distance between us and them." I spout ignorantly.

I trail close behind her as she refuses to reply and keeps moving forward.

Eventually we start walking and I pass her up, finally stopping her.

"What is going on? I honestly need you to explain this to me." I demand as I cut her off, blocking her from traveling forward.

"I don't have to tell you anything." She hisses back in a rude and disrespectful tone.

"Well, then I guess you won't be getting this then, now will you"? I chuckle, holding the gem in my hand.

"Tell me why you need this sacred relic and I'll allow us to move forward." I order.

"Please Justin, just trust me. We need to get further away, but I promise once we do, I'll tell you everything. You can even lead the way. We just need to keep moving forward." She begs.

"Hmm, she knows my name. I guess she must know me from somewhere." I ponder to myself.

Debating my options, I lead the way and we continue our trek in the snow. Over time, the wind picks up and the snow becomes even more blinding than before. With a hand over my eyes, I struggle to see what's in front of me. In my other hand I am gripping the gem tightly when suddenly something tears through my Achilles!

I stumble to the ground, spilling the gem forward and it glows vividly in the snow.

Suddenly, an explosion goes off, shaking the very earth we stand on! As I turn around, I see a giant ship up in flames as explosive debris covers the pure white snow, staining it.

"Yo!! There were so many innocent people on that ship! I don't understand. What's going on? What happened my foot"? I question.

The lady trots forward and picks up the gem. She stares back at me and attempts to run off!

"Oh no you don't"! I shout and launch a giant Sathonic hand outward to grab her.

Once my grip is around her waist, I yank her back and slam her in the snow. She stands up quickly and the vile wind sends her hood flapping off her head!

Once the hood flops off, my heart sinks like a rock. I realize who it is, as her unmistakable white glossy hair blows majestically in the wind.

"Jacqui"!? I shout bewildered.

"I'm sorry Justin, it wasn't supposed to end like this." She whimpers mournfully.

"You're a fake! You tricked me! My best friend died to save you. Why... why are you doing this"? I demand as I feel warm blood trickle down from my ankle onto my hands.

Jacqui tosses me a roll of bandages.

"Wrap that, I know you'll be fine. I just need you out of the way when I do this." She claims.

She seems lost and unaware of what she is looking for.

"Jacqui, you killed all those people on that ship back there. There were hundreds of prisoners and you just killed them without any hesitation." I comment, petrified.

As small streams of tears attempt to race down my face, they quickly freeze in the blistering weather.

"I'm sorry. I know, I know. You just need to stay away from me. I'm sorry Justin. I wish I could explain, but I can't." Jacqui chokes out.

"We were supposed to be together, you're really going to betray me too? After everything that just happened"? I scream irately.

"We should be together. Just not now... maybe in another lifetime... loser". Jacqui gives me a painful smile as she sobs and races off.

Runaways

I sit here, watching her disappear off into the distance as she abandons me, cold and frozen in the snow.

Justin Avery

Runaways

Justin Avery

Dedication

First, I want to thank God for giving me the patience to complete this novel. It has been a strenuous and time-consuming process. However, now that I have completed this novel, I want to give a huge thanks to everyone who took time out of their day to help me create this! Even if you consider your contribution small, it played a vital role in my growth as a writer. To the individuals that stayed up many nights while I searched for character names or just common terms, thank you so much! Each and every one of you are greatly appreciated and I just want to thank you for your massive contribution to my dream of finally becoming a published author. All of your help was imperative for me to slowly mold character designs, attack names, animal fusion designs, and so much more.

Enormous thanks to Hailey Jack! She did the lion share of the artwork in this novel and sat with me for countless hours as I could always rely on her assistance. Hailey was the backbone to this novel's creation, and I can confidently say that it would not be the same without her support.

Runaways

There are too many names to thank, but I would be remiss if I didn't mention Bryan and Dwight. These two individuals have sat on call listening to me for ages. I could always bounce ideas off of them and they would give me constructive criticism and great feedback. They both intentionally or unintentionally inspired a plethora of ideas that are stored inside of this book. Again, a huge thank you to everyone that took part in this!

I do appreciate all of your contributions and feedback! I am an independent author still searching for an agent and new illustrators so for business inquiries only, you can reach out to me through my writing email.

Justloading11@gmail.com

I hope you all enjoy your day and thank you again for the support!

www.ingramcontent.com/pod-product-compliance
Lightning Source LLC
Chambersburg PA
CBHW030543020726
47494CB00005B/1463

* 9 7 8 1 7 3 7 3 2 6 1 0 6 *